Tammy
JO BURNS

The Beast of Yorkshire

THOSE SCANDALOUS TAGGARTS
BOOK ONE

Copyright

The Beast of Yorkshire, Those Scandalous Taggarts, Book 1

This book is a work of fiction. The names, characters, places, and incidents are products of the writer's imagination or have been used fictitiously and are not to be construed as real. Any resemblance to persons, living or dead, actual events, locales or organizations is entirely coincidental.

Cover design and Interior format by The Killion Group, Inc.

DEDICATION

For all the women who have ever believed in "happily ever afters," this book's for you.

PROLOGUE

"Sit down, Penelope," the old man said gruffly from behind his desk.

Penelope took the seat indicated. All she wanted to do was to slouch against the back of the chair, to relax, but the man sitting across from her would not approve. Instead, she sat ramrod straight, her slightly upward tilted chin was the only sign of rebellion in her posture. She smoothed her hands over the charcoal gray dress she wore, representing her transition from full mourning to living life once more. This had been the longest year of her life. "You asked for me, Grandfather?"

"'Tis time, Penelope."

"Time for what?"

"Don't play the dunce with me, girl. You know exactly what I mean. It's time you took your sister's place."

Penelope's pulse pounded so hard she could hear it in her ears. *What is he planning now?* she wondered worriedly. She schooled her features so as not to give away her concern. "What are you talking about, Grandfather?" she asked again, attempting to give a hint of vacuousness to her question. She found on most occasions her grandfather preferred to believe women had nothing between their ears but air.

"I'm talking about her marriage that never happened. I have put the bloody Beast off long enough for you to observe your mourning."

"It hasn't been a full year, Grandfather," she argued.

"It's been long enough, and you should feel grateful I've let you carry on this long."

"Carry on?"

"Yes. What else would you call being allowed to mourn a traitor and would-be murderer? It's time everyone put this behind us and recovered our good name and the family coffers. Your father—"

"Don't you mean *your son*?" Penelope interrupted the old man, unable to remain quiet a moment longer.

"Do not speak unless spoken to, girl," the old man bellowed.

Penelope did not so much as flinch. She refused to give the old man any indication that she feared him. She calmly observed his appearance. The last year had been hard on him. He had lost so much weight he looked to be a shadow of his former self. His face was drawn and redness had begun to travel up his neck. Little drops of spittle formed at the corners of his mouth.

"As I was saying, *your father*," he said emphatically, "singlehandedly ruined this family. First he ruins us financially, and then he turns traitor in an attempt to recoup the money. The marriage agreement I made with Yorkshire will see us well on our way back to financial solvency."

"And pray tell, Grandfather, how is this marriage going to re-establish our good family name? Especially since you are forcing me into a family known throughout the *ton* as the Scandalous Taggarts."

"It won't, but with the right amount of money, your brother and I will put this family back where it should be."

"Going to buy your way back into everyone's good graces? Do you really think it will be that easy?"

"I told you to shut your mouth," the old man ground out.

Penelope clamped her mouth shut, becoming fearful that she had pushed him too far and would soon suffer physical repercussions. She stared over his right shoulder, refusing to make eye contact with him. Her hands were so tightly clasped in her lap, her knuckles had turned white.

"I have been in contact with Yorkshire, and he is sending a carriage for you at the end of the week along with half of the money. He is sending it in good faith that you will follow through with the wedding once you arrive. As soon as the vows have been spoken and the ink dry on the marriage certificate, he will send the rest of the money. Then—"

"Then you begin to corrupt my brother. Are you going to turn him into a greedy money monger like you, that thinks nothing of his family but only how many pounds he has in the bank?" The old man stood and knocked his chair back against the wall, but Penelope had been pushed too far. She was tired of being overrun by this…this tyrant. "You are despicable and I *despise* you. My father only ever wanted to rusticate in the country, but he felt compelled to try and please you. And what did it lead to? Nothing but death and destruction." The entire time she had been speaking, the old Marquess had stalked around the desk until he stood in front of her. Refusing to allow him to feel superior, Penelope stood, and looked him in the eye. "I hate you and what you have done to this family," she snarled through her teeth, her hands fisted at her sides.

She was not expecting what happened next. The back of the old man's gnarled right hand lashed across her right cheek. Penelope lost her balance and fell backwards. The chair scooted back, and she fell in an unceremonious heap on the floor, cradling her cheek. Her eye felt as if it would pop out of its socket, and she could taste a trickle of blood where she had bit the inside of her mouth. Her eyes were tearing up, but she refused to let them fall, refused to show any sign of weakness to this man.

"Since you do not seem to understand the situation quite well enough, I'll go over it one more time," the Marquess of Bolingbroke said, staring down his granddaughter.

"What's going on in here?" A young man stood in the doorway, demanding to know.

"Go to your room," Bolingbroke ordered her brother.

"No, let him stay," Penelope countered, getting to her feet and putting the chair between her and her grandfather. "Allow him to see what type of man he's going to have to become to live up to your standards. Let him see how he should treat his family members," Penelope challenged.

"Fine. Come in, Grandson. Now, Granddaughter, this is what you will do. You will travel to Yorkshire. You will marry the Duke of Yorkshire in your sister's place."

"But he's killed three women!" Her brother, the Earl of Blackstock, argued. "We can't allow Pen to go. We'll never see her again!"

"It's done," Penelope answered. "Half of the money up front and half upon delivery of one reluctant wife. Correct, Lord Bolingbroke?"

"No," her brother denied shakily.

"And with all that blood money, Grandfather is going to teach *you* how to be a proper earl and rebuild the family fortune. He wants to groom you to be just like him, Sam."

"I will renounce the title."

"The bloody hell you will," Grandfather said. "And to make sure you," he pointed to Penelope, "follow through with your end—"

"What more could you do to me? You've already condemned me to death. What now?"

"If you do not marry within seventy-two hours of arriving, I will have your mother committed to Bedlam."

"You wouldn't," Samuel gasped, still standing by the doorway.

"He would," Penelope replied, feeling the nails being pounded into her coffin.

CHAPTER 1

Certificate of Marriage," Penelope Presley read the words aloud again for what must be the thousandth time. Each time she unfolded it, she only managed to read those three words before her stomach began to churn sickeningly, and she quickly closed it once more. She rested her head against the luxurious leather squabs of the well-equipped coach and looked out the window. The beautiful Yorkshire wilderness was lost to her even though it seemed as if she were engrossed. Today was the last day of life as she knew it. She would be arriving at her fiancé's house in Yorkshire this evening, and they would marry as soon as possible. She supposed she should be thankful for the respite the time of mourning had given her to brace herself for her upcoming nuptials. Instead, she felt angry, resentful, and…tired, so…very…tired…

"Miss Presley. Miss Presley."

Penelope heard a voice calling for her as if from a deep well. The carriage was inordinately still. She peeked out the window and noticed that twilight had descended. "Did I fall asleep?" she asked even as she stretched her stiff muscles and rotated her neck to remove the kinks from it.

"It would appear so, miss," the footman said as he stood at the door, holding it open.

"Where are we?"

"Taggart Hall, Miss Presley."

"Already?"

"Yes, miss. May I help you down?"

"Yes," she said as she gathered up her reticule and the piece of paper that would tie her to the *Beast of Yorkshire* for the rest of her life, however long that would be. Her reticule hung from her wrist, and she clutched the marriage certificate to her chest with her right hand while extending her left to the footman. Her legs felt like jelly after her time on the road. She swayed just the slightest bit, and the footman looked unsure as to what to do.

"Are you all right, miss?"

"Yes, just getting my land legs back underneath me."

"Oh, yes, Miss Presley."

"Thank you for escorting me from London, and give my thanks to the coachman for getting us here safely, as well."

"Yes, Miss Presley. It was our pleasure," the man said with a nod before turning to unload her few bags.

Penelope turned and studied at the house looming before her. It looked like a giant, dark smudge on the horizon with light glowing in windows here and there making it look garish. A strong wind carrying the slightest hint of the sea came whipping through trying to tear her hair free of its mooring. A crashing sound reached her ears, and she looked up in time to see a large, hulking figure braced on the parapet walk. Distant lightning lit the sky showing the man's cape flying up around him reminding her of some winged phantom of her nightmares.

The door opened, shining a welcoming light on her, chasing off the encroaching darkness. A well-dressed older man opened the door. "Miss Presley, I presume?"

She looked back up, but whoever had been there earlier was now gone. A shiver raced up her spine before she shook it off and answered his question, "Yes."

"We've been expecting you. Welcome to Taggart Hall."

Duncan watched the carriage lumber up the drive. It drew to a stop in front of the Hall, and the footman jumped nimbly to the ground. He held his breath as the man opened the door and stood there. Was she in there? Was she refusing to leave the relative safety of the coach? The wind picked up pulling at his cape and overly long hair. He put his foot up on the low part of the parapet and leaned on the taller piece with his left arm. His body relaxed when he saw her stepping down from the coach.

She was here. After the long wait, the fighting with the Marquess of Bolingbroke, back and forth through their solicitors, she was finally here. He had won her hand by default and agreed to pay a king's ransom for her. He could now start over and put the past behind him. She would help him. Penelope. At that moment a distant bolt of lightning lit the sky enough that he could see she had found him on the parapet. He stood frozen, unsure what to do. *When have you ever been unsure of yourself?* he questioned himself. *Since women seem to choose death rather than being with you, Beast*, he mocked himself.

But Penelope was made of sterner stuff. Together they would forge a new life. They would prove all the gossips wrong. He really wasn't the beast they accused him of being. She was not like her family. She was strong. She would help him prove to everyone he was not a killer. She would live. She had to. He would keep her at a distance. He would make certain this marriage stayed exactly what it was meant to be—a business arrangement, nothing more, nothing less.

He closed his eyes and thought back to that ball when he had first seen her. She had been so quiet and reserved compared to her sister. Penelope hid in the shadows and watched the world pass her by. He understood why. Anytime she stood next to her twin, she had been completely and utterly ignored, invisible. She was quiet, stoic, and had a strength of character that would serve her well here in the wilds of the moors.

Duncan turned to go inside but heard the distant drumming begin. "Not tonight," he groaned and lifted his face to the sky as it was lit by another lightning strike. The drumming crescendoed until the thunder sounded as if it were part of it. "Bloody hell." He raced inside, down the stairs, and across to the stable.

"Heard the drums, Your Grace. Cyclops is ready," he said, indicating a black horse with a patch of white that covered both eyes.

"Guns are in your saddlebags," another man said, holding out a sword in a scabbard.

"Many thanks," Duncan said, wrapping the scabbard's belt about his waist and fastening it. He grabbed a fistful of Cyclops' midnight mane and catapulted himself onto the horse's back. Energized, the horse pawed the air as Duncan turned him. They left the stables as fast as Duncan dared with the moon dancing in and out of the clouds.

The butler escorted Penelope to a room that appeared to be an office. She couldn't ignore the pitying glances he sent her direction whenever he believed she wasn't looking. If she had been in the man's position, she would have done the same thing. No, she would have been screaming at the poor girl to run as fast as she could.

"His Grace will be along momentarily."

"Once he's finished with his walk five stories in the air with a gale blowing in, you mean?" The calmness in her voice belied the fear and nervousness she felt inside.

"If you would have a seat, I will have tea and biscuits brought in shortly."

"Thank you." It did not go without notice that he had ignored her question.

The man bobbed politely then quickly left the room.

Unable to sit, Penelope walked over to the window and looked out, unsure as to what she should do with herself. A man wearing a cloak practically flew down the drive on the back of a dark horse. She heard the rattle of the tray and spun around. "Who was that?"

"I'm not sure I know what you mean."

"The man racing down the drive on the back of a horse. The one that looked as if he were trying to escape the very devil himself. It looked to be the same man walking the parapets when I arrived."

"I can't rightly say, Miss Presley, since I didn't see either one of them," the butler answered evasively.

"Was it His Grace?"

"Again, Miss Presely, without having seen them, I couldn't answer truthfully."

Penelope crossed her arms and stared at the servant.

"Perhaps you would like to be shown to your room? You have had a long trip, after all."

"Of which I had a lengthy nap on the final leg of our journey. No, I believe I will wait right here. Besides, I would hate for this delicious fare you have put together for me to go to waste."

"Yes, miss." He bowed and let himself out of the room, closing the door behind him.

Penelope was angry. She had traveled for three days, and as soon as she sets foot in his house, her betrothed takes off for parts unknown. *You are assuming that he is your betrothed*, her conscience chastised her. *Never once did the butler confirm that either person you saw was the Duke of Yorkshire.* "Nor did he deny it," she argued. She paced the room until her feet hurt, and she grew weary. A lightning bolt so bright it lit the majority of the room was quickly followed by rumbling thunder that shook the bric-a-brac that was scattered on shelves and tables about the room. A driving rain started soon after.

Penelope drug a chair from in front of the desk to the window. She pulled back the heavy velvet drape and watched the storm alter the dark landscape. Once the lightning and thunder passed, it left behind a gentle rain that pinged against the windows. The sound lulled Penelope into a restless, albeit dreamless, sleep.

Bright sunlight filtered through the window, causing Penelope to blink awake.

A man on horseback caught her eye as he came tearing up the drive. He looked quite handsome, even though he was defying convention by wearing only his polished Hessians, black breeches, and dark shirtsleeves. If this was the same man from last night, he had lost his cloak. He had a sword at his side and what looked to be several rips in his shirt. His dark hair was wind-blown, giving him a piratical appearance. He stopped in front of the house, dismounted, then handed the horse off to a footman. If only her future husband looked like that, then perhaps this upcoming marriage might be tolerable. Instead, she expected a decrepit, old man with one foot in the grave and the other on a slippery slope, for the man had already buried three women.

Wait, was that blood peeking through the ripped place on his arm? Where had this man been all night, and what had he been doing? He looked up and made eye contact with her. Penelope gasped and let the sheer curtain fall into place. It gave a soft, filtered light to the room, taking the edge off the harsh masculinity that could be seen on every surface. Penelope paced the confines of the study in an attempt to expel her nervous energy. Who was that man? Was he dangerous? She should have escaped last night while she had been left alone, but instead she had slept. She was so lost in her thoughts that the soft, feminine voice made her jump.

"You must be the new bride. I'm sorry, I didn't mean to startle you."

Penelope looked the young woman over. She was quite pretty with sable ringlets that framed her elfin features. She had long, dark lashes that enhanced her emerald green eyes. She was a perfect model of what a man of the *ton* would be looking for. Compared to this woman, Penelope felt very plain indeed with her lackluster blonde hair that had to be forced to hold a curl and brown eyes that only rivaled the color of mud.

"Well?" she prompted when Penelope showed no sign of answering.

"Yes, it would appear as if I am the new bride. Penelope Presley," she curtsied politely, still unsure of the rank of the woman standing in front of her.

"Lucy Varley. Let me be the first to welcome you to the family."

"Thank you. I don't know much about my future husband. Are you His Grace's granddaughter?"

"Most definitely not." Lucy laughed uproariously.

"Did I miss the joke?"

"You do at least know his horrible nickname, don't you?" Lucy asked, still laughing.

Penelope felt her cheeks redden. Lucy was correct. The only thing she really knew about her husband was that he was called the *Beast of Yorkshire*. She could not suppress the shiver that traveled up her spine.

"So, you *have* heard," Lucy laughed delicately. "And I am *not* his granddaughter," she explained, emphasizing the word not.

"Oh?" Penelope wanted to scream at the young woman to just explain herself and be done with it. Instead, she pulled on every social grace her mother had ever taught her, remained calm, and appeared to be interested in every word the young woman said.

"I'm Duncan's step-aunt. My mother and his grandfather were married for a brief time before the sixth Duke of Yorkshire passed away leaving Duncan to inherit the title. Duncan would have had to father a child when he was just out of leading strings for me to be his granddaughter." Lucy wiped at the tears leaking from her eyes.

"I see. Do you and your mother both live here?" Penelope asked, trying to stem the tide of Lucy's laughter.

"Yes. I do hope we can become very good friends," Lucy said, finally getting herself under control.

Her words seemed to sound sincere, and Penelope found herself agreeing with the young woman.

"I best be going. Duncan should be here any moment. I passed him in the hall earlier." She turned to walk out of the room and paused a moment. "Good luck," she tossed over her shoulder before leaving the room.

Good luck? Penelope thought silently, *I'm going to need a miracle.* Penelope continued pacing the room when she heard the sound of a heavy tread in the hallway outside the door. She stopped, looked across the room, and prepared herself for her first viewing of the *Beast of Yorkshire.*

CHAPTER 2

Duncan walked into the study and halted at the vision before him. He didn't know if she would look as he remembered. She looked better. Miss Penelope Presley stood in front of the window haloed by the light about her. It gave her an ethereal appearance. Everything about her screamed fastidiousness, then she looked at him. Rebellion and anger glinted in her eyes. No, she did not want to be here. He could easily tell that, but then he couldn't blame her. After all, he was the *Beast of Yorkshire* and had already buried two wives and a fiancée.

"Miss Presley?"

"Yes? Are you taking me to meet the Duke of Yorkshire? I must admit I am quite anxious and would like to get this meeting over with."

"Then you shall wait no more. Miss Presley, I am Duncan Taggart, the Duke of Yorkshire."

"You...you are the *Beast*?"

He watched her slap a hand over her mouth and saw the horrified expression that slipped over her face. Duncan almost felt pity for the poor girl. Almost, until he remembered how much he was paying her grandfather for her when it should be the other way around. Then there was the stigma attached to her family name, as well as the fact that he should have been married almost a year ago. No, he was done pitying people. This was a business arrangement in which, at the end, he would have an heir who would carry on the family name and inherit the title.

"Yes," he replied with a smirk.

"I'm sorry. It merely slipped out. I thought, well it really doesn't matter anymore. Oh," she fell into a deep curtsy as she realized she had yet to address him properly. "Your Grace."

"Enough. Come sit," he held out his hand for her to sit on one of the chairs in front of the desk.

"If you don't mind, I've been sitting in this chair all night," she said with a dig.

"Already waiting up for me, and us not yet married? Perhaps you will be a dutiful wife."

"Yes, Your Grace," Penelope gritted out between her teeth.

"Do you have the marriage certificate?"

He watched her bend her head as she dug through her reticule. "Here it is," she extracted the piece of paper and held it up triumphantly.

"Thank you." He took the paper from her and shoved it in a drawer in his desk without ever looking at it. "How was your trip here?"

"Uneventful. Thank you for asking, Your Grace."

"If we are to be married, I think it is a little much for you to keep calling me *Your Grace*. My name is Duncan."

"Yes, Your Grace," she stubbornly replied.

He let out a sigh of frustration.

"When are we to be married?"

"Tomorrow," he replied succinctly. He studied her but could not determine if she looked anxious or relieved.

"What are your expectations of me as a wife?"

"I would say what any man expects of his wife. You will play hostess for me when we have events, whether here or in London. You will run the household for me. And, of course, you will provide me with an heir and hopefully a spare or two. Do you have any other questions for me?"

"What if I cannot give you an heir?"

"Do you have any reason to believe you can't?"

"No."

"Then we shall not worry about it, shall we?"

"I have one more question. My mother is not well. Ever since my father…died, and my sister's actions…well, Mother hasn't been of sound mind since."

"And?"

"I would like to move her here so I can oversee her care."

"Is there any possibility that she could harm herself or others?"

"I suppose there is always that possibility, but she has shown no sign thus far."

"Then I don't see any harm in bringing her here. I will send my coach and a maid to fetch her. If you will let me know where she is, I'll take care of everything."

"Thank you. I fear that if she is left under Grandfather's care for too long that he will see her put in Bedlam."

"He would do that?"

"You ask that after he sold me to you?" she countered. "The man has no scruples. I fear for what he will turn my brother into, but I have to trust that Samuel is strong enough not to fall under Grandfather's dictates."

"I will wait until the marriage ceremony is performed and send my secretary along with the marriage certificate so that he can have it processed in London. I will have him meet with Lord Bolingbroke and settle everything."

"That might be best. I don't know if Grandfather will be relieved to have Mother off his hands, or angry at having his power over her stripped."

"May I ask you something?" Duncan asked.

"Of course."

"What do *you* expect from this marriage?"

"Much of what you confirmed earlier, but in addition I ask to be respected. If you choose to have a mistress, I ask that you be discreet. I do not want any more scandal surrounding my name or my future children's names than what is already there."

"That's all?"

"Yes."

"Why?"

"I know I was not your first choice as a wife. In fact I wasn't even your second or third. Then I became a consolation upon my sister's death. You have been kind enough to allow me to grieve for my family, despite their wrongdoings. I believe that nothing you could ask of me would be that difficult to endure. You helped me escape my Grandfather's house, and for that I am extremely thankful. I am fully aware you are only marrying me so that you can have children to carry on your name. I do not expect anything more from this marriage."

"You don't appear to be the least bit worried that people consider me responsible for the deaths of my previous wives and fiancée."

"Oh, I believe their deaths are somehow connected to you, but no, I do not believe that you actually killed them. If I did, I would not be here."

"You're not worried about your life?"

"I'll be frightened for my life every day I am here, but I have also decided that I will be your last wife. I do not take kindly to having my life snuffed out like a candle. I plan to be around a long while, Your Grace. Now, the trip from London was long and tedious, and as you say, I performed my first wifely duty by keeping vigil all night for my betrothed to arrive home safely. I find I would like to wash the road off of me and perhaps lay down for a bit."

"Of course. I will have a maid show you to the duchess' chamber. Can you give me directions to where your mother is being housed? If so, I will begin making arrangements for her transfer."

"Thank you," she said and gave him the information he requested. A maid arrived at the door ready to show her up to the room.

"If you feel up to it, I would like you to join me for supper."

"Perhaps," she answered cooly before leaving the room.

He sat behind his desk, contemplating the woman who was to become his new wife. Despite all that had happened to her, she appeared to be strong-willed and confident. She was not living under any false assumptions of what their marriage would entail.

"At least she's pleasant to look at," he murmured to himself. Duncan pulled a piece of paper close, along with an inkwell and quill, then he began composing a letter to Penelope's grandfather in regards to her concerns.

Penelope followed the maid silently up the elegant stairs and down a long hallway until they almost reached the end. She had counted at least four doors on each side and there were two more hallways on this floor. She tried not to think about the massiveness of the house or the fact that she would be mistress of it all. The maid opened the door of the next to the last room on the right.

"This is the duchess' chamber, Miss Presley."

"Thank you."

"My name is Mary. I have been assigned to you until you can interview for a personal maid. Is there anything you'll be needing?"

"I would like a bath."

"We will have it set up as soon as possible. I'll be back shortly to begin unpacking your bags."

"No rush," Penelope said, then quietly closed the door on the maid's departing figure. She turned around and leaned against the carved, dark wood. She saw nothing of the room itself, instead she kept seeing her fiancé. Her burly, handsome fiancé. The man she had wished was her fiancé as he rode up the drive on his horse. *Sometimes dreams* do *come true*, she thought to herself with a smirk on her lips. If she were forced to guess his age, she would have to say he was in his early thirties, meaning the man was no more ready to meet his maker than she was. If she had met him in a London ballroom, she would have been breathless, as would every other young woman, as well as most of their mothers.

Instead, he was the man she had been sold to. A shudder passed through her, but she didn't know if it was because she was frightened or excited. Perhaps marriage to that handsome man downstairs would not be so difficult after all.

"But what of the dead women?" Her stomach churned sickeningly. Despite what she said downstairs, what if she once again caused him to be labeled a widower? What if he was doing away with his wives? Her stomach churned even more. A knock at the door made her jump away from it.

"Yes?"

"We have your bath, miss."

She opened the door and held it as the footmen carried in the tub, followed by more men and women carrying buckets full of water, some steaming, some not. Penelope moved out of their way and crossed the room to the window. She looked outside and studied her surroundings. Her window looked over the cliff that sat several hundred yards away. Sea grass, lavender, and native brush dotted the landscape and danced in the sea breeze. To her right, she saw a village trailing over the cliff.

"What's that village over there?"

"That's Robin Hood's Bay," Mary answered from where she was directing the footmen and maids.

"Robin Hood's Bay? As in *the* Robin Hood?" Penelope asked, laughter in her voice.

"Aye, miss, but no one knows if he ever really lived there. It's a fishing village."

"I see." Penelope looked out over the sparkling waters. The view was breathtaking. "Perhaps living here won't be so terrible after all," she said.

"Oh, no, miss. It's quite a lovely place to live, and the sea air is good for so many ailments."

"What of being forced into a marriage?" Penelope rested her forehead against the windowpane. An eery silence fell in the room punctuated by the sound of sloshing water and clanking buckets. She wished there were tears for her to cry, but there was only a deep, aching emptiness. Her father and then her sister had deadened whatever emotions she had felt. Her grandfather had not improved the situation.

"Miss," Mary tapped on Penelope's shoulder.

Penelope jumped and spun around to face the attractive maid.

"I'm sorry to startle you, but your bath is ready."

"Thank you."

"I'll help you out of your dress. Is there any particular scent you'd like added to your bath?"

"It doesn't matter."

"I have just the thing to relax you after your long trip."

The young woman made quick work of unbuttoning Penelope's dress. She then left her alone and moved to the bath and began mixing something that smelled heavenly. Penelope walked to the tub, shed her clothes, and quickly climbed into the steaming water. "What is this?"

"A lavender milk bath. The lavender will relax you, and the milk is good for your skin."

Penelope closed her eyes and felt a cool, damp cloth placed across them. She laid her head back against the rim of the bathtub and let the scent and warmth comfort her. She could hear Mary working in the background and found the noise surprisingly soothing.

"Mary?"

"Yes, miss?"

"What can you tell me of His Grace's previous wives?"

"Oh, miss, you don't want to be thinking about them now."

"Yes, I do," Penelope countered. She lifted a corner of the cloth covering her eyes and looked pointedly at the young woman.

"I didn't know his wives."

"But you've heard things," Penelope guessed.

"Yes."

"I'll tell her, Mary. You just keep unpacking Miss Presley's bags."

"Yes, Miss Varley." Mary quickly curtsied then turned back to the luggage and the wardrobe.

"You knew *all* of His Grace's wives?" Penelope asked Lucy.

"Yes. They were all so very sweet. It's so sad that they…"

"They what?"

"Well, that they died so young."

"Can you tell me about them?"

"I'm the least familiar with his first wife, Isabelle. Mother and I moved here just a few months before the accident."

"Accident?"

"Isabelle loved to walk the cliffs. She was raised near here, and she and Duncan were sweethearts, I suppose. Well, they seemed to be. They had known each other for so long that no one was surprised when they married, at least that's what I've been told. But like any married couple, they quarreled, especially towards the end. They had an awful row about something and didn't speak for days. They were civil to one another after that, but they were never like they had been in the beginning. Anyway, no one is quite sure what happened, but one afternoon Isabelle went for a walk and didn't return for the evening meal. Duncan went searching for her…"

"And?" Penelope prompted when the young woman drifted off.

"He found her at the base of the cliff. Dead. They had announced to the family just a few days prior that they were expecting their first child."

"That's horrible." Penelope sat up in the bath, sloshing water about.

"Yes, it was. It took Duncan several years to recover from the loss. His grandfather set up his next marriage. Samantha was nice enough, but quiet and kept to herself. She loved to read."

"What happened to her?"

"She took the ague and no matter what we gave her, she just grew weaker. I remember sitting next to her bed and reading to her for hours on end. She loved books, and it seemed she rested easier the times I read to her. She never recovered her health and a few weeks later she just never woke up."

"I'm scared to ask about his fiancée," Penelope said. She took the bath sheet and wrapped it about her as she stood from the water. She stepped gingerly from the bathtub and left a trail of damp footprints across the room

"Francis was frightened of her own shadow. She believed that Duncan was responsible for Isabelle and Samantha's deaths. She locked herself in her room and refused to allow him inside."

"How long?"

"The night before they were to be married," Lucy said ominously.

"What happened?" Penelope whispered.

"Lucy, you aren't carrying tales to our newest family member are you?"

"Of course not, Mother." Lucy stood and moved to the side of a beautiful, older version of herself. "Mother, this is Duncan's fiancée, Penelope Presley. Penelope, this is my mother, Rosalie Taggart, Duchess of Yorkshire."

"Soon to be *Dowager* Duchess of Yorkshire," the older woman corrected.

Penelope tried to curtsy while clutching her towel close. "Your Grace."

"Please, we will be family very shortly, and it looks as if I have caught you at an inconvenient time. Excuse me. Lucy, come along."

"Yes, Mother." Lucy winked and smiled at Penelope before she left the room trailing her mother.

Mary quietly closed the door before returning to assist Penelope.

"Mary, do you know what happened to His Grace's fiancée?"

"Yes, miss," Mary said softly.

Several minutes passed. A thick silence fell over them. "Mary, tell me," Penelope pleaded when she could wait no longer. A sickening dread filled her.

"His Grace found her the next morning, only he hadn't yet inherited his title."

"Mary," Penelope drawled out the maid's name. "What happened to Francis?"

"She killed herself. She found drinking poison preferable to being married to His Grace."

"Oh, my," Penelope said softly. She collapsed onto her bed and clutched the towel tightly about her.

"Are you going to stay?"

"I have no choice, Mary."

"I don't believe His Grace is responsible for any of their deaths."

"Mary, I'd like to be alone for a while."

"Yes, miss."

Penelope waited until the young woman left her, then she crossed and locked the door. She also locked the door that she assumed joined the duchess' and duke's chamber. Once she felt she was sufficiently secured within her room, she crawled up on the bed, curled into a ball, and stared into the empty space. The entire time she silently cursed her grandfather, sister, and father, but most especially, her grandfather.

"Hello, big brother," a cheery voice penetrated Duncan's concentration on the wording of the letter. He had decided Lord Bolingbroke would not appreciate control being yanked from him, and he would have to involve his own solicitor in order to secure Penelope's mother's move to Taggart Hall. Duncan stiffened as his brother's voice reached his ears.

"Reese!"

"Lucy!"

Duncan watched as the slight figure of his step-aunt threw herself into his brother's arms. His body stiffened as he controlled what he wanted to shout. His hand tightened around the quill until a snapping sound penetrated his hearing. He opened his hand, looked down, and saw the writing utensil lying in two distinct pieces across his palm.

"Easy there, big brother. You wouldn't want people to think all those rumors about you are true, would you?"

"Reese!" Lucy said, shocked.

"It's all right, Lucy. He won't do away with me as long as people know I'm here."

"What are you doing here?" Duncan demanded.

"I heard my big brother was getting married, *again*. You didn't expect me to miss that, did you? Besides you're going to need a witness to sign the death, I mean, marriage certificate."

"Reese, stop that right now! Duncan has never harmed anyone in his life."

"Leave us, Lucy," Duncan ordered.

"No. If I leave, the two of you might kill one another."

"Get out."

"Perhaps you should do what he asks, love." Reese led their dark-haired step-aunt to the door and gently pushed her through. "I promise we won't kill one another."

"I'm going to get Mother," Lucy threatened.

"I would love to see Rosalie," Reese answered easily.

"Humph." Lucy picked up her skirts and flounced off down the hall.

"Why are you really here?" Duncan demanded once Lucy had left them alone.

"Do you really want me to say it out loud?"

"I asked, didn't I?"

"Fine. I'm here to make certain another sister-in-law doesn't end up in an early grave."

"That's quite a comment coming from you," Duncan said as he yanked open a drawer and searched for another quill.

"What's that supposed to mean?"

"I want you gone. Now."

"That's just too damn bad," Reese said, his jovial attitude gone. "I'm not going to stand by while another Duchess of Yorkshire is laid to rest."

"Are you accusing me of killing my wives?"

"I—"

"Am I interrupting something?"

Duncan looked up, shocked to see his fiancée standing in the open doorway. "Miss Presley, it would be best if you returned to your room," Duncan ordered her as if she were a recalcitrant child.

"Hello, I'm Penelope Presley," she said, ignoring his command.

Duncan watched his fiancée walk across the room and hold out her hand to Reese. He wanted to yell at her to stay away from him. Instead, he clenched his fists where they rested on the top of his desk.

"Penelope, such a lovely name for such a beautiful woman." Reese bent over Penelope's hand and placed a kiss on the back of it. "It's too bad that my brother found you first."

"I would say that you are in need of spectacles, sir, if you think I am beautiful. Also, I don't know that you could say he *found* me, but rather he *bought* me."

"Miss Presley," Duncan growled.

"There's no need to hide the truth, is there, Your Grace?" Penelope turned and gave Duncan a sarcastic smile before facing Reese once more. "And so you will be my brother-in-law?"

"Yes, Miss Presley."

"Please, call me Penelope. We are to be family, after all, and I find myself rather short in that area as of late. You look extremely familiar. Have we met before?"

Neither of them saw the bigger man stiffen.

"Presley," Reese seemed to take a moment to process the name, as if it had taken a moment to trigger a memory. "Do you know a man named Samuel Presley?"

"Why, yes, he's my brother. Do you know Sam?"

"Indeed. In fact, I believe I visited your house a few years ago," he mused.

"Oh, yes, now I remember. You were one of several friends Sam brought round. One of the older men that my grandfather said was being a bad influence on my brother. I'm guessing he did not meet you at university. Grandfather was quite angry that you all ate so much food."

"He's a bit of a sourpuss, isn't he?"

"Yes. I remember Whitney, my sister, was also quite smitten with you."

"You know each other?" Duncan interrupted, his tone tinged with anger.

"I suppose we do," Penelope answered, "though not well. If I remember, you play a mean game of whist."

"I had a wonderful partner," Reese teased her.

"Miss Presley, please leave us," Duncan growled. "Reese and I have unfinished business to discuss." His anger was intensifying with every moment his brother flirted with his fiancée.

"You best do as he asks, sister dear. You know his nickname is not just because people believe he killed three women."

"Reese, that's enough," a new feminine voice chastised.

"Hello, Rosalie, or should I say Grandmother?"

"You call me Grandmother, and I will have you thrown out of this house right now, you wicked boy. Now come and give me a hug," she ordered.

Duncan watched his brother easily walk across the floor and into the other woman's open arms. Rosalie hugged Reese warmly when all Duncan wanted to do was force him to leave the house, and make him stay away from Penelope.

"Rosalie, have you met our newest family member yet?"

"Briefly," the older woman said before she crossed to her, took her in her arms, and gave her a warm hug.

Duncan remained on tenterhooks, still sitting behind his desk. They were not supposed to welcome her into the family fold. This was merely a business arrangement. Anytime it was anything else, it had not ended well. He refused to have another woman on his conscience.

"Ladies, if you will leave us, Reese and I have much to discuss."

"Come, my dear. Cook almost has the evening meal ready."

"Shouldn't we..."

"The boys won't kill one another. They know better," Rosalie said pointedly as she closed the door.

"Now, back to why you're here," Duncan said.

"I'm here to make certain my future sister-in-law outlives you."

"And who is going to see that she outlives you?"

"What is that supposed to mean, Duncan?"

"It means that every time something happened to one of my wives or my fiancée, it coincided with you making an unscheduled visit."

"Are you blaming their deaths on me?"

"Should I?"

"Damn you, Duncan!" Reese leaned over the desk. "I never touched a hair on any of their hea—"

"I beg to differ," Duncan challenged.

"You know what I meant."

"Do I?"

"Dammit, quit being a bloody arse. I never hurt any of them, and I'm telling you right now, if any harm comes to Penelope, I'll do everything in my power to help her escape your clutches. And if she dies…"

"What?" Duncan growled, almost sounding like the beast people accused him of being.

"I'll see you hang for your crimes. *All* of them. Do you understand?"

"I have committed no crimes, and *you* will stay away from her. Do *you* understand?"

"Well, it looks like we're at a stalemate, doesn't it, big brother?"

Penelope allowed Rosalie to lead her out of the study. "Are you certain they won't hurt one another?" she asked the older woman. *Why am I even concerning myself with two strangers who are behaving like children?* she fumed silently.

"They know better. Now, stop worrying about those two boys. Tell me all about yourself. After all, you will be joining the family."

"There's really nothing to tell," Penelope mumbled.

"Here now, don't you know that you're marrying into an already scandalous family? Besides, word travels quickly, especially when it contains the hint of scandal."

"You know?" Penelope jerked her head around to stare at Rosalie.

"Yes, my dear, I know." Rosalie patted Penelope's hand that was draped over her arm. "I am quite used to being whispered about. When I married the boys' grandfather, well, you can only imagine what people said about our age difference. Besides that, I was not a member of the *ton*. My husband was a captain in the military, killed in the war. I have heard people say that I married Thomas only for his money." The other woman was silent for several moments before she continued. "In a way I did."

"What do you mean?"

"I had a young daughter to raise. I needed to see she had the best chance possible. I want her to have a better life than what I did. I must admit, I threw myself at Thomas, and luckily, he took an interest in me. So, you see, I am not above reproach and refuse to judge anyone else."

"Thank you," Penelope said softly. "I have asked His Grace to bring my mother here after we are married. She's not the same woman she used to be."

"We'll help you care for her. When we go to London for the season, we'll hire a nurse to stay with her."

"Thank you, again." The two women walked on quietly until they came to a beautiful salon.

"Let's sit and visit until supper is ready."

Penelope sat on one end of the brocade settee and Rosalie at the other. She looked nervously at the older woman, wrung her hands, and twisted her fingers together. The woman looked to be slightly younger than her own mother. She estimated her age to be her late forties to early fifties. There were a few silver threads in her otherwise dark hair that caught the light just right and sparkled in the setting sun.

"Your Grace—"

"Please, call me Rosalie."

"Rosalie, may I ask you a question?"

"Of course."

"I would normally ask my mother or sister, but well…"

"What is it, dear?"

"It seems as if tomorrow shall be my wedding night."

"And you haven't a clue as to what you're facing, do you?"

Penelope blushed a deep shade of pink. "No, I don't. Not really. You see, I've always lived in London, so I don't even know what goes on in the country among the animals. I don't want to go in unprepared."

"You poor thing. Wait here."

Penelope watched Rosalie stand and cross the room to shut the door. The older woman then returned and reoccupied her seat on the settee. The woman began to talk slowly and descriptively. Penelope could feel her face becoming warmer the longer Rosalie spoke.

"I'm supposed to do that with *him*?" Penelope held her hands against her flushed cheeks. "I don't even know him, and he's going to expect me to allow him to stick *that*," she waved one of her hands, unable to say the word, "in me? I just…I can't!"

"I know it's going to be difficult, my dear. Perhaps it would be best if you just lay there and close your eyes. Sometimes they say that's easiest."

A tap sounded on the door.

"Yes?" Rosalie asked.

"The meal is ready, Your Grace."

"Thank you. Come, you'll feel much better after you've eaten."

"Oh, no, I can't sit in there and face him after what you've told me."

"You're going to have to see him sooner or later," Rosalie reasoned. "It might as well be now." Rosalie stood and tugged Penelope's hand until she stood. "Now, come along."

Penelope reluctantly allowed the older woman to pull her across the room. "I just can't," she said.

"You can. Tomorrow night you will be facing him in truth. Don't you think you should begin over a shared table with people around to serve as a buffer?"

"Perhaps you're right."

"Of course I'm right. Now, come along."

Penelope followed several feet behind Rosalie. She drifted further behind her as they left the room. As she approached the stairs, Penelope started to turn. She was on the fifth step, escaping to the freedom of her bedroom when a deep voice sounded to her right.

"Aren't you joining us?"

"Uhm…I…"

"Yes?" Duncan asked.

"Can't you see she's nervous around you, big brother?" Reese asked. "Come, sister dear, you can sit by me. I won't let the big, bad beast hurt you." The younger Taggart held out his hand for her. "Come on, Penelope," he coaxed.

Penelope hesitated a few more moments before she placed her hand in her future brother-in-law's. She felt him gently squeeze her hand and saw him give her a warm smile.

"What's wrong with her?" Lucy asked.

"Don't you worry about it," Rosalie said.

The meal was a tense affair with Lucy, Rosalie, and Reese the only ones contributing to the conversation. Penelope found herself pushing her food around her plate and answering questions only when they were directed at her. She avoided Duncan's gaze as much as possible, embarrassed after Rosalie's frank discussion with her regarding the wedding night. When the servants began delivering the dessert, Penelope decided she could not stand the stiff politeness a moment longer.

"If you all will excuse me, I've had a long few days." She placed the napkin next to the small plate.

"Miss Presley," the deep voice of her fiancé stopped her in the hallway.

"Your Grace?"

"Is something wrong? Do you feel ill?"

"No."

"I noticed that you didn't eat very much, and quite honestly, there are few that can resist Cook's desserts."

"Yes, well, you'll come to find that I'm a woman who can resist many things."

"That's excellent to know for the future," Duncan said.

"Excuse me," she said, once more, stepping around him.

"You can't hide from me forever."

"No, but I do believe I have approximately sixteen hours left, don't I?"

"Use them wisely, Miss Presley."

"I intend to, Your Grace." Penelope swept up the stairs as regally as she could and entered her new bedchamber. She shut the door and turned the lock before collapsing on the bed and staring at the ceiling. Tomorrow her life would change forever. Whether for better or worse remained to be seen. One thing she knew for certain, she had no one to rely on but herself. She prayed there would be a child soon, and then he could seek his pleasure with some other unfortunate woman and leave her alone.

CHAPTER 3

The next day, Penelope considered her reflection in the mirror. She decided she looked passable as a bride. Her dress was light blue with a white lace overlay that split down the front. The empire waist, highlighted by a navy satin ribbon tied beneath her bosom, emphasized the bounty nature had blessed her with. A matching ribbon wrapped about her head held her blonde hair up and back. Mary had worked hours curling her hair, and by some miracle most could still be seen, bouncing merrily every time she moved her head. Matching slippers completed the ensemble.

She studied her eyes in the mirror and was surprised at what she saw. When she thought of her future husband, her eyes brightened just the tiniest bit. Why was that? He's the *Beast of Yorkshire*. She shouldn't be anticipating anything about this man, let alone what they would be doing together tonight after all the lights had been extinguished. Penelope caressed a delicate box that had an Indian look about it. It had been her grandmother's, her mother's, her sister's, and now hers. She had secretly taken the beautiful box with a complicated inlaid design of wood, jewels, and metal upon Whitney's death. Although it had been passed through the family, it had last belonged to Whitney, and she had wanted something to remember her sister by.

Penelope opened the lid and studied the contents of the box. It had once overflowed with jewels, but now they barely covered the bottom. A strand of pearls, a locket on a gold chain, and a cameo brooch with a light blue background lay nestled inside. A pair of pearl earrings finished the jewelry collection. She clipped the earrings to her ears and couldn't resist shaking her head and watching them jangle. The cool pearls that made up the necklace slipped through her fingers. Penelope put the strand of pearls around her neck and closed the delicate clasp.

She glanced in the mirror and a wave of nostalgia swept over her. She remembered when she and Whitney were little girls, and they would watch Mother get ready for the balls and parties she attended with Father. Her mother would put jewels on the girls and they would take turns walking around the room in her slippers. They would laugh and giggle as they twirled about, then Mother would pick up each one of them and press kisses against their cheeks. It was one of the few happy memories Penelope had of her childhood. One of the few times she had felt loved and wanted. There were so many others when she felt like she had merely been an after thought. She wasn't the beautiful daughter or the son and heir.

"Stop it," she ordered herself. "Nothing about the past is going to help you now." She slammed the lid shut on the box and couldn't help but wince at the loud sound it made. Penelope braced her arms against the delicate vanity, her head drooped forward. "All right, Penelope, it's time to pull yourself together. Mother would not approve of this behavior. After all, it's your wedding day. You should have a smile on your face, ready to enjoy the festivities. Make them believe you're happy if nothing else."

Penelope looked up in the mirror once more and practiced her smile until it looked more natural and less strained. She crossed the room and opened her bedroom door to see Rosalie standing on the other side, her hand raised as if to knock.

"I was just coming to check on you. The minister has arrived, and may I say, you look absolutely beautiful. You will take Duncan's breath away, my dear."

"Please, there's no need to say things like that. I know my looks are passable, but—"

"Passable? I don't know who filled your head with that nonsense, but thank goodness you're here now and I can work on setting you straight," she said, drawing Penelope into the circle of her arms and giving her a hug. "You go on down. I have something in my room I would like you to wear. I'll be down momentarily."

Penelope nodded and walked down the hall that doubled as a gallery of all the Taggarts that had lived before, including husbands, wives, and children. In some cases there were even hunting dogs and racehorses. Medieval armor, complete with battle axes and javelins, stood sentinel every few feet. Who, in their right mind, would consider this mausoleum a perfectly sound place to raise children? Most women would be all agog that they lived in a castle. Penelope silently dared them to spend a night in one. Between thinking about her upcoming nuptials and listening to the wind whine through the cracks, she'd scarcely gotten any sleep.

Voices drifted up to her as she reached the balcony. It sounded as if Reese and her future husband were arguing and there was another male voice attempting to calm the two men. She took a deep breath and let it out as she took her first step down the stairs. She had only made it down to the third step when something caught her foot and her world tilted precariously.

"I don't want you at my wedding!"

"And I told you, I don't give a damn. You'll continue to see me until I'm good and ready to leave."

"Gentlemen, please. Remember, you are brothers. Family. The Lord says—"

"Aaaahhhhh!!!!"

"What the bloody hell is that?"

Both Duncan and Reese raced from the room in time to see Penelope falling backwards down the stairs, trying to grab the bannister to stop her momentum.

"Penelope!" Duncan roared as he raced to the staircase. He vaulted over the railing of the lower portion of the stairs so that he could reach her before Reese did. He had vowed to himself he would keep Penelope safe from harm and here she was, catapulting down the staircase. Duncan reached her just as she came to a sudden, jarring stop on the landing halfway down the stairs. "Are you all right?" he asked, pushing back stray strands of her hair that had pulled free from its coiffure.

"Don't touch me!" she shouted and tried to move away from him.

"Penelope, I promise I'm not trying to hurt you. I only want to make certain you're unharmed."

"Perhaps you should let me see to her," Reese said.

"No!" both Duncan and Penelope snarled at him.

"What's going on?" Rosalie stood at the top of the stairs, a decorated horseshoe in one hand.

"Mother, what happened?" Lucy asked, joining her mother.

"I'm trying to find out, dear."

The two women started to make their way down the stairs when Penelope halted their progress. "Stop!"

"What is it, dear?" Rosalie asked.

"Fourth or fifth step from the top," she said, wincing as she tried to push herself up. "Something is strung across the step. My foot caught in it and caused me to fall."

Reese raced up the stairs and meticulously studied the area Penelope indicated.

"Well?" Duncan demanded.

"Nothing."

"That's insane! I felt it. It cut across my foot."

"I believe you," Duncan said softly. "Now, I insist that you allow *someone*," he held up his hand to halt her speech when she looked to argue, "to make certain you're not severely injured."

"My maid," she grumbled.

"But, my dear," Rosalie said, starting down the stairs.

"My maid," Penelope growled.

"Of course," Rosalie replied softly.

"Jameson!" Duncan yelled.

"Sir?"

"Get Mary, now!"

"Yes, sir."

"My pearls!" Penelope cried out when she saw the iridescent beads scattered all over the stairs and the floor below.

"I'll gather them for you," Lucy said.

"Thank you."

"Your Grace?" the maid asked, puzzlement in her voice.

"Miss Presley has had an accident. Come up here and help me check her for signs of injury."

"Yes, Your Grace." Mary joined the couple on the landing. "Do you hurt anywhere, Miss Presley?"

"My ankle and wrist."

"It looks like you have a knot forming on your forehead, as well." Mary swiftly and expertly checked her wrist and ankle as well as her back. "We need to get your ankle and wrist bound. You also need something cool on that bump. Can you make it to your bedroom?"

"I'll carry her upstairs," Duncan spoke up.

"You'll do no such thing," Penelope argued.

"Your sixteen hours are up," Duncan said meaningfully, referencing the end of their conversation last night. He picked up her slight frame in his arms. She felt so feminine compared to him. Penelope cradled her wrist against her chest.

"Please be careful where you step. Those are my mother's pearls."

"Lucy."

"I've gathered all between you and the top of the stairs."

Duncan walked up the stairs with his future wife in his arms. "Reese, please let Reverend Meecham know there will be a delay. I will send word in a few days when we are ready."

"No," Penelope countered.

"Yes."

"Reverend Meecham," she said, looking over Duncan's shoulder at the forgotten man looking bewildered at the goings-on. "If you will just give us a few moments, the wedding will go on as scheduled."

"Miss Presley, it can be postponed," the cleric said.

"No, Reverend, it cannot. It has already been postponed long enough."

"Yes, miss."

Duncan carried her down the gallery hall she had just passed through back to her room. He gently placed her on her bed, but refused to leave her. Instead, he alternated between pacing and looking out the windows. *This can't be happening again*, he fretted. *There's no way that I'll allow another woman to be killed because I need an heir and a spare.* So lost was he in thought that it took several minutes before he realized he was being spoken to.

"What?"

"You're making Mary nervous. Please quit pacing."

Duncan came to an abrupt halt and observed the maid wrapping both Penelope's ankle and wrist with strips of white fabric. He watched as she made Mary place her slipper back on her swollen foot.

"There you go, Miss Presley. It will offer you some support, but you shouldn't walk on it for a few days. You also need to keep it elevated."

"Thank you, Mary, I'll see that she does all of the above."

"Yes, Your Grace." Mary curtsied deeply in acknowledgement of his authority.

"Mary, would you collect my pearls from Lucy and put them in the jewelry box. I'll restring them later."

"Yes, miss." Mary quickly dipped into another, more shallow curtsy then left the room.

"I'm letting you out of the contract," Duncan said, looking out the window.

"What?"

"I'm letting you out of the contract," he repeated and turned to look at Penelope.

"Why?"

"I refuse to be responsible for another woman's death."

"Well, I'm sorry that you feel that way, but my grandfather has an agreement with you, and he's very particular about his wishes being carried out. He would have us thrown in Newgate for breech of contract."

"In other words, he needs the money."

Penelope remained silent.

"I'll give him the bloody money," Duncan said as he speared his fingers through his hair. "I will *not* have another death on my conscience."

"I am made of sterner stuff. Do you forget my family history? I *will* be your wife. I *will* give you an heir. And I *will* live to be an old woman."

"Before we exchange vows, you need to know everything about—"

"I do."

Duncan looked up, startled.

"Please, Your Grace. Do you think in a house this big there isn't going to be someone willing to share the ghastly history of the *Beast of Yorkshire* with his new fiancée? I know how much you cared for your first wife. That you were very dear friends and perhaps you loved each other just a bit and there was to be a child when she had her accident. Perhaps that is what hurts you most about her. Then to watch the second linger with a long, suffering illness that no one was able to cure. And to have the third one cowardly take her own life. No, Your Grace, I am made of sterner stuff than that.

"I have survived gossip and scandal. I lived through my father turning traitor because he went through the family coffers. Then he turned a pistol on himself rather than face the hangman. And then there was Whitney. She was my twin sister, and I thought I knew everything about her. I was so very wrong. You know, she tried to kill the wife of the Director of the War Office."

"I had heard that," Duncan replied, keeping his answer to a minimum. It seemed as if Penelope needed to vent her spleen and he would allow her the opportunity.

"She almost succeeded, except the other woman had some unexpected talents. Mother lost her mind and my brother was sent to the country estate to be tutored in private and taught how the estate operates. He visits London occasionally, but not enough in my opinion. Therefore, since the deaths of my father and sister, it has only been me to take the brunt of my grandfather's temper, and pardon me for saying this Your Grace, but I will be damned if I go back to his house. I would rather stay here and face whatever fate awaits me."

"What did Lord Bolingbroke do to you?"

"It's not important. Also, you should know that if we're not married by tomorrow evening, Grandfather will have Mother committed to Bedlam. Now that you know all about me, I guess I should ask if *you* still want to marry *me*?"

Duncan studied the woman sitting before him. Her chin was tilted at a proud, but determined angle, and her uninjured hand was tightly fisted in her lap as she waited for him to announce his verdict. What was he going to do? Condemn her to a life with him or her grandfather? Duncan did the only thing he felt he could do.

"Miss Presley, I will leave the decision entirely up to you. I will be downstairs in the study with the minister. If you do not arrive within thirty minutes, I will send him away and begin making arrangements to send you wherever you would like to go." With that, Duncan turned and left her room knowing it would probably be one of the last times he would ever see her. For when given the opportunity, who would stay around to marry the *Beast of Yorkshire* when they could live without the fear of death hovering about them elsewhere?

Penelope sat on the bed, cradling her throbbing wrist. Had she truly told the *Beast of Yorkshire* she preferred marriage to him rather than living with Grandfather? She had never admitted to anyone how much she despised the old man. How much she blamed him for all that had befallen her family. How much she would hate him if he turned Sam into a replica of himself.

"No, there is *nothing* that could entice me to spend another second in Grandfather's house," she announced to the empty room. She gingerly stood and hobbled across the floor to reach the bell pull. Then she rested, most unladylike, on the little table next to the bed. In moments Mary stood in the open doorway.

"Did you need something, miss?"

"Yes, Mary. Please send for Lord Reese, then I need your assistance in making me presentable once more. I have a wedding to attend."

"But, miss…"

"Yes?" Penelope asked, raising an eyebrow at the young woman's hesitation.

"Nothing, Miss Presley." Mary pulled on the bell pull and then assisted Penelope awkwardly across the room. The maid went right to work reworking the ribbon through Penelope's golden curls and repinning the strands that had escaped during the fall. In the meantime, another maid appeared and was instructed to bring Lord Reese immediately.

Soon the man stood in the doorway, a concerned look on his face. He waited until Mary left before speaking. "I can't believe he tried anything before the marriage. I'll kill him for you, just say the word."

"Please, calm down."

"Calm down? How can you act as if nothing happened? Your wrist and ankle are wrapped and you have a bump the size of a chicken egg on your head."

"You exaggerate." But she still checked her reflection in the mirror. True, there was a bump, but it was nowhere near the size of a chicken egg. A robin's egg, perhaps, but definitely not a chicken's egg.

"Penelope, why did you send for me if you're going to go through with this?"

"I want you to give me away, Reese."

"No."

"Please. I would ask my brother, but he isn't here. I wouldn't ask you, but you've been so kind to me, and you do know Sam."

"You want me to escort you to your death?"

"Your brother is not a killer," Penelope steadfastly replied.

"You truly believe that, don't you?"

"Yes, I do."

"Fine. I'll stand in for your brother, but I'm not leaving after the vows have been spoken. I plan to stay around and make certain you're safe. Do you understand?"

"I would expect no less from my brother. Thank you, Reese." Penelope stood with his assistance and hugged him tightly. Neither saw the person standing in the hallway spying on them.

Duncan stood in the study, quietly talking to the vicar when Reese entered the room with Penelope in his arms. Rage coursed through him upon seeing his brother holding his fiancée so intimately. He took a deep breath and exhaled slowly. It would be better this way. She'd be safe and live a long, fruitful life—albeit without him. What was it about this woman that he felt like she was already his?

"…can go on as planned," Reese said.

"What?" Duncan asked, pulling himself back to the present. He noticed that Penelope now stood next to Reese on one foot, an arm wrapped about his to help her keep her balance. The bump on her forehead was turning mottled shades of blue, purple, green, and yellow. He imagined she had a terrible headache but doubted she would say anything about it. He found himself wanting to take her in his arms, to protect her from the world, but she had made her choice. Duncan just prayed that Reese was not the killer he suspected him to be.

"…marriage to take place?"

"Pardon?" Duncan asked for clarification once more.

Reese helped Penelope sit down before walking to his brother, grabbing his arm, and pulling him into the foyer. "What is wrong with you?" Reese demanded of Duncan.

"Nothing."

"Well, it sure as hell doesn't seem like it. For some reason, unbeknownst to me, that woman in there wants to go through with marrying you. You, at least, could act like you want to go through with it as well."

"She what?"

"Where have you been?" Reese asked the ceiling and let his hands flop against his outer thighs. "Listen to me, big brother, and listen well. Penelope wants to go through with this marriage. I am taking her brother's place and giving her away. Do *not* make me regret going through with this."

"She needs to leave. She isn't safe in this house. No woman connected to me is."

"I agree, but if you haven't noticed, your future wife is quite stubborn. Once she makes up her mind I think it is very hard to coerce her to change it. So, to ensure her health stays intact, I will be staying on, as I said earlier."

"And you think *that* is going to keep her safe?" Duncan scoffed.

"How many times do I have to tell you that I had nothing to do with their deaths?"

"So it was just a coincidence you were always here when one of them died?"

"Yes."

"I doubt that very much."

"I don't care if you believe me or not. The truth is I'm not a murderer, and I *will* be staying to see that Penelope receives adequate protection."

"And are you going to spend the night in our bedroom each night?"

"If necessary."

"You are a sick bastard," Duncan growled. "I can't believe you think me capable of murdering my wives."

"Yet you think *me* capable of murdering them. Explain to me how that makes any sense at all. Now, you have a beautiful woman in there willing to sacrifice herself for her family. Are you going to embarrass her and send her away, or are you going to marry her?"

Duncan remained quiet, staring down his brother.

"Well, what are you going to do, Duncan?" Penelope's challenge floated to his ears. He turned his head to see her standing in the doorway, a grimace the only thing marring her beautiful face, as she leaned heavily on Reverend Meecham.

Penelope sat in the chair where Reese had left her. Her head pounded as did her wrist and ankle. She shifted uncomfortably and tried very hard to suppress the moan that wanted to escape. She could feel bruised areas popping up all over her body, especially her back.

"For some reason, unbeknownst to me, that woman in there wants to go through with marrying you. You, at least, could act like you want to go through with it as well."

"She what?"

When Reese dragged Duncan into the foyer, he had not closed the door behind them and now their conversation was filtering into the study. *No, their argument*, she corrected herself. It sounded as if both men thought the other responsible for the death of the three women. At that time the enormity of what Penelope was about to do overwhelmed her. She was willing to risk her life in order to not return to her grandfather's house, to rescue her mother from the man's clutches, and to hopefully save her brother as well.

"And are you going to spend the night in our bedroom each night?"

"If necessary."

Penelope's head snapped up as the brother's argument once again penetrated her rampant thoughts. She looked up to see the minister blushing and tugging at his collar. She gave the man an awkward smile before pushing herself out of the chair, careful not to use her wrapped hand. Penelope tried to put pressure on her bandaged foot and almost collapsed. She grabbed the chair to stay upright.

"Miss Presley, allow me." Reverend Meecham lay his Bible down on a table then rushed to her side.

"You are a sick bastard," Duncan growled. "I can't believe you think me capable of murdering them."

"Please help me to the door," she begged the cleric.

"Are you certain that is wise?"

"Yet you think *me* capable of murdering them. Explain to me how that makes any sense at all. Now, you have a beautiful woman in there willing to sacrifice herself for her family. Are you going to embarrass her and send her away, or are you going to marry her?" They heard Reese ask.

"Not in the least, Reverend Meecham, but I fear it must be done."

"At least take a drink and fortify yourself," the older man lifted the cup someone had sat on the small nesting table beside her.

"I think that is a wonderful idea." Penelope took the drink from Reverend Meecham and made quick work of it. It was light, flavorful, and refreshing. Feeling much better, she looked at the older man and said, "I am ready for your assistance."

"Of course."

Penelope and the reverend crossed the room as quickly as possible, considering. The two entered the foyer and saw the brothers staring one another down. Duncan looked pensive, angry, and something else that she couldn't quite name. "Well, what are you going to do, Duncan?"

She knew that she had startled him. Penelope had used his Christian name for the first time, and she found it rolled off her tongue much easier than it should. She also knew the exact moment he realized she stood there.

"You shouldn't be standing."

"I repeat, what are you going to do, Duncan?" she asked again.

"I suppose I'm going to marry you."

"Reese, will you still give me away?"

"Yes," he answered reluctantly.

Lucy walked into the house with a tiny nosegay consisting of red and white roses and some greenery. She held them out to Penelope. “I picked these for you.”

“Thank you, Lucy.”

“I’ll get mother so we can start the ceremony.”

Penelope nodded quickly and inhaled the sweet and spicy smell of the roses.

“Penelope, are you—”

“Don’t.”

“But, I want to make sure that—”

“Reese, I have no more options left open to me.” She did not mean for them to, but the words drifted across the room to her future husband.

Once everyone had gathered, the ceremony proceeded quickly. A ring was slipped onto the ring finger of her right hand due to the swelling from her sprained, left wrist. She would move it to the correct hand as soon as she could. Throughout the ceremony, she clutched the nosegay as if it were a lifeline, the aromatic scent of the roses wafted up to her, calming her. Several times during the ceremony, she brought the flowers up to her nose to inhale more deeply of their smell, not really caring what anyone thought of her behavior.

At the end of the ceremony something strange started to happen. Penelope felt like it was a combination of stress and her earlier fall, but her vision became slightly blurred and she was seeing two of the big man in front of her. A lightness washed over her body and she felt as if she were floating. She weaved and felt herself falling only to be brought up tight against Duncan, her fia…no, her husband.

“Are you all right?” he whispered to her.

“Just a little dizzy.”

“Your Graces, I need you to sign the marriage certificate.”

“Of course,” Duncan said.

Penelope heard the scratching of a quill, but her husband never relinquished his hold on her. She was tethered to his side as a boat was to a dock. For some reason that thought made her giggle hysterically. He placed the quill in her hand and lowered the writing utensil to the line she had to sign.

"Sign here," he ordered her. She scrawled her name as best she could without really seeing it or anything else on the paper.

"And now the witnesses," Reverend Meecham said.

"Rosalie, Reese, will you sign the certificate?"

"Of course. What's wrong with Penelope?" Reese asked.

"Aftereffects, I believe."

Everyone quickly signed their parts on the certificate, keeping a close eye on the bride. It was passed to Duncan who tucked it into a hidden pocket on his coat, then he bent and swung Penelope up in his arms.

"I'm flying!" Penelope announced, flopping her arms like bird's wings.

"Where are you going?" Rosalie asked.

"My wife needs to rest."

"But the festival—"

"Will have to wait. The townsfolk will understand," Duncan said. "As you can see, she is in no condition to attend a festival."

"But I want to dance and be festive," Penelope whined, then she flung her head back and giggled hysterically. "Duncan, why're you being so mean to me? I'm a duchess now. You must do as I say, and I say take me to the festival!" she shouted.

"No."

"Reese will take me, won't you, Reese?" she asked her brother-in-law pitifully. She perched her chin on Duncan's shoulder, wrapped her arms loosely about his neck, and peered at Reese as she pouted childishly.

"Not if he knows what's good for him," Duncan growled low in her ear as he carried her up the stairs.

There would be talk, he thought to himself, but there was nothing to be had. "Send Mary to Penelope's room," he called over his shoulder, not caring who followed through with the order as long as someone did. Penelope needed to rest. He left the study and the others behind and climbed the stairs. Over halfway up he took a step and heard a crunch beneath his foot.

"Mama's pearls!" the woman in his arms wailed. Duncan sighed and looked heavenward. He knew that if he looked, there would be a crushed pearl where his boot had been. Instead, he continued up the stairs.

"What has gotten into you? This is more than aftereffects from a fall."

"What were they talking about downstairs?" Penelope asked, squinting up at him. "Oh, yes, a festival. I want to go." Suddenly the tears stopped and she squirmed in his arms.

"Don't worry about it now, and you aren't going anywhere. You need to rest and recover."

"I'll be fine."

"After you rest," he said again. "Mary is going to stay with you." Was it just him, or did he feel her relax a bit when he said that? Halfway down the hall he heard scurrying feet. Mary passed them and held the door open. He gently placed her on the bed.

"You made a beautiful bride," he said.

"Thank you, Duncan."

"Rest now. Mary, stay with her, and don't let anyone in or out other than me. Do you understand?"

"Yes, Your Grace."

"I have some things to see to, but I will be back. Take care of her."

"I will, Your Grace."

"My flowers! Duncan, I want my flowers."

"I'll have them sent up to you."

He left the two women alone, enclosing them in the duchess' chamber. For a moment he considered locking them inside, but changed his mind in the end.

What is going on with her? he wondered once he was in the hallway. The way she was acting had nothing to do with her fall down the stairs. "It's already started," he announced to the suits of armor lining the hall. "Dammit," he slammed the flat of his palm against the wooden door frame.

The door opened a crack and Mary stood on the other side, a concerned look on her face. "Your Grace, did you need something?"

"No, I'm sorry." Duncan turned and walked away from the duchess' bedchamber. Once he reached the bottom of the stairs, he looked at the people gathered around with anxious looks on their faces. "In the study, now," he growled, leaving no room for argument. "Shut the door," he ordered, not caring who did it.

Once he heard the tell-tale click, he turned on the group. “Who drugged my wife?”

“What in bloody hell are you talking about?” Reese demanded.

“Did you not see how she was acting?”

“The fall—” Lucy started only to be interrupted by Duncan.

“The fall did not cause her to yell she was flying to one and all when I picked her up.”

“I suggested she take a drink to help fortify her before we joined you in the foyer.”

“Where’s the glass?”

“Here, Your Grace.” Reverend Meecham quickly grabbed the glass and handed it over to Duncan.

He took the glass from the cleric and sniffed. Next, he swiped the inside with a finger then tentatively tasted it. There was just a hint of bitterness on his tongue, but it was so masked by all the other flavors that it would be easy for one to miss it.

“Well?” Reese demanded.

“There was something in here besides just the wine.”

“Damn you, Duncan. I warned you—”

“And I didn’t touch a hair on her head.”

“Boys,” Rosalie said.

“Reverend Meecham, thank you for coming and performing the ceremony,” Duncan held his hand out to the cleric.

“It was my pleasure, Your Grace.”

“Rosalie, Lucy, would you mind showing Reverend Meecham out?”

“Of course, Duncan. Come, Lucy,” Rosalie called for her daughter to follow her.

“What are you going to do?” Reese asked once the others had left the room.

Duncan remained silent, not ready to share his thoughts with anyone, let alone his brother.

“Did you hear me?”

“Yes.”

“Well?”

“This is not something I’m willing to talk to you about.” Duncan walked past his brother only to feel a heavy hand on his upper arm halting him. He looked down at the hand and followed it upward until he reached his brother's face. Rather than saying anything, he merely cocked a brow at Reese.

"I warned you that I would do whatever I could to protect her from you."

"And I told you that I have never hurt a wife of mine, nor do I intend to begin with Penelope. Now, are you done with your accusations?" When silence met him, Duncan jerked his arm free of his brother's grip.

"I'm going to stand guard outside of Penelope's door."

"That's not necessary. Mary is with her."

"I believe it is." Duncan watched Reese leave the room then he saw a concerned Rosalie standing in the doorway.

"It's started again, Duncan."

"Leave me alone and shut the door," he ordered his step-grandmother.

"But Duncan—"

"Shut. The. Door," he barked the order. He saw the hurt look flitter across the woman's face before she obeyed his command. Duncan could see she was truly concerned by the latest turn of events, but he didn't have the energy to pacify her. He walked to his desk and pounded on the top of it in time with the words he uttered, "Damn! Damn! Damn!" Duncan collapsed into the large chair behind his desk. "What am I going to do?" he asked the empty room, cradling his head in his hands, his elbows braced on the top of the desk.

Somehow, the crinkle of the paper in his inner coat pocket penetrated his thoughts. He took out the folded piece of paper and tapped it against the palm of his hand before laying it aside. Duncan pulled out a sheet of vellum as well as ink and a quill. He carefully wrote out instructions for his secretary regarding the filing of the marriage certificate and acquiring Penelope's mother from Lord Bolingbroke's clutches.

Duncan stood and tugged on the bell pull. Jameson entered the room after a polite knock.

"Yes, Your Grace?"

"See that Mr. Phillips gets this."

"Yes, Your Grace. Is there anything else that you need?"

"No, that's all." Duncan looked around the room as if to check that there was anything else he needed to attend to before returning upstairs. He came to an awkward halt when he saw Reese sitting on a chair across from Penelope's bedroom. His brother was reclining in the chair on two legs. He was so very tempted to kick them out from under him and watch him go flying. Instead, he stalked over to him and stared down at him. "You can leave now."

"I don't think so."

"I don't need you camping outside our suite."

"I beg to differ."

"Damn you!" Duncan grabbed the lapels of Reese's superfine and jerked him upright. "Leave this house."

"I don't trust you to be alone with your wife."

"I didn't—"

"Boys, this is enough! Reese, go to your room now."

"But Rosalie—"

"Go."

"Thank you, Rosalie," Duncan said.

She nodded before walking down the hall and disappearing around the corner. Duncan watched his brother reluctantly follow suit, then he turned and entered her room. "How is she?" he asked Mary.

"She's been asleep almost the entire time you've been gone."

"Good. Thank you, Mary. You may go." She curtsied and left the room.

Duncan locked the door behind the maid then turned and took in the room. Penelope remained lying on top of the bed covers in the dress she wore for the wedding. She looked so innocent, asleep as she was. Too innocent to be married to the likes of him and forced to live in this cursed house. But he had to remain here. Had to protect his people, keep them safe.

He checked all of the windows in her room, along with the doors that led onto the balcony shared with his chamber. Duncan checked the two wardrobes in her bedroom to make certain no one lurked inside. He even dropped to his hands and knees and checked beneath her bed. Nothing.

"Careful, my husband is lurking around here somewhere." The slurred words reached his ears. "They call him the *Beast of Yorkshire*. I should be scared of him."

"You aren't?" He couldn't stop from asking the question.

"No. I'm scared of this house. There's evil here…" A snuffling sound filled the air.

Duncan peeked over the edge of the bed and saw that Penelope was asleep once more. He climbed to his booted feet, heaved a sigh, and rested his left fist on his hip while he tunneled his right through his thick, dark hair. "What am I going to do?" He shook his head and crossed the room to enter his bedchamber.

CHAPTER 4

Penelope woke to a strange room. *Where am I?* she wondered worriedly. The full moon filtered through the sheer curtains hanging over the French doors and the windows. She shifted and couldn't help the moan that escaped. Every part of her body ached. Her head throbbed like someone was beating a drum and wouldn't stop. She studied the room and tried to move as little as possible. Slowly the room began to look familiar to her. She was in the duchess' chamber in Taggart Hall. She was now the Duchess of Yorkshire from what little she could remember of yesterday.

Her eyes flew open as she had a sudden, overwhelming urge to visit the necessary. She rolled to her side with a loud groan and winced as she struggled to push herself upright. Once she managed to sit up and swing her legs over the side of the bed, her ankle throbbed in time with the pounding in her head. She sat there for several minutes hoping everything would calm down, but soon her body demanded she see to its needs.

She put her good foot on the floor and used her good hand to balance. The throbbing slowed to a dull ache, and she decided to take her chance. The first hobble wasn't terrible. She was still standing up at least. But by the time she reached the halfway point, tears had come to her eyes and her leg throbbed all the way to her hip.

"What are you doing out of bed?"

The low-pitched voice broke her concentration, and as she spun to see who had infiltrated her room, she lost her balance. She gritted her teeth and prepared herself for a fall that never happened. Instead she was gathered up in two strong arms and cradled against a firm, bare chest.

"Put me down." She struggled against him.

"Where exactly? You aren't supposed to put any weight on that ankle. Now, what where you doing?"

She refused to make eye contact with him.

"I can stay here the rest of the night, just like this," her husband threatened huskily.

They stared at each other, until Penelope looked away. "Water closet," she mumbled.

"What was that?"

"Water closet," she managed to get out between her gritted teeth.

"Oh, yes, um, I see," he said.

"You can send for Mary," she suggested.

"Who is already asleep, more than likely. I'll see to your needs. After all we're married now, aren't we?"

Penelope was mortified when he put her on her feet outside of the water closet. She waited for him to light a lamp, place it inside, and then leave her in solitude. She considered just staying in there the rest of the night, perhaps the rest of her life. It would be infinitely easier than facing him again. Unfortunately, the knocking on the door indicated that would not be the case. Penelope stood balancing on one foot, silently praying that he would give up and go away. More pounding followed by a concerned inquiry.

"Penelope, are you all right in there?"

"I'm fine," she ground out.

"Do you need more, um, time?"

As her mind followed his train of thought, she immediately shouted, "No! No, I'm finished." Penelope pushed open the door refusing to meet his eyes. She felt herself swept up in his powerful arms once more and deposited in front of the stand containing the pitcher and basin.

"Yell out when you're finished," he said.

"Thank you," she muttered. Penelope went through the motions of washing. Afterwards, she looked down and realized she was still wearing the gown she was married in. What exactly had happened to her? She began to work at the buttons along the back of her dress, but found it difficult to do one handed.

"Allow me," Duncan's deep voice rolled over her.

Penelope's back went ramrod straight as she heard him so near. The single light he had lit earlier cast them in shadows. She looked in the mirror and saw him standing behind her. He looked so very intent on the job before him. She felt the buttons slipping free, one-by-one, and decided to talk in order to take her mind off of what he was doing.

"I remember so little of last night. What happened?" She met his gaze in the mirror.

"I believe someone drugged your drink."

"I see."

"You don't sound surprised."

"After taking a fall down the stairs, I fear nothing is going to surprise me. Was anything ever found around the stairs?"

"No."

"Of course not." He slipped the last button free just as the sound of drums being beaten reached their ears. She put a hand to her head and muttered, "I wish that drumming would stop."

"Drums. I must get dressed."

"You can hear them? They're not just in my head?"

"Not this time."

"Not funny, Your Grace," she called after him, holding her head. She watched him slip through the door that joined their rooms. Penelope slipped her dress off her shoulders and let it fall to the floor while trying to maintain her balance. The drums continued to beat loudly. She also heard a pounding filter from the duke's bedchamber. There was a low quick conversation, then he was back in her room.

She leaned on the washstand and turned her head to look at him. What she saw took her breath away. Her husband was dressed in all black from head to toe making him look quite piratical, much like he had that first night.

"What's happening?" Penelope questioned him.

"An emergency. I'll be back as soon as I can." He helped her to the bed. "I want you to keep the doors locked until I get back."

"All right," she agreed.

"I'm serious about the doors."

"I said I would keep them locked," she tossed back.

"I'm sorry your wedding day has been so—"

"Memorable?" Penelope finished with a smirk.

"Yes."

Then he surprised her when he leaned over her and placed a gentle kiss on her lips. "Stay safe," he said.

"Duncan! Let's go!" Reese pounded on the door that connected their rooms.

"I'm coming!" Duncan called back. He bent down and kissed her once more before disappearing through the adjoining door.

Penelope sat on the bed and stared where her new husband disappeared. She found that her body pulsed in time with the drums. Her fingers on her unwrapped hand drifted up to her lips that tingled from her husband's kisses—something she had never expected to happen.

Duncan and Reese rode towards the seaside village as fast as their horses would carry them. Clouds drifted over the waning moon, casting the land in shadows. It was dangerous to push the horses so hard, but the drums were being pounded louder and louder.

"Will your bride be safe?" Reese yelled over the rushing wind.

"I locked her in her chambers, so I can only hope."

"And if something should happen to you?"

"Then you must be hale enough to return and set her free," Duncan threw back at his younger brother, finding himself jealous of the man's easy camaraderie with Penelope. "Go south and I'll head north." He veered his horse in the direction he had indicated he would take, not bothering to check that his brother followed his order. He rode his stallion, Cyclops, to the top of the cliff and looked out at the channel.

There, bobbing on the water was the cause of the drumming. A good sized ship sat just beyond the bay, and rowboats were being lowered into the water.

"Damn press gangs," he muttered.

"Third one this month, Duncan," a burly man with Viking ancestry running through his blood came up beside him.

"Yes," he muttered.

"Same as usual?"

"Yes, Gavin. And this time, let's make an impression on them. I grow weary of this game they're playing."

"Right away, sir. Boys, you heard him. Man your positions."

The sound of chorused agreement reached Duncan's ears. He sat atop his stallion, blending in with the darkening skies as he watched the village men prepare to fight off another press gang. He should be grateful they had not lost more men to them, but the ones they had lost were good men and would probably never be seen again. The rowboats were pulling into the shallows and sailors were jumping into thigh-deep water.

"Now!" Duncan yelled, and the first round of gunshots could be heard along both sides of the cliffs. Flashes from the end of the rifles gave away locations of the village men. Another round of gunshots could be heard from down below. Duncan gave a smirk because he knew the women of the village refused to be left behind in the battle.

"You took my brother, you bloody bastards! You killed my mother!" An accusatory voice had Duncan searching to find the person. The clouds parted, giving both him and the press gang a view of the person running towards the water. The loud bang of a solitary gun filled the air, falling one of the sailors.

"Anna! Come back!" a frantic female stood in the darkened doorway of a house screaming.

"Did you hear that, Duncan?"

"Aye," he yelled spurring Cyclops into action. Cyclops made quick work of the steep trail down to the beach. The sound of random gunshots could be heard echoing off the cliffs. Thankfully, the woman was no longer yelling for Anna. Unfortunately, the sailors had begun to return fire, and Duncan found himself caught between the enemy and the ally.

Anna's slight figure continued to run towards the water, shooting, and discarding weapons as she went. She was making sure that every shot counted, too. *How many bloody guns does the girl have?* he wondered as he watched her shoot. He quickly followed that thought with, *Damn, I'm proud of her*. He blinked as he watched Anna fall to her knees in the surf before falling forward. "No!" he yelled at one of the sailors in the water moving toward the fallen girl. Duncan pulled his gun and shot the man, but not before he felt a searing pain in his own arm.

He heard a shout as fire lit arrows arced through the sky. Two of them met their target and caught one of the uppermost sails on fire. The call for retreat from the ship sounded followed by a cheer from the cliffs. The commanding officer of the ship would know he had precious little time to get the fire put out before it engulfed the vessel, leaving the men to face the angry villagers.

Duncan shook his head as he guided Cyclops to where he last saw Anna. He dropped heavily into the surf and used both the fire and scant light of the moon to search for the girl. A bit of her white shirt fluttered on the wind teasing Duncan. He grabbed at it once, twice before he had a firm grasp and pulled her close. He flipped her over and the sight that met him caused him to fall to his knees and cradle her close. A wave crashed over them.

"Duncan! Duncan!" The firm grip on his injured arm, along with the burn of the salty water brought him to his senses. "Come on!" Reese dragged him to his feet and grabbed Cyclops' reins. The two men stumbled and fought their way through the water to the beach. Duncan cradled the girl's lifeless body close.

The young woman that had screamed at Anna earlier came running toward them. "Keep her back!" Duncan ordered. Someone grabbed her, but he could hear her thrashing about in the background, trying to break free. He gently laid the girl on the rocky beach, her sightless eyes stared at nothing. The bullet had proven fatal. Duncan gently closed her eyes and bowed his head over the girl.

"No!"

"Sarah!" A young man came scrambling down one of the rock-strewn paths. Soon the girl was wrapped up in the arms of a strong young villager.

"Sarah, what happened?" Reese asked.

"When the drums started, she got this wild look on her face. After Caleb left, she gathered every weapon she could find. I tried…tried to take them from…from her," she sobbed.

"It's all right, love," Caleb soothed.

"It's not all right," Sarah said. "My *sister*, my only family is lying there dead because *he* can't protect us from the press gangs!" she yelled, pointing at Duncan. "Instead, a *girl* feels like it's her responsibility and ends up losing her life. It's true what they say, you really are a beast!" Sarah picked up her skirts and shouldered her way to the body of her sister before dropping to the ground once more. She gently cradled the younger girl in her arms, while she cried and rocked back and forth.

Reese helped Duncan to his feet. Even though Duncan stood several inches taller than Reese, he felt minuscule. Gavin reached them as Duncan was just about to mount his stallion.

"Anna?"

Duncan looked at his old friend and shook his head. "It would seem the curse has struck once more, only now it's affecting the villagers as well," he said as he mounted Cyclops. The coal black horse with the lone white patch around his eyes shied nervously, feeling his master's emotions. "I'll take care of all the costs of the funeral, but I won't be there."

"Duncan," Gavin stopped him.

The giant of a man paused and looked down at him from his great height.

"Sarah's anger will pass," the big, blonde man said, guessing at what had transpired. "Anna acted out and paid the price."

"Perhaps, but look at how they stare at me. They believe in the curse. They know I was married this very evening, yet there were no festivities because my wife was injured on her first night in my home as a married woman. I don't know, Gavin, perhaps I *am* cursed." Duncan nodded, turned his horse to the path leading to the top of the cliff, and spurred him forward, leaving the village behind.

Duncan and Reese entered the dark, looming house after leaving their horses with the stable hands. Duncan turned to his brother and studied him.

"I know we don't always agree on things, but thank you for your help tonight." He held out his hand to Reese.

"Let's get one thing straight. Those people are my friends, too," Reese said, as he took Duncan's hand firmly in his. "And another thing, as long as I think you are telling the truth, I *will* support your and stand beside you, because that's what brothers do."

The unspoken threat was not lost on Duncan.

"Is everyone all right?" Lucy asked breathlessly at the top of the stairs.

"Go to bed," Duncan said.

"But I heard the drums—"

"I said, 'Go to bed,' Lucy."

"It's been a long night, love," Reese said, softening Duncan's words.

"Your arm," Lucy gasped and stepped close to him when she saw the streaks of blood as Duncan passed her.

"Will be fine," he said as he brushed past her. He didn't even hear the whispering between his brother and Lucy. Duncan reached his bedroom door, dug for the key, and came up empty-handed. "Dammit!" He slammed the palm of his hand against the doorframe. "Jameson!" he shouted to the rafters, not caring who he disturbed.

"Yes, Your Grace?" the man summoned asked a few minutes later. He wore his nightshirt over his pants with his jacket pulled over it. The ensemble was completed with his slippers and a nightcap.

Duncan might have laughed if he wasn't so devastated from the events this day had brought. "I need the key to my rooms."

"Of course, Your Grace." Jameson handed over the key. "Your Grace, you're injured. Do you need assistance?"

"No. Go back to bed."

"Yes, Your Grace."

Duncan let himself into his room then locked the door behind him. A bottle of amber liquid sat on a low table near a chair. He walked across the room and poured himself a healthy amount before quickly downing it. He poured himself another drink and tossed it back, too. Duncan reared back and threw the glass across the room. It shattered across the far wall, falling in hundreds of pieces.

"Who's there?" a muffled feminine voice came through the wall.

He took the decanter and tipped it backwards, taking deep drinks, trying to ease the ache in his chest. All he could see was Anna's blank stare and hear her sister's accusatory words ringing in his ears. It brought to mind other women from his past. Isabelle's broken body lying among the rocks. Samantha fading away before their eyes. Francis choosing to end her life rather than be tied to him. Soon the dainty table followed the path of the glass. Splintered wood lay on the floor mixed among the broken glass that sparkled like diamonds.

"Duncan? Duncan, are you all right? Help! Someone help!" Pounding sounded both on the adjoining door and down the hall.

Duncan heard a muffled discussion outside his bedroom door that led to the hallway.

"Open the door, Duncan," Reese ordered.

He remained mute and tipped back the decanter once more.

"Duncan, please answer us." The feminine plea had him scowling at the connecting door. How in hell could she sound so concerned about him when they didn't even know each other? True, they were married, but she didn't want him. Nobody wanted him anymore, and he couldn't blame them. Who would want to be associated with the *Beast of Yorkshire*? He gave a soft laugh and took another drink from the decanter.

"Duncan, open the damn door!" his brother tried to order him.

"Go to hell," he slurred, the liquor had started to catch up with him.

"You're going to feel like hell in the morning," Reese predicted through the door.

"Too late," Duncan muttered. He emptied the rest of the bottle with just a few deep gulps.

"Open the door."

"I've no need for a nanny." He threw the empty container, enjoying the cacophony of sound as the glass made contact with the wood. Dark rivulets ran down the door.

"Fine. Enjoy your misery."

"I plan on it," he answered, saluting the door. He made his shaky way across the room to a free-standing cabinet. He smiled after he opened the door and found a bottle located inside. Duncan broke the seal on his smuggled French brandy as he continued to get well and truly drunk.

"Penelope, open up." She heard her brother-in-law urge from the other side of the large, wooden door.

"I can't. His Grace took the key and locked me inside before he left."

"The bloody bastard," he muttered.

"He was trying to protect me," she rushed to her husband's defense. *And why are you doing that?* she asked herself. "I have no idea," she murmured.

"Well, you're not going anywhere for the time being. He has the only key without us rousing the entire household."

"No, don't do that," she pleaded as a flush covered her skin. *There's no need for the staff to know that your new husband has kept you locked in your room like you're a captive,* she thought, mortified. "Jameson?" she asked, after taking a moment to remember the butler's name.

"Gave his key to Duncan."

"I see," she said softly, leaning her forehead against the cool wood. "Is he all right?"

"Who?"

"My husband." The word still felt foreign on her tongue.

"As well as he can be considering the circumstances."

"Yes, of course." Her thoughts, what few she could remember, went to their disastrous wedding hours earlier.

"No, Penelope, you misunderstand—"

"Please, Reese, don't say anymore. I understand perfectly. I'll be fine until morning. It's really not that many hours away. Good night."

"Damn…I mean—"

"Goodnight, Reese," she said more forcefully.

"Goodnight, Penelope," he returned on a sigh.

She pressed her ear against the door and heard his footsteps fade and then pause. Was that whispering? Yes. Who was he speaking to? What were they saying? Were they laughing at how her husband had her caged like a wild animal? Finally, the sound of closing doors greeted her ears.

"Did your protector go to bed?" Her husband asked through the door.

She hobbled as quickly and as best she could to the connecting door. "I hate you. Before morning, the entire household will know you have me locked up."

"It's our weddin' night," he slurred, "isn't that s'posed to hap'n?"

"Together, not separately," she hissed. She heard deep laughter from his bedroom. "This is not funny in the least."

"How's it feel to be sold to the *Beast*?"

"What?" she asked, straightening.

"How's it feel to be sold? Especially to a man who's killed three women already?"

"Are you drunk?" she asked suspiciously.

"Have they told you all the gory details yet? Have they made sure you know how each one died? That one took her life rather than marry me?"

"Duncan, stop."

"Less than twelve hours from the time the wedding was to happen…"

"Duncan," she ground out.

"And then tonight…"

"What happened tonight?" she asked, her curiosity piqued. She touched the connecting door as if she could touch him.

"She was so young," he slurred.

A thud and a tinkling sound reached her ears, followed by something strange and difficult to describe. Penelope winced as she fell to her knees and peered under the door. Her vision was blocked almost entirely, but there in the corner, just out of reach of her long, slim fingers was the key to her freedom. She reached under the door once more until the top of her hand was scraped, leaving behind white and red marks. She slammed her good hand against the floor.

"Think," she ordered herself, and blew a wayward piece of hair out of her face. Just as quickly the thought came to her. Penelope tugged four hairpins from her falling coiffure and twisted them together, wincing when they put pressure on her sprained wrist. At the end she bent it just a little. Once more, she peeped under the door and worked at moving the makeshift hook towards the key. She misjudged the distance and had to pause to add another pin to the length.

Biting back her frustration, she fed the hook under the door once more. This time it made the slightest contact with the key. She held her breath as she gently pulled the key toward her. Several times she had to pause and readjust the connection between the hook and key. When she finally had it in her hands, she almost screamed with delight. But the strangest thing happened next. Instead of hobbling across the room to freedom, she jammed the key in the lock of the door that connected her chamber to her husband's. She unlocked it and twisted the handle. Then two things happened. The door flew open on her, and her very drunk, very unconscious husband landed in a sprawled heap at her knees.

Penelope uprighted the bottle that lay haphazardly beside him before it spilled out any more of its amber contents, then she stared at the man she had been sold to. *No*, she corrected herself, *the man I married. No more will I blame people for the predicament I find myself in.* Even in a drunken sleep his brow looked marred with worry. *What exactly have you been through tonight?* she wondered.

She scooted around the door and leaned over him, feeling around his waist. She removed two pistols and gently laid them aside. Penelope peered into the room and saw shattered glass, splintered wood, and trails of liquid flowing down a wall. She shook her head and found herself sitting next to him and running a finger over his brow. A lullaby came to mind that her nurse used to sing to her and her siblings when they were ill or their sleep was plagued with nightmares. Penelope softly began to hum to the giant of a man. Was it her imagination, or did he seem to relax some?

When he seemed to be resting more peacefully, she managed to stand. She gathered the half-empty bottle and the two pistols and limped into her room. Knowing she couldn't move Duncan, she left him on the hard floor to sleep off his drunken stupor. She looked at him once more and found herself thinking that he had not earned the harsh nickname he'd been given. Then she turned and took care of the things that she must.

CHAPTER 5

Duncan woke to a pounding in his head, the likes of which he had never quite felt before. He groaned as light pierced his eyes. Ever so slowly, he rolled over onto his stomach, cradling his head. *What did I do last night*? Then in a flash everything came back to him. Well, almost everything. He slowly squinted one eye open and saw a doorframe and below him was the floor. *What the hell?*

"Coming back to life?"

The melodious voice of a female reached his ears. A female that wasn't Lucy or Rosalie. He managed to raise his head and track the origin of the voice. In a chair, backlighted by the light coming through the window, sat a blonde, ethereal looking woman. His wife if he remembered correctly. "Pen…Pene—"

"My name is Penelope," she reminded him, enunciating each syllable.

"I remember," he reassured her before allowing himself to collapse on the floor once more. The smell of whisky and smuggled brandy reached his nostrils making his stomach roil. He groaned again.

"I'm surprised you can remember anything after last night," Penelope said, just the hint of snarkiness in her voice.

He snapped his head up and looked at her. She had a brow cocked haughtily at him. Duncan glanced down and saw a cocked gun held firmly in her hand. He blinked, willing the blurriness to go away. Duncan looked once more. His wife was definitely pointing a gun at him. So this was going to be how it ended. The *Beast of Yorkshire* was finally going to be bested by one of his wives before the same could be done to her. He chuckled until it expanded the pounding in his head.

"I suggest you find a more comfortable position. We're going to have a discussion."

"You're not going to shoot me?"

"Not right now," she replied.

A mixture of relief and disappointment vied for dominance in him. He struggled to push up to his hands and knees.

"There's a chair to your left."

Duncan turned his head. Sure enough, there sat a chair, a rather comfortable looking one at that. He crawled over to it and pulled himself into it. "How much did I drink last night?" he asked. His head was propped against the chair's soft, high back.

"I really don't know. I found a bottle more than half empty next to you, but I doubt that was the first one."

"I very much doubt it, too," Duncan agreed. "What exactly do you want to talk about? I'm not certain how well I can focus, but I'll do my best."

"Fair enough. First of all, did you kill your wives?"

"Cutting straight to the heart of the matter, aren't you? I thought you believed me innocent."

"One will say anything when they feel like an endangered species. Answer the question," she ordered.

"No."

"What do you think happened to them?"

"I really wish I knew," he said the last on a sigh.

"Do you believe I am in danger?"

"Very much so."

"Thank you for being honest."

"I wish I had another answer to give you." He opened one eye in time to see her shrug one shoulder.

"I have found life to not be very kind to me over the last two years. Why should my marriage to you be any different?"

"I will do everything in my power to protect you."

"Thank you for that, at least. What were the drums last night?"

"Press gang," he answered succinctly.

"I'm sorry? I have vaguely heard of them, but I don't guess I quite comprehend what you mean."

"Robin Hood's Bay is a fishing village. Fishermen are supposed to be safe from the press gangs if they choose not to join His Majesty's Navy. This war has dragged on longer than anyone thought, and depleted our manpower. The Navy is desperate for sailors."

"Therefore, they come after men that live in villages along the coastline?"

"Yes, especially when they can't find any enemy ships to overtake."

"The drums are a warning," she guessed.

"And a summons. The women beat the drums as a warning while the men retreat to the cliffs. Those of us that live further away from the village ride in to help. Then gunfire ensues, and we run them off once more. Hopefully, without anyone being taken."

"Sometimes it doesn't work out that way?"

"No."

"What happened last night? What caused you to come back and drink so much? Was it a celebration?"

"No." *Why am I sharing all this with her?* he wondered. *Because you're tired of being alone. Tired of being treated like a pariah. Tired of keeping everything to yourself.* "No, it was not a celebration. We have been attacked randomly by press gangs in the past, but this is the third time this month."

"Isn't that a lot?"

"It feels like it." He paused and studied Penelope. She really seemed to be concerned with what was going on in their little part of England. Duncan straightened up and continued with the story, keeping eye contact with his new wife. "The first press gang that attacked this month took a young man with them. His mother was a widow and had been ill for some time. She died a few days after he left, leaving behind two daughters. Sarah is newly married and Anna is no more than fifteen. Anna has always been a spitfire. When she was younger she would often accompany her father on his fishing trips." He sat there quietly for several minutes, visions of last night flashing before him.

"Duncan?"

"She ran out of the house, screamed at the sailors, and called them filthy names. Her mother would have been horrified at the language coming out of her daughter. I think Anna killed two and injured at least one more before she fell into the water."

"They shot her?"

"She was dressed like a boy. The only reason we knew it was Anna was because her sister called her name as she ran from the house. I guided my horse down the cliffside as quickly as possible, but when I got to her…"

"She was dead?"

"Yes," he said roughly. He rubbed his hands over his face. "I can't get the way she looked out of my mind. Her sightless eyes. She was so damn young."

"I'm sorry," Penelope offered.

"It's not your fault."

"No, but I truly am sorry. I do know what it's like to lose people you are close to. The villagers are like family to you, aren't they?"

"Yes."

"I thought so," she said.

They both remained quiet for many minutes, but he noticed the gun never wavered. His wife had determination. She rose several notches in his estimation. The piercing light of the sun shining into the room felt like a pick to his brain. He scowled and rubbed one temple before he felt some relief when shade fell over him. Duncan looked up and saw the drape pulled partially over the window. "Thank you."

"Tell me about you and your brother."

"We're like any siblings. We get along sometimes, we fight sometimes."

"It seems like you fight more than just sometimes. It also sounded like he believes you *were* responsible for what happened to your wives and fiancée and vice versa."

"Yes."

"Can I trust him?"

"I don't know."

"Rosalie and Lucy?"

"I don't know."

"The staff?"

"I don't know."

"What *do* you know?"

“That you should trust no one?”

“Not even you?”

“Not if you’re wise,” he said.

“I don’t suppose I’m very wise then,” she replied.

“Then you can put the gun down.”

“Not quite yet. There’s the matter of our marriage to discuss.”

“Oh?”

“Yes. I’m tired of being the one who is whispered about. I think I might like the quietness of Yorkshire.”

“You’re staying? Despite the accident?”

“We’re married. Of course I’m staying. There’s something else. You need an heir—”

“About that—”

“I want a child and, if I’m lucky enough, children.”

“What are you saying?”

“I want someone who will love me unconditionally. Someone I can take care of. Someone that won’t look at me in horror. Someone who hasn’t heard all the rumors, or worse, the ugly truth. Someone innocent of the world’s ugliness.”

“I see.”

“So when my sprained ankle and wrist heal…”

“Of course.” He cleared his throat nervously. “Can you put the gun away?”

“Ask nicely.”

“Please.” Click. The sound echoed in his ears as he watched her pull the trigger. “It was empty?” he asked incredulously.

“I cleaned it.”

“What? How?”

“Never underestimate me, Duncan.”

“No, I can see that I shouldn’t. I suppose I should get cleaned up now if that is all for our discussion.” He indicated his stiffened, salt-encrusted clothes. Duncan pushed up and winced before he collapsed back into the chair and grabbed his arm.

“What’s wrong?”

“I forgot I was shot last night.”

“And how does one just forget something like that?”

He watched her ease to her feet and struggle for balance. Duncan put out his good arm to steady her. “I don’t know. I guess the events just kind of made it not important. Then I got drunk and really didn't feel anything. When I woke up, my pounding head overruled everything else. Oh, and there was that little matter of my new wife pointing a gun at me."

"Stay where you are. Do not move. Understand?"

"Yes," he said, watching Penelope limp around her room, gathering up things and placing them in a basket.

Penelope placed the basket on the table and willed her hands to stop trembling. "Take off your shirt," she ordered, proud that her voice sounded strong. She limped across the room and gathered a pitcher, bowl, and wash cloth. When she turned around she almost dropped the items in her hand. *He's magnificent,* was the only thought that came to her. She stood there, taking in the breadth of his chest covered in dark hair. The way it tapered to a narrow waist. His stomach was made up of ripples that had the tips of her fingers tingling, aching to touch him.

"Penelope, is something wrong?"

"What?"

"Is something wrong?"

"No," she shook her head and slowly made her way back to his side. She shifted the basket to the floor and placed the bowl where it had been sitting. Penelope poured water in the bowl before setting the pitcher aside. After dipping the cloth in the water and wringing it out, she forced herself to look at her husband. "This will probably hurt."

"Go ahead," he muttered.

Penelope gently lifted his arm and began cleaning. "It looks as if it went through the fleshy part of your arm. There's no bullet, so I'll just clean it, stitch it, and pack it with some healing herbs."

"All right."

She worked on his arm, wincing when she had to flush the wound. It bled once more. She took some bandages, wrapped his arm tightly, and put pressure on the wound's entry and exit point, putting her in close proximity to her husband. She took the opportunity to study him. His head lay against the back of the chair, and his eyes were closed. His brow was furrowed as if he had the weight of the world on his shoulders. Penelope used the thumb on her free hand and smoothed his brow. He opened his eyes and studied her. "It's not your fault," she said softly.

"I wouldn't be so trusting if I were you."

"It's not your fault," she said more firmly.

"What exactly?"

"That girl. Anna."

"I think the villagers believe differently."

"They're wrong. She made the decision to challenge the enemy and knew that it could lead to her death. You shouldn't be held responsible. The British Navy should be."

"Hmph," he grunted.

Once she was satisfied that the bleeding had slowed enough, she sanitized the needle and thread and sewed the wound closed.

"Where'd you learn how to do this?" he asked.

"My brother got into enough scrapes. I paid attention when our housekeeper would mend his battle scars. When the money ran out, we had to let servants go, and could not afford to call for a physician. I mended everyone."

"It sounds like your grandfather lost a valuable part of his household when you left."

"He doesn't believe so. To him, I'm merely a female with nothing in her mind and an extra mouth to feed."

"You'll never be that here. I will always seek your opinion on matters."

"You needn't say that. I understand my role here, and I am perfectly fine with it."

"Pardon my saying, but your grandfather must be a right bastard"

"In all but truth," she agreed. Once she was finished, she wrapped his arm in a bandage. "There, now don't get that wet."

"Thank you." Duncan managed to stand. He approached his bedchamber and paused.

Penelope looked up and saw him studying her. "Is something the matter?"

"Why?"

"Why what?"

"Why didn't you use the key to escape?"

"Because I'm not running from you. That was never my intention. You are my future, and we're facing it together." She watched him nod before he walked out of her room. She waited until the door closed before she collapsed in a heap on the chair that he had just moments before occupied. Her stomach churned nervously and beads of sweat popped up on her brow. "Did I really tell him I wanted a normal marriage?" She asked herself incredulously. "No, you told him you wanted the outcome of a normal marriage — children. Pull yourself together. You have a house to learn how to run. And now you're talking to yourself." Penelope shook her head and sighed audibly, irritated with herself.

In the next room, Duncan struggled to get his body under control. His wife's touch had had a powerful effect on him. More powerful than he expected. He found himself attracted to Penelope, and he feared that would prove a danger to her. He wasn't one that believed in such superstitions as curses, but he found himself praying to God to keep his new wife safe from harm.

When she had said that she wanted children earlier, he had felt an energy course through his body that he had not felt in a very long while. Penelope was beautiful, though she seemed to not realize it from the plain clothes she wore. She was also confident and feisty to have held him at bay with an empty gun, his own no less. A gun that she knew how to clean. Then she had cleaned and stitched his injury like a seasoned physician, never once blinking an eye. No, he would never underestimate her. And he would do everything in his power to keep her safe. The question was, who could be trusted?

Duncan sank gratefully into the steaming water of his bath, careful not to get the bandage wet as Penelope had instructed. He let his head fall back against the rim. He had this tub specially commissioned to accommodate his large frame. It was a luxury to be certain.

As the water soothed him, he came to terms with what happened the previous night. He knew Anna's sister had spoken in the heat of the moment. The poor girl had lost the last of her family upon Anna's death. Anna had harbored such bitterness and anger that she thought she could take them all. The entire situation had been doomed. They should have realized what

Anna was feeling, should have found a way to help her. However, nothing could be done now. He would make sure that Sarah and her husband were well provided for. If Sarah wanted to leave the village and the memories it held behind, he would see it all taken care of.

Once again, his thoughts turned to Penelope. His body was reacting once more. How long before her wrist and ankle would be healed enough? One week? Two? He cared little about his arm. In the meantime he would be walking about in a state of agony, attempting to keep his mind on business, or would he? Duncan's eyes popped open and he stared at the ceiling. He could spend the next two weeks courting his bride. True, they were married, but didn't all women wish to be courted? Yes, that's what he would do. He would court her, and perhaps introduce her to a little seduction along the way. A wickedly handsome smile lit his face as he plotted his strategy to woo his wife.

CHAPTER 6

Several evenings later, as the family gathered for their supper, Duncan assisted Penelope in taking her place at the foot of the table. They had avoided each other for several days. She had stayed in her room, nursed her wrist and ankle, and told herself she was out of her mind. She told herself over and over that his touch had not affected her as she believed it had. Speaking of his touch, was it her imagination, or did his touch linger just a little longer than necessary? No, perhaps she was just overly sensitive to being near him after having seen him half naked. After touching him... *Snap out of it!* She scolded herself silently.

"Thank you to whomever for finding the cane for me to use. It has made moving about so much easier."

"You're welcome," Reese piped up. "I remembered Grandfather had one he used and dug for it in the attic. How are you feeling?"

"Better. As long as I take things slow and easy, I should be fine. I'm also very careful where I step. I suppose you never found anything, did you?" she addressed the question to Duncan.

"No."

"I surmised as much. Perhaps it was my mind playing tricks on me."

"I doubt that very much," Reese assured her.

The first course was delivered and everyone ate in comfortable silence.

That silence was broken when Duncan spoke, "Would you like to see some of the sights tomorrow?"

"I would love to," Lucy spoke up excitedly.

"Lucy, you've seen the sights. I was speaking to Penelope."

"Oh," the girl said, disheartened, and returned to her soup with much less gusto.

"I would like that and would very much like for Lucy to join us if she would care to," Penelope said.

"Thank you," Lucy said excitedly. "I can point out the best shops and introduce you to some of the ladies in the village."

"Lucy, I think Duncan wanted to be alone with Penelope," Rosalie interjected.

"But she said…"

"Oh, bloody hell, if you want to come, come. For that matter, let the whole bloody family come along."

"Duncan," Penelope admonished.

"The coach will be out front in the morning. If you aren't there by eight, you'll be left behind."

"But that's so early," Lucy whined.

"Be there, or stay behind," he said between clenched teeth.

An uneasy silence settled over the table for the remaining courses. Duncan, Reese, and Penelope retired to the study after the meal. Penelope used the cane, but couldn't contain the small thrill that went through her when Duncan came to her side and offered his arm.

"I would like to look at the books you have," she said and silently perused the bookshelves while Duncan and Reese discussed estate business. A short time later, Lucy and Rosalie entered.

"Penelope, what is London like?" Lucy asked when she and Rosalie joined them.

"You're going to London?" Penelope asked.

"Yes. I am to have my introduction to society this year."

"You don't seem very enthused about it."

"I've come to love it here," she said.

"I can understand that. Perhaps I can give you some pointers on dealing with the debutantes of the *beau monde*?"

"I would like that," Lucy nodded, though with not much enthusiasm. "I believe I will turn in for the night. Goodnight everyone."

Similar sentiments were echoed around the room back to Lucy.

"Duncan, I'm sorry," Rosalie spoke up after Lucy had left the room. "I fear she may have a bit of a crush on you."

"What?" Duncan and Reese asked simultaneously.

"Surely you jest," Reese scoffed. "I am by far more handsome than Duncan. Besides, I thought she was always smitten with me."

"Stuff it," Duncan said. "Rosalie, I have never encouraged any romantic relationship with Lucy."

"Nor have I, for the record."

"No, you just flirt with every woman you see, regardless of their age. Surely you only need to remember Isabelle for proof," Duncan argued.

"Boys, that's enough. Duncan, I know you have always been quite solicitous around Lucy. One cannot control the infatuations of a young, impressionable girl. The trip to London will do her good. She needs to meet new people, especially those that are her age. Goodnight, boys."

The three left in the room remained mute. After a pregnant pause, Duncan shook his head in bewilderment.

"I don't understand. I haven't done anything special…"

"Hmph," Penelope muttered, a bit irritated, before turning back to the books.

"And I really don't understand why she would choose *you* to be infatuated with," Reese said.

Penelope heard the tinkling of glass behind her followed by Duncan's refusal. A small smirk played on her lips.

"I mean, I am the more handsome of the two of us. I am also the more congenial."

"You are also a flirt, and dare I hazard a guess that you are not around very much?" Penelope asked as she continued searching for a book.

"I do come and go, but I don't see what that has to do with anything. Duncan's a grouch."

"Not to Lucy," she surmised as she pulled a book off the shelf and turned around. "And I would imagine that you see that she wants for nothing."

"I do my best, but I still don't understand why she would be infatuated with me."

"Men," Penelope muttered. "Adolescence is not as easy for young ladies as it is for boys. Especially when the young lady in question comes from a genteel background rather than a titled background. She sees Duncan as her protector and often times that can turn into a bit of hero worship."

"Speaking from experience, sister dear?" Reese playfully asked.

"Perhaps," she said, thinking back to the handsome, dark-headed director of the War Office. Even when doling out bad news, he had always been kind to her. He had often stopped by to check on their family, despite what her father and sister had done. But now he was married, and last she heard expecting a child with his wife. Perhaps it had already been born. And now she, too, was married.

"It looks as if you may have some competition for your wife's affections, big brother," Reese teased.

"All I'm saying is be gentle with her feelings," Penelope went on quickly before Reese could go any further. "If Lucy wants to join us tomorrow, let her join us. What would it hurt?"

"Perhaps you're right," he grudgingly replied.

"I think I would like to retire for the night as well."

"Let me escort you upstairs," Reese started to cross the room.

"*I'll* escort her," Duncan rushed over.

"Gentlemen, I'm not a piece of meat to be fought over, nor are the two of you rabid wolves. I am perfectly capable of finding my way to my bedchamber on my own," she said.

"Nevertheless, it would be my honor and privilege to escort you," Duncan said.

"Then by all means, escort away." Penelope sighed in irritation, yet found herself secretly thrilled when he took her book for her and held out his arm for her to take. She secretly wondered why he was being so solicitous towards her. *Should I be concerned?* she wondered.

"*Robinson Crusoe*," Duncan mused, bringing Penelope out of her silent reverie.

"What?"

"I'm just surprised of your choice of reading material," he said as they slowly walked up the stairs.

"I thought I warned you to never underestimate me?"

"So you did. How are you feeling?"

"Bruised and sore, but better. Thank you for asking. And you?"

"Pounding head and throbbing arm."

"How many marriages do you think begin as ours has?" Penelope inquired.

"I would hazard a guess that we are in the minority."

"Duncan, why are you being so solicitous towards me? We both know it isn't necessary for you to escort me to my room."

"Perhaps I just want to make a better impression on you. Maybe I want to show you that I can be kind. Perhaps I think every woman should be properly courted, even if she *is* already married," he finished huskily as they reached the door to her bedchamber.

"That is very thoughtful, but not necessary." She reached out and took the book from his grasp.

"I believe otherwise. My first gift to you is this," he reached into his pocket and pulled out a key.

"What is this to?"

"This fits the lock for the three doors to our bedchambers—yours, mine, and the connecting door."

"Don't you remember I already have one? The one from the other morning," she clarified.

"I have not forgotten. My key came up missing somewhere between here and the channel, I imagine forever lost. The one you retracted was the butler's. This is the housekeeper's. You now have, in your possession, the only two keys for our rooms. You are absolutely safe from everyone, including me." He unlocked her door and opened it for her before placing the smooth piece of metal in her hand.

"Thank you." Penelope took it and closed her fingers tightly around it, trying to hold both it and the book in the same hand, while her other hand clutched the top of the cane.

"There's one more thing." Duncan gently placed a hand on her upper arm, halting her.

"Yes?" Penelope asked, curious. What happened next left her stunned and fighting for air. Duncan used both hands and gently cupped her face, tilting it upwards as he lowered his. His firm lips brushed hers, ever so softly at first. Then the oddest thing happened and she could have sworn she felt his tongue snaking along the seam of her lips. There it was again.

"Wha—" Before she could complete the word, his tongue swept within her mouth, making a quick foray to claim his territory before slipping out again. He placed several more lingering kisses on her lips that had her following him for more when he pulled away.

"Goodnight, wife," he said huskily before turning down the hall to retreat to his room.

"Goodnight," she said in a bit of a daze as she entered her room. Penelope somehow managed to close and lock the door and set the book aside, then she lifted trembling fingers to her tingling lips. "Gracious," she said on a sigh, "what have I gotten myself into?" Little did she know that in the adjoining room, her husband was feeling just as shocked from the effects of their shared kiss.

The next morning they met at the agreed upon time and found they were the only two there.

"Where is everyone?" Duncan growled.

"Lucy has a headache and chose not to come. Rosalie decided it would be best if she stayed with Lucy. I've no idea about Reese."

"Here I am," the man in question answered jovially as he cantered up on a dappled gray and white horse.

"Of course," Duncan muttered. "Since it's going to be just the two of us in the carriage, I'm going to have the curricle readied instead. It will take a few minutes…"

"That's perfect. I just realized I forgot my bonnet. I'll be back shortly." As she entered the upstairs hall, she saw Lucy. "Are you feeling better then? Would you like to go with us?"

"No. I'm so embarrassed by my behavior. I couldn't stand to be in the same room with him right now. What must he think of me?"

"There, there, Lucy. I promise you, men are dense when it comes to such matters. All will be well. Now, are you positive you won't come with us? The weather is beautiful."

"No. I really do have a headache and I just need…time, I suppose."

"I understand. I'm just going to get my bonnet then. You get some rest." Penelope hugged her close before Lucy retreated to her room. Penelope shook her head sadly, knowing that things would likely never be the same between the young woman and Duncan. She quickly retrieved a bonnet and made her way back downstairs. When she stepped outside, a polished two-wheeled curricle sat at the ready, and a midnight black horse stood in the traces. "It's lovely," she said, admiring it.

"Where's your bonnet?" Duncan asked.

She held up her hand indicating she had it, but had not put it on yet.

"You're going to have to help me up," she told him.

"It will be my pleasure," he said.

She forced herself to not take a step back as he approached her. Penelope found she didn't trust herself around him after last night's kiss. She couldn't believe that she had followed his retreating lips like they were her life source. Suddenly, she was being swept off her feet and into the air until their faces were even with one another. Penelope found herself mesmerized by his face with its lines etched from worry. Then his lips were caressing hers, still tender, but perhaps just a bit more forcefully than last night. She clutched his bicep with her good hand while the other arm was hooked about his neck. Then two things happened simultaneously—she felt the curricle seat against her back and legs, and he broke off the kiss. Was that disappointment she felt? Yes, and that same tingling sensation she had felt last night.

She sat there, stunned for several moments. Her cane and bonnet were being thrust at her, breaking her out of her stupor.

"Here," Duncan said gruffly.

"Thank you," she replied, then quickly looked around, horrified. "Where's your brother? Oh my goodness, did anyone see us? I can't believe you did that here in the open."

"Why not? We're married, aren't we? Remember, I said I would be courting you."

"Well, yes, but *physical affection*," she whispered the last two words, "is something that takes place in the bedchamber, behind closed doors."

"Is that how your family was?"

"My family was very proper," she huffed.

"Yes, was," he said, emphasizing the last word as he pulled his large frame into the curricle.

Penelope slid as close to the far side as she could, but still felt every part of her left side touching his firm, muscled body.

"Put your bonnet on," he ordered and flicked the reins to get the horse moving.

How had she forgotten it? She took the gloves out of the inside and laid them across her lap, then she took the bonnet, tugged it firmly on her head, and tied the bow under her chin. Thankfully the bonnet blocked him from her vision, now if only she could ignore the feel of him next to her, the heat his body generated, or the firmness of his arms and legs. *Stop it!* She ordered herself. Penelope jerked on the first glove, winced, and grabbed her throbbing wrist.

The curricle came to a halt, and she flinched when she felt Duncan reach for her arm.

"Easy," he said softly, like he would if talking to a high-strung horse.

"It will be fine. I just wasn't thinking and pulled too hard."

"You don't have to wear the gloves at all," he said.

"I am a duchess now. It will be expected of me."

"By whom?"

"Everyone. Our peers, our servants, those that live in your shire."

"Perhaps when we have to go to London, but you'll find country life is much different, but," he said when he saw her begin to argue, "if you insist, allow me to assist you. You just hold your arm still and let me do the rest."

"I'm not a child," she muttered mutinously.

"I insist."

Penelope watched him turn, albeit a bit awkwardly, and gently work her gloves up her arms, first one and then the other. He ended each with a kiss on the tender inner-skin of her elbows. She couldn't help the shiver that raced through her body.

"Cold?"

"No," she said, sounding breathless to her own ears.

"Good." He turned, took the reins, and they were moving once more.

"Where's your brother?" she asked in an attempt to end the awkward silence that had settled between them.

"Why?"

"Just curious. He was about earlier. I assumed he was going to accompany us."

"Do you want him to?"

"I don't suppose it really matters one way or the other." She shrugged.

"His horse was growing restless. He said he would catch up with us later."

She nodded.

They rode for a while before she heard Duncan mutter, "I apologize."

"For?"

"The comment about your family. It was uncalled for."

"Oh, thank you, but I suppose you are right. Perhaps if my parents and grandfather had not put so much emphasis on outward appearances, things would have ended up much differently."

"No one should have to go through all that you did."

"Thank you. I suppose it made me stronger, made me realize how fickle society is. Women I once thought to be dear friends will no longer look at me, let alone speak to me. The only men that had anything to do with me only wanted me for a mistress, and Grandfather decided that would not make him as much money as selling me off whole. Even most of our servants left because of the stigma surrounding my family."

"I'm truly sorry, and point out the men to me so that I can kill them myself."

"Oh, no," Penelope replied with a self-deprecating chuckle. "I took care of the one or two that snuck past Grandfather."

"You shouldn't have had to. Your fa…"

"Yes, my father should have, but that is impossible since he committed suicide. Perhaps my brother? Grandfather had him sent away. Then it should fall to my grandfather. Remember this is the man that sold me to you in marriage to take my sister's place. So, Duncan, tell me who I should have relied on these past years?"

"You have me, now and forever," he said.

"I wish you hadn't said that."

"Why not?"

"I have this strange sense of foreboding when you use the word forever. As if fate is teasing us. I just want to have a normal life. A peaceful life. A caring husband, children, perhaps a dog and a cat."

"You make it sound as if anyone will do as long as they slot into the position you have planned for them," he said. He sounded a bit petulant. Funny for a man of his size to resemble a child being denied his favorite toy.

"I suppose so. Except, of course, for the children. I want them to be mine. I don't know why I feel so strongly about that. Perhaps it comes from having people ripped away from me so recently. It's difficult remembering I will never see my sister again. That she made choices that changed my perception of her forever. There's that word again, creeping into our conversation. I'm sick to death of this morose talk. No more. My family is what it is. Now, where are we going?"

"Whitby."

"I thought you were going to take me to see Robin Hood's Bay?"

"I don't think they are ready to see me yet."

"So what can I expect to see in Whitby?"

Penelope listened as he extolled the virtues of Whitby, another seaside village that he had jurisdiction over as the Duke of Yorkshire.

"Is Whitby also attacked by the press gangs?"

"Not as often. The village does not sit as close to the water as Robin Hood's Bay."

"I see. It's not as easy to get in, take, and get away."

"Correct." He stopped the horse, set the brake, and wrapped the reins around a bar before jumping out of the curricle.

"What are you doing?"

"I want to show you one of the most beautiful sights you'll ever see in your life," he said as he walked around the buggy. He scooped her out and gently placed her on her feet. After handing her the cane, he offered her his other arm and led her to the cliff. "Hold on tight to me. I don't want you to lose your balance in this wind."

She bestowed a grateful smile upon him before looking out at the view in front of her.

Duncan placed his hand securely over her arm that was wrapped around his, careful of her injured wrist. He observed her as she looked out over the water. The wind was blowing so that her pale pink dress hugged every curve of her body, making his pants grow uncomfortably tight. Her honey blonde hair was loose and blowing in the wind from beneath the bonnet. His fingers ached to run through the loose strands, to feel their silky texture, and bring them up to his nose and inhale deeply of her scent. He still couldn't quite place it and it was driving him mad.

She took a step towards the cliff, jarring him out of his study of her. He shifted his grip so that he could wrap an arm around her, anchoring her firmly to his side. "Careful," he instructed her as she peered over the ledge. A strong gust of wind knocked her off balance, and he took a step back with her in tow.

"Thank you," she said loud enough to be heard over the gales. "That's quite a long way down, isn't it?"

"Yes," he replied.

"What?" she asked louder.

"Yes," he almost shouted to be heard.

"It's so beautiful here," she said. "The water is entrancing."

"You should see it when a storm is upon us. It can be terrifying."

"I would love to see that, too." The wind calmed a bit, and she edged close to the cliff once more and looked over.

"There are trails and caves all through here. Though you never want to get caught in one of the lower ones as the tide is coming in. Very seldom do people ever make it out alive if that happens."

"I'll remember that."

"Would you like to look some more or return to the curricle?"

She looked wistfully out over the water, but turned back to him and said, "I think perhaps we should go back."

Duncan very solicitously helped her back to the conveyance and then once again lifted her and set her on the seat. This time, when he leaned in to kiss her, he was relieved that she neither jumped or pulled away. Instead she met him. When he broke the kiss, they studied each other for several long moments.

"We've only just met," Penelope said, as if trying to point out things against them.

"You're right," Duncan agreed with her, unable to fight the truth.

"I don't even know you. Not really."

"Again, I can't argue with the truth."

"I fully expected to hate you."

"I have no doubt."

"Stop being so agreeable and get in the curricle," she ordered, irritated.

"Yes, Your Grace." He performed an exaggerated bow just to annoy her. He found he liked doing things that would make her slightly cross with him, for then he could kiss her happy. Duncan bounded into the curricle, unwrapped the reins, and gave them a shake to start the horse moving.

"How far until we reach Whitby?"

"Not long."

"I wonder what happened to Reese."

"I don't know," he answered, feeling jealousy unfurl within his gut. *Will Reese always be a competitor for the affections of the women in my life?* he wondered morosely.

"Tell me about Isabelle."

"Why?" Surprise filled his voice.

"Curiosity. What was she like?"

His mind went back in time, conjuring up an image of Isabelle. He found this harder to do as the years passed.

"Duncan?"

"We were good friends growing up. Our marriage was arranged when we were babes and we thought it lucky that we got along so well. She came to my chin, tall for a woman, and had blue eyes and light brown hair. She always had a ready smile and a kind word."

"How did the two of you get along?"

"Well, until…"

"Yes?"

"I'd rather not discuss it."

"All right."

They traveled on a bit before he felt a gentle, gloved hand cover his.

"The reins didn't do anything to deserve being mangled," she said, a teasing note in her voice.

"I was away on business when Reese arrived home from university and gallivanting about the world. When I came back from my business trip, Isabelle told me that she and Reese had fallen in love."

"Oh, Duncan."

"I seem to remember saying something naïve and stupid about the two of us having been in love. She told me that the love we had was based on friendship and caring for one another, but what she felt for Reese caused her pulse to race. She said she felt like a giddy schoolgirl every time he walked through the door. They were already sleeping together. They tried to fight it, she said."

"What did you do?"

"I stormed off, locked myself in the study, and got thoroughly foxed. I didn't speak to either of them for days. Finally, I offered her a divorce. At first she declined, but then she and Reese talked about it. They were going to agree and move to a sugar plantation the family owns on a Caribbean island, but fate intervened. She was expecting a child and she couldn't be sure if it was mine or my brother's."

"Oh, no."

"If the child was mine, I couldn't give up my heir. Hell, if it had been a daughter, I wouldn't have been able to let her go either. To be raised by another man, even if it was my brother, I just couldn't do it."

"And I'm sure Reese felt the same way."

"We fought, Reese and I, and it turned physical. Soon the only people speaking to one another were Lucy and Rosalie. One afternoon, Isabelle walked to the cliffs. She loved walking them and looking over the ocean. Whenever she needed to think, she would walk them for hours on end. She didn't return for supper, and Reese and I went looking for her. I found her lying among the rocks at the base of the cliff, dead."

"Did she jump?"

"I don't know. There was a ripped piece of white cloth clutched in her hand. I suspected that she and Reese had had an argument and… I'm sure it was an accident, but…"

"You believe he killed her."

"And he believes the same of me, which is why whenever I marry, he shows up at the Hall. He feels it is his duty to protect his new sister-in-law from her husband."

"What of the other two?"

"Samantha loved to read and insisted we add many of the titles in the library that we have today. She took the ague a few weeks after she arrived. We put her to bed immediately, and she continued to worsen. Lucy sat with her almost constantly, nursing her, since they had become great friends. One morning, she just didn't wake up."

"How sad."

"And then there was Francis. Her father was looking to attach himself to a title regardless of the cost. By now, as you can imagine, there have been all sorts of rumors surrounding the *Beast of Yorkshire*. She must have believed every one of them, for the night before our wedding she locked herself in her bedchamber. When she didn't come out the next morning, and didn't answer when anyone knocked, we forced our way in. She was lying on top of the bed. Francis preferred poison over a lifetime of being married to me, however short it would have been."

"Don't say that, not even in jest," Penelope said.

"Your right, I shouldn't joke about the lives of three lovely and kind young women. How do you feel now that you know my sordid history and the background of the curse?"

"Sad for you," she said morosely. "How do you not hate your brother?"

"I think part of me does. I tolerate him. We have family business interests together, but we will never again be as close as we were as children."

"I can't blame you," she swiped at a trail of water running down her cheek.

"There's no need to cry for me," Duncan said, wondering how this woman could find the compassion to care for him as she was.

"I'm not," Penelope countered.

"What do you call this?" he asked as he swiped at another drop tracking its way towards her pointed chin. Let her attempt to deny she had shed not one, but two tears for him.

"Rain," Penelope replied as they were both peppered by fat rain drops.

"What?" Duncan asked sounding somewhat stunned.

"Rain," Penelope drawled out so that he could understand. "You know, the liquid that falls from the clouds in the sky."

Duncan looked around dumbfounded. "When did the clouds roll in?"

"You were truly lost in the past, weren't you?"

"I suppose." He reached around and pulled the canopy of the curricle up over their heads. "Perhaps that will help," he said as he turned back around and urged the horse to travel faster.

"As long as the brunt of the storm holds off, I imagine we'll be fine," Penelope said. "I don't know about you, but I have never been in danger of melting from a bit of rain."

"That's not what I'm worried about," he muttered, remembering another wife and another time.

"What?"

"I had taken Samantha for a ride when she caught the ague. A summer storm caught us unawares, and we had no shelter."

"I'm made of sterner stuff," she assured him. "Look, what's that?" she asked pointing to something just coming into their vision.

"Whitby Abbey. It's nothing but an old pile of ruins."

"Surely there is some shelter to be had?" Penelope yelled to be heard over the gale that was unleashing itself upon them. The canopy was doing little good to protect them from the storm that had rolled in. Instead of trying to answer her or argue against her point, he merely nodded and guided the horse that direction.

The rain grew heavier as they reached their destination. Duncan jumped out of the curricle, tied the reins to an old post, and was just rounding the carriage when he saw Penelope falling.

CHAPTER 7

Determined to not be a nuisance or a burden, Penelope awkwardly stood while trying to remain hunched over so she wouldn't hit the canopy. She tried to turn around, but her good foot slipped out from under her on the rain-slick floor of the curricle. The next thing Penelope saw was the sky. She closed her eyes and scrunched her face as she stiffened and braced herself for the impact of the hard ground when she felt herself brought up against something firm and warm. Her eyes opened in shock and she saw her husband cradling her close.

"You have taken ten years off my life in just the few days that I've known you," he said as he struggled from his knees to his feet.

"I suppose I should have told you that I am not known for my gracefulness."

"Somehow I can believe that." He smirked as a bolt of lightning lit the sky, quickly echoed by rumbling thunder.

"I think we should carry on this conversation after we find a dry place."

"I agree."

Penelope held onto him as he picked his way to the abbey. Most of the abbey was roofless and what little remained leaked like mad. There was a far corner that looked relatively dry.

"There," Penelope said and pointed in the direction she wanted him to go.

"Your Grace, I do believe you have found the only dry spot in this old monastery." He lowered her so she sat braced against one wall, and he stood back up. "I forgot something in the curricle. I'll be back in a moment."

Penelope watched her husband make a mad dash to the buggy, grab something that, as he grew closer, appeared to be a basket, and then run back towards her. Just as he reached the abbey, the storm truly let loose its ferocity and the rain came down in buckets. Even soaking wet with his hair plastered to his head, he made a fine figure of a man. She watched him bend over and observed the tight fit of his breeches and felt a curl of something warm spread from a place she really shouldn't be thinking about, especially in an abbey, ruins or not, throughout the rest of her body. She was sprinkled with droplets of water, breaking her out of her admiration.

"What are you doing?" she shrieked, holding her hands up in front of her like a shield.

"Shaking off the water," he said sheepishly.

"Like a wet, mangy dog?" she asked. The man did not even have the decency to apologize. He just gave her a sheepish grin and tried to tug off his superfine coat. She untied and removed her bonnet as she watched him struggle for several minutes. Finally, she looked at him and asked, "Trouble?"

"Usually, I have my valet to assist me."

"Well, it's too bad you don't have him here, isn't it? What's in the basket?"

"I had Cook prepare us a picnic. It isn't anything special—cold chicken, fruit, cheese, wine. A dry blanket to sit on."

"Hmmm, perhaps since you were so nice as to do that, I could return the favor and help you with your coat."

"Thank you." He sat, turned to her and within a few moments he was free of the wet material.

"You're welcome. How is your arm?"

"It throbs, but I try to ignore it as much as possible. You did an excellent job of sewing me up."

"Thank you."

She pulled the basket between them and started going through its contents.

"And your injuries?"

"I'll be fine before long," she said, then blushed as she realized what that meant for their relationship.

“You sit back and I’ll take care of everything,” he said, moving the basket out of her reach. He removed the blanket and spread it out on the dry ground.

Instead of arguing, she did as he instructed. Soon everything was laid out on the blanket. “This looks wonderful, thank you. I must say, there is something to this courting business. First there were the fresh flowers every morning and the accompanying notes wishing me well. Now this picnic,” she spread her hands to indicate the food spread out between then. “I don’t know that I would have ever been treated like this in London. You know, you really did not do well when you got me. Whitney was far more beautiful.”

“I don’t believe that.”

She was mesmerized a moment by Duncan tearing into the chicken with his beautiful, perfectly straight, and gloriously bright, white teeth. How many men had approached her in London that made her want to cast up her accounts with their fetid breath and rotting, yellow teeth? Too many to count, certainly.

“Penelope?”

“Hmm?”

“I said, ‘I don’t believe that.’”

“Oh, right,” she forced herself back to the present and their conversation. “Well, it’s true. Whitney was absolutely gorgeous, a true diamond of the first water. She was the most sought after girl during our lone Season. Well, her lone Season. Then everything happened,” she waved her hand dismissively.

“You were twins, correct?”

“Yes. We favored, but were not identical. I miss her so much. Not the person she had turned into, but the way she was. We used to confide everything to one another. We had secret words that only the two of us understood. I was more than happy to stand aside and let her have her time to shine. Keep in mind, we never lived anywhere but London, but she was the epitome of London society. She loved to attend the balls and soirees. Even when we were little, she would beg mother to tell her every little detail about the ball or party they had attended the evening before. Then she would put on mother’s ball gown and party dresses and shoes and dance about the room.”

"What changed?" he asked as they continued to eat. The rain beat down around them, on the barely there roof, and on the old stones of the abbey.

"Father. He gambled away money we didn't have, then he partook of traitorous activities in an attempt to get the money back. You know the rest. Father was caught and killed himself in lieu of hanging. Whitney blamed a young woman whose father had been a bargaining tool and tried to kill her, but in the process died herself. Not only are we now poor and the family name tainted, but I have had to live under my grandfather's thumb for the last year."

"We've both been through a lot."

"So it would seem," Penelope said before taking a sip of wine.

"What did you look forward to in a husband?"

"Would you believe I never thought about it?"

"You're right, I wouldn't believe it."

"I had hoped to find someone who needed a companion that liked to travel."

"You want to travel?"

"Perhaps not all the time, but there are things I have read about and would like to see."

"You are definitely full of surprises, Your Grace."

"Yorkshire will have to be enough for me to explore, though," she said as an afterthought.

"It does have quite a lot to see, but why do you say that?"

"Well, you oversee all of this, and then you will have to be in London for Parliament."

"I imagine I can still take my wife to see the sights she wishes to see. That's why I have a steward. He can make the important decisions without my presence, and I fully trust him."

"Perhaps," she said noncommittally.

"I have to ask, why a desirable young woman, such as yourself, would not consider what you would want in a husband?"

"Didn't you hear me tell you about my family? I had no idea any man in his right mind would willingly marry me with my family history. So why get my hope up by dreaming?"

"I believe that's even more sad than being saddled with the title the *Beast of Yorkshire*."

"Yes, well, we all have our own burdens to bear." She repacked the basket with the food they hadn't eaten. Once she finished, Duncan moved the basket from between them and scooted close to her, pulling her into the cradle of his arm. Penelope held herself stiffly for several minutes, unsure what was happening.

"Relax and enjoy the rain," he coaxed.

Finally she did, allowing his body heat and the sound of the rain to lull her into relaxing. She felt Duncan's fingers comb through her hair from root to end, over and over. At first she thought to pull away, but the longer she sat there, the more right and tranquil she felt. Then he lifted a handful of her hair and inhaled deeply.

"What are you doing?"

"Honey!" he exclaimed triumphantly.

"What?"

"Your hair smells like honey and a warm summer day on the moors."

"You're waxing poetic," she accused.

"And your skin," he bent low and pressed a kiss along her neck, "smells like lavender."

"You only had to ask, and I could have told you all that."

"I preferred to figure it out on my own."

"Hmmm," she muttered. He continued to play with her hair, soothing her. Before long the combination of his ministrations and the sound of the rain had her drifting off to sleep.

Duncan could tell by the change of her breathing that she had fallen asleep. The storm raged on, punctuated by the occasional lightning and thunder. He prayed that this was one of those storms that lasted for hours and would allow them to remain secluded, even if she slept through most of it.

Speaking of sleep, he thought. There were parts of his anatomy, mainly his posterior that was going numb sitting on this old, stone floor. He tried to reach for his superfine without disturbing Penelope, but had no luck. He ended up propping her against the wall while he created a make-shift bed. Duncan took his damp superfine and rolled it up to form a lumpy pillow, then he laid down and gently maneuvered Penelope back into his embrace without waking her.

How long has it been since I've held a woman in my arms like this? he wondered idly. He and Isabelle had shared the same bed, but had rarely held one another. Samantha had preferred separate beds entirely.

Duncan's thoughts were interrupted when he heard Penelope mumble in her sleep. She shifted towards him, moved an arm across his stomach, and hitched a leg upon his thigh. He felt his body react to hers. He counted, and somewhere around seven hundred, finally drifted off to sleep as well.

Penelope jumped awake at a particularly loud clap of thunder. The ground vibrated beneath her. She felt a large hand rub up and down her back in a soothing manner. She felt herself relax once more until she realized she was laying horizontally against a very warm and very male form. She struggled to rise up on her forearm and looked up at her husband's face.

"How did we end up like this?" she demanded.

"There were parts of my person becoming quite numb, and I thought this would be more comfortable. And I was correct."

"Hmph," she muttered and tried to push up when she realized she had also draped her leg across his. She felt herself turn red with embarrassment.

"There's nothing to be embarrassed about," Duncan said, his voice low. "We're married after all."

"Married and out here in the wide open for anyone to see," she hissed.

"If you haven't noticed, it's been a full on storm for the last hour and doesn't show signs of stopping anytime soon. Not long enough for us to return to Taggart Hall, at least."

"What do you suggest?"

"I'm comfortable where I'm at, and we still have food."

"What if…"

"Yes?"

"What if one of us has to, well, you know…"

"Ah, well it's quite primitive, but I assure you that people have been surviving without a water closet for centuries."

"You're joking." Penelope looked at his face and what she saw deflated her spirits. "You're serious."

"Consider this an adventure."

"I've never been outside of London until I traveled here. Even then we only stopped at inns that were fully functional."

"Then I would say you are long past an adventure, wouldn't you?"

"This roof could give way any minute."

"Just part of the adventure," he said.

"Adventure," she said along with him, and gave him what she considered her best imitation of an evil eye.

"What was that?" he asked.

"I just gave you the evil eye," she said. She reared back, studying him as he threw his head back, laughing. He wasn't just chuckling, this was a full belly laugh. "It's not supposed to be funny," Penelope said, her ego slightly damaged.

"I'm sorry, it's just knowing that you were trying to hex me, and you looked so cute while doing it. I just found it rather funny."

Penelope studied him as he was still lost in laughter. The stress lines that bracketed his mouth and furrowed his brow disappeared, and he looked years younger. "You should laugh more often."

"Perhaps I'll have a reason to now," he replied, a smile still flirting with his lips.

She watched as a curly lock of dark hair fell rakishly onto his forehead and before she realized what she was doing, she reached up and brushed it back with the rest. She had removed her gloves earlier so they wouldn't become stained while they ate, and now she was glad of it. His hair was thick and coarser than hers. The waves and curls wrapped around her fingers in a gentle caress. She wiggled up and smelled his hair like he had done to her earlier, but unlike him, she couldn't place the scent. "What does your hair smell like?"

"Sandalwood." There was a roughness to his voice.

"I want to kiss you," Penelope said nervously. She licked her dry lips with the tip of her tongue and noticed he was transfixed by her innocent move. "Does that make me a harlot?"

"No, it makes you a woman, and by all means, please proceed."

"I'm not sure how to go about it."

"Just put your lips against mine. Instinct will take care of the rest."

"Are you certain?"

"Yes."

Penelope readjusted herself, leaned over Duncan, and gently brushed her lips against his. "Like that?" she asked.

"Sort of," he said in a husky voice.

She leaned back over him, laying on him as if he were a comfortable mattress, and brushed another kiss against his lips. Penelope looked down and saw him staring at her. She could feel his chest rising and falling, somewhat erratically, beneath her. "Are you all—"

The question was cut off when his mouth suddenly covered hers. She felt his fingers spear through her hair as his hand cupped the back of her head and pulled her down, unwilling to let her retreat from the kiss. If what he was doing could be called a kiss. His tongue had invaded her mouth as it had that one other time. It swept in and tangled with her tongue before exploring other parts of her moist cavern. Just when she thought she would scream in frustration, his tongue returned to hers and then it was like he said—instinct took over.

She met every plunge and stroke of his tongue with her own, doing what felt right and good. She rested against his chest, no longer stiff, but soft and pliant. The hand at the back of her head went from being forceful to caressing. A heat started low in her pelvis and she felt a flush spread up and down her body. Penelope felt Duncan's other hand splay across her lower back. They continued kissing, and exploring until he pulled away. She moaned at the loss of his mouth pressed to hers until he started pressing kisses elsewhere.

Duncan rolled so that now she lay with the ground pressed against her back. The blanket provided a warm barrier between her and the stone floor. He kissed the apples of her cheeks, then fluttered kisses as light as the caress of a butterfly's wing against her closed eyes. She bit her lower lip as he took the lobe of one ear between his teeth and gently nipped it before suckling it. He moved onto a spot on her neck, right behind her ear that she had never before realized was sensitive. Her body buzzed with something she couldn't put a name to. The ache low in her pelvis, that she had felt earlier, intensified.

"What are you doing to me?" she asked breathlessly.

"Introducing you to passion," he replied.

"And I was willing to pass this up to become a companion and see the world?"

"Now you can have both. I'll take you wherever you want to go," he promised.

"I don't know that I can survive the excitement of both."

"I have every faith that you can," he countered as he dropped kisses on her upper chest.

"How did you do that?"

"What?"

"Unbutton my spencer without my realizing it?" Shock laced her question.

"You became quite distracted by my expert kisses. Besides, it was hiding the most delectable treasure." She watched him bend over her and brush another kiss against her exposed chest.

"This is highly improper."

"We're husband and wife."

"Anyone could pass by."

"Not likely with the storm raging."

"Are you talking about the storm swirling about us, or the one consuming me?"

"Take your pick." He grinned wickedly.

"Do you know how devilishly handsome you are?" she asked, studying his face. She reached up and cupped his cheek. He had shaved this morning, but already, she felt stubble tickling her palm.

"Well—"

"Distract me again," Penelope ordered. This time she was the one cupping his head and bringing his lips down to meet hers. As she engaged her husband in a sensual kiss, she mentally tracked the movement of his hand. It went from her lower back to her posterior, giving it a gentle squeeze. Next, it skimmed her hip and slowly moved up her side with a slight foray onto her flat stomach before moving up over her ribs. *Will he?* She wondered, unable to complete the thought. Her breasts, something she thought were only created to give sustenance to babies, were tingling and swelling slightly. *What's wrong with me?* she thought. She tried to remember the things that Rosalie had told her, but his touch pushed all thoughts out of her mind.

Instead, she focused on his kisses and that straying hand. He really was a wonderful kisser. *Poor Francis didn't know what she was going to get to partake in, or she might have decided to live*, Penelope found herself thinking. *Thank goodness fate interceded*, she thought and was immediately overcome with guilt, until Duncan's hand cupped one of her swollen, aching breasts. A moan reached her ears. *Was that me? Did I actually moan, thankful that he's touching me so intimately?* she wondered, mortified.

Then he began doing things, all the while still kissing her. He gently squeezed her globe, then tweaked the turgid peak that had formed. She waited for Duncan to pull back, disgusted at her body's response, but instead, he only seemed to turn more ravenous. He threw a leg over hers, pinning her down, and leaving her to feel him intimately. Was that the rod that Rosalie had told her about that was pressed against her hip? Goodness help her, but instead of embarrassed, she found herself intrigued, curious as to what that part of him actually looked like. Her womanhood must be curious as well, for suddenly she felt a wetness down *there* she had never felt before.

She tried to follow his lips, but instead he looked down at her like he was a man half-starved, and she was a banquet. His eyes tracked downward and she looked too, trying to determine what he was studying so intently. Then she knew. He gave a tug and reached inside her bodice to lift her breasts free for his inspection. Embarrassed, she tried to cover herself with one arm.

"No. You've seen my bare chest, it's only fair that I see yours."

"That was different," she argued.

"Penelope, you're so beautiful," he murmured. He took her hand that was trying desperately to cover her assets from his eyes and brushed a kiss along her palm before pinning it beside her head.

She watched him bend low and place a kiss on her left breast. She laid back and closed her eyes tightly, relying on her senses. Penelope began to relax and enjoy the randomness of his kisses on her breasts. She gasped when she thought she felt his tongue lick across her areola and nipple.

"Did you just lick me?" she hoarsely demanded. She raised her head up and stared at him, aghast.

"Yes," he said with a wicked grin as he did it again.

"Don't do that," she ordered. "It's unseemly."

"All right," he agreed readily. Too readily.

She lay back, relieved, until she felt his mouth close over her breast and suckle her. "Duncan," she squeaked his name.

"Should I stop?" he queried. While waiting for her answer, he gently blew on the peak, causing it to stiffen even more.

"Please, no," she said, guiding his head back to her throbbing breast. Penelope arched her back to give him greater access. Suddenly her hand was free and both hands were holding him to her, afraid he would pull away, afraid he would stop bestowing this wonderful attention on her. She was so wrapped up in what he was doing to her that she didn't realize he had shifted and no longer had a leg thrown across hers. Penelope was also unaware that he was ever so slowly pulling up the hem of her dress until his hand rested on her hip. A hip covered only by pantaloons.

Abruptly, Penelope realized his hand felt much warmer against her hip than it had earlier. That is when she realized her legs were bare to the elements and her skirts were bunched about her waist. "What—"

"Relax." Duncan returned to her mouth and kissed her once more.

She tried by staring at the decaying roof above her while he trailed kisses along her neck.

"Do you want me to tell you what I'm going to do next?"

"Stick your rod in me?"

"What?" he asked laughing.

"Rosalie said that's what men do. They stick their rod in women."

"There's a little more finesse involved, and you need to stop letting Rosalie give you advice," he said before kissing her deeply. "I am going to seduce you and introduce you to a small portion of the world of passion. When I make you my wife, it will not be on the floor of some ruin, but in a nice, soft bed where I can take my time with you."

"Then what are you going to do now?"

"Do you feel a tightness inside you? It feels like you might snap at any moment?"

"Yes," she said, licking her lips nervously.

"I can make that go away," he whispered, then suckled her earlobe. "Would you like me to take care of that for you? Would you let me help you?"

"Yes," she whispered and stared at him, her teeth worrying her lower lip.

Duncan kissed her deeply, gratefully, rescuing her lower lip from those beautiful, white teeth of hers. He placed kisses along her neck down to the place where it met her collarbone. He suckled lightly then laved the spot with his tongue. Duncan returned to worshipping her breasts. He gently moved her legs apart and felt her stiffen. "Trust me," he said as he lifted his head and looked at her. "You're a beautiful woman," he told her.

"No. I'm just plain."

"You're anything but plain," he countered. He brushed her mound and felt a slit in her pantaloons.

"What are you doing?" She halted his progress by gripping his wrist.

"Remember, that ache will go away if you will trust me."

"I don't know if I can." He could hear the insecurity in her voice.

"Give me a chance."

He relaxed as she slowly released his hand. Duncan took her hand and put it beside her head once more. "I want you to grip my coat anytime you feel unsure. All right?"

"Yes," she whispered.

He noticed she was already gripping the coat as if it were her lifeline. He gave her a devastating smile and then kissed her soundly. Duncan was still kissing her when he returned his hand to her leg. He pushed her ankle towards her hip, making her leg form a peak, then gently pushed it to fall outward. Once more, he returned his attention to her breasts as he used his finger to rub along the entrance to her femininity.

"Duncan!" she yelled, twisting the coat mercilessly.

"Should I stop?"

"I don't know," she whimpered, as a tear slipped from the corner of her eye.

"What's wrong? Did I hurt you?"

"No," she shook her head. "Is this wrong to feel this? When we barely know one another?"

"I hope it's a sign."

"A sign for what?"

"That we belong together. I think we are very lucky to feel this powerful attraction already. Now, I'll ask you again. Should I stop?"

"No."

"Thank you," he said before continuing. He returned to suckling her breasts while he taught her about lovemaking. He moved up to her ear and praised her. "You're so passionate," Duncan whispered to her. "This wet heat is your body's way of telling me you like what I'm doing to you. And this," he said, pressing on her little piece of flesh, "this is going to give you release."

Her body tightened, she let out a gut wrenching moan that reached his ears, then he watched her wilt to the ground.

CHAPTER 8

When Penelope came back to herself, she felt a languidness she had never before experienced. Her center still felt dewy in the aftermath of their passionate afternoon. Her dress once more covered her legs and bosom. She looked up to see Duncan watching her, a silly smile on his face. He bent down and kissed her softly.

“Thank you,” he said.

“For what?”

“For sharing your first time with me.”

“Everything we do will be my first time,” she reminded him.

“Thank you just the same.”

“You’ve had at least two first times before me,” Penelope stated bluntly.

“No, I haven’t.”

“Need I remind you ”

“Neither of my other wives were virgins when they came to our marriage bed.”

“Oh.”

“Isabelle turned out to be a rather lusty young woman and apparently Samantha fancied herself in love with someone else.”

“I see.” Penelope thoughtfully studied him while he caressed her cheek, her lips, her brow. He was playing with her loosened hair when she quietly suggested, “You know we could—”

“No, the storm is letting up. We should return home.”

“If you insist.”

“I do.”

“Help me up,” she said. “I must look a mess.”

“You look beautiful,” he countered.

Penelope felt a blush steal over her. She straightened her pelisse and buttoned it once more. She kept fidgeting with her dress, gloves, and bonnet until finally a pair of masculine hands clasped hers tightly.

"You look wonderful. No one will be able to tell anything happened."

Penelope nodded, then felt a finger gently lift her chin until she was forced to meet his gaze. She watched him as he leaned down and settled his lips over hers once more. Her eyes fluttered shut and she leaned against him, savoring the kiss. She found she was sorry when it ended. She opened her eyes to see him staring at her.

"Remember, whenever you're ready to take this further we will. It's your choice."

"Kiss me again, Duncan," she ordered. She lifted up on her tiptoes and wrapped her arms about his neck. Penelope luxuriated once more in the feel of his lips against hers and their tongues tangling together. She was so lost in the kiss that when he pulled away, she tried to follow his lips.

"Pen, we have to stop, or your initiation to lovemaking will be here, on the hard ground, after all."

"I don't think I would mind," she mused.

"As long as there is a doubt in your mind, we will wait."

She felt disappointment mingled with something else. How could anyone think him a beast or that he murdered those women when he made her feel infinitely cared for? It just amazed her. "Shall we go home then?" she asked.

"Yes," he said, leading her back to the curricle.

They were halfway to Taggart Hall when they met up with Reese. The look on the other man's face could only be described as frantic.

"What's wrong?" Duncan asked.

"The two of you are what's wrong. Where the devil have you been? I've been all over, looking for you," Reese returned.

"The Bay?" Penelope asked, a perplexed look on her face.

"It's the shortened version of Robin's Hood Bay. It's how the locals refer to it," Duncan explained to her.

"Yes, and no one saw you today."

"No, we decided to go to Whitby," Duncan answered over her head.

"Whitby? Why the hell would you go there?"

"Because I'm currently not welcome in the Bay, remember?"

Penelope could hear the hurt in his words. She placed a gentle hand on her husband's tense thigh. How could anyone believe Duncan a murderer when he cared so much about the people around him? She had to stop this interrogation before it got out of hand and resulted in the two brothers turning to fisticuffs. "Reese, Duncan and I had a lovely afternoon. He showed me some of this beautiful landscape."

"Oh, really? What?"

"Well, Whitby Abbey, for one. It's some of the loveliest ruins I've ever seen. We were caught by the rain, and decided to picnic there and well…"

"Yes?" Reese asked impatiently.

"We got to know one another better."

"Just how well did you get to *know one another*?" Reese asked sarcastically. "You look a little worse for the wear."

"Reese," Duncan growled.

"We talked," Penelope raised her voice to be heard over the bickering siblings, "about our *pasts*." She emphasized the last word and gave Reese a meaningful look. She noted that he at least looked chastised. "We have decided to make the best of our marriage. There are things, mutual things, that we both want out of it, such as children. We would appreciate the opportunity to get to know one another without everyone always hovering about."

"I see how the wind blows," Reese mused. "But I will not stand aside while another Duchess of Yorkshire meets her untimely death. I will be in the background, making certain that you remain safe at all times."

"Why you—"

Penelope squeezed Duncan's leg when he leaned across her as if he were going to jump out and strangle his younger brother. She was afraid that was exactly what he wanted to do. "Reese," she said softly, "it's not necessary, because I am absolutely safe with your brother, but if you feel the need, do what you must."

"Rest assured, I will," he said.

"Duncan, shall we go home before it begins to rain once more?"

"Yes."

Penelope winced as Duncan slapped the reins against the horse's back a little harsher than necessary. "The horse didn't do anything wrong," she admonished.

"You're correct."

She looked back and saw Reese trailing behind them at a sedate pace. "Are the two of you ever going to make amends?"

"It's doubtful."

What had started out as a pleasant ride back to the Hall ended up being a quiet and tense affair. When they reached the front door, he helped her down and inside the rambling castle.

"I'll see you at supper," Duncan said.

"I think I'll eat in my room tonight," she said. Was that disappointment on his face? Regardless, she needed time to think. Time to review today's events, all of them. And time to herself.

Duncan watched her disappear inside the Hall and felt like they had just taken two steps backwards, if not more.

"Did she wizen up and leave you behind?" Reese taunted.

"Walk away," Duncan muttered repeatedly to himself, but his brother wouldn't let it go. He could feel Reese standing close behind him. He took a step toward the house, but halted when he heard him speak.

"Don't let anything happen to her."

"Why? So you can have a chance to win her over like you did Isabelle?"

"Go to hell," Reese replied.

"I've been there for years," Duncan countered before he turned and walked into the house. How could a day that had started so well end up being so disappointing? That seemed to be the story of his life. He walked in the house, let the butler know he would not be joining the rest of the family for supper, and locked himself in his study to work on estate matters.

Upstairs, Penelope reclined in the large bed wondering, not for the first time, how wise this decision was. Then she would think back over the afternoon they had spent together and her body would catch on fire once more. *What kind of power is it that he wields over me?* she wondered. She hadn't been expecting this physical connection between them. She thought she would have to endure his touch, not look forward to it. At least the idea of begetting children was no longer repulsive. Penelope fought sleep as the seconds turned into minutes and the minutes into hours, but in the end she lost the battle.

Sometime later she was startled awake by the sound of a door slamming shut. A deep darkness descended upon the room. She looked to the side and saw that the candle she had lit earlier had gone out. Penelope let her eyes adjust to the inkiness. She lay very still as she watched him move around without lighting a single lamp or candle. His body was silhouetted by the light of the soft moonlight just breaking through the sheers. He tossed something dark over a chair and then there was a grunt, followed by a thud. Penelope started to ask him if he was all right, but changed her mind and remained silent.

She watched as he poured liquid from the decanter into a glass. He tossed back the liquid, drinking it down in one gulp. She studied him as he unwrapped his cravat and placed it on the dresser. Next, he tugged his shirt free of his breeches and she could feel her heart race and her body heat up. Before too long, the shirt slid down his arms, revealing his broad back to her. She could see the bandage that was wrapped around his upper arm covering the wound that she had seen to almost a week ago. *I really should check it to make certain it's healing properly*, she thought. Penelope held her breath as he bent over and worked his second boot free. His posterior looked firm and her hands ached to squeeze him as he had her. *What madness has overtaken me?* She wondered silently.

Her breath stuck in her throat as he worked the buttons of his breeches free. He pushed the material over his hips and downward, then he kicked them free. The man was as nude as a newborn babe, but the similarities stopped there. No, this man looked like the marble statues she had seen in the museum and gardens in London. When he turned sideways, it took all of her willpower to keep from gasping. Penelope watched in awe as the part that made him a man grew and slowly went from being flaccid to pointing towards the ceiling. *Is it supposed to do that, or is there something wrong with him?* she wondered. She felt her skin heat in a flush beneath the shift she wore and the bed clothes on top of her. Penelope wanted to squirm, but she didn't dare move. No. She would remain still and pray he fell asleep before he realized she was in his bed. Then she would slip out, undetected. After all, the bed was quite large, and she was almost on the edge. *This was a* very *bad idea*, she berated herself.

She held her breath as he approached the bed. He tossed the covers to the side, on top of her, and laid back on the bed. Penelope heard him groan and peeked over the covers, curious as to what was wrong. Her eyes widened at what she saw. He had wrapped his hand around his manhood and was rubbing up and down. *Why is he doing that?* She didn't have long to wait to get her answer. Duncan groaned and jerked, and then he was covering that part of him with a cloth, but not before Penelope saw something shoot out of him.

"Eeek!" She threw the covers over her head, mortified.

CHAPTER 9

"What the bloody hell is going on?" Duncan demanded. He stood, swept the coverlet off the bed, and wrapped it around his hips. Duncan dropped the other cloth in his haste to cover himself. "How long have you been there?"

"A while," she murmured from beneath the sheet and blanket.

"Why?" He grew impatient as he waited for an answer. "Well?" he demanded when it looked as if she would just remain silent, hiding beneath the sheets. He took a moment to light a lamp so that soft light kept the darkness at bay.

"Because…"

"Yes?"

"Because I want a child."

Not him, but a child. But he was the means to the end. And just like that, his earlier erection that had been caused by thoughts of their afternoon together returned with a vengeance. Could he live with the knowledge that he was being used like a stud? *But aren't you willing to use her like a broodmare?* he questioned himself. Both comparisons were harsh, but true. The only thing they both agreed they wanted out of this marriage was children, and there was only one way to go about creating those children. He felt himself grow harder, which should be impossible after what happened just moments earlier.

"Come out from under the covers," he ordered. He watched her peek at him from beneath the sheet. "You'll have to come out from under there if we are to do what you want us to do."

"I've changed my mind," she said.

"Why?" He waited, but she remained silent. "Penelope, do you still want a child?"

"Yes."

"Then why the change of heart?"

"I saw…"

"What?"

"Everything."

"And during your viewing *of everything*, when did you change your mind?" He watched Penelope twist the sheet and blanket in her hands. She refused to look at him. "Penelope?"

"Your thing," she muttered.

"My member, you mean?"

"Yes."

She closed her eyes and seemed to cringe. Did she find him so distasteful? "What about it?" he persisted.

"It g…grew, and moved."

"It has to do that to create children," he explained. "Rosalie said she talked with you, and this afternoon didn't you feel me, it, pressing against your hip?"

"Yes," she answered.

"Well?" He watched her shake her head in the negative. "Let me hazard a guess. You watched what I was doing to myself, didn't you?"

She nodded her agreement.

"That was because of you," he answered honestly, his voice husky as his need for her grew.

"Me?" she asked, somewhat breathily.

"Yes. My member came to life because I was thinking about this afternoon, about you, and how responsive you were. It was aching and needed release. I didn't know that I only had to look on the other side of my bed to find my lovely wife there, ready to take the next step. So, I took matters into my own hands, so to speak."

"But something spewed from you at the end."

"That creates children, it's my seed."

"You must be joking. That can't be what Rosalie was talking about."

"She probably romanticized it, but that's exactly what it is."

"And it goes inside me?"

"Yes."

"Where you touched me earlier?"

"Yes, but deeper."

He watched her process the information as he fought to keep his body in check. Had he managed to undo the progress he had made with her this afternoon? He was just about to suggest she return to her room when he heard her say, "I'm being quite silly aren't I?"

"No."

"Yes, I am. I'm a woman and this is an expectation of me, isn't it. I am to lay with a man and create children so man, as a species, can continue to flourish?"

"I suppose."

"Please forgive me for acting like a ninny. Yes, we should continue. As we discussed earlier, we both want children, but for different reasons. So, if you wish to continue tonight, I am agreeable."

Was this the same woman that only moments ago hid beneath the covers like a frightened child? "Are you certain about this?"

"Yes."

His member throbbed painfully. *Control*, he commanded himself silently. *You must remain in control or tonight may be your only night with Penelope.*

"I have one question before we begin."

"Go ahead," he replied, wondering how she could sound so analytical at a time like this. All he could think about was losing himself inside her.

"How are we going to fit?"

He heard the slight tremor in her voice and knew at that moment that she wanted to be brave, but her fear of the unknown was quickly overcoming her desire for a child. "Trust me," he said, his voice taking on a distinctly husky tone, "we'll make it work." He held his breath as he watched her consider his words. "Penelope, I promise you that whatever happens tonight, your pleasure will equal or exceed what you felt this afternoon." He watched her eyes light and sparkle as she remembered their earlier interlude. Hope blossomed in his chest.

"All right," she said.

"Are you certain? Because when I begin to touch you, I won't be able to stop. Not this time."

"I'm positive."

"Excellent." He climbed back onto the bed, the cover still wrapped around his waist.

"Aren't you going to take that off?" she queried.

"I think it would be best if I didn't at this point." Then he leaned over her and captured her soft, pliant lips with his.

Penelope sighed against the masculine lips that moved insistently against hers. Her hand slowly unclenched from the sheet and combed back the loose locks of his hair that had fallen forward. She opened her mouth to the persistent tracing of his tongue against the seam of her lips. When she did, she let another sigh slip free as they began to kiss as he had taught her earlier. Their tongues tangled with one another in a sensual manner, and tingles coursed through her body as the kiss continued. Penelope let her hand slip downward, until she touched the smooth skin of his bare shoulder. Her other hand let go and gripped his other shoulder.

She looked up at him when he pulled away. Her body quickened when he gave her a devilish smile.

"Are you still certain you want to go through with this?"

"Oh, yes," she agreed while nodding her head.

"Wonderful," he said.

"How's your arm?"

"Well enough," he grunted.

Penelope studied him as he swooped down for another kiss, then he lowered his body over hers and dropped kisses along her jaw to her ears. She closed her eyes and bit her lower lip when his teeth gently nipped her earlobe before suckling it. She turned her head to the side to allow him greater access. Penelope reveled in the sensation as he used his teeth and gently scraped down her neck, light enough that he wouldn't leave a mark. He moved back up, then he followed the same trail with his tongue and lips until he reached the spot where her neck joined her shoulder. Duncan laved the spot, following the ridge of her collarbone with his tongue to the indention at the base of her throat. He repeated all of his actions on the other side of her neck until he was once more playing with that delicate indentation.

He brushed kisses across the upper part of her chest, never breaching the fabric of her shift. She felt his lips replaced with the backs of his fingers. Each time he made a pass, his fingers moved a bit lower, until they slipped beneath the shift she wore. Penelope inhaled sharply when he grazed her tender peaks.

"Might we remove this?" he asked, indicating the shift.

"Yes," she managed to say. She wiggled and shimmied until the shift passed over her head and floated to the floor. Still lying beneath the protection of the sheet and blanket, she felt relatively safe. Penelope reached up and cupped his bristly cheeks to guide his lips back down to hers. She kissed him as if he was her sustenance, and was so overcome with the kiss that she didn't feel him move off of her until it was too late. He flicked the covers back. Her only protection from him removed. She fisted her hand in the bedsheets beneath her, refusing to cover her breasts from his view, but she couldn't stop the blush that covered her skin.

"What's this?" he asked, a hand resting on a silk-clad hip.

"Pantaloons," she answered.

"They're beautiful but must go."

"No," Penelope protested, mortified. "There's a slit," she clarified, blushing even more.

"That's wonderful to know for future reference," he said cryptically before kissing her once more.

Her stiffened posture melted away. When his hand cupped an alabaster globe, she couldn't help but shiver. When his thumb raked back and forth against the tip, she was forced to stop the kiss and take a gasping breath.

"Is something wrong?" he whispered at her ear.

"No," she managed to say.

"Good."

Penelope rolled her head to the side to allow him better access as he dragged his lips along an imaginary line that led him from her ear, down her neck, and to her breast. She gasped and gripped his upper arms, careful of his wound, as he took her deep into his mouth and suckled, first softly then more ardently. Penelope clenched her thighs together as the more attention he payed to her bosom, the more she tingled below, as if the two were directly related to one another. She bit her lip as one of his hands moved caressingly along her ribs. She felt the slow tug of the tie on her pantaloons, and her eyes flew open. "What are you doing?" she asked as the bow came free.

"The next step," Duncan said before returning to suckle her bounty once more.

Penelope bit her lip and stared into the darkness that should be the ceiling, but the lamp's glow didn't penetrate the darkness that high up. She worried her lower lip when she felt his hand slip beneath the waist of her pantaloons and caress her quivering tummy. The strangest thing began to happen. A few inches lower her body felt like it was weeping. She found herself both embarrassed and afraid, but then she recalled what Duncan had done to her at the ruins and how her body seemed to take over. Penelope mentally gave herself a thorough tongue-lashing for being so uptight.

Duncan sat back on his heels and studied her.

"Why did you stop?"

"Oh, I'm just pausing the events for a moment. I believe it's time we do away with these, don't you?" he asked as he slowly tugged the pantaloons down her body.

Penelope felt each excruciating inch as they traveled down her legs, leaving her fully exposed to her husband's view. She fisted her hands tightly by her side. She lay there, waiting for him to cover her with his body, but instead she remained exposed for what felt to be an eternity. Unable to take another moment of scrutiny, she reached for the sheet he had flicked away earlier. "I knew this was a mistake. I never should have—"

"You're so beautiful," he said, entwining his fingers with her hand, to keep her from reaching the sheet. "You take my breath away."

Penelope's eyes flew up to his. "You don't have to say that," she said, feeling awkward and exposed all at once. "I know how plain I look. Whitney was the beauty." She attempted to cover herself from his view, but he halted her progress again. He caught her other hand, seductively kissed her palm, and placed it beside her once more.

"I will not listen to anyone put down my wife, not even you, understand?" His words were softened when he leaned in and kissed her. "Now, where was I? Oh, yes, I remember," he teased as he returned to her breasts.

"You are rather good at this, aren't you?"

"I've been out of practice, but am quickly remembering. You taste like nectar from a flower," he said.

"I believe I married a poet."

"Perhaps I just have the perfect muse," he countered. He slipped a finger gently inside her wet heat while she was distracted.

"Duncan!" she squeaked and grabbed his wrist with her free hand. "What are you doing?"

"Remember at the ruins?"

"Yes."

"We're going a step further. One step at a time. All right?"

"Yes," she whispered as her body began to adjust.

"Excellent," he said as he seduced her into a state of full-blown arousal. "Another step," he whispered as he added another finger, gently stretching her.

Penelope grew restless and allowed her legs to fall open, to grant him easier access to her body. She squeezed his hand, hoping to convey the need that was coursing through her body. Her body throbbed, most especially where his fingers plied her. "Duncan," she said, his name sounded like a plea.

"Do you need release?"

"Yes."

"Do you need to fly?"

"Yes," she whimpered.

"Fly for me then," he said.

Penelope felt him strum that special place that he had introduced her to earlier and then she was, indeed, flying. Her body bowed on the bed, and her mouth opened in a silent scream. She was still experiencing her wonderful climax when Duncan moved over her and she felt something large probe past her entrance and enter her pulsating channel. When had he divested himself of the cover?

"Relax," he whispered and kissed her tenderly when she would have stiffened against the invasion. Instead, she relished the languidness that had washed over her body leaving it soft and pliant. “That’s it,” he praised her and she couldn’t help but smile. “I’m honored to be your husband, to be the one introducing you to passion.” His words were a balm to her battered soul, even if they were spoken in the heat of passion.

Penelope took stock of how she felt as his body took possession of hers. It was a strange sensation, but at the same time, it felt incredibly right, perfect even. He came to a stop and they were so close she felt his body kissing hers where they met. “Is that all there is?” she asked a bit disconcerted. She looked into his deep blue eyes, and brushed back his haphazard locks that made him appear younger than he was.

“No,” he rasped. “Wrap your legs around me, like this.” He guided one of her legs about him with his free hand and let her follow suit with the other. She gasped when he shifted just a bit closer, that part of his body fully embedded within her. They were as close as two people could be. “Yes,” he said. “It’s exquisite, isn’t it?”

“Amazing,” she responded.

“Now, we really fly.”

Penelope felt him entwine his fingers with her other hand so now they were completely connected. She felt him slowly pull away. “Where—” she began to ask only to gasp when he plunged back into her. Over and over he repeated the process until she could no longer think, no longer recall her own name. She felt her body tightening as it had earlier. Penelope experimentally squeezed her inner muscle and was surprised when she heard a deep groan come from her husband. She looked up in time to see Duncan’s blue eyes darken to almost black. He let go of her hand and manipulated that little nubbin as he slammed into her one last time, and she felt the strangest gush fill her before her body exploded.

“Duncan!” his name erupted from her lips.

Duncan collapsed beside her, pulling her into his arms. His breathing was erratic, but so was hers. Shivers traveled up and down her body in the aftermath of their sexual encounter. They were still intimately joined, but somehow Duncan reached over her and pulled the blanket over them. He tipped her chin and forced her to look into his passion-filled eyes. “Are you all right?" he asked, placing a tender kiss on her forehead, her eyes, the tip of her nose, and finally her lips.

"Yes," she whispered. "Please tell me I imagined yelling out your name."

"Oh, it was no trick of your imagination," he gave her a twisted grin that had her heart galloping.

"What was that…that…gush?" she blurted out.

"My seed. What you witnessed earlier," he clarified.

"Oh. Well, I should go to my bed."

"Oh, no. We should remain just like this to make absolutely certain our effort was successful," Duncan kissed her and held her close before they both drifted off.

"Where are you going?" Duncan asked Penelope when she slipped from the bed.

"Back to my room," she replied, retrieving her shift from the floor.

"Why?" He raised up on an elbow and looked her over from head to toe. What he could see of her, that is. She was currently using the shift like a shield. The room was now dark, the lantern having snuffed itself out hours ago.

"We've done…well…you know," she answered, waving between them with the hand that wasn't clutching the garment to her body.

"Do you think once was enough?"

"Twice," she corrected him, holding up two fingers while still clasping the shift to her body. "And wasn't it?" she challenged.

"Wasn't it what?" he asked as he peeked over the mattress and took in her shapely legs and dainty feet.

"Would you focus for a moment?"

"Oh, I am," he gave her a mischievous gleam.

"Was it enough to create a babe?" she growled.

"We can wait to find out, or…" He let the sentence taper off.

"Or what?" she demanded.

"Or we can continue on in our pursuits in order to make certain that we have created the child we both want." Duncan watched her eye him warily. He could see her weighing her options. "How long has it been since your last courses?"

"That's a bit personal to ask, isn't it?"

"We are now husband and wife. We are attempting to create a child. It seems I know a great deal more about the process than you do. Please, correct me if I'm wrong about any of this."

"No," she mumbled.

"Now," he softened his tone considerably, "when was the last time you had your courses?" He studied her and had begun to believe she wouldn't answer him when he finally heard a shy reply.

"Almost two months."

"What?" he demanded, as he slipped from the bed, no care for his nudity. "Are you already with child? Did your grandfather send me soiled goods?"

"No. How can you think that? After what we just did? What are you even talking about?" She took several steps backwards as he approached her.

"Don't act innocent. Your grandfather put you up to this didn't he? Whose child are you foisting onto me? You said you knew Reese. Is it *his*? I've been made a fool of once, I'll be damned if it didn't happen again."

"You're mad," she whispered, her eyes wide with a mix of fear and anger. What had happened to the man who only hours earlier had made her feel, not loved, but at least special? Standing before her now was a stranger.

"I'm angry, but I'm not crazy. That's your bloody family." He pointed at her, too angry to see how she flinched at the accusation. "Perhaps it's a good thing your bloodline is not mixing with mine. I wouldn't want madness to be a possibility with any of my children." Duncan pinned an arm across her chest, ripped the shift from her hand, and threw it to the ground. "You hide your body as if you were a virgin."

"I am…was," she argued, "until a few hours ago."

"You're going to keep up the pretense that I was your first lover?"

"It's the truth," she argued. Penelope tried to push him away, but he kept her pinned against the wall. She felt his erect manhood pressing against her stomach. It twitched as if it had a mind of its own, and her body responded in kind. She silently cursed them both. Penelope despised herself as she felt herself growing weak and shivery as she had during their lovemaking.

She craved his touch. That most intimate part of herself, where he joined with her was growing moist once more. What power did this man have over her? Or had he taught her something about her body, and now any man would do? No, she couldn't imagine allowing anyone else do to her what Duncan had done.

"You lie, you witch," he practically spit the moniker at her. "You lied about your virginity. You carry another man's babe, and yet I still want you. Not even Isabelle had that control over me. Once I knew she had been with my brother, I wanted no part of her, but you…I…I can't get enough of you. What spell have you cast on me?"

"None, you *beast*!" she spat the derogatory moniker at him with all the venom she could muster. "I am not a witch, and I am *not* with child, unless it's yours. How can you even think that when I came to you a virgin? When I let you—"

"Let me? You *begged* me. You *screamed* my name," he growled. "The entire household heard you, and they're about to hear you again."

Penelope felt herself being lifted in the air. "What are you doing?"

"Wrap your legs around my waist."

"No. Put me down." She struggled in his arms and pushed at his shoulders. She felt his lips on the base of her neck, suckling hard. "Ow, stop! What are you doing?"

"Marking you as mine."

His right hand cupped, ground, and shaped her left breast, pinching the nipple until it stood erect, while his left cradled her bottom, and squeezed it. His bare right leg was wedged between hers, keeping her exactly where he wanted her. She sucked in a breath when he lowered his head and strongly suckled at her right breast while he still manipulated her left with his hand. This was not her tender lover of earlier, and she tried desperately not to respond to his touch. She attempted to remain stiff and uncaring after all the hateful things he had just said to her, but soon her fisted hands were gripping his shoulders instead of pushing him away.

He removed his hand from her breast and she heard a whimper. Had that come from her? Then there was a moan when his finger prodded her feminine core. How could she still want him so badly and be so angry at him? What had he done to her? He had turned her body into a traitor. He found that hidden jewel that drove her mad, that she had not known existed less than twenty-four hours earlier. Penelope felt her body tightening as he continued to toy with her. Then he stopped. She shifted her hips in a silent plea for release, but his finger stayed just far enough away.

He hovered, letting her feel his presence, but refusing to give her the relief she craved. "Beg me," he demanded.

"What?" she asked, dumbfounded, trying to make sense of what he said. She was too lost in the sensual haze, her body craving the experience once more that his had taught her to expect from him. A spark shot through Penelope when he lightly pinched that bud.

"Beg me. Tell me what you want from me," he ordered.

"I want you to put me down and leave me alone."

"I don't believe that, Pen," he said, shortening her name. "If you wanted that, you wouldn't be holding onto my shoulders or wrapping your legs around me. You'd push me away, not pull me closer. Now, tell me what you want."

"I hate you," she growled before she wrapped her arms tightly around his neck and kissed him as he had taught her.

Duncan ripped their mouths apart then fisted his hand in her hair and pulled her head back. He dropped kisses along her graceful, slender neck. "Tell me how much you need me. How much your body is weeping for mine," he whispered in her ear.

"No," she said, but couldn't contain the shiver of desire his words caused.

"Don't deny it, I can feel it." To prove his point, he plunged a finger deep into her feminine core. "Your body is crying for me, witch," he whispered against her ear.

She was embarrassed to admit it was true. Her sheath was drenched with wanting him, even though he was being an accusatory ass. She could feel his manhood teasing her entrance after he removed his finger. She tried to shift, to take him inside her, but he kept her pinned right where he wanted her. "Why are doing this? I haven't done anything. I swear I came here a virgin." She didn't know it was possible for him to get any angrier, but he did.

"Damn him, and damn you." He placed her on her feet and went to his knees.

"What are you doing?" she asked dazedly.

"You'll beg me before the night is through."

She yelped when his mouth replaced where his finger had been moments earlier. Her body was taut with sexual tension. He spent his time pushing her ever closer to the precipice but refusing to let her crash. She gripped his shoulders then fisted her hands in his hair in a non-verbal attempt to demand he give her release, but he refused to comply. Finally, she could take no more. "Please," she whimpered.

"What?" he demand as he pulled away and rose.

"Please, *Beast*," she snarled.

He made no comment, merely lifted her up, spread her wide, and pushed forcefully into her.

She threw her head back, her breath stolen with his possession. Yes, it was primitive and he was rough, but goodness help her, she liked it. Not every time perhaps, but she found it exciting as he pulled out quickly then slammed back into her. She wrapped her legs around his waist, using the leverage to pull him closer. Penelope heard the sounds escaping her and couldn't stop them, the whimpers, the moans, the mewling.

"Look at me." Duncan's words somehow reached her ears. "Bloody hell, look at me. I want you to know that it's me and not him inside you."

His words shocked her into looking at him.

"You're my wife, dammit, and only mine. Un…der…stand?" Each syllable was punctuated by a thrust. "Who *am* I?"

"Duncan," her voice caught.

"Who?"

"The *Beast*," she repeated.

"Who?"

"My *husband*," she replied tearfully. Penelope was so close to the precipice that she shook. She wrapped her legs tighter around his waist and plunged downward forcefully as he moved upwards into her one last time, and together they reached the pinnacle. She held him tightly as he leaned against her while they both recovered, letting their breathing return to normal. He slipped from her, and it felt as if a chasm had developed between them. Penelope let out a squeal as he tossed her onto his bed.

"You'll sleep here from now on, where I can watch you. When you begin to show, I'll send you and your mother away for a time on the pretense of you getting help for her. I expect you to give the child away. I refuse to raise another man's bastard. When you return, we shall begin working on begetting an heir. In the meantime, you'll be the perfect wife, in every way, including in the bedroom. Do you understand?"

"No, I don't understand," she stood up, fisted hands on hips, uncaring of her nudity. "I came to you a virgin. If I am with child, it is *yours*. I don't understand why you're angry or why you would want me to give away our child, which I will *not* do."

"You should get a job on Drury Lane."

"I thought we were to trust one another."

"That was before I realized I had married a lying, scheming bitch. I'm done talking about this. Get in bed and go to sleep, I'm tired."

"No."

"Suit yourself and sleep on the floor if you want, but you *will* stay in this room."

"I hate you."

"I believe you already said that once tonight."

"I thought you were going to court me. To prove that we would be good together."

"You put paid to that," he said and looked pointedly at her flat stomach before turning his back to her and pulling the sheet and blanket over his body.

CHAPTER 10

The next few weeks were strained between them and the entire household felt it. They rarely said a few words to one another during the day. During the afternoons Penelope often walked the garden or toured the local sights. Most of the time someone accompanied her. Other times, like today, she was able to slip away undetected. Several times she went back to the ruins where she had been so blissfully naïve. On more than one of those occasions, Duncan had joined her there and new, even more passionate memories had been created, because no matter how much she disliked him at the moment she couldn't deny him using her body. She wanted to hate him, but she was a willing participant in their carnal activities. Her body had become addicted to his, and she hated herself for it.

She went to Robin's Hood Bay and found the people quite friendly to her face, but what she heard them say behind her back was damning and hurtful. It had not taken long for the villagers to find out that her grandfather had sold her to Duncan. She vaguely wondered who told them, but shrugged it off deciding it really didn't matter since it was the truth.

Penelope had continued on, trying to ignore the mean things they were saying about her. She had even visited with the sister of the girl who had died the night of the press gang's attack on the village. She had taken her a gift and commiserated with her on what it felt like to lose a sister. The young woman still held resentment towards Duncan for not doing more. Despite everything, Penelope defended him and told her how guilty he felt about Anna's death. The two hugged and promised to visit again.

Penelope walked back to the top of the village and then followed the cliff for some time until no one could be seen in either direction. She found a trail and carefully picked her way down to the solitary beach. *Why did I defend him?* She wondered, angry with herself. He has been nothing but a beast, using your body to slake his lust every night as one might with a harlot, and acting like you don't even exist during the day. *But you're enjoying your nights together and the things he's teaching you*, the devil on her shoulder taunted.

"Shut up," she muttered to herself. Penelope removed her bonnet and the pins from her hair and let it fall down her back. In London, she would have never been allowed to do this. But this was not London. She sat down, removed her sturdy walking boots and stockings, and dug her toes into the moist sand. She giggled like a young girl in leading strings at the feeling. "This is delightful," she said laughing. The laughter died as she realized she had no one to share it with. She tossed the items she removed further up the beach, away from the water.

Penelope walked along the edge of the surf and after the initial temperature shock, she found she liked it. *Perhaps because it's cooling your overheated body from thinking about your husband. The way he touches you. The way you touch him.*

"Shut. Up," she growled, kicking at the foamy waves in frustration. She lifted her dress to just above her knees and walked further into the water. Penelope stood there getting caught up in the rhythm of the waves. She enjoyed the way they crashed into her and then sucked the sand from around her feet as the water was pulled back to create another wave. She looked around and saw no one. Before she could change her mind, she stripped off her dress and petticoats until she only wore her shift. She raced back up to the beach, folded them, and placed them under her boots so the wind wouldn't scatter them.

She walked into the water again and shivered a bit before her body became accustomed once more. This time she went into her waist, allowing the surf to rock against her. She took a step and felt something speed away under her foot causing her to lose her balance and fall. The water quickly covered her head and tossed her about. Her lungs burned for air when she felt the sandy floor against her cheek. Penelope put her hands out and pushed off the bottom, hoping to break the surface of the water soon. She did and quickly gulped in air. She got her legs beneath her, but couldn't feel the bottom.

How had the beach gotten so far away so fast? She wondered just before panic sunk in. She looked at the sky just before a wave crashed over her head. *Wonderful, a storm, too,* Penelope thought. She fought her way back to the surface purely out of instinct and a need for survival, because she didn't know how to swim. She took another breath and let out a short lived cry for help before she was once again forced under. She flailed and grew weaker and more tired every time another wave pushed her under. And now the sky had opened up releasing the rain in a deluge, causing the water to churn where only minutes before it had been calm and soothing. *How much longer can I last? Will Duncan remarry, or will he give up believing he really is cursed? And what if there is a baby now?* That thought gave her a renewed sense of fight. She broke the surface and screamed for all she was worth.

"Did you hear that?" Duncan shouted over the rain to the men in the fishing boat. He had gone out with them needing to expel some of the pent-up tension he had felt since the night he and Penelope consummated their marriage. Now he thought it might have been serendipitous that he chose today of all days over the last few weeks to help the fishermen.

"No," they chorused, eager to be home and out of the weather that had quickly turned sour.

"Listen," he urged them all to focus.

"Help!"

"Over there!" Duncan pointed in the direction he had seen a head bob out of the water, shouting to be heard over the storm. "Turn the boat."

"Can't, Your Grace, we'll hit rocks and break up. We'll lower a dinghy."

"Take too long." He was already pulling off his boots. He climbed over the railing and propelled himself into the intense water. Every time he spotted the person, they were a little further out of reach. Using his body, he rode the waves toward the person. It was a trick he and Reese used to do when they were children. Never did he think he could use child's play to save someone's life. He saw a hand barely sticking up out of the water. He encircled the wrist like a manacle, barely noting how slim it was in his grasp.

The combination of his powerful strokes and the waves had him reaching the quickly shrinking beach in no time. He managed to signal to the fishermen he had worked with today that they had reached safety and saw the boat continue on. Duncan looked beside him and noticed two things almost simultaneously, the person he rescued was his wife and she wasn't breathing.

When Penelope became aware of her surroundings, unfortunately it was accompanied by her expelling water from her body in a most hideous way and a rather large someone straddling her back and pushing on her over and over. If they didn't stop, she was afraid she would be eating the sand beneath her. She tried to buck them off of her, but she was so weak. *Why?* She wondered. Then it all came back to her. She had played in the waves when something moved under her foot and caused her to fall. She had been sucked out to sea and fought for her life. The person managed to purge her body of more ocean water and then crawled off her and turned her over.

"You're alive. Thank God, you're alive." Duncan pulled her into a fierce hug as the rain poured around them. "What were you doing?" He gripped her arms and shook her. "Do you realize how dangerous the water is for someone who doesn't know how to swim? And in a storm, no less. Were you trying to kill yourself?"

All she could manage was to shake her head in the negative.

"Then explain to me what you were doing!" he yelled at her, his demand punctuated by a lightning bolt and clap of thunder that caused them both to jump. "Bloody hell, we've got to get off this beach."

He looked around and the next thing she knew, he stood up, tossed her over his shoulder, and headed towards the rocky cliff face. She wiggled around to try and see where they were going when she felt his hand swat her almost bare posterior.

"Be still or both of us will go crashing into those rocks and crack our skulls open."

About halfway up the cliff face, after several close calls, they entered a shallow cave. It was about twelve feet deep and seven feet tall, but was only wide enough for two people to sit or lay side by side with very little extra space to spare. He put her down. After he helped her scurry into the cave, he quickly followed. Shivers began to run up and down her body and she broke out in gooseflesh, but she wasn't sure if it was because of the storm, the fact that she was wet, or that she had nearly died.

"What in bloody hell were you thinking?"

She bit her lip to try to keep the tears at bay that threatened to fall.

"Was there anyone else with you?"

"No," she managed.

"Was this your way of fixing things? To take your own life?"

"No!" she turned and yelled at him. "I was doing something I had never done before. I was playing in the surf. I was enjoying myself. I was *not* thinking about you or me or our horrible marriage. Then something moved under my foot and I lost my balance. The next thing I knew, I was swept away from the beach and fighting to stay above water."

"A combination of the storm and high tide coming in. Horrible marriage, huh?"

"What would you call it? You only use me to satisfy your physical needs."

"Are you going to tell me you aren't enjoying yourself?"

"I'm going to sleep. Wake me when we can leave, unless of course I need to take care of you first."

"As a matter of fact," he said before pushing her backwards.

Penelope tried to remain immune to his touch, tried to remain stiff and unyielding, but she couldn't. He had learned her body too well. Learned what it liked and what it demanded. By the time he slowly entered her, she was on fire with need. She pulled him to her, held him close, and encouraged him. Just as she was about to climax, he pulled free of her.

"What?" she asked, devastated, her body tormented with unfulfilled passion.

"Face the ocean and get on your hands and knees," he said.

"Why?"

"So you can watch the beauty and fury of the storm and ocean while I bring you to your peak."

Unsure, but ready to answer her body's demands, she did as he instructed. Soon, her breath was coming in gasps as he entered her from behind. He felt so incredibly deep this way. Every time a wave crashed, he plunged into her. He teased her breasts to perky attention. Before long, she slammed backwards to meet his every thrust as she watched the waves crash onto the rocks below. The shoreline had disappeared with the rising tide. Her clothes floated out to sea, but all she cared about was this man she had unwillingly married. This man who had been hurt so often, he was like a frightened animal, afraid to trust anyone with his heart. She fought to keep the wall she had erected around hers in place, but it became increasingly hard to keep it from crumbling into bits.

Penelope brazenly took his hand and tried to move it where she wanted him to touch her. She was so close to flying she just needed him, there.

"Touch yourself," he bent over and whispered at her ear.

"No," she shook her head as he continued to work in and out of her.

"I'm not going to do it. This is a new lesson."

"Please," she begged. "Don't turn me into a harlot."

"I'm not. You're my wife and I'm showing you pleasure."

He took her hand and guided it to where she had tried to move his. He ground her finger against that magical jewel and her whole body shook. Her groan echoed off the walls of the cave. Her inner muscles caressed and stroked him until he threw back his head and yelled his release.

"Well?" he asked sometime later. They were lying next to one another, not touching. His pants were back to rights as was her shift.

"What?"

"What are you thinking?"

"That the villagers are right. That I am the *Beast's* whore." She rolled away from him, pulled her knees up to her chest, and tried to go to sleep.

CHAPTER 11

The next morning they returned to the Hall by horseback. Penelope had a blanket wrapped tightly around her, but could not stop the shivering that had set in during the night. Her throat felt like it was being cut by glass every time she swallowed, and her ears and eyes itched uncontrollably. The sneezes began on the ride home. She wanted nothing more than to lean against him and soak up the heat that emanated from his body, but instead, she held herself stiff and upright. She pulled the blanket tighter in an attempt to ward off the chill that had penetrated her bones. They spoke not one word to each other, or touched one another, unless necessary, since their interlude last night.

The door burst open when they reached the Hall and Reese approached them just in time to help Penelope down from the horse. "Where have the two of you been?" he demanded.

She felt his arms tighten around her as she was wracked by a coughing fit.

"Get your hands off my wife," Duncan ordered. He slid off the horse and threw the reins to a stable hand that had rushed over upon their arrival. He jerked Penelope out of Reese's arms and gripped her upper arm to keep her upright.

"Careful," Reese admonished. "She's ill."

"I'll take care of her. You've done enough."

"What are you talking about?"

"Get out of the way," Duncan snarled. When Reese showed no sign of moving, Duncan pushed him aside and drug Penelope behind him.

"Duncan," she wheezed and stumbled.

"What's going on?" Rosalie demanded as she entered the foyer, Lucy not far behind.

"That's what I'm trying to find out," Reese said, "but my brother's talking in riddles. Now, what happened?"

Penelope felt Duncan step away from her. She stumbled as he let go of her and put her hand out to grab the banister before she went down. She heard a horrible sound and saw Reese crash backwards into the foyer table.

"Reese," she called out at the same time Lucy did. Both of them moved to help Reese, but Penelope's progress was halted by a large arm wrapped around her waist. Next she knew, she was lifted off the floor. "Put me down," she fought him and kicked at him, but her energy quickly diminished and left her hanging limp in his arms.

"What the hell was that for?" Reese called after them.

"Get out of my house," Duncan growled.

"Why?"

Duncan stopped at the top of the stairs and looked down at his brother, "Because you've ruined my life and my marriages."

"Reese, Rosalie, Lucy," Penelope pleaded, holding a hand out to them.

"Duncan, be sensible." Rosalie's words floated up to her.

"Why are you doing this, Duncan?" Lucy echoed Rosalie's concern.

Reese charged up the stairs and her world spun sickeningly as Duncan did an about face and stared down his brother. "If you lay one hand on her, I'll kill you, brother be damned," Duncan growled.

"Duncan," Penelope moaned pitifully.

"Send for a hot bath and her maid," he tossed out the order and continued down the hall to his bedchamber.

She bounced on the mattress when he dumped her on the bed. She sat there shivering, unable to bring her body under control. Every muscle ached and her head swam sickeningly. "Why did you do that?" She had hoped to make her demand more forceful, but instead it turned into a whisper.

"I told you before, I am not discussing this any more. Just looking at you angers me. Get out of my room."

"I thought you wanted to keep an eye on me."

"I don't have to have you in my bed to know you aren't going anywhere."

Somehow Penelope managed to get to her feet and shuffle across the floor. Her bedroom door banged open and her head snapped upward to see both Rosalie and Lucy rushing towards her with open arms. She fell to her knees and let the tears fall freely. She cried harder when she felt the two women's arms wrap around her.

"She's burning up. Mary, send for Mrs. Helms immediately. Tell her to bring her bag," Rosalie ordered.

"Yes, Your Grace," Mary forgot to curtsy in her haste to carry out the order.

"She's fine," Duncan said from the connecting door.

"She's not. Now leave us alone before I have you horsewhipped," Rosalie ordered.

"How dare—"

His words were cut off when she reached over and slammed the door in his face.

Duncan piled his stiff clothes in a messy heap on the floor and climbed into the bath that awaited him. He closed his eyes, but every time he did, he either saw Penelope dipping beneath a wave or heard her condemnation of his treatment of her. Had he really turned her into a whore? No, he refused to believe he had. She had been as eager to receive his touch as he had been to give it.

Almost two months. Her words echoed in his head, taunting him, yet he still wanted her. "Why, dammit, why?" he asked himself. When Isabelle had told him about her and Reese's affair, it had instantaneously killed any physical attraction he had felt towards her. Penelope was another story entirely. He ached with the need to have her. He ached so much that he was willing to force her to remain with him, to fulfill his sexual desires. *I am the* Beast's *whore*. The accusatory words taunted him. Is that really what people were saying about her? Why wouldn't they? He had bought her, hadn't he? Had haggled with her grandfather so that he could purchase her instead of her sister because he was more attracted to her? He had been willing to sacrifice another woman to the curse, because he needed a bloody heir.

"What did you do to Penelope?"

His brother's voice brought him out of his reverie. "What in bloody hell are you doing in here? I thought I told you to leave my house."

"And I will, as soon as I am convinced that Penelope will be safe, and right now, I'm not certain that will ever happen," Reese said, unperturbed by Duncan's gruffness. "What happened?"

"She decided to go swimming in the bay with a storm rolling in," Duncan grudgingly answered.

"Damnation, what was going through her mind?"

"Nothing, evidently. Now leave. You've done enough."

"What are you talking about?"

"I know about the two of you, so you might as well stop the pretense. You are no longer my brother. I want you gone by morning."

"You've lost your bloody mind," Reese replied.

"Are you telling me I have no reason not to trust you?" Duncan saw that Reese could not meet his gaze. "Get out. You sicken me."

"Dunc—"

"Get out!" he roared.

"You're going to regret this," Reese predicted before slamming the door shut.

He was just going to step out of the tub when the connecting door opened and Rosalie entered. He quickly sat back in the water and pulled the bath sheet over his chest. "What are you doing?"

"Oh, you act as if I've never seen a naked man before."

"What do you want?"

"I want you to cease this yelling that you're doing. It isn't good for Penelope. She's quite ill."

"She did it to herself. Now, if you'll kindly leave, I would like to get dressed."

"Duncan, I have always been your champion. I've thought the reputation that surrounds you was uncalled for, until now. I abhor the way you are treating that dear girl."

"*Dear girl*? That's rich," he tilted his head back and barked his laughter.

"Shhh, you're going to wake her."

His laughter stopped abruptly and met his step-grandmother's fierce gaze with an even fiercer gaze of his own. "I find I really don't care how I inconvenience her. Her grandfather sold me used goods. More so, I suspect her innocent act was just that. She's with child."

"That's wonderful," Rosalie said.

"It's not mine. She knew Reese before she arrived, and I don't find it a particular coincidence that they arrived here within hours of each other. Do you?"

"You aren't suggesting—"

"Why not? It's happened before. Now, get out of my room Rosalie." The older woman huffed and slammed the connecting door shut. Finally, he was left in peace.

The fever set in with a vengeance. Penelope only woke when someone prodded her to take medicine or to force broth down her. Her breathing was raspy to her own ears, when she was lucid enough to care. She ached all over and even the hair on her head hurt. She was burning up and kicked the covers so they gathered in a pile at the foot of the bed. Soon, she was shivering once more.

The cloth of her nightdress irritated her skin and she whimpered as she fought to remove it.

"Shhh, easy." The voice that sounded like Duncan's tickled her ears, and seemed to care, but no, that can't be right. He hated her. Soon she was free of the cloth and she almost shouted with relief. Then she felt the coolness of tepid water being sponged along her body. Tears trickled down her temples into her hair. "Don't cry."

"Hurt," she mumbled.

"I know."

"Duncan hates me."

Silence.

"Don't know why." She began to shake uncontrollably and felt the blankets cover her, but it did no good. The shaking continued. The mattress dipped and she felt herself pulled against a broad, hair-covered chest that felt so incredibly warm she couldn't help but cuddle into him. She took a deep breath and smelled Duncan. That's when she decided she must be delirious because he hated her.

The next time she woke, she was alone in bed and her night dress was on her once more. Mary was working in the room. She must have made a noise, for the maid quickly turned and looked at her. "Oh, Your Grace, you're awake."

"Yes," Penelope croaked.

Mary rushed over and placed her inner wrist against Penelope's forehead and cheek. "No fever, praise be. We were worried about you."

"How long?"

"Three days. When you become ill, you do a good job of it. Did you really try to drown yourself?"

"No," she muttered. "Drink."

"Yes." Mary scurried to bring her some broth to sip on that had been kept on a warmer. "No more than a couple of spoonfuls now." Mary helped Penelope lean up. Penelope sipped it gratefully, enjoying the saltiness of the liquid. When Mary took it away she collapsed against the pillows once more. "I'll be back in just a moment, Your Grace."

Penelope tried to nod her head, but had the feeling she failed miserably. The next time she opened her eyes, three concerned faces studied her—Duncan, Rosalie, and Lucy.

"So, you're still with us," Duncan surmised. He made it sound like an accusation.

"Of course she is," Rosalie said, "it was just a bit of the ague."

"I was so worried about you," Lucy said, her eyes red with unshed tears.

"I'm fine," Penelope lifted one side of her lip in a half-hearted smile. "Reese?" she managed to say, surprised at not seeing him gathered around.

"Bloody hell," Duncan muttered and stormed from the room.

"Duncan!" Lucy called after him.

"Leave him be, bloody stupid fool," Rosalie muttered. "Reese is staying in the dowager's cottage, but don't tell Duncan. As you can see, they aren't speaking."

Penelope squinted, trying to make her scattered thoughts coalesce.

"Now, now, you relax and go to sleep. Brothers have been fighting since Cain and Abel and will continue to do so."

"Cain killed Abel," Lucy muttered.

"Hush now, don't worry the poor thing anymore than she already is. You just go back to sleep. I'll have Mary sit with you."

CHAPTER 12

Duncan stormed outside after hearing his brother's name on his wife's lips. *Damn! Damn! Bloody damn!* He stomped around the perimeter of the Hall until he spied a stack of logs. He went to the gardener's shed and started rifling through the tools when he heard a throat being cleared behind him.

"Can I help ye, Your Grace?"

Duncan turned to see Old Clancy, the long-time gardener, standing behind him.

"I need an axe, Clancy."

"An axe?"

"Yes."

Clancy stepped around him, dug for a moment, and handed him the requested tool. "It's dull. Haven't had time to sharpen it."

"All the better," Duncan said, carrying it back to the logs so that it rested on his shoulder. He put down the axe then adjusted one log so that it was elevated between two others.

"We were going to take care of that, Your Grace," the old man said.

"Now you don't have to worry about it anymore, Clancy." Duncan picked up the axe once more, took a stance, and felt, as well as heard, a satisfying thwack as the blade cut into the log. Over and over he hit the log with the tool, finding a release for his anger. Over and over he fought with the log to relinquish the axe back to him. When the log split, he paused, readjusted, then began again. He continued on, hacking the first log into five pieces before he moved on to the next one. When he made the last two pieces of the last log, he was covered in sweat and his shirt stuck to his body.

"Duncan, I brought you something to drink."

"Go away, Lucy."

"But I—"

"Now, Lucy."

"Yes, Duncan."

She left the glass of cool liquid behind. He walked over, picked it up, and drank it down in only a few gulps.

"Son," Clancy said, joining him where he sat, "that new wife got you tied up in knots?"

"It could be the estate. It could be—"

"Stop telling me what it could be and tell me what it is."

"As you said, my wife."

"Ah. She's a pretty lass."

"Yes."

"What's the problem?"

"The curse."

"Explain yourself, lad."

"She came to me carrying another man's child."

"Ach, I can't believe it."

"It's true."

"Do you know whose it is?"

"My brother's," he said and couldn't hide the anguish in his voice. "He betrayed me again, and her grandfather defrauded me."

"What are you going to do?"

"Send her away until the babe is born. She'll have to give it up, and then we can begin our family."

"You still want her?"

"That's the hell of it all, Clancy. I want her more than any woman that's ever come into my life."

The two men sat in silence, both contemplating Duncan's future.

"You seem to be doing better," Rosalie said as she carried in a tray of food.

"I feel like I'm getting stronger," Penelope replied as she shifted to a sitting position. She allowed Rosalie to place the tray across her lap before she picked up a piece of lightly browned toast and nibbled at it.

"Now, tell me why Duncan seems to think you are expecting a child that isn't his."

Penelope carefully watched Rosalie as she moved to a chair, sat down, and draped her arm over the back. The woman looked at her expectantly, and Penelope knew that regardless of how embarrassing this conversation was going to be, Rosalie would not leave until she had her answer. Unfortunately, Penelope didn't know what that answer was either.

"Well?" the older woman prodded.

"I don't know."

"Tell me what you do know about having children."

Penelope thought back throughout her life. She recalled the ladies her mother visited, her so-called friends that had disappeared when Mother had needed them most. Several of them throughout the years had confided to her mother that they were going to have a child. She remembered Mother only visited them once or twice more, often within that same month, and didn't see them again until the baby was a few months old. Even when Mother had Samuel, she was so little that she barely remembered, but what she did recollect was the amount of time Mother spent in her bedchamber, most specifically in bed. It was as if she had been sick for months. Then one night she and Whitney awoke to terrible screams coming from her mother's room. She and her sister had scampered out of the nursery and downstairs to her parents bedchamber. Only they had been stopped in the hallway when they saw their father pacing up and down the corridor. Another scream had rent the air and Father had looked worriedly at the door.

"Mama," the girls had chorused and gone straight for the door, only to be gathered up in their father's arms.

"Here, now, what are you two doing out of bed?"

"Someone's hurting Mama," Penelope had said, almost in tears.

Next, a feminine roar filtered out into the hall, and all three of them stared at the door.

"What was that?" Whitney asked fearfully.

"Your wonderful mother," Father had said with admiration in his voice. "Girls, you are going to be big sisters after a while. Your mother is having a baby."

"Like our dollies?" Whitney asked.

Father had chuckled at that. "I suppose there is some resemblance. Only this baby will eat, sleep, and cry. Eventually it will walk and talk like you two little ladies. And I pray it be a boy this time," he muttered the last part under his breath, but the girls had heard.

"Don't you like little girls, Papa?"

But he had never answered for at that moment a piercing wail, that could in no way be their Mother, filled the air. Their father put them on the floor and stood at the door. Mrs. Childs, the housekeeper opened Mother's door.

"It's a boy, my lord, with a fine set of lungs."

"Thank God," he had said. "Did you hear that girls? You have a little brother! Now, go back to bed. You'll see him soon enough."

The girls had climbed the stairs slowly to their room in the nursery, holding hands. They fell back asleep, holding tightly to one another, knowing their lives would never be the same.

"Penelope, Penelope, are you all right?" Rosalie asked as she started to rise from her seat.

"I'm fine."

"You're crying."

Penelope swiped a hand across her cheek, surprised when she felt dampness. She stared at the tears glistening in the lamp light as if seeing something unknown. She dropped her hand, reclined against the pillows, and retold her tale. When she finished, Rosalie snorted in disgust.

"Society," she said in contemptuously.

"But aren't you—"

"Do not compare me to people born to it. You need not know how it was done, but I fought my way to my title. I'm not proud of some of the things I've done to get it, but it was always with the hope that Lucy would have a better life than what I had. I've also seen enough babe's die to know that they are all precious, regardless of if they are boys or girls. Now tell me what exactly made Duncan so angry that he believes you carry his brother's child."

"You know?"

"It's difficult not to know after he punched Reese then kicked him out of the house."

"He didn't!"

"Don't you remember? You were there."

"No," Penelope's head pounded, and she lifted a shaky hand to press against her temple. She closed her eyes and tried to remember. She recalled some yelling and accusations, but she had been in the full throes of the fever by that point. A gentle hand cupped the back of her head, lifting her up a bit while placing a glass against her lips.

"Here, now, take a sip. Just a sip."

Penelope did as told and began coughing as the liquid burned its way down her throat to her belly. "What was that?"

"Whisky."

She licked her lips and wondered if she should like the taste as much as she did once she became accustomed to the burn.

"Now, why does Duncan think you are having Reese's child?" Rosalie asked once more.

Penelope thought back in her memory to the night they consummated their union. How she had been about to slip back to her room. The questions about when her last menses had been. When she had told him, he had become irrational. Penelope repeated the conversation to Rosalie.

"Two months?!" Rosalie exclaimed. "Are you sure you're not with child?"

"I came to Duncan a virgin."

Rosalie began to ask more questions that had Penelope thinking back over the last horrible two years and longer. Each question she asked involved Penelope thinking back to her menses. She grew more and more embarrassed with each question. Her mother had never shown this much interest in her daughters, leaving nannies, governesses, and maids to see to their needs.

"You were a virgin, and Duncan is a bloody idiot. He's so caught up in this curse that he can't see past it."

"You believe me?"

"You are too naïve for your own good. Your mother did you an injustice by not discussing such matters with you, as I am sure her mother did her as well. You need to learn something of the world, and here is your first lesson."

Rosalie continued on, talking very frankly about a woman's body. Penelope blushed, though she listened attentively. She even dared to ask the occasional question.

Finally, she asked the most important question of all, "So, because I told him it had been almost two months since my menses, that's why he thinks I'm going to have a baby?"

"Yes."

"But if what you say is true, it is because the turmoil my life has been, and continues to be."

"Yes."

"Why would he think that?"

"Because he is a man," Rosalie said.

"I have to tell him, explain to him."

"He will not believe you. Let me explain to him."

"But won't you be embarrassed?"

"Dear, hardly anything embarrasses me anymore. Now, finish eating and get some rest."

Duncan was looking over tenant complaints when Rosalie stormed into the study. The door bounced off the bookcase, and she appeared angry. He idly wondered what had riled her. "Won't you come in?" he asked, sarcastically.

"Don't take that tone with me, young man." The older woman shook her finger at him.

She was still a stunning beauty in her early fifties. His grandfather had done well in choosing her as his wife. He remembered how the old man had enjoyed their lively arguments, and then the two would disappear for hours. That's how he wanted to end his life—fighting and making love. He looked towards the ceiling and couldn't help the feelings of disappointment, resentment, and anger that coursed through him.

"Duncan James Taggart, I'm speaking to you." Rosalie slammed the door shut and crossed to his desk.

"Rosalie, you're in quite a snit. What, or who, has caused it?"

"You have, because you're a man and a bloody idiot. You jump to conclusions, believe in a bloody curse, and have no faith in women."

He stiffened at the accusations she threw his way. "Rosalie, I would be very careful as to what I said if I were you."

"I am being careful and you do not frighten me. Do you know what you have accused that poor girl of?"

"It's not an accusation! It's the truth, and I will not speak of it with you."

"You do not have to speak, you just listen. That girl came to you an innocent in every sense of the word. My little finger knows more about the reproduction process than your wife does, or did. Thanks to me, she is now much more educated."

"She's a great actress, you mean. Besides, you already talked to her."

"Duncan, I told her what to expect on her wedding night. I should have explained more to her, but I had surmised that surely her mother had shared *some* pertinent information with her. I couldn't have been more wrong. When her courses came the first time, she thought she was dying. Her twin sister told her otherwise, and that was only because a maid had told her."

"I am not speaking of such things with you. Now, get out of my study and leave me in peace."

"If you are going to accuse her of infidelity, then I am going to defend her and prove you wrong, and you are bloody well going to listen to me!" She slammed her hands down on the desk and leaned over it, glaring at him. "Her courses were regular until two years ago when her family life fell apart. It was never wonderful to begin with, if you ask me, but the girls had to leave the finishing school they attended because there was no money. Talk, of course, spread rapidly since they only had a few weeks left and couldn't even afford that. They had to let servants go, and the girls had to fill in, mostly Penelope. I get the idea that her sister thought she was too good for menial tasks. They went from being waited on to doing the work."

"The clothes she wears," he guessed.

"Yes. She sold all of her dresses to bring in money. Her sister kept hers, for they were hoping Whitney, at least, would make a match. Then her father and sister further sullied the family name and lost their lives in the process. Her courses have been sporadic for the last two years. If you had questioned her further, you would have found that out before you jumped to conclusions."

"She could be making up these stories."

"Your wife, sweet young woman that she is, is clueless about what it takes to create a child. I have just spent the afternoon schooling her on the making and birthing of babies, down to every last detail that I have knowledge of. All she knew of childbirth was that it took place behind closed doors and entailed a lot of screaming. She's never even seen a woman heavy with child, not even her own mother. The woman stayed confined to her bedroom throughout most of her pregnancy for whatever reason. Knowing the *ton* as I do, I imagine she was embarrassed over her body concerning a very normal process."

"You jest."

"Do I look as if I am joking, Duncan? She and her sister were practically forgotten the moment their brother was born. Her parents did their daughters a grave injustice in so many ways. Now one is dead, and one has been accused of adultery."

"But she knew Reese."

"A coincidence."

"They arrived within hours of each other."

"Duncan Taggart, you placed the bans in the papers from here to London. Reese is reckless, but he isn't stupid. He keeps up with what is going on in the world just like any other man. He reads newspapers."

"I've been an idiot."

"I'd say you have."

"I'll go and talk to her."

"Not now, she's resting. What you need to do now is go make peace with your brother."

"I—"

Rosalie held up her hand and stopped whatever he was going to say. "He is staying in the dowager's cottage."

"I told him to leave."

"And I told him he could use my future house. Now, I know the situation was different in the past, but I can't fix that. But you should apologize to him for this situation, because I can guarantee you, your wife had a difficult enough time consummating her marriage with you. She's not one to sleep with every man that crosses her path."

Duncan watched Rosalie retreat from the room, leaving him alone with his thoughts. Could he have been so wrong about Penelope? Was it easy to accuse Reese because of the past? Why couldn't he just not care? He picked up the glass of whisky that had been sitting next to his hand on the desk. He tossed back the remaining liquid, then threw the glass across the room. It shattered into hundreds of tiny pieces in the fireplace.

"Duncan, are you all right?" Lucy asked with concern as she peeked her head into the room.

"Go away, Lucy."

"But—"

"Leave me alone," he practically growled, like a wolf with a wounded paw. He heard the door shut once more and knew that Lucy had left him alone to lick his wounds. "Pen won't ever let me close to her now." Duncan laid his head against the back of the chair and closed his eyes, calling himself all sorts of names.

CHAPTER 13

Duncan let himself into Penelope's room. The moon was bright tonight, and she had the drapes pulled back, so he could see her fairly well. She sat in a chair with her feet pulled up and a blanket tucked around her. She had lost weight from her illness. Weight that, in his opinion, she did not need to lose.

"Is there something you needed?" she asked when he remained standing there, silent.

"You're awake," he said, stating the obvious like a nervous fool.

"Yes. I think I've gotten too much rest."

"Yes, I could see where that could happen. When I get back, I think perhaps you should learn how to swim."

"When you get back? Where are you going?"

"I have some business to attend in York. I'll only be gone three or four days."

"I see."

"Would you like to learn how to swim?"

"I don't know," she shivered as she remembered the water tossing her to and fro.

"If you know what to expect of the water, it can be quite fun to splash about in and swim. But you have to respect it."

"Perhaps."

"Think about it."

"I will," she promised.

"Penelope—"

"Duncan—"

They both tried to speak at the same time.

"Normally, I would say lady's first, but I need to get this out. Rosalie spoke to me."

Penelope dropped her face in her hands. "Please don't say another word," she muttered, her words muffled.

"I owe you an apology. I didn't realize how…well, how…"

"Stupid I was? How little I know of my own body? Instead of apologizing, you should either be laughing at just how bird-brained your wife is or crying because you are now forever attached to someone like me. I can't believe I have been so stupid."

"Pen—"

"No. Never again will I be so innocent in the ways of the world. And you have nothing to apologize for. Any man in your place would have thought the same thing. If anyone should be apologizing, it should be my mother to me, for not educating me and Whitney. And both of my parents should apologize for loving their son more than their daughters. And my grandfather for being a manipulative old man who forced us into a marriage."

"He didn't force me," Duncan admitted, but Penelope was too wound up to hear him.

"I'm sure you want nothing to do with me, especially with people calling me a whore and my actions verifying their words."

"You're not a whore, and I will hurt anyone who says it."

"How are you going to hurt an entire village, Duncan? And they're right. You paid for me like a man would pay for a mistress. Wives are supposed to lie still and accept their husband's advances. That's the only thing Mother ever told us. Only mistresses, whores, and courtesans enjoy what goes on in the bedroom. So, you see, they're right. I am your whore in every sense of the word. Now, please, I would like to go to sleep. I am quite tired."

"But I thought you said you had gotten too much rest."

"I'm tired," she repeated. "Safe travels."

"We will discuss this more when I return."

"I wish we wouldn't," she said.

"You don't always get what you wish for," he replied.

"I'm sorry," she said softly.

He went back through the connecting door and quietly closed it. He braced his hand against it, recalling how ethereal she looked with the moon shining on her. Then he thought back to how she had responded to his touch previously. Any man would give all he possessed to have a wife that was as responsive in bed as Penelope was. But now, thanks to the villagers and the rumors that had filtered among them, she believed the worst of herself. How was he going to get close enough to court her now? He looked thoughtfully at the barrier that kept him from his wife.

"Sometimes you get more than you wished for."

Reese returned to the house. Penelope sat in the parlor reading when he entered the Hall. "Reese, it's so good to see you," Penelope held out her arms as he bent down and hugged her.

"My brother apologized to me for being an ass."

"You must admit, he had reason to think it was true," Penelope said, blushing.

"Isabelle was different. I was in love with her. There will never be another woman for me."

"I doubt that very much. I think you will also find that one of the things that attracted you to Isabelle was the fact that you couldn't have her," Penelope said sagely.

"I don't want to discuss this now."

"You can't continue to run from the past."

"You had us quite worried, you know," he said, changing the subject. "Even my hard-headed brother. Rosalie said he didn't leave your side through the worst of the fever."

"I doubt that," she countered. "Ah, here comes the tea tray." This time she was the one to change the subject. A flash of memory infiltrated itself into her mind. The feel of a large, hot body, pulling her shivering form close and warming her when she thought she would never be warm again.

"Reese!" Lucy ran into his arms when she saw him standing in the parlor.

"You look as beautiful as ever, little one," he said dropping a kiss on the top of her head and hugging her tightly.

"I guess this means that Duncan visited with you," Rosalie surmised, trailing behind her daughter.

"Yes, I did, Grandmama," Duncan teased as he entered the room.

"You call me that again, and I'll have you drawn and quartered," the older woman said with a lack of menace.

The group sat down together. Lucy and Rosalie passed out the tea and Reese passed out the treats. Duncan hovered. They were chatting and visiting gaily, when Penelope started to feel unwell. She felt her heart pick up speed, and it felt exceptionally hot in the room. She put down her teacup with an abrupt thump, the cookie slipped off the edge of the table and fell to the floor. The people around her began to swirl in a sickening mass, making her dizzy. Her stomach churned, and it felt as if what she had drunk and eaten were soon to make a reappearance. She clasped her hand over her mouth, stood, and clumsily pushed past Lucy who sat next to her.

"Pen, what's wrong?"

She thought maybe Duncan was asking the question, but his words sounded disjointed. Someone grabbed her shoulders and led her down a hallway and through a door before she was embarrassingly sick.

When she came back to herself, she realized she was kneeling outside the servants entrance of the Hall. She had cast up her accounts and felt utterly drained. As she tried to stand, she found she was still dizzy and beads of perspiration popped up on her brow.

"Easy," Rosalie said at her elbow. "Duncan, help her up."

"Now, just lean against the house for a moment," Duncan said.

A maid appeared with a glass of water. "Bring a wet cloth," Rosalie instructed the maid before turning to Penelope. "Rinse and then take a sip."

Penelope did so gratefully. "I don't know what that was about. I thought I was getting better." She used the back of her hand to wipe at her brow.

"Lean your head back."

"Here you are, Mama. Is she all right?" Lucy joined them holding out a washcloth, and Reese stood in the doorway. Both looked concerned.

"She'll be just fine, I suspect, in a few months."

Penelope enjoyed the cool, damp cloth trailing over her face. How long had she gone without a mother's care? Almost her entire life. True, she had Mother, but she had been too wrapped up in society. To her, children had been a requirement to carry on the family name and title.

"Do you mean she's going to have a baby?" Lucy squealed excitedly.

"The signs are good," Rosalie said, smiling.

"Congratulations, Penelope!" Reese hugged her tightly. "Aren't you going to hug your wife?" he asked his brother.

She felt his arms go awkwardly around her, and then he kissed her forehead.

"I think I would like to go lay down for a while," she said.

"Of course. Duncan, take her upstairs."

"Yes, ma'am." He sounded meek.

"Thank you," she said gratefully when they entered her bedroom. She sat on the bed, and they looked at each other awkwardly.

"The best thing for you is to rest," he said before leaving her alone.

She waited until she heard Duncan's footsteps disappear down the hall and then she scurried across the room and locked first that door then the one that connected her room to his. She opened the dresser drawer and stared at the stack of clean linen she had had to send Mary for that morning because her courses had started. Her legs felt like jelly and she floated to the floor right where she had been standing. No, she definitely was not going to have a baby, but she wasn't ready to tell anyone else that. She had a horrible feeling that somebody wanted her to be the next deceased Duchess of Yorkshire, and she trusted no one.

Duncan postponed his trip to York for a few days.

"I want to make sure you're all right."

"Hundreds of women have babies every day. I will be fine."

"Those women aren't my wife, and those babies aren't mine."

"Go to York, I'll be fine." But she wasn't fine. When Mary brought her breakfast tray up, Penelope had been foolish enough to eat. Her stomach cramped ominously, and she had quickly cast up her accounts and dry heaved for several long, excruciating minutes afterward. Tremors wracked her body and she was covered in perspiration. Her stomach contracted painfully and her vision blurred. She was frightened to even drink the water in her pitcher and had ended up sneaking into Duncan's room. She took a swig of the whisky he kept in his bedchamber and used it to rinse her mouth. After that, whenever a tray of food was brought to her, she waited until she was alone, then walked to the window and dumped the food into the shrubs below her window. When she was forced to eat with the family, she pushed the food around on her plate to make it look as if she were eating.

"You need to eat more, dear," Rosalie said, the evening after Duncan had left for York. "You are growing incredibly thin, and that isn't good in your condition."

She had been thankful when he left, because that meant one less pair of eyes watched her every move. It was also one less person she had to worry about. "My stomach is just upset," she said. Yes, it was upset because she had not ingested anything in almost two days because she was fearful for her life. Just this morning, when she had looked out her bedroom window, she had seen one of the cats that roamed the grounds lying incredibly still. She had immediately rung for Mary who, in turn, had asked her beau to check on the creature. Her stomach plunged when Mary confirmed it was dead. Penelope knew without a doubt that the cat had eaten some of the food she had thrown out. It was no coincidence that he lay dead so close to those bushes hiding the tainted food.

She grew weaker every day since she had not fully recovered from that nasty case of the ague. Now she wondered if there was a reason she hadn't gotten over it completely. Had someone been trying to kill her all along? "I think I'll go upstairs and rest."

"That's a good idea, dear," Rosalie said.

Penelope went up the stairs and locked herself in her room. She lay down on her bed and tried to force herself to go to sleep, but had no luck. She went from staring at walls to staring at the ceiling. Then she began to count. "One. Two. Three…"

Her stomach growled loudly, startling her awake. She looked around the room as if it were a strange place she'd never seen before. That's because it wasn't her room, it was Duncan's. She was clutching his pillow as if it were her lifeline. She inhaled deeply and smelled him all around her. Then she remembered. She had reached one hundred and still had not fallen asleep. So, she had gone to Duncan's room and curled up in his bed since he was gone. Evidently, it had done the trick. But now her stomach cramped so badly from hunger, she feared she would be sick again. She quickly changed back into one of her serviceable dresses, tugged on her slippers and crept out of the room.

Penelope skulked down the servant's stairs to the kitchen. She lit a candle and dug for food. Surely whoever was slipping poison into her food would not risk the lives of the entire household. She found a chicken that had been cooked on the spit and began to tear off chunks of meat. She wanted to devour the food but made herself eat slowly so that everything she ate would not make a reappearance. She found some crusty bread and cheese as well. Penelope ate until she could eat no more, then she found a pitcher of water. She poured herself a glass and enjoyed the taste of the refreshing liquid. She was refilling the glass when she heard the servant's entrance door open.

She almost dropped the glass but quickly recovered. Heavy footsteps came towards the kitchen. It didn't sound like Duncan. Besides, he wasn't supposed to return home for several more days. A man entered the kitchen, but it was neither Duncan nor Reese. It was Duncan's secretary, Mr. Chester.

"Oh, Mr. Chester, it's good to see you again," she said awkwardly.

"And you, Miss…I mean, Your Grace," he bowed. "Is His Grace upstairs?"

"No. He had business in York. He should be home in a few days."

"Yes, well, good evening," the little man said, a worried, pinched look about him. She watched him walk to the study and leave some papers on Duncan's desk. He also scribbled a note before he left the house again. Both he and the gamekeeper had little cottages on the land where they lived.

Penelope was curious as to what was so important that Mr. Chester had wished to speak to Duncan tonight. It was well past midnight. She tiptoed to the study so as not to alert anyone that she was up and about. She very carefully closed the door and locked it behind her. Less careful, but still quiet, she lit a candle and sat in his chair behind the desk. She picked up the paper Mr. Chester had written on and read the man's note:

Your Grace,

No good news any way around. The marriage certificate was not accepted by the magistrate. If you will look, it was issued too long ago and had the sister's name on it. The mother has been sent to Bedlam. Because you are not legally married, I was not able to seek her release. Also…

The letter fluttered from her frozen fingers to the floor. She ripped open the first package which contained the original marriage certificate. Her eyes flew to Whitney's name printed beneath the line. *How could I have missed that? Because your life was spinning out of control!* The second package contained the new marriage certificate with the correct names. The third package contained information about an investigator by the name of Grantham.

She looked at the new certificate. She had the opportunity to be free. To start over. To get away from this condemned relationship. To live. Someone was trying to kill her, much like someone had killed Duncan's previous wives. She had to leave before Duncan returned, because he would force her to make their marriage permanent. She sprinted up to her room. She needed to be able to travel quickly, so she decided she would only take one bag with her. Penelope packed only the items that she deemed necessary for her existence, everything else she left behind.

Penelope was walking towards the door when she heard a knock. Time had passed quickly, for the sky was turning light gray and pink with the dawn. She dropped her bag and pushed it beneath the bed then quickly crawled beneath the covers.

"Come in," she called as she realized she was still wearing her bonnet. She hastily removed it and hid it beneath the covers.

"I'm sorry to bother you so early, Your Grace, but the dowager duchess and Miss Lucy need my help packing for their trip to London," Mary prattled away as she entered Penelope's room.

"Just put the tray on the table," Penelope said. "I'm not feeling well this morning. I think I will rest a while longer."

"Is there anything I can do for you, Your Grace?"

"I'm certain I'll be fine," she replied, feeling horrible for lying to the young maid, but this was her opportunity, and she had to take it.

"Yes, Your Grace. I'll pull the drapes, so you can rest better."

"Thank you."

Penelope closed her eyes, feigning sleep as Mary left and pulled the door closed behind her. She waited as long as she possibly could, threw back the covers, and bent low to grab her satchel. She pulled the bonnet on, slipped from her room, and down the servant's stairs just as she heard voices in the hallway. Her heart raced as she picked her way across the grounds and attempted to keep from being seen. She had very little money and her only plan was to somehow get her mother out of that horrible place.

"Samuel will help me," she thought, her spirit lifting slightly as she began to walk.

CHAPTER 14

Duncan arrived home early from York. Thoughts of Penelope kept him from concentrating on business. When he walked into the Hall, it was a madhouse.

"What's going on?" he asked Lucy as she dashed past him.

"Oh, Duncan, you're home. We leave for London tomorrow. Isn't it exciting? I'll be attending balls and musicales."

"Has anyone seen Mary?" Rosalie asked from the stairs. "Oh, hello, Duncan. We didn't expect you back so soon. I need Mary to help me finish packing, but can't find her anywhere. She was here just a few hours ago. If she's sneaking around with one of the footmen—"

"Have you checked in Penelope's room?" Lucy asked, interrupting her mother's rant.

"No. Mary said she was feeling unwell again this morning, so I haven't wanted to bother her."

"I'll check. I'd like to look in on my wife," Duncan said.

"Of course," Rosalie said, and floated off down the hall towards her room.

"I'm sure she'll be happy to see you," Lucy patted his arm as she passed him on the stairs and followed her mother.

"I sincerely doubt that," he muttered, climbing the stairs, and tightly gripping a bouquet of flowers he had picked on the way home. He was not a romantic man by any means, so this was going to be difficult for him, especially since she probably didn't want to see him. Halfway up the stairs, he changed his mind. He wasn't quite ready to face her yet. He turned around and retraced his steps down the stairs and ended up in his study. Papers were scattered across his desk. Ignoring them, he placed the flowers on top of them and then poured himself a drink. He was tired and dreaded the conversation he and Penelope needed to have. She was right, he had not treated her with the respect a wife should receive from her husband. Although he had enjoyed the bed sport and hoped she had as well, there had been some finer points he had been evading ever since he believed he had been swindled by her and her grandfather. He would send her away as soon as her mother arrived. It would be best for everyone. Then after she had the babe and healed, she could return and they would begin as if nothing had happened.

He quickly drank the amber liquid and poured himself a second then ambled to the desk. He heard the crunch of a piece of paper beneath his foot, bent over, and retrieved it. "No," he groaned as he read the contents. "Bloody hell!" he roared and sent his fist into the desk. The pain that radiated up his arm only made him angrier. There was no way he would be able to talk her into marrying him again after the way he treated her. He sat down in his chair and studied each paper—the false certificate, the new one, and the information on the investigator. Suddenly, he realized that all the papers were out of their envelopes and Mr. Chester's letter had been on the floor. Someone knew about this already, he realized. Dread washed over him.

He drank the rest of the whisky, stood, and exited the room. He found himself climbing the stairs a second time. Duncan reached her door and tapped lightly on it. It swung partially open. A frown marred his features. She always kept the door shut, whether or not she was in the room.

"Pen, are you there?" Silence. He pushed the door back a little more and saw that the bed was empty and unkempt. The drapes were still pulled closed, leaving the room in a gray dimness. Duncan was about to leave the room when he saw sturdy shoes and the hem of a serviceable dress peeking from around the end of the bed. He noticed a chair was on its side beneath the window. He raced to the side of the woman lying prone on the floor. As he rolled her over, he said a silent prayer that it not be Penelope. He was greeted by Mary's unseeing eyes. He bowed his head, feeling guilty at the relief coursing through him.

Duncan gently placed her back on the floor and closed her eyes. He opened the drapes, allowing in what little light there was from the setting sun. He studied the room. There were two trays of food. One was untouched on a small table and the other was on the dresser. The one on the dresser was fresher, some of the food still warm. It was missing a teacup. He found the empty teacup on the floor next to Mary's body. Some of the food on the tray had been picked at as well. The chamberpot was lying close to the maid and looked as if someone had cast up their accounts in it. Signs of vomit could also be seen around Mary's lips. He gingerly picked up the teacup and smelled the inside. There was another smell besides that of tea, cream, and sugar. Unfortunately, he couldn't put a name to it. He was placing the dainty cup back on the tray when he heard the sound of footsteps outside the open door of Penelope's bedroom.

There had to be some reason Mary had felt confident enough to eat food off of her mistress' plate. Duncan looked at the dead woman, trying to guess her secrets.

"What's going on?" Reese asked from the doorway.

"That's a very good question," Duncan replied. "Send for the gravediggers."

"Gravediggers?" Reese asked, taking a step forward. "Not Penelope—"

"No, not Penelope, thank God. Mary, her maid. But I fear Penelope was the target. I want to speak with Jameson as well."

"I'm not your bloody servant—"

"Bloody hell, Reese, grow up. This isn't about you. This is about Penelope and keeping her alive. Now, go find Jameson and send him up right away."

Reese looked as if he might argue, but instead disappeared. Duncan continued to prowl about the room. He found a bin of soiled linens that clearly stated there was no child as of yet. It seemed as if Rosalie was wrong in her assumption as to what had caused Penelope's illness before he had left for York. He felt relieved and silently chastised himself for it. *There is a woman lying dead because she ate and drank what was meant for your wi...Pen.* Duncan continued to move around the room, looking for clues.

"Your Grace, I was told you wanted to see me," the butler said at the door.

"A footman has been sent for the gravediggers," Reese announced.

"Good. Jameson, Mary is dead. It looks to be poison. What can you tell me about her?"

"Oh, dear. Mary has worked for us for several years. Never had a problem with her, Your Grace."

"She seemed to be competent in her position," Reese observed.

"Yes, my lord, she was."

"Do you know if she was seeing anyone?" Duncan asked.

"We do not encourage that sort of behavior, Your Grace," the butler said, sounding affronted.

"Of course you don't, but we know that sometimes human nature takes over."

"Yes, Your Grace. I believe I've seen her speaking to one of the stable hands, a young lad by the name of Will."

"Thank you." Duncan stepped out of the room leaving Reese and the butler behind. He left the house and headed toward the stables. There were several men in the paddock working with the horses. There were others polishing the carriage and readying it for the trip to London. Still others milled about the stable performing different jobs. He walked up to one of the men and said, "I need to speak to Will."

"Yes, Your Grace," the man said, dipping into a deep, respectful bow. "Will," he turned and yelled at a young man mending a piece of leather. "Lord Taggart wants a word with you."

Instead of leaving his work behind, Duncan went to him where they could talk privately.

"Your Grace," the man bowed respectfully.

"Will, were you friends with a maid in my house named Mary?"

"Yes. I know Mr. Jameson said no to that sort of thing, but I'm in love with her."

"I understand."

"You do?"

"Yes, which makes this all the more difficult. Will, I have something to tell you, and I'm afraid it isn't good news."

"About Mary?"

"Yes. She's dead, Will."

"What?"

"I found her earlier in my wife's bedchamber. It looks as if she had eaten some of the food off the trays, and perhaps that food was poisoned."

"Just like that bloody cat." The man took several staccato steps before he spun around and hurled accusations at Duncan, "It's the curse! I told her we needed to get away from here, but she said she liked the new duchess too much to do that. You killed my Mary!" The man shoved Duncan angrily. "No wonder Her Grace left you! Who could blame her? Not me! I should have bundled my Mary up and taken her away from here."

Duncan saw men approaching them to intervene, but held his hand out to stop their progress. "Left? Penelope left?"

"Yes," the man's words dripped with hatred.

"Did you see her leave?"

"Yes. I told Mary, but she didn't believe me. She ran to the house to check on her mistress and that was the last time I saw her. I thought she was just mad at me because I was right. I quit. I'll gather my things and be on my way."

"Will, I am sorry about Mary. I had nothing to do with her death."

"I don't believe you."

"What direction did Her Grace leave? I fear for her safety."

"She's better off far away from you, if you ask me," Will replied.

"He didn't ask you, and you *will* answer His Grace," one of the older stable hands said.

"He killed Mary!" Will spat the words.

"No, His Grace was gone from here until an hour ago."

"Then it was the curse, and he's just as much to blame," the inconsolable young man argued.

"The curse part might be true, but you best respect your master. Now, answer his question," the older man ordered.

Will reluctantly told Duncan where he last saw Penelope, and the direction she had went. "And when was this?"

"Just after dawn."

"Bloody hell." He looked outside and saw darkness start to descend on the Yorkshire countryside. She had started out on foot but could have easily convinced someone to give her a ride by this point. She could be anywhere.

"You mentioned something about a cat earlier. What was that about?"

"Her Grace saw a cat outside her window. Mary had me check on it. It was dead. There were some scraps of food that it had drug from the bushes beneath her window. That's when I tried to get Mary to leave."

"Did you tell her about the food?"

"No."

Duncan wanted to tell him that he should have, but refrained. "Thank you for the information, Will. I know this does nothing to console you, but it will help you move away from here should you so choose." He stood and handed Will some coins he had on him.

"I don't want your blood money." The man let the coins fall to the ground.

"Neither do I," Duncan replied. Feeling responsible for the young maid's death, he left the coins where they fell. When he reached the house, it was to see the gravediggers had arrived and were carrying Mary's sheet-covered body down the stairs. He heard wailing inside, and was tempted to walk until he was lost in the darkness of the moors. Instead, he took a deep, steadying breath and stepped inside. Lucy stood at the top of the stairs wailing like a banshee while her mother attempted to soothe her.

"Where's Penelope?" Reese asked.

"Seems to be headed towards London."

"What are you going to do?"

"Go after her."

"Perhaps we should postpone our trip," Lucy said between sobs.

"No. You and your mother will take the carriage and go to London as planned. We will all stay in the house in Mayfair. Perhaps I'll hire an investigator to search for my errant wife."

Reese followed Duncan into the study. "Did I hear you correctly? You *might* hire an investigator to search for your wife?"

"That's what I said. Now, I would really like to be left alone." Duncan was pouring himself a glass of whisky when he saw Reese reading the letter from Chester.

"So the two of you aren't married, Penelope is missing, and her maid is dead."

"Yes."

"All in the span of time when you were conveniently away and just as quickly decided to return," Reese accused.

"I didn't kill that maid, nor did I plot any of this!" Duncan growled. "I believe you were here the entire bloody time."

"Why would I want to kill Penelope?"

"Why did you kill Isabelle?"

"I didn't kill her! We were going to run away together that very night. We knew the child was mine and we were going to go abroad and disappear. Start our lives over."

"And what of me?"

"We were going to pay the ship's captain to report that she had been swept overboard during a storm and I drowned trying to save her. It was going to be tragic, but you could have remarried because we were dead."

"Only you weren't. You were so irresponsible, and you pulled Isabelle down with you. I want you to leave."

"I am. I'm accompanying the ladies to London."

"You're not staying in the Mayfair house with us. Damn you, I want my marriage to last."

"According to this, your marriage is already over." Reese waved the letter at Duncan like a flag blowing on the breeze.

"I like Penelope," he continued, ignoring Reese's taunting. "I want to have children with her. I don't want you to interfere with our relationship. Do you understand that?"

"I do. But I'm still going to be around to make certain she's safe."

"I'm not trying to kill her," Duncan growled in frustration.

"Someone is. Where do you think she's gone? To her grandfather?"

"No, not that bastard. To her brother."

"Who do you think this investigator is that looks like Grayson? Grantham, isn't it?"

"I don't know. Perhaps I'll visit Aunt Aggie while I'm there. I'm traveling by horseback. I want to get there as quickly as possible," Duncan said. "Hopefully I'll overtake her on the way to London." He gathered up all of the papers and stuffed them into a leather portfolio.

"Well, we'll see you in London then, won't we?" Reese followed Duncan into the hallway.

"Do what you must." Duncan turned and pulled his great coat on, the back fanned out about him like the wings of some large, phantom beast. He strode out of the study and house with purposeful strides.

"Brother, don't do anything you'll regret," Reese called to him, still nursing his whisky.

"I'll regret nothing, but I will have my wife back."

"And what if she doesn't want to be your wife? Have you not realized that she is once again on the market? She could have anyone, and you've broken her in nicely," Reese said caustically.

"You bloody bastard," Duncan turned on his heel until he stood in front of his younger brother. He dropped the portfolio, pulled back his arm, and let it fly. His fist drilled into Reese's stomach followed by an upper-cut to the chin. Duncan looked down at his brother's prone figure. Reese stared back at him with a dazed look on his face. "You will keep your bloody hands off Penelope. Do you understand?" Duncan tired of waiting for Reese to acquiesce, grabbed a fistful of his collar, and lifted his smirking brother to a reclining position before he let loose a right cross.

"Duncan! What have you done?" Lucy yelled and dropped to Reese's side. She gently lifted the man's head and placed it in her lap.

A footman had his horse waiting for him. He grabbed the portfolio and approached Cyclops on the left side. He shoved the leather folder into a saddlebag then swung up into the saddle. The stallion shied sideways as it felt the tension of the man on his back. He ignored the young woman, dug his heels into the horse's flanks, and rode as if the devil himself were after him.

By the time she reached London, Penelope was hungry, sore, and filthy. She longed for a hot bath and a soft bed. It had taken many days for her to make the journey. She had ridden in the back of wagons with livestock, and she had walked. She had paid the people for their generosity with part of her pin money. She had also used part of the money to purchase food. One meal a day was all she allowed herself. She needed as much money as possible to get her mother out of Bedlam.

She was so tired by the time she reached London that she walked to the house she had grown up in by mistake. She twisted the knob to enter the house only to be greeted by a beautiful young woman dressed in the finest clothes and ready for an outing.

"Yes?" the girl asked, looking down her nose at Penelope.

Only then did Penelope realize her mistake. "I'm sorry. I must be disoriented."

"I should think you are," the young woman said. "Now, be off. We do not allow your type around here, and we're in no need of extra servants."

Penelope took a moment to survey herself, then spun on her heel and quickly left, fighting back the tears that longed to fall. "What do I do now?" she wondered aloud. She had been completely honest with the young woman. She had walked to her old house purely out of habit and memories. She had yet to formulate a plan on how to get her mother out of the prison Grandfather had placed her in. Samuel was her only chance. Hopefully, he had yet to return to university and together they could figure out how to free their mother.

Armed with a plan, she made her way through the streets of London, ignoring the looks that followed her, especially as she moved towards the finer houses of the city. Penelope wound her way through the city streets until she stood in the finest neighborhood in Mayfair. The house in front of her had been her home for a little over a year. The worst time of her life. She took a deep breath and steeled herself for the altercation to come. She knocked on the door and waited for it to open.

"Ye…Miss Penelope, is that you?"

"Yes, Giles. I would like to speak to Samuel."

"Wait here," the man said, looking her over carefully. Even the servant looked at her in disgust. She brushed at her clothes and poked the stray strands of her hair beneath her crushed bonnet. "His Lordship will see you in his study. Please follow me."

Penelope rolled her eyes as she did. As if she didn't know where Grandfather's study was located.

"Miss Presley, my lord."

"Shut the door, Giles," the man ordered.

"Yes, my lord."

Was that a look of pity the butler had just bestowed upon her? Well, she didn't need it. She knew what she was getting herself into. She knew she was dancing with the devil. Penelope stood, waiting until she was spoken to, for that is just one of the many games the old man liked to play, and the more you twitched, the longer you waited. She found she was rather twitchy, because she had not even wanted to see this man in front of her. Something was amiss and she wasn't certain as to what it was.

"What is it you want, Penelope?" her grandfather inquired almost an hour later.

"I want to speak to Samuel."

"That's going to be difficult to accomplish."

The man appeared even angrier than usual. How had she not picked up on this earlier? "Why?" she asked tentatively.

"Your brother left. Said he did not appreciate the way I forced you into marriage with a murderer. I told him when I was in my grave, he could do as he saw fit, until that time, he would do as I say. He said he was leaving. I told him I would disown him if he stepped out the door. He walked out and has yet to return."

"Good for him," she said, but knew she had no one to help her free Mother now.

"You smell rank and look horrendous. Why are you here smelling up my house and looking like that?" he asked, pulling a handkerchief from his pocket and holding it to his nose.

"As if you didn't know."

"Know what?"

"That you are so far in debt that you failed to get a new marriage certificate. Therefore, my marriage is null and void."

"Sounds as if you have a bit of an issue on your hands, don't you?"

"Me? Because of you, I'm no better than a whore. I've slept with a man outside the bonds of marriage, because of you. My issue is *you*."

"You best remember who you're speaking to, girl."

"I'm speaking to the man who ruined my family. My father died trying to please you. My sister died trying to claw her way back into society. You've had my mother committed to Bedlam. I was forced into a farce of a marriage that turned out to be a fake. I was almost murdered. And now my brother, my only family, has disappeared to get away from you. You are a horrible old man and I despise you."

"You go too far."

"I didn't go far enough. Now, if you have any decency, you will get my mother out of Bedlam. It's the least you can do."

"I'm not doing anything to help you after the way you just spoke to me. Get out of my house, right now, before I call the Runners."

"You would do that?"

"It seems someone stole some silver right before you disappeared a few months ago."

"You're a liar. You sold it all."

"And who do you think the Runners will believe?"

"I hope you rot in hell." She stormed out of the room and slammed the door behind her. She walked through the house and opened the door to leave when it was pushed shut with a loud thud. The doorknob slipped through her fingers and she looked up to see Giles with his hand braced against the door.

"Come with me, Miss Penelope," he said.

"Why? Am I not good enough for the front door anymore?"

"No, miss. We, the few of us staff that remain, like and miss you and your brother. We abhor what the master's done to your mother, but we need our jobs. We've packed you some food to see you through at least a few days. One of the maids also has you a fresh change of clothes."

"Oh, Giles," she choked, her voice husky with tears.

"Shh, we must hurry before he catches us. Come," he encouraged her to follow him, which she gratefully did.

In the bowels of the large mansion, she was ushered into a small room. “Mrs. Giles,” she said, and moved to throw her arms about the older woman when the rotund lady halted her.

“Not that I’m not glad to see you, Miss Penelope, but you smell quite ripe. We don’t want your grandfather knowing that we’re helping you.”

“Of course.” She swiped at the tears that threatened to fall.

“Get out of those clothes and we’ll clean you up a bit before you change.”

“Thank you.”

“We thought we’d never see you again. We were afraid that…”

“I would die at the hands of my husband?” she prompted.

“Yes.”

“He’s not my husband,” she replied.

“You sound a bit sad about that.”

“We don’t have much time, do we?” Penelope asked in an attempt to get the woman to move onto a different topic.

“No, we don’t,” the housekeeper agreed. Soon Penelope smelled better and looked better. She stepped out of the room and into the kitchen. Two rough-hewn sacks sat on the table. “Take these with you, miss.”

“What are they?” Penelope asked after picking them both up and hearing rattling come from one of the sacks. They were tied together with a thin rope so she could easily carry them draped over her shoulders, if necessary.

“Something to tide you over,” Mrs. Giles said shrewdly Suddenly, there was a pounding on the door. “Giles, go answer that. We’ll slip her out the back.”

“Yes, Mother,” the butler said to his wife.

“But take your time,” Mrs. Giles called after him.

Penelope almost giggled as the man slowed his steps tremendously. If he wasn’t careful, Grandfather would storm out of his office, yelling until he turned red for someone to answer the door.

“Now, you go, Miss Presley. Slip out the back door. Go to the mews behind the house. Let one of the lads see you to an inn.” The older woman pressed several coins into Penelope’s hand and closed her fingers about them.

"I can't take this."

"Yes, you can. You've always been so kind to us. We'd like to do this for you."

"If I'm ever able, I'll come back and take you all with me. You don't deserve to have to live for Grandfather's every whim."

"We'll be fine. Now, go on with ye. Be safe." This time the housekeeper hugged Penelope fiercely before she slipped out the back door and into the evening light.

Duncan beat on the door until it calmly swung open to reveal an aged butler. The man looked to be ninety if he was a day, and he seemed to be unflappable.

"I want to see Blackstock."

"And may I tell my lord who is calling?" the man asked with a supercilious arched brow.

"The Duke of Yorkshire."

"Your Grace," the servant bowed low in deference to Duncan's title, "Lord Bolingbroke will be happy to see you."

"I want to see Penelope's brother."

"Lord Blackstock is away—"

"I thought I told you never to refer to that insolent boy as Lord Blackstock again," a voice drifted from a room to the right.

"I'll save you the trouble of showing me to Bolingbroke's study."

"Of course, Your Grace."

Was that a smirk on the butler's face? Duncan strode across the foyer and down a slight hall to where he had heard Bolingbroke's voice emanate from. He pushed the door back, not flinching when it slammed against the wooden bookcase behind it.

"Who gave you leave to come in here unannounced?"

"I did. I'm Duncan Taggart and I'm here for my wife."

"I know who you are, and I don't believe she's your wife. Another fine scandal you've drug my family name into."

"I did?" Duncan roared. "You, old man, are the one who has ruined everything. You are the one who has brought shame not only on your family, but also mine. Now, have you seen her?"

"She was here," the old man said, never once looking up from the papers spread out on his desk.

"Where. Is. She?" Duncan ground out.

"How am I to know where your whore went? Told her I didn't want her here. I'll not abide having a woman in my house who slept with a man outside the bonds of matrimony."

Duncan could no longer contain the anger that coursed through his veins. He swept the papers and everything else off the old man's desk, then the desk itself was flipped over with a loud crash. The old man tried to sputter, to call for help, but before he could Duncan had him out of his chair and pinned against the wall. "You listen here old man, and you listen well, because your very life depends upon it. Should anything happen to Penelope, I *will* come after you. Should one hair on her head become crinkled, you will pay the price. She has done nothing untoward and does not deserve your ill treatment. Now, where is she?"

"If I knew, I wouldn't tell the likes of you," the old man wheezed.

"I should kill you now. It would be so very easy to snap your neck with my bare hands. Instead, I'm going to let you continue to live your miserable existence, but will do everything within my power to ruin you. I *will* get Penelope back. I *will* rescue her mother. But most importantly, I *will* ruin you for all you have done to my wife. You will not receive another penny from me, and if I never see you again it will be too soon." Duncan pulled back his right arm and punched the wall beside Bolingbroke's head. He greatly enjoyed watching the man flinch and his eyes roll back in his head. When he let the old man go, he slid to the floor in a heap. Duncan turned around and walked out of the room to applause.

"Here, Your Grace," a maid handed him a towel for the bleeding knuckles he had been unaware of until that moment.

Duncan looked at the small grouping in front of him. Four people of varying ages stood there, clapping with smiles spread across their faces. "Shouldn't you be supporting your employer?"

"Pardon my bluntness, Your Grace," said the old man who had opened the door earlier, "but our employer is a cruel man. We only stayed because of Miss Penelope and Master Samuel. Now that they're gone we can leave, except he will not write us letters to take with us so that we can seek jobs elsewhere. We are as good as enslaved."

"How does he treat you?" Duncan knew it was a useless question, knew what the answer would be.

"Worse than his family, and that was horrid."

"Gather your things. See the house right across from here?" Duncan opened the door and pointed across the square. A warm breeze blew, ruffling his hair. "Tell them I sent you, and that they're to find positions for you."

"Your Grace…I…" the old man who had opened the door tried to speak, but couldn't. His eyes were rheumy with unshed tears. "Mother, I told you we would escape from here someday."

"You certainly did, Mr. Giles, you certainly did."

Duncan watched as the man and woman, he assumed to be husband and wife, kissed one another and danced a merry jig. Since he first viewed the man, it seemed as if Mr. Giles had shed twenty years from his life, perhaps more. Everyone was laughing or crying. "You should get your things before he awakens."

"His Grace is right. Ten minutes everyone. Less if you can manage it. If he hears the celebrating, and we're still here, he'll likely shoot us on sight. Now, hop to it," the woman he assumed to be Mrs. Giles clapped her hands and everyone quickly sprang into action. In less than ten minutes they had cleared out their belongings and left the house.

Duncan paced outside the house while waiting on the servants. Mr. and Mrs. Giles were the first outside. The couple waited patiently, and he felt their eyes watching him with each pass he made. Finally, unable to take it anymore, he turned on them. "What is it? Have I grown a horn or a third eye?"

"I apologize Your Grace, you just seem to be overly worried," the rotund little woman said.

"Of course I'm worried. My wife has disappeared. She has nowhere to go. She has very little money and no food. London is full of danger."

"It's my understanding she isn't your wife," Mrs. Giles prodded.

"A mere oversight, no thanks to *him*," he said scathingly, pointing to the house with his head. "Dammit, everything was going fine. Well, not fine exactly, but I thought she liked me. I care for her. I want to make certain she's safe. I want to make this right. I want us to be truly married. I want to keep her safe."

"Have you tried to harm her?"

"No. Those rumors are lies. I would never harm another human unless it was under dire circumstances." He looked pointedly at the window to Bolingbroke's study once more.

"Tell him, Mother," Giles prompted his wife.

The older woman wrung her hands and looked extremely worried. "She was here. As you were knocking on the front door, she slipped out the back. We gave her food, a change of clothes, and…"

"And what?"

"We took some of Lord Bolingbroke's finer things that she could exchange for money and put them in her bag."

"Where did she go?"

"I honestly don't know, Your Grace." Mrs. Giles held her breath after answering all of his questions. One look at her and one could see she wondered if he would tell them they weren't needed after all, that they were to return to Lord Bolingbroke's manor and live out the rest of their lives under his horrible and hateful tutelage.

"She can't have gotten far. I must go. Tell Hastings I sent you over."

"You still want us?"

"You helped her and for that I thank you. You did what you could. I'll be back, hopefully with Penelope in tow."

"I hope so, too, Your Grace." The two older servants wrapped their arms about one another, hoping that he did indeed find Miss Penelope before something bad happened to her.

CHAPTER 15

Penelope stumbled along the darkening street. The bags she carried were heavy. One of them jangled, drawing unwanted attention to her. She attempted to keep her head down and move onward, but exhaustion weighed heavily upon her. All she wanted to do was lie down, sleep for a week, and forget about her problems.

"Hello," a decidedly masculine voice called out.

Penelope stiffened her shoulders and kept walking, ignoring the man.

"I said, 'Hello,'" he repeated himself.

Penelope continued on, praying that he would take the hint and leave her alone. He didn't.

"Come now, don't be like that. It's getting late. I thought I would offer you a ride," he said.

She pursed her lips and kept walking. Tears burned the backs of her eyes. *Why won't this man just leave me alone? Can't he see I want nothing to do with him?* In her exhausted state, she failed to notice the loose cobblestone in the sidewalk. Her toe caught on the uprooted edge and she flew forward, landing on her stomach and face. The sacks landed with a loud crash beside her, their tops coming open, and their contents of food and silverware spilled onto the walk. She pushed herself up so she could gather everything to her. She winced as a pain shot up from her wrist, and she saw a small pool of blood on the ground. Penelope swiped a hand under her nose and balked when she saw it come away covered with red.

At the same time, she quickly brought both hands up to try and staunch the flow, people seemed to appear from nowhere.

They came from the recesses of the alleyways and the darkened stoops, making their way to the spilled food and silverware. Penelope tried to fight them off, but there were just too many of them. They were scavengers and would go to any length to survive. She was too innocent still and had never seen this harsh reality of the world. She had nowhere to go, no food, no money, and nothing to trade for money, except herself.

A strong arm wrapped itself around her, and she tried to shy away, but the person refused to leave her side. If she could have smelled through her nose, she would have smelled an exotic perfume wafting about her instead of a manly scent. She looked over and was shocked to see a woman in a beautiful dress that hugged her curves. It looked to be dampened in a way that she knew was only worn by scandalous women. She had heard her mother speak poorly of women that dressed in such a manner, but at the moment she found she couldn't care less. The man seemed to have disappeared and left her alone.

"You poor dear, are you all right?"

"I don't know," Penelope replied honestly.

"Cecil, bring me my shawl," the woman called over her shoulder. Soon the two women were joined by a man dressed in livery. He held out a beautiful, silk shawl in a shade that favored garnets. The woman carefully folded it and gently removed Penelope's hands. "Here."

"No, I'll ruin it," Penelope argued.

"Shh, I have plenty more where this one came from, and can easily get more should I choose to. Now, hold that tight against your nose and tilt your head back. Cecil, help me get her standing."

Penelope swayed unsteadily once she regained her feet. The woman and her servant stood on either side of her, each gripping an arm. "Where can we take you?"

"Nowhere," Penelope said, her voice muffled through the cloth. "I have nowhere to go." She could no longer hold back her tears or the fear she felt. Sobs racked her slight body. The woman once again put an arm around her, and Penelope found she just wanted to curl up and let this stranger soothe her as her mother never had.

"Now, now, those tears are going to do nothing for your nose. That settles it, you're coming with me."

"No, I couldn't."

"You can and you will."

"You don't even know me. I could be a thief or a murderer."

"Shouldn't you worry the same about me?"

"What would it matter at this point?"

"You need to trust me," the older woman instructed.

"Why would you want to help me?" Penelope asked suspiciously.

"Let's just say I see a bit of myself in you," the woman said serenely. "Now, let's get you settled in the carriage, and we'll be on our way. Before too long, we'll have you clean and fed. How does that sound?"

Penelope couldn't help it, she started crying once more. Somehow she managed to get into the carriage with the assistance of the kind woman and Cecil. As they drove off, the forgotten bags and a bloody, embroidered handkerchief that had come loose were the only things that remained behind on the walk.

The clip-clopping of his horse's hooves against the brick road echoed loudly in Duncan's ears. She couldn't have gotten far, but she wasn't on any of the streets he had traveled down. Nor was she in any of the alleys. He had stopped at several shops and asked after her, but no one had seen her. Even an extra coin dropped here and there couldn't bring him the information he wanted.

He turned off a main road and onto a side one. In the distance he saw a carriage turn and disappear into the night, almost becoming one with the darkness. Duncan could hear the sound of scurrying creatures, both large and small, as they tried to escape from his prying eyes. His gaze swept from side to side as he searched for his errant wife. He had no doubt that she would be his, regardless of her grandfather's interference, or rather lack thereof. On his left, a slight figure crept out from the dark shadows and approached a heap of something on the walk. A sliver of light from the barely there moon glinted off of something in the person's hand.

Duncan pulled his horse to a halt and slid to the ground. He flipped the reins around an unlit street lamp and approached the person. He dropped to one knee and inspected the cloth lying on the ground. There were two cloth bags and a handkerchief, all of which had various amounts of what looked to be blood on them. Duncan picked up the handkerchief and saw on one corner the monogrammed initials done in what appeared to be a delicate, feminine hand. "P. P. A," he read the letters out loud in the order they appeared on the handkerchief and knew immediately whose initials they were.

The small form tried to scurry away when Duncan's hand fisted in their collar, holding them immobile. The person was so covered in grime, he couldn't tell if it was a man or woman, child or adult.

"Let me go!" The person struggled to free themselves.

"Did you see what happened here?"

"Let go!"

"I'll pay you. I just want the truth." The struggles slowed until they became non-existent.

"How much?"

"Enough that you won't have to worry about where your food is coming from for a year, if you're careful." He watched the person eye him carefully before making her decision. For the first time he noticed that the person was wearing a dress indicating that it must be a woman. If he didn't find Penelope, this could very well be her in a short time.

"I'll take the money now," the woman said snapping him out of his thoughts.

"Half now. Half after." Duncan waited until she nodded her agreement. He withdrew the money and pressed it into her palm. "Now, what happened here?"

"A woman fell and blood went everywhere. People came out and took everything that fell out of those bags she carried. A coach stopped. A woman got out and helped her. They disappeared right before you came up."

"Bloody hell." Duncan roughly pushed the rest of the money towards the woman, tucked Penelope's bloodied handkerchief into the pocket of his weskit, then quickly untied and mounted his horse. He dug his heels into the stallion's flanks and shot off down the road. He turned the corner and traveled almost ten minutes before pulling the horse to a stop. Duncan stood in the stirrups and looked in every direction. “Penelope!” he yelled, his voice reverberating off of the buildings around him. “Penelope!” It was useless. She had melted into the darkness with some stranger. In that moment, he wondered if he would ever see her again, or if all he would ever have to remember her by was a blood-stained handkerchief with her initials on it that smelled faintly of lavender. Dejected, he turned his horse and slowly made his way to the Mayfair mansion.

“Giles!” the old man yelled from his position on the floor. When no one answered his calls, he slowly pushed himself up, cursing all the way. Never in his life had he fainted before, and he would never admit to anyone that he had. He walked out of his study towards the foyer. An eerie hush greeted him. “Giles! Hortense!” Silence. The front door stood open. He walked to it and just as he was shutting it, he saw a male servant wearing his livery disappear in the house across the way.

The old man slammed the door. Anger coursed through his veins. He stormed through the house taking inventory of the meager items he had left. The silver that had been in the family for several generations was gone.

“They’ll pay,” he growled. “First, that little whore will rue the day she came crawling back to me, and that bastard of a beast will pay for stealing my servants out from under me.” He stomped back into the study and sat behind his upside down desk and began plotting.

CHAPTER 16

Penelope lay curled up on a bed that was made of soft goose down and smelled of roses. She now wore a clean night rail provided by the kind woman who had literally picked her up off the street. Her nose and face throbbed. A brute of a man the woman called Abram had set her broken nose. She had blacked out for several minutes when that had happened. When she came to, there had been a hot bath ready for her. After bathing she had made the mistake of looking in a mirror. Not only was her nose swollen from the cloth they had used to pack it, but both of her eyes were blackened. She looked a sight and probably would for quite a while.

The older woman's name was Helena, but she knew nothing else about her. Her house was tastefully decorated, but there was something that Penelope felt slightly uneasy about. She couldn't quite pinpoint what it was, and found herself too exhausted to try and figure it out. Penelope felt alone and heartily wished for Duncan's large frame to be next to her. What she wouldn't give to feel his arms wrap around her and pull her close to him, for him to push her hair aside and his lips to brush kisses along the nape of her neck.

"Stop it," she ordered herself. She had no means of finding her way back to Yorkshire. Would he even want her if she did find a way back to him?

"No, he doesn't want me. I'm no better than a harlot thanks to Grandfather," she whispered. "If only he would come after me," she voiced her most fervent wish aloud. "But why would he?"

"Henry, keep your voice down. I have a guest," Penelope heard Helena say as she walked past her room.

"And just who is this guest? It had better not be another man. You are mine and mine alone."

"I think I'll make you wonder just a bit longer exactly who lies beyond that door," Helena taunted. "There's no need for you to remain complacent and think I'll always be here for you. You expect me to be only yours, but what of you?"

"I didn't come here to fight. I could have stayed at home if I had wanted that."

"Then what did you come here for?" Penelope could hear the sauciness in the other woman's voice. There was a male growl followed by feminine giggles, and a door slammed shut farther down the hall.

Silent tears slipped onto the pillow. She found herself growing jealous of what the couple was sharing behind that closed door, even if it did appear to be rather illicit. She wrapped her arms tightly around herself as she attempted to go to sleep. Tomorrow was soon enough to come up with a plan for her future.

Penelope had been up for hours. When she tired of the lonely bed, she paced the length of the room. Now her stomach growled reminding her how long it had been since she had last eaten. Her clothes had been taken from her last night and had yet to be returned. A light robe lay across the foot of the bed. Even though she couldn't smell because her nose was packed with bandages, her stomach continued to rumble loudly. When her stomach growled a third time, she worried her bottom lip and pressed a hand against her cramping stomach.

Her decision made, she pulled on the robe over her night rail, left the room, and made her way downstairs. She sniffed the air as well as she could and followed the wonderful aromas into the depths of the house. Penelope ended up in the kitchen and was greeted warmly by the staff that was present. One of the women that had helped her bathe last night guided her to what she assumed to be the breakfast room. There was a small buffet that stood along one wall. A small table sat in front of the window where the morning sun attempted to infiltrate the clouds, with no luck. Fat raindrops splattered against the window before sliding slowly downward.

She stared out the window, her chin propped in her hand, as the servants carried in dish after dish. Once they had finished traipsing in and out, Penelope picked up her plate, stood, and crossed to the buffet. She quickly piled food on the plate, sat at the table, and devoured everything edible. She cared very little that she couldn't taste most of it, she only knew she had to stop the ache of her stomach from lack of food.

"Good morning, Penelope. How are you this morning?" Helena asked as she breezed into the room. She too wore a night rail and robe.

"Better," Penelope replied before taking another bite.

"I'm glad to hear it." The older woman filled her plate before taking her seat and joining Penelope. "Now, tell me all about yourself. Why were you all alone?"

"I found out my husband and I weren't really married."

"Pardon?"

Penelope launched into her story. Helena interrupted occasionally to ask a question. Penelope noticed that as she continued on with her story, Helena got extremely quiet. "And that is how you came to find me last night," she finished on a sigh and pushed around what little food remained on her plate.

"So you were married."

"No, I thought I was, but thanks to the machinations of my Grandfather, I am nothing more than a woman who has slept with a man outside of the sanctity of marriage," she said as bitterness dripped from her words. She realized what she had said, inhaled a sharp breath, and looked up at Helena. "I'm sorry, I didn't mean—"

"No, don't apologize, once upon a time, I had ideals as well, then men ripped them away from me."

"What happened?" Penelope asked.

"Let's just say that often times what is required of you overrules what you want."

"I understand that all too well," Penelope said. "What I need to do first and foremost is get my mother out of Bedlam. She isn't crazy, she's sad, and terrified. She's never had to live any other way, and she's lost so much."

"The easiest way is going to be to find yourself a powerful protector."

“Protector? But that means I will be somebody’s mistress,” she said, unsteadily.

“It can have its benefits,” Helena said before taking a sip of tea.

“Henry?” Penelope asked.

“For almost thirty years.”

“Does he have a wife and family?”

“A wife that he was forced to marry. His children only use him for his money and how he can advance them in society.”

“And you want nothing from him?”

“No. Everything that he gives me is a gift between two lovers.”

“I don’t know…”

“Do you want your mother out of Bedlam?”

“Yes.”

“Are you willing to go back to your husband after the attempts on your life?”

“No.”

“I don’t think you have any other choice,” Helena said wisely.

Penelope pushed the almost empty plate away as her stomach churned sickeningly at the idea of what she had to do, and what she was going to have to become. “When do the lessons begin?”

“Today. There is a courtesan ball in three weeks. It is a ball for men to take their mistresses to, as well as to look for new ones. It will be a perfect opportunity for you to be presented, and your nose and eyes should be healed by then.”

“All right,” she said with resignation in her voice.

“This is wonderful! I’m going to have so much fun teaching you everything,” as an afterthought she added, “and dressing you.”

“It’s been a bloody week and I haven’t been able to locate her anywhere,” Duncan growled as he paced the study of his Mayfair mansion.

“I’ve told you what I think you should do,” Reese said. He looked as relaxed as a cat, reclining on the tufted leather chair, his legs sprawled in front of him. It was quite the opposite of Duncan who looked as if he was ready to suffer apoplexy at any moment.

"Your curiosity only lies with who this detective is. You care not one bit where my wife is."

"Need I remind you, she isn't your wife." Reese held his hands up in supplication at the look he received from Duncan. "You may live in your delusional world, but I think if you are going to find her, you need more than the two of us searching for her. Besides, if we hire this Grantham fellow, we can also see if he really does look like Grayson."

"Fine," Duncan growled, mainly because he had no other suggestions. Twenty minutes later, the two men were tying their mounts in front of an office building. A shingle squeaked above them as it blew in the breeze. It read *D. Grantham, Investigator*. There was a young boy loitering about. The two brothers secured him to watch over their horses then entered the office. It was clean and tidy, consisting only of a desk with a chair behind it and four chairs occupying the area in front of it. A man sat behind the desk and when he looked up, Duncan had to steel his features. Despite the fact that this man wore a patch over one eye, he could be their cousin Grayson's twin.

"Can I help you gentlemen?" the man asked as he stood. He held out a hand to shake theirs.

"I need assistance finding my wife," Duncan replied as he firmly gripped the other man's hand. He noted that the other man was not weak by any means, a good sign in his opinion.

"I see. And she is missing because?" the investigator prompted.

"It is rather a long and sordid story that I do not wish to get into. Now, will you help me?"

Grantham leaned back in his chair and steepled his fingers in front of him. Finally, he spoke. "Mr…"

"Duncan Taggart, Duke of Yorkshire," he said, emphasizing his title. Now, why had he done that? Never before had he thrown his title about expecting some sort of special treatment. Why now?

"Your Grace," the investigator bowed his head but remained sitting. He continued speaking, "I will not help a husband find his errant wife just so that he can return to mistreating her. Likely, in my opinion, if she ran, she had good cause, and you have just enforced that by not wishing to explain the situation. So, I'll bid you good day. I'm sorry I cannot help you."

"I haven't mistreated my wife."

"You're the *Beast of Yorkshire*. You have two deceased wives and a deceased fiancée. That you have not been brought up before the hangman only goes to prove how far money will reach. Now, I'll kindly thank you to leave my office, Your Grace."

"No, you listen here. I will agree something sinister is going on in my house, but I have had nothing to do with it. My last wife, Penelope, found out moments before I did that our marriage was a fake." He held up a hand to stop the investigator from talking. "An error on her grandfather's part that was unfortunately overlooked by both of us on our wedding day. Her grandfather will not have her in his house, and she has but a few meager items to see her through. I have been looking for her the entire time I traveled from Yorkshire to London and for the week I have been in residence here. All I have found is one of her handkerchiefs covered in blood. I fear for her life, and I need help finding her. I've been told you are the best in London. I'm willing to compensate you greatly if you can help me."

"How do you know the handkerchief belongs to her?"

"It has her initials embroidered on it."

Duncan eyed the other man as he sat there contemplating all he had just told him. He could also feel his brother's eyes on him as well. He no longer cared. Let them stare. Let them see how worried he was about her.

"I'm intrigued. I'll take the case, Your Grace. I suggest you tell me everything so that I'll know where to begin my search."

Reluctantly, Duncan sat down and told the story. Reese interjected parts here and there as necessary.

"So you believe her life could actually be in danger?"

"Yes," Duncan answered matter-of-factly, without any hesitation.

"And you are not the person responsible?"

"No."

"And you, sir?" The investigator turned on Reese.

"Pardon?"

"In my estimation, you stand to gain quite a bit with your brother out of the way. That would mean you would inherit the title, monies, and land."

"Well, I suppose…"

"Come now, my lord, it is a much greater weight than merely supposing, isn't it? You would be the Duke of Yorkshire. Lesser men than you have killed for such a title."

"Not me," Reese argued.

Grantham ran down a list of questions. He scribbled out beside them as Duncan answered. They discussed the deposit and then the fee once he found her. He seemed to be very confident that he would, indeed, find her. The men shook hands, and then Duncan and Reese left the office.

They were about to mount their steeds when Duncan paused. "He never formally bowed to me."

"Nor to me," Reese concurred. "Sometimes you need to realize there's more to life than titles and kowtowing to people. What I'm curious about is Grantham's story. He could very well be Grayson's brother they look that much alike," Reese said as he mounted his horse.

"I agree, it is strange," Duncan said. Soon they were both mounted and clip-clopping down the street.

"Where are we going?" Reese asked.

"To search for Penelope."

"Why? You've hired an investigator. Let him do his job."

"If you don't want to help me, that's fine. Go home and leave me be."

"I'll ask that group of men up ahead," Reese sighed, sounding resigned.

Duncan just wanted her found safe. He wanted to be able to wrap her in his arms. He patted the crisp, new marriage certificate in his pocket that he carried with him everyday, all day. She was his and no one else's, and if it hadn't been for her grandfather they would be back in Yorkshire. Every time he thought of the old man, rage shot through him. Then he would have visions of the maid he had found dead in her room. He could only be grateful that Penelope had left when she did, that she had been wise enough to suspect her food was poisoned. Otherwise, instead of looking for her, he could be mourning her.

Duncan pulled his thoughts away from the could have beens and focused on looking for Penelope. He had to find her before something horrible happened to her.

CHAPTER 17

Helena, I can't let you spend all your money on me," Penelope argued as they sat in a dressmaker's shop on Bond Street. Penelope's broken nose and blackened eyes were healing nicely, and Helena had tricked Penelope into an outing. Helena had told her that she, herself, needed new clothes, when, in fact, they were on a shopping trip for Penelope.

"Pish," the older woman said. "When was the last time you had a new dress?"

"Years," Penelope said softly. Even when she had gone to Yorkshire, she had continued wearing her old dresses.

"And you want to get your mother out of Bedlam, don't you?" the older woman asked quietly so as not to be overheard.

"Yes."

"Well, then, you need the type of clothes that will get you noticed by the men that will help you reach your goal. Now, I never had a daughter, so allow me this one concession."

Penelope thought to refuse, to call this entire plan off, then she remembered her mother. "If I allow you to do this and teach me all that I need to know in order to secure a b…ben…benefactor," she stumbled over the word, "I want to try to see my mother today."

"Of course. Right after we get you a wardrobe. Now, Margaurite, please take Penelope back and have her try on different dresses. She must have all sorts. She will also need two riding habits, and don't forget the ball gowns," Helena called after them as they disappeared behind a curtain.

By the end of the fitting, Penelope didn't think she could be poked or prodded anymore than she had been. After they left the modiste, they went next door to the cobbler's. Her foot was measured, and he was told that he could check with Margaurite for the various colors needed. Afterward they went to the haberdashery where she picked out several different hats and bonnets. They also chose the finest kid and satin gloves in several different colors. The hosiery and undergarments would be delivered with the clothes. Penelope also picked out a beautiful set of handkerchiefs. She had lost the last one her mother had presented to her on her sixteenth birthday the night she had landed in Helena's life. These would never replace that one, but her mother had always said that one could tell the class of a lady by her kerchief. She would decorate these to rival any that a debutante might carry.

Penelope flopped back in the coach, exhausted, after they left the last store. "I knew that it took a lot of money to attract a husband of the *ton*, but I never realized it required as much to attract a protector."

"More, my dear," Helena corrected her. "Most of the time you are attempting to lure a man from a wife or fiancée. He has to be willing to support you on top of a family. You must make sure he knows you're worth the effort."

"But we don't even know who my protector will be yet," she argued.

"It doesn't matter. Men want to be bowled over when they see their mistress. They want to know that you took extra time preparing to see them, making yourself beautiful."

"I see." Penelope looked out the window at the city she had grown up in. It seemed to have turned on her, becoming cold and ugly all at once. People she once considered friends wanted nothing to do with her. Her family had either been ripped from her or left her. Someone even tried to kill her in her husband's house. *Not your husband*, she reminded herself for what had to be the thousandth time since she left Yorkshire over a week ago.

What is he doing now? She idly wondered. *Does he even care that I left? Is he already looking for someone to take my place? Did he miss me at all?* She swiped at the lone tear that trickled down her cheek. *How am I going to allow another man to touch me the way he did?* Somehow she repressed the shiver that trailed down her spine.

"We're here," Helena announced. She reached under the bench and pulled a basket free.

"What's that?" Penelope asked curiously.

"Food for your mother."

"Oh, Helena," Penelope said, tears pricking her eyes.

"Now, stop that. Crying is not good for your nose at this point in time. Now, come with me and let's see if we can't get in to see her. If they won't believe us that you are her daughter, I have secured two tickets."

"Tickets?"

"Yes. You see for a small fee, you can walk through Bethlem Royal Hospital and survey the inmates much like visiting the Tower Menagerie," she said, referring to Bedlam by its official name.

"But that's horrible and cruel."

"Indeed. Now, come and let's see what we can do."

Penelope allowed Helena to take the lead. She realized that she was far more naïve than she had ever thought herself. They approached the inner gate on foot, and it was then that she noticed a line of people moving slowly inside. There were two young couples ahead of them. She recognized the girls from finishing school. The young men they were with passed over slips of paper, and then they were ushered in, giggling and talking all the while. Penelope felt sick to her stomach. These people had come to gawk and laugh at the people considered by society's standards to be insane, and her mother was one of those people.

Suddenly, anger propelled Penelope to take the lead. They approached the guardhouse and she stiffened her spine.

"Two tickets."

"I'm here to see my mother. She is a patient."

"Name."

"Lady Blackstock," Penelope said loud and proud, not caring that people around her whispered behind their hands. Many took a step or two back, as if they would catch a disease from her for just hearing the name.

"One ticket," he said on a sigh.

"This is my aunt." Penelope clutched Helena's arm.

"One ticket," he repeated.

"But—"

"It's fine," Helena patted Penelope's hand. "I have a ticket." The older woman passed the slip of paper to the man. He gave them brief directions to Lady Blackstock's room before turning to the people behind them. "Come, my dear."

Helena slipped an arm around Penelope and led her through the maze of hallways. They came to a room that housed several women. Penelope scanned the room and saw her mother sitting in front of a dirty window in a rocking chair.

"Mother!" Penelope rushed to her mother's side, but was greeted with a blank stare. "Mother, it's me, Penelope."

"My turn," her mother mumbled, clutching the arms of the rocking chair.

"Yes, Mother, it's your turn," she said, finger combing the lank strands of hair out of the older woman's face. Her hair had faded from a once vibrant blonde, to a duller shade with hints of gray sprinkled throughout. "Mother, this is my friend, Helena. We brought you food."

"Hello, Lady Blackstock," Helena said. "You've raised a fine daughter." Nothing. "I hope you enjoy this food." Helena handed the basket over to the older woman, then she gently took Penelope's shoulders and pulled her back.

"No," Penelope tried to break free, to remain close to her mother.

"You do *not* want to be in the midst of what is about to happen," Helena said, her voice laced with wisdom.

Penelope watched astounded, as Lady Blackstock tried to eat the food as quickly as possible while also fending off her roommates. The other women surrounded her and there were feral sounds emanated from them. The basket flew across the room and all the patients in the room, except for Lady Blackstock, chased after it. Penelope rushed to her mother's side once more. There were scratches and bite marks on the woman's hands and arms. Penelope ripped a portion of her petticoat and dabbed at the wounds. "Mother, I promise I *will* get you out of here, and Grandfather *will* pay for putting you in here."

"We should go," Helena said at Penelope's side.

"I will be back for you, Mother, I promise." She squeezed her mother's hands before standing. Helena led her out of the room and out the exit, missing the handsome man with the eyepatch by mere minutes. "That is a horrid place. Do people know how awful it is?"

"I think the true question is do people *care*?" Helena asked, bitterness in her voice.

"Helena, you seemed to know the workings of it rather well."

"Too well," Helena replied.

Penelope sat patiently while the older woman seemed lost in memories.

"I was a patient there myself many years ago."

"Oh, Helena," Penelope said. She crossed the carriage so that she sat beside her. She wrapped a comforting arm around the older woman.

"I was a young woman and had fallen in love. Unfortunately, he was forced into a marriage he did not want. We tried to not have anything to do with one another. I was even engaged to a duke, you see I am the daughter of a duke."

"But…"

"Yes, fate had other ideas for me. We fell in love and had a torrid affair. We kept it secret, but then I fell pregnant. The morning of his wedding, I was going to tell him, to convince him we should defy our families, run away, and get married."

"What happened?" Penelope prodded when Helena acted lost in thought.

"My father caught me sneaking out of the house and had me locked in my room with men stationed under my window so that I couldn't leave. I was soon sent off to have the child. I was in mourning for the loss of my lover to another and did not take care of myself. The birth did not go well. I almost died. I was in and out of consciousness and heard the child give one weak wail before they took him from me. I named him, but they told me he didn't survive. A few months later, I returned to London. I was depressed about the babe and the loss of my lover. I went wild. My father's answer was to have me committed to Bedlam."

"Your father did that to you?"

"I was scandalizing the family name and had to be brought to heel. It was all done very quietly. I didn't see any of my family when they took me away. In fact, I haven't seen them since before I was sent away to have the baby."

"You haven't seen your family for thirty years?" Penelope asked, unbelieving of what she had just heard.

"No, I haven't," Helena replied softly. "When Henry found out where I was, he rescued me. He was the only person to come see me. No one ever brought me food. I'm not proud to admit this, but I was one of those women that attacked your mother."

"Henry? You mean…"

"Yes, Henry and I have been together for over thirty years. He is all I have. My family disowned me. He bribed the director of the hospital and had me released into his care. I've had to share him with his family, and we never had anymore children. I couldn't choose who I fell in love with and I didn't want the men my father kept foisting off on me. My deepest regret is having lost my son. When I told Henry about little Henry Dominic, he cried. He had tried to find out where I was but no one from my family was allowed to speak to him. Perhaps if they had things would have turned out differently."

Penelope looked at the tough, older woman, surprised to see tears running down her cheeks. After all these years, she still mourned the child she had lost and the marriage that was forbidden to her. Penelope hugged the woman tightly, feeling her pain. She would always mourn what could have been with Duncan, what should have been if fate had not turned against them.

"What do you mean you keep missing her?" Duncan demanded, slamming his hands down on his desk and staring down the investigator.

"I mean exactly what I said," Grantham replied, showing no sign of being intimated by the large duke hovering over him. "I have other clients I am working for."

"You've already had a fortnight. In that time period, you keep *just missing her*? What will it take for you to make my case a priority? I want her found!"

"*All* of my clients are important to me and just because you have a grand title and money behind your name does not make you more important. I will continue to work at finding your wife.

Now, if you require nothing else of me, this discussion is keeping me from doing my job."

"You're bloody insolent," Duncan growled.

"It's what makes me good at my job. Now, if that's all, I'll be on my way. I have several meetings I must keep today."

"About Penelope?" Duncan demanded.

"One of them is."

"Excellent. I want to know what you find out."

"As always, I will keep you informed *when* I find information that is worth sharing. Good day, Your Grace." Grantham gave a slight bow before he left the room.

"Damn it," he went to swipe his desk clean when a calm, feminine voice greeted him from the doorway.

"You might rethink that," Lucy said as she entered the study and sat down. "It would make a terrible mess."

"I'm not in the mood for company."

"That's entirely too bad. I'm here, wether you want me or not."

He looked up and she gave him an impish smile. "What do you want, Lucy?" he asked on a sigh as he fell into his chair.

"There's a ball coming up that I want both you and Reese to escort me and mother to."

"I'm not going anywhere. Not until I've found Penelope."

"You've become no fun at all," she said with a pout before standing. "If she wouldn't stay, you're better off without her."

"No one asked your opinion, Lucy."

"Why are you being so mean to me? *She's* the one that left."

Duncan watched her flounce out of the room. He sat back in his chair and stared at the ceiling. His fingers were linked together across his taut stomach.

"What did you do to Lucy?" Reese interrupted his musings.

"Nothing."

"You must have done something. She just threw herself into my arms, crying that you were ruining her Season."

"She needs to grow up. Everyone has coddled her far too long. It's time she sees that the world around her is more than just titles and money."

"You need a woman," Reese said.

"I need Penelope. Bloody hell, where could she be?"

"There is a masquerade to be held at Vauxhall Gardens tomorrow night. You should come with me. I've heard there are going to be several women present in need of protectors."

"No."

"You can't continue to sulk about the house. You must realize that you may never see Penelope again. She could even be dead for all we know."

Suddenly, Duncan was out of his chair and around his desk in a matter of seconds. He quickly had Reese pinned against the wall. "Do you know something you're not telling me?"

"No."

"You had better not be responsible for the lives of any of the others."

"I'll not waste breath on this conversation again. Now, if you have nothing else to say, let me go."

Duncan did, then took a step back. "I'll not be going with you tomorrow."

"Suit yourself."

He watched Reese leave. Duncan was running off all of his family, and he really didn't care. Penelope had truly gotten under his skin. He had to find her and she had to be alive. He refused to believe anything else.

CHAPTER 18

It was a gorgeous night for an outdoor masquerade. Helena had her maid put Penelope's hair up in an intricate updo. She wore nothing but a thin, silk shift and fine hosiery beneath her dress. The maid helped her get into a beautiful aquamarine dress that looked like shimmering water when she moved. The bosom was cut so low, that her rouged nipples and areolae could almost be seen. She started to tug on the dress when feminine hands stayed her from behind.

"You look beautiful, my dear."

"I'm indecent."

"You are not showing them anything they do not already know exists. Besides, the true treasure is hidden from view," Helena answered with a throaty laugh. "Here, this will help." She brought out a beautiful mask designed with feathers and jewels. Helena quickly tied Penelope's mask in place. It sparkled in the light when she turned just the right way, and the feathers bounced and swayed. "And one more thing."

"What are you doing?" Penelope shrieked when Helena and the maid began wetting her dress. It caused the fabric to shrivel up in some areas and cling to her in others. It left very little to the imagination.

"Showing off your assets," Helena said. When she was satisfied with the look, she set down the bowl and sponge and asked, "Shall we go?"

"I suppose, though I don't see why I'm wearing clothes at all," Penelope muttered as she tugged on her gloves.

"Penelope, dear, you want to entice without giving everything away. The damp cloth eludes to the beauty that lies beneath the fabric. The rest requires them to use their imagination."

"And you guarantee I will be able to acquire a benefactor?"

"I promise you will have one before the week is over."

"Then I'm ready."

"Excellent."

"Why aren't you wearing a mask?"

"I'm much too old and tired to play these games. They are for the young. I will go as myself and enjoy watching the young bucks fight over you."

"But if I arrive with you and you aren't wearing a mask, won't they all assume that I am staying with you?"

"Of course, my dear. How else will they know where to send their proposals?" Helena smiled. "I promise you that you will survive this. Come now, your coach awaits."

Penelope's stomach flip-flopped as they traveled to Vauxhall Gardens. She had never been to Vauxhall before because of the semi-scandalous reputation it had. She remembered how the girls at Mrs. Lambert's Finishing School had talked about girls who had been ruined because of things that had gone on at Vauxhall Gardens. She couldn't help feeling both nervous and excited that she was going somewhere that society did not wholly approve of. Penelope plucked nervously at her gloves until she felt a calm hand settle over both of hers.

"Calm down. You look beautiful, and I will be watching over you."

"You've only ever been with Henry. Helena, how am I going to allow some man to touch me the way Duncan did?"

"It's not easy, and I have been with men other than Henry. Remember, I said I went a bit wild after coming back to London. I didn't believe Henry wanted me, so I turned to other men. It's not easy when you care strongly for someone else to give yourself to another. I can't give you any advice to make it easier. You just have to decide what is most important to you—keeping yourself pure or getting your mother out of Bedlam."

"You're right," Penelope said, straightening her spine. She looked out the window and watched as they approached the gardens. It was brightly lit with beautiful paper lanterns. Music greeted them as they were helped out of the carriage. As they made their way to the masquerade, the music grew louder. Voices wafted to them on the warm summer breeze. This was not a formal ball where people were introduced to the attendees since most of them wished to remain anonymous.

"Here is your dance card, Penelope."

Penelope took the pencil and held out her wrist so that Helena could tie the ribbon around it. She looked around the outdoor dance floor and could see that she was already garnering a good amount of attention.

"You can afford to be selective," Helena said in her ear. "Come, let's go to my box and watch the fun begin."

As soon as they were settled, a group of young men wearing dominos began pushing one another out of the way to be the first to get to their box. They acted like bulls, fighting over who would get to rut with her. Her stomach turned, disgusted at their behavior. "Are you certain this is fun?"

"Of course. Remember, first name only, or even a shortened version. Yes, I think you should be Penny tonight. Men do not want to be bored by your past or your problems. Promise each man only one dance, no more. They are only interested in their needs at this point and whether or not you can fulfill them. It is all right for them to steal an occasional kiss, but be coy. Turn your head at the very last minute. Leave them frustrated and wanting more. Understand?"

"Yes," she said, running her tongue along her lips, leaving them glistening in the lantern light.

"Good girl," Helena said, patting Penelope's leg. "Let the games begin."

Penelope's dance card had filled in a matter of seconds. Needing a moment of peace about halfway through the evening, she slipped behind some bushes, hoping to be undetected for just a few moments. She looked down at her dance card and saw that every line had been filled. John. Will. Sam. Tom. James. Alfred. The list went on and on. She had been dancing every dance almost since she arrived. Her feet ached and her head pounded from gritting her teeth in a forced smile. She had listened to the men brag about their prowess in everything from the hunting fields to the boudoir. Of the ones she had met thus far, she could not consider doing with any of them what she had done with Duncan. Evidently she had not hidden well enough, for her next partner showed up at her side, intruding on her thoughts and her momentary reprieve from the world.

"Pardon, but I believe this dance is mine."

That voice! Penelope's head snapped up and she quickly looked at the card on her wrist. Her next partner was supposed to be a man named Martin. Why did he sound suspiciously like Reese? She quickly stood and placed her hand in his as he escorted her to the dance floor. Of course this dance would have to be a waltz. There was no chance of them being apart for even a short while.

Martin lead her around the dance floor, and Penelope tried to get Helena's attention, but it was no use. The older woman was occupied with a handsome, older man wearing a black domino. The color off-set his silver hair quite nicely. From the way they cuddled and whispered, she imagined this was the elusive Henry. Penelope had lived in the woman's house for over two weeks and this was the first time she had seen the older gentleman. She could see why she was in love with him and willing to be his mistress, if nothing else.

"What can I call you?" *Martin* brought Penelope's attention back to him.

"Helena," she said huskily, in an attempt to disguise her voice. Panicked, she used her friend's name, still unable to let go of the thought that he sounded very much like Reese. She had been using a false name, couldn't he be doing the same?

"Ah, Helena. Such a beautiful name for a beautiful woman. Is this your first time at an event such as this?"

"Yes," she replied, staying as close to the truth as possible.

"And where are you from?"

"London."

"You're a lovely dancer."

"Thank you."

They went around the dance floor several more times before he spun her off onto one of the walks. "There, this is much better, don't you think? It was getting to be quite crowded on the dance floor."

He continued to dance with her, holding her much closer than he should. If it had been Duncan's arms around her, she would have welcomed them. Instead, she tried to push away, to put space between them.

"Now, now, is that any way to treat your future protector? There's no need to look any further, my dear Helena."

Penelope tried to twist her head away, but he was determined. "No, Reese, stop!" she pleaded, vocalizing her suspicion.

His head snapped up. "Penelope?"

She used the confusion to slip free of his arms and ran to Helena's box. "We have to leave," she whispered, looking over her shoulder.

"What happened?"

At that time, several things happened at once. Reese came pounding through the shrubbery and gripped Penelope's arm.

"Duncan has been looking everywhere for you. Do you realize how worried he's been?"

Another young man came up at that time, also wearing a domino. "Father, I figured you would be here with your whore. I thought I should tell you that Mother has sent me for you. The physician says she won't last through the night. I don't know why she would want you by her side as she leaves this world."

"Henry, I'm so sorry," Helena replied.

"Aunt Aggie, what are you doing here and where is Uncle Davis? Who is this man?"

"Helena, what is this young man talking about?"

In all the confusion, Penelope twisted free of Reese's loosened grip. She picked up her skirts and ran across the dance area and slipped down the path that would lead her to the carriages. She ripped off her mask in her haste to leave because it impeded her vision. The carriage was not hers to take, but she did have a few coins that Helena had given her. She hailed a hack and told the jarvey to drive as far as her coins would take her. When the conveyance came to a stop, she found herself in front of The Green Park. She paid the driver and watched the coach rumble down the road, leaving her alone. If she had had extra coin, she would have tipped the driver for depositing her in her favorite place in all of London. Many people preferred Hyde Park, but there was a quietness here that soothed one's soul.

The park was closed, but she had nowhere else to go. She found a way into the park and meandered down The Queen's Walk. Never before had she been here after dark. It was beautiful. The moonlight filtered through the trees, leaving everything dappled in silver. She walked until she came to the Queen's Basin. She sat along the bank and watched the swans glide effortlessly on the water. The moon acted as a spotlight on them. Penelope lay down on soft grass that trailed to the water's edge and watched the beautiful creatures until her eyes grew too heavy to keep them open any longer.

"Duncan! Duncan!" Reese yelled as he entered the Mayfair Mansion. "Duncan! Dammit, where are you?!"

"Here!" Duncan called from the doorway of the study. He was still dressed for the most part. He was only missing his weskit and coat. He held a glass of amber liquid in one hand, and his hair looked as if he had just run his fingers through it. "What are you trying to do? Wake the entire house?"

"I found her!"

"You what?"

"I found her!"

Duncan put the glass down unsteadily on the table in the foyer. "Where?"

"Vauxhall Gardens. She was at that ball I tried to get you to go to."

"You mean…"

"She was looking for a protector. I danced with her," he ducked and twisted as Duncan charged at him. "Now, hold on. She and I both wore masks. She used a false name, and I used my middle name. Something about her seemed familiar and when I figured it out, she was trying to get away. Then she ran to Aunt Aggie, who was with a man that wasn't Uncle Davis, but then it turned out it wasn't really Agatha either. And then this young buck came up and told the older man his wife was dying, and Penelope managed to get away—"

"Stop!" Duncan roared and placed a hand on each side of his pounding head. "Did you find Penelope or not?"

"Yes, but—"

"But what?"

"She disappeared again."

"How?"

"In the confusion she slipped away. I think she took a hack."

"From Vauxhall?"

"Yes."

"It's likely the driver will return there to pick up more passengers."

"Good thinking! I'll get your horse ready and go with you."

"You're going nowhere."

"Oh, yes, I am. I know how she's dressed, remember."

"Tell me."

"Absolutely not. It's time you realize you need me to help you and that we are *not* enemies. Now, do whatever you need to do to make yourself presentable. I'll have your horse ready by the time you are." With that, Reese turned and left the house.

Duncan looked down at himself. He was in shirtsleeves, pants, and boots. He decided that he didn't care about society, he had to find Penelope. He rushed out of the house, slammed the door behind him, and joined his brother. Soon the two were racing down the street. They were just leaving Mayfair when Duncan heard a familiar voice calling for him. Investigator Grantham came into view.

"What is it, man? I'm on my way to collect my wife."

"You found her then?"

"Yes, or I am about to."

"So you don't know exactly where she is?"

"Bloody hell, no, and you are costing me valuable time."

"I know exactly where she is, Your Grace."

"And where would that be?"

"The Green Park."

"Ha! She was at Vauxhall," Reese threw in confidently.

"Yes, she *was*, and I followed her when she left. She took a hack and ended up at The Green Park. Miss Presley slipped inside. I stopped the driver and asked if she specifically wanted to be let off there. He said, and I quote, 'No, the poor miss only had a bit of coin. Asked me to take her as far as I could. The park was a little beyond her coin, but seemed the safest place to leave a young girl like herself.'"

"I see," Duncan said.

"I tracked her down inside, as well. She went to the pond. There's a man watching the entrance to see if she leaves. He's also not to let anyone in either without me or without a passcode. I have a lead on another case that I need to see to, so the passcode you will need to give him is 'black swan'. He will expect some form of payment."

"Thank you, Grantham. I will of course follow up on this. If she *is* there, I will send you the rest of your fee in the morning."

"I look forward to receiving it, Your Grace," the man said confidently, nodding before he turned his horse away. He shifted in his saddle and looked at Duncan once more, "By the way, I tipped the hack driver wee for his concern over the welfare of Miss Presley." He turned, made a clicking sound, and horse and rider were disappearing into the night.

"I have a feeling we haven't seen the last of him," Reese said prophetically.

"At the moment, I don't care. I'm going to get Penelope."

"Do you think she's really there?"

"I have no reason to believe otherwise." When they reached the entrance of the park, Duncan ordered Reese to stay behind. If Penelope was in there, he didn't want their reunion to be observed by his brother, because he was unsure how it would go himself. Reese would wait with the horses until Duncan reappeared, with or without Penelope.

He dismounted, and a man approached from the shadows. "Park's closed, guv'nor."

"Black swan," Duncan said feeling foolish, but getting the desired result.

"The miss is still in there, guv'nor."

"Thank you," Duncan said and placed several notes in the man's hand.

"Thank ye, guv'nor!" The man tugged on his hat and walked off, a whistle on his lips, his step light, and his pocket full.

Duncan walked along the edge of the Queen's Walk, on the grass. He didn't want the gravel crunching under his boots to give away his presence. He followed the path to the reservoir. There was a lump lying on the bank. He put his hands on his hips and blew out a breath. After almost three weeks of searching and worrying, there she was. Duncan rounded the reservoir, squinting in the moonlight. It looked like she had fallen asleep. He crept silently around and lowered himself to the ground behind her. Just for a moment, he wanted to take her in his arms, to relish in the feel of her body against his. Then he would spank her until she couldn't sit down for a week for leaving him.

CHAPTER 19

Penelope smiled as she dreamed. She lay next to Duncan and burrowed further into his warm embrace. He ran his fingers through her hair. She could even smell the masculine scent that was uniquely him. She threw an arm about him and held him close. If she could only have him in her dreams, then she would fully embrace it.

"I've missed you," she murmured in her sleep.

"Then why did you leave me?"

"I had to. Someone wanted me dead. Besides, we aren't married." And that is where she had always woken up in the past. Her dream would end and Duncan would disappear, but this time he continued talking.

"I told you I'd protect you."

"But you didn't," she said sadly. "I think someone tried to poison me."

"You're right. Mary ate some of your food. I found her dead in your bedroom."

"You what?!" Penelope sat up quickly, pulling free of Duncan's embrace. She looked around and saw that the moon was still high in the sky and her husband, no, her…what should she call him? Duncan, she decided to just call him Duncan. Duncan lay on the ground next to her. The swans honked loudly as she startled them from their slumber. She placed a hand on him and pushed on his chest. She tried to pull her hand back, but he quickly caught it and entwined their fingers as he propped himself up on one elbow. "You're truly here."

"Yes, I am."

"I thought I was dreaming."

"You dream of me?"

"Yes," she answered somewhat mutinously. "Though I've no idea why after the way you treated me."

"You're right. I treated you horribly." They were both quiet for several minutes. "Do you know how worried I've been about you?" He rubbed the back of her hand with his thumb.

"I was fine," she muttered.

"You have a bump on your nose. How did you break it?"

"I fell," she answered evasively. "It's still tender, but healing nicely. Is Mary really dead?"

"Yes."

"Someone was poisoning my food," she repeated his earlier explanation. "I suspected it when I became so ill and couldn't regain my strength. I've never been sick like that before. I quit eating and even though I was hungry, I got better, stronger. I snuck into the kitchen at night when everyone slept and ate from the larger portions. I doubted that anyone wanted to poison the entire household. Poor Mary."

"We have to get out of here before someone comes along." Duncan stood and pulled her to a standing position. He reached out to tug the bodice up on her dress. "I don't want anyone else to see what belongs to me," he growled.

Penelope slapped his hands away. "They do not belong to you either," she said. "This dress is made to be worn as-is."

"Including dampened and showing off *all* of your assets to any man with a roving eye?"

"Yes. How else am I to find a protector?"

"Dammit, I'm your husband, you do *not* need a protector."

"First of all, you are *not* my husband. Second, I have to get my mother out of that horrid hospital, and the only way I can do that is to find a wealthy protector. Third, someone in your household wants me dead. And fourth…"

"Yes?"

"I suppose there's really only those three."

"Oh, how I've missed you," he growled. He pulled her into his arms and settled his mouth firmly over hers. Penelope couldn't help kissing him back. She had missed him, too, had missed his kisses and his touch. When his hands started to travel lower, she stopped him and took a step away, breaking contact with him. "Let's go home." He tried to grab her hand, but she slipped free of his grasp.

"I can't go with you," she said. She heard the huskiness in her voice and tried to steel herself.

"Of course you can. I have a new marriage license. We can be married on the way home."

"I'm not going to live with your family."

"Why not?"

"I value my life too much."

"Do you believe I was poisoning you?"

"No, but I believe someone in that house was. Even you cannot deny that. Either a family member is doing it themselves or they are paying a servant to do it. Either way, I refuse to put myself at risk again. Not until the person is caught."

"How do you suggest we do that?"

"I don't know, but if you want me as your wife, you'll come up with a solution."

"Where do you plan to go until then?"

"I suppose I'll return to Helena's," she said.

"Helena?"

"The woman I was staying with."

"If I purchase a separate house, far away from Mayfair, will you consider living there?"

"If it has a room for my mother as well, and perhaps a nurse for her."

"You're willing to live like my mistress, but not my wife?"

"I'm not a threat to whomever wanted to end my life by being your mistress."

"Bloody hell, Penelope."

"This is the way it has to be, Duncan," she said softly.

"I'll take you to this Helena."

"No. I would rather we not risk being seen together. I know that Reese is the one that told you about seeing me at the ball. I don't know how you found me from there, but it doesn't matter. We need people to not know where I am until we come up with a way to find the murderer."

"I hate this."

"So do I. Believe it or not, I have truly missed you."

"Yet, you could search for a protector."

"It wasn't my proudest moment, but I had to do it for my mother."

"The same woman who never really cared that much for you? Didn't you say that Whitney was the one that was her pride and joy? The one she hoped would make the perfect match that would save the family? And you aren't Samuel, the son that will carry on the family name. You are the forgotten child that is still making all the sacrifices. Tell me, Penelope, how is that working out for you?"

"It brought me to you," she said softly, "and for that I would do anything in my power to help Mother." She knew she was saying so much without saying the most important words of all, but she couldn't. This would be as close as he came to knowing how she felt about him…for now. They stood there in the quiet aftermath of her words and stared at one another as if trying to see into each other's soul.

"I'm going to give you money for a hack. I want the address for Helena's house." She recited it as he pressed a handful of notes and coins into her open palm. "You better bloody well be there when I collect you tomorrow. If you're not, I will hunt you down and you *will* regret running away from me again. Do you understand?"

"Yes."

He cupped her faced and kissed her gently and thoroughly, leaving her breathless. "No other man will ever touch you. You are mine, paper or no. Understand?"

"No, I don't, and there is no need for you to feel beholden to take care of me. There isn't going to be a child," she muttered guiltily.

"I know."

"What?"

"I found the evidence of your courses in your room."

"Oh."

"Why did you let me believe there was one?"

"I just didn't correct you that evening."

"Why not?"

"I was frightened for my life. I thought perhaps if everyone thought I was expecting they wouldn't hurt me. I was wrong. I should have remembered what happened to Isabelle."

Duncan pulled her into his arms and held her tightly once more. “This doesn’t change the fact that I do not want you in the arms of another man. Do you understand?”

“Yes.” She thought she heard something. *Perhaps it was the death knell on our relationship*, she thought idly. She soaked in as much of Duncan as she could, just in case he backed out of his promise now that he knew there wouldn’t be a child.

Duncan slipped out of the park and found Reese sitting on the walk, back braced against the high fence. He held the horse’s reins loosely in one hand. “Did you find her?”

“No.”

“What do you mean no? Did Grantham lie to you?”

“There was someone there, but it wasn’t her.”

“You’ve got to be kidding me. You mean he led us on a wild goose chase when we could have been searching for her elsewhere?”

“Swans,” Duncan interjected.

“What?”

“Never mind. I don’t want to talk about it.”

“Well, if it wasn’t Penelope, what took you so long?”

“I needed to think.”

“I *think* we should pay Grantham a visit. It would be a cold day in Hell when I—”

“I *said*, I bloody well don’t want to discuss it with anyone,” Duncan growled. “Now, I have matters to attend to.” He turned his horse towards Mayfair, leaving Reese to either follow or stay behind. Reese only waited a few seconds before following his older brother.

Penelope waited patiently until the two men disappeared into the darkness. She looked carefully through the metal fencing and shrubbery but saw no hacks. Depending on how one looked at it, it was extremely late in the night or early in the morning. She decided it would be best to wait until the park opened for the day then find a way to slip out. Penelope looked down at the expanse of exposed skin between her throat and the neckline of her dress. She lifted the hem of her dress and ripped off a large piece of the shift. She tucked it into the neckline of the dress, turning it into a make-shift fichu. Now she felt modest enough to be seen in the daylight.

She spent the rest of the time reflecting on all that Duncan had told her. Mary was dead. Mary had eaten food meant for her and had lost her life because of it. She started shivering and couldn't stop. Duncan had left Yorkshire searching for her. That should have warmed her, but she couldn't stop thinking about Mary and how that could have been her.

Voices reached her ears. They must have opened the gardens. *How long have I been sitting here?* She wondered silently. *And when did the dawn break?* She had been so lost in thought she had missed the sunrise. "You have to pull yourself together," she muttered. She slipped into some shrubbery and saw men, who looked to be gardeners, walk past her. Penelope waited until they left before she crept towards the gate. She waited until she thought she could sneak out without being seen. In a few minutes, she walked out without anyone ever knowing of her presence. After traversing several blocks she spotted a hack, hailed the driver, and gave him Helena's address before climbing inside. The hack rocked back and forth, and the ride was incredibly bumpy, but Penelope noticed none of that. Finally, it drew to a stop. She sat there so long that the driver had to beat on the top of the coach to get her attention. She slipped out, paid him, and gave him an extra coin for her inattentiveness. She walked up to the door, and it flew open before she could even knock.

"Oh, my dear, I've been so worried about you! What happened? Where did you go? Who was that man?" Helena threw her arms around Penelope, pulling her into a tight hug.

"Oh, Helena," Penelope sighed as she wrapped her arms about the older woman.

"Come. Tell me everything." Helena ushered her into the parlor where a maid was carrying in a tea tray. "Are you cold? You're shaking horribly."

"I'm not…not cold," Penelope managed to get the words out from between her chattering teeth.

"Bring a blanket." The older woman's words barely penetrated the fog that she found herself engulfed in. "And the brandy."

Soon, Penelope felt a comforting warmth around her shoulders. A cup was lifted to her lips and she was forced to take a sip. The liquid made her cough, and when she recovered the liquid was forced upon her once more. Once she had drunk all the contents of the teacup, she felt a warmth spread throughout her body to her extremities. The shaking slowly subsided, and she was able to set aside the blanket as well.

"The man I was dancing with at the end was Reese, Duncan's brother."

"Oh," Helena said softly.

"Are you all right? You look pale."

"I'm sorry dear, but I'm not feeling well all of a sudden. I think I'll go lay down for a bit. It was a long night, after all."

"Yes, it was," Penelope agreed. "I'm sorry for worrying you. I just didn't know what to do. I had to get away from there, from him." She and Helena stood and wrapped a comforting arm around each other before climbing the stairs. "I'll see you in a bit."

"Yes."

"And Helena." The other woman paused and looked at Penelope questioningly. "I'm sorry about Henry's wife."

"I never wanted any harm to come to her," Helena replied softly. "She was a good woman that was forced to marry a man she didn't love, like so many others. She has been a good mother and served Henry well as a hostess, even if they were not close. I feel for her children. I just wish they could see that I love their father, and he loves me."

"Give them time."

"They've had almost thirty years," she said sadly.

"Thirty years of seeing their father preferring to be with someone other than their mother. Even in the *ton* that must be difficult for children to understand. I think all children want their parents to be happy and in love. Then the bitterness and disillusionment sets in," Penelope said, sounding jaded.

"Are you speaking from experience?"

"Perhaps," Penelope answered.

"Rest, we'll visit more later," Helena said, patting her arm before disappearing into her bedroom.

Penelope entered her own room as she thought about the other woman. She had lived over thirty years as someone's mistress. It's true they had, and lost, a child together, and he had saved her from the horror of Bedlam, but she was the resented *other* woman by everyone else's standards. If Penelope found a protector that was single, eventually they would have to marry, and she would become the *other* woman. Some would even consider her to be that during the courting process.

Duncan had a perfectly good marriage license. One with her name on it, not her sister's.

"Am I mad to pass up marrying him? I care about him, perhaps even love him. I believe he cares about me, but someone wants me dead and out of the way." She walked to the window and stared outside. It suddenly hit her what struck her as odd about this area of London. Her mother insisted they never come over here because this was where the undesirables lived.

Mother pulled down the shades of the coach as they passed through a particular neighborhood.

"Mother, I was looking at—"

"Sit back," Mother ordered Whitney. "I will not risk seeing them together, nor having my children suffer that."

Penelope remember having wondered what her mother had been talking about, but now she had a very clear picture. "Can I live with being an *undesirable*? I'll forever be shunned by society. But how is that different from now? What if we are able to keep our marriage a secret? Look how well that worked for Romeo and Juliet," she said, only half joking. "I have to get a grip on myself, or I'll be in Bedlam right next to my mother."

Penelope slowly backed up until she felt the mattress against the back of her legs and sat down heavily. She fell backwards and stared at the ceiling. "What am I going to do?" The events of the night and morning caught up with her, along with the brandy-laced tea, and her eyelids grew heavy until she could no longer keep them open.

CHAPTER 20

Grantham, I have another job for you," Duncan announced, barging into the man's office.

"Sir, I'll be with you as soon as I've finished with this client," Grantham said pointedly.

"I'll wait outside."

"That would be best. There's a coffee house next door. I'll get you when I'm finished here."

Duncan raised a supercilious brow at the other man but did as instructed. He made it through one strong cup of tea when he saw the investigator enter the establishment. He stood, tossed some coins down on the table and waded his way through the tables to the door. "It's about time."

"Pardon me, *Your Grace*, but some of us have to work for our living."

"You should expand your office," Duncan said as he followed the investigator. "You know, hire a secretary, have a waiting area."

"Again, some of us are not born into money, *Your Grace*."

"Fine, Grantham. I have another job for you."

"You've yet to pay me for the one I completed."

"Is that all you think about is money?"

"Again, *Your—*"

"I know, born into money and all that nonsense. First of all, I want you to pretend I never asked you to find Penelope."

"Was she not where I told you she would be?"

"She was, but I suspect others are looking for her as well. I don't want her found by them if at all possible."

"Penelope who?" Grantham asked.

"Excellent. Secondly, I need you to purchase a house for me."

"Oh?"

"Yes." He laid out the physical specifications he wanted the house to have. "It needs to be in a shabby, but genteel area of London. An area where the neighbors do not necessarily care what is going on at the house next door."

"All right."

"And find out where I can be married quietly, or a person willing to perform a ceremony without a lot of fuss. I already have the special license. I merely want to expedite the proceedings, yet keep it buried in paperwork for as long as possible."

"All right."

"There's one more thing."

"Yes?"

"I need your help finding out who has been killing the women in my life and why."

"Now this is my type of case, Your Grace," Grantham said, rubbing his hands together in glee. "I believe it's time you told me everything, but before you do," he said halting Duncan's progress. He stood and walked around the desk. Grantham locked the front door and pulled the curtains over the windows. Only the glow of the lantern lit the room and he turned up the wick so that it shone brighter. "There are some tales that should not be interrupted or overheard."

And so Duncan settled back and told Grantham, practically a stranger to him, the same story he had told Penelope. He had only confided everything to these two people. Not even Reese knew everything. When he finished, he felt as if a weight had been lifted from his shoulders.

Grantham let out a long, low whistle. "May I ask you something, Your Grace?"

"I believe we are past the point of formality. Call me Duncan or Taggart. What was your question?"

"How have you escaped the hangman's noose this long?"

"What do you mean?"

"If I were a magistrate, one death might be an accident, but three? And one from the top of a cliff? I'd have had you swinging at the end of a rope."

Duncan stared at him, his mouth gaping open and closed like a fish.

"I know you didn't do it, Your…Taggart. I pride myself on being a good judge of character, and the accusation has shocked you to your very core. So now we have some questions to answer. Is someone obsessed with you and wanted the other women out of the way? Does someone want *you* out of the way? Who can be trusted in your household?"

"No one," he answered sadly. "Except Penelope."

"I agree. I don't think she would try to kill herself through poison. Not a pleasant way to die. I assume the shabby genteel house is for her?"

"And her mother."

"I have a suggestion, if I may."

"Yes?"

"Two separate houses." He lifted his hand and halted the duke's words. "I realize she wants to take care of her mother, but convince her that if her mother is in the same house she is, her life is in danger."

"You're right. What do you plan on doing?"

"Creating two false identities and purchasing them that way. In the end, the seller doesn't care who's buying them as long as they have money in their hands."

"Do what you must."

"You also need to stop showing up here unannounced, and I can't trust sending word to your house."

"What do you suggest?"

"Parliament."

"No. I have successfully avoided Parliament for the last two years, ever since Grandfather's death."

"People will expect you to take your seat in Parliament. You will always receive missives there. Besides, you're going to have to make it seem like you truly didn't find Penelope and that I'm still searching for her. You have to stay busy. What better way than to take your place in Parliament?"

"Do you always know so much about your clients and have an answer for every dilemma?"

"I'm not an investigator for the thrill of it," he said. "Well, maybe I am," he add with a grin, his one eye glinting mischievously. "You send correspondence here, if necessary."

"What if we need to meet?"

"Let's not get ahead of ourselves. Like a well-played chess game, Taggart, we take it one move at a time."

"If anything happens to Penelope…"

"I'm on the first ship to parts unknown where you'll never find me, and I can keep all my body parts and live to be a ripe old age."

"I'm glad we understand one another. Here's the money you'll need to make all the transactions. You'll also find what is owed to you for finding Penelope, and the reimbursement for the generous tip you gave the driver."

"Thank you. I'll also get her mother out of that hell hole."

"I appreciate that."

"I was told my mother died in there shortly after I was born. She was young and alone. No one deserves that fate."

"I agree."

The two men shook hands, before Grantham led him to the front. He pulled back the drape just enough to peek out. "No one appears to be watching. Be careful out there, and I'll take care of everything."

"I have no one else to trust at this point."

"Perhaps I should relocate Penelope to the new house," Grantham suggested.

"Absolutely not. That is one point that is non-negotiable. I will hire an unidentifiable hack, but *I* will be the one to see her transferred and settled in. You take care of the rest. A cleric is top priority after the housing situation. Understand?"

"Yes. We'll get to the bottom of this, Taggart." Grantham clapped him on the back before he slipped out the door.

Instead of leaving right away, Duncan returned to the coffee house and settled in with another cup of strong tea. He spent the next hour or so mulling over what his future was going to look like as a member of Parliament. For the second time in his life, he felt terrified. The first had been when he realized Penelope had left him, and her life was in danger. What would Parliament do when they found out the *Beast of Yorkshire* was going to take his place amongst them? He shook his head and tossed back the now cool tea. "Those Scandalous Taggarts strike again," he murmured in a low voice, chuckling softly.

The two women living in Helena's house alternated between morose and jumpy. Every time a knock sounded at the front door, they would crane their necks to see who waited on the other side. There were many notes of inquiry as to Penelope's availability as a potential mistress. She sighed as she added another one to the growing stack.

"What's wrong?" Helena asked, looking up from the book that she had not turned a page on since picking it up an hour ago.

"Men," Penelope muttered.

"I'm sorry, dear, but you're going to have to be more forthcoming than that."

"These." Penelope swiped up the stack of letters as she stood. She thumped them rhythmically against her hand as she paced across the room. Her agitation was clear in every step she took.

"What about them?" Helena asked, sounding both confused and tired.

Penelope turned around and stared at Helena as if she had grown two heads. "It doesn't unsettle you at all that there are at least a dozen men of the *ton*, both married and not, that have inquired as to whether I would be their mistress?"

"That's what you set out to do, isn't it? You needed someone wealthy and with enough standing in society to get your mother out of Bedlam. That's what you're holding in your hand—your future, and the answer to your prayers. So you must decide if you're going to follow through and choose someone or continue to sit around here and wait for someone to show up on the other side of that door who never will."

Penelope watched, dumbfounded, as Helena slammed her unread book down on the side table and stood from her chair. Just before the older woman walked out of the room, Penelope spoke, "Are you sure you aren't talking about yourself?"

"No," the older woman said softly before taking a step down the hall. A knock sounded on the door and Helena spun around to open it. "Yes?" she demanded before saying, "Oh, Henry."

Penelope peeked around the corner and saw the man from the ball holding Helena tight. He wasn't wearing a domino now, and she could see why Helena was in love with him. He was quite handsome. Neither was aware the door stood open and anyone driving by could see the couple. Tears pricked the backs of her eyes as she ached to feel Duncan's strong arms around her. But Duncan wasn't here. Duncan had failed to make an appearance for almost a week. He had promised he would get her the next day. She sighed and walked back into the parlor. She sat on the settee once more.

One by one she opened each envelope and read the letter inside. Three more arrived while she went through them. She placed them into different piles—yes, no, and maybe. She was going through the maybe stack again when another knock sounded on the door. Shadows had started to fall in the room, indicating that evening approached.

"If that's another proposal, I'm going to scream," she muttered.

"Miss Penelope, the Duke of Yorkshire would like to see you," the housekeeper announced.

"What proposal?" a deep voice came from the doorway.

"Duncan." She stood up, and the letters fluttered to the floor.

"What proposal?" he repeated.

"Where have you been?" she demanded.

"I've been taking care of things. What are those?"

"None of your business." Penelope squatted and quickly gathered the letters.

"Bastards." The word drifted down to Penelope. She looked up to see the big man shuffling through the letters on the settee. "I'll kill every one of them."

"You'll do no such thing. Now, give me those." Penelope stood and jerked them out of his hands. "What right do you have to threaten the men that wrote these letters?" she challenged and flicked the letters against his chest. "At least these men have made contact with me in the last *week*. You promised to come for me the next day, but you lied!" She shoved him when he tried to wrap his arms around her. "What *things* have you been taking care of? What was so much more important than coming here to see me? To make certain that I hadn't left again?"

"Nothing."

"You prom… What did you say?"

"Nothing is more important than me coming to see you."

"Somehow, I find that hard to believe, since you didn't do it. This man has offered me my own home."

"I can match that."

"And this one has told me I could have a thousand pounds a year."

"I can give you more money than that."

"And this one has promised me sensual pleasure beyond any I have ever known." Before she could walk away, Duncan swept her into his arms and his mouth took control of hers. It didn't take long for Penelope to respond, entwining her arms around his neck. She moaned softly when Duncan pulled away.

"I'm the *only* man that will give you pleasure, and you know just how pleasurable it can be," he said huskily.

Penelope tried to admonish him, but couldn't get the words out. She watched as Duncan ripped the letters out of her hands and tore them in half. "Stop that," she ordered uselessly. She looked down and saw one letter peeking out from under the settee. Penelope quickly scooped it up. "It appears Lord Jameson will be the one," she mused as she walked away from Duncan and the piled of shredded paper on the floor. "Hmm, he's young, heir to a dukedom—"

"I'm a bloody duke!"

"My own house, carriage, servants—"

"I can give you all that!"

"He says he's prompt and—"

"Bloody hell, I had things to attend to!"

"Quite a lover," she continued, ignoring his interruption.

"No other man is laying hands on my wife," he growled.

She turned on him, looking like a tigress, and snarled, "I'm. Not. Your. Wife."

"And I'm going to remedy that."

Duncan stalked her like a hunter closing in on its prey, and she held her hand up to ward him off. "You stay where you are. You aren't going to promise to come for me and then not show up and just expect me to fall gratefully at your feet when you do. And as long as a possible murderer is still out there somewhere, I am not, I repeat, *not* marrying you. Do you understand me, *Your Grace*?"

"I wish everyone would quit throwing my title at me as if it were the plague," Duncan muttered.

Penelope ignored him and stomped past him when she felt his big hand grip her upper arm. The next thing she knew, she felt a hard shoulder against her stomach, and was viewing the world upside down. "Let me go," she struggled against him. She pummeled his back with her fisted hands.

"Stop that," he growled, swatting her derrière.

"Let me down!" She wiggled and pushed, but his grip remained firm.

"What is going on down here?"

Penelope covered her flushed face in mortification as Helena's voice reached her ears.

"Put that young woman down this minute," a seasoned male voice added.

"Aunt Agatha?" Duncan queried, sounding very confused.

"No, it can't be."

"Helena!" the older man called out.

"What's going on?" Penelope asked, twisting around in time to see Helena being swooped up into a pair of manly arms. "Let me down." She squirmed until Duncan was forced to put her down. "Bring her in here," she ordered the silver-haired gentleman. "Place her on the settee." She rushed out of the room, found the housekeeper, quickly gave her instructions, then returned back to the two men and the inert woman.

"And just who the hell are you?" Duncan was demanding of the older man.

"Duncan, not now."

"Yes, now. I want to know who this man is with Agatha, and why it isn't my uncle."

"For one thing, she isn't Agatha and I don't know why you would think that. Her name is Helena," Penelope explained.

"No, it can't be."

CHAPTER 21

Duncan studied the woman lying on the settee, the woman that bore a remarkable resemblance to his Aunt Agatha. A woman who had the same name of his deceased aunt.

"Help him to a chair," he heard Penelope order someone. Then he felt a pair of hands guiding him backwards until he felt something at the back of his legs.

"Sit."

Duncan did so, his eyes never leaving the woman lying unconscious on the settee. "Are you positive her name is Helena?" His voice sounded funny even to his own ears.

"Duncan, what's the matter? You look as if you've seen a ghost," Penelope said.

"I think I have."

"What?"

"Last name. What's her last name?"

"Smith," Penelope said

At the same time, Henry said, "Taggart."

"What?!" Penelope demanded again.

"I've got to tell Agatha. She has to know. All these years." He raised shaking hands and scrubbed them up and down his face.

A moan interrupted the thoughts running rampant through his mind. Duncan watched Helena slowly regain consciousness.

"Easy," Penelope said gently when Helena acted as if she would flee.

"What happened," the older woman asked.

Duncan took turns studying all of them, wondering what had happened to her during the last thirty years. He watched her eyes grow wide, but this time she didn't faint, the two just stared at one another.

"You look like Jamie," Helena said.

"I'm Duncan, James' oldest son. You look exactly like Aunt Aggie," he almost made it sound like an accusation.

"And how is Jamie?" Helena asked. She couldn't hide the bitterness that seeped into her voice.

"Passed on. Almost ten years ago. Mother took a fever and declined quickly. He refused to leave her side and quickly caught her illness. We lost them within a few days of one another. Father lost the will to live when Mother passed away." Duncan watched as twin rivers of tears streaked down the older woman's cheeks. The gentleman hovering over her pressed a handkerchief into her hand.

"You know one another?" Penelope inserted the question in the quiet lull that followed Duncan's words.

"I believe she's my aunt."

"You believe? What's that supposed to mean? Do you not know for certain?" Penelope demanded.

"I was told she died."

"What? Why?"

"I had shamed my family and refused to be what they wanted me to be," Helena spoke up.

"And that was?" Penelope prompted.

"A dutiful daughter who did as she was told. Instead I followed my heart." She looked up at Henry and gave him a sad smile.

"So they told everyone you died? That's ridiculous and a bit extreme, isn't it?" Penelope asked.

"No. I was only one more in a long line of scandals that plagued our family. Father was determined to turn the family name into one that was respectable. When I didn't conform to his demands, he disowned me. I just didn't realize he had done it so permanently."

"That's not what I've been told," Duncan said, a frown marring his features.

"This is all my fault," Henry sighed.

"No, Henry, it is my father's fault for being more concerned with how the *ton* viewed him than he was about his family. And what of Agatha?"

"She's here in London. The *Season* is starting up, and she wouldn't be anywhere else."

"She always did love parties."

"Henry, if you don't mind my asking, how have you spent all these years among the *ton* and not run into Aunt Agatha? She and Uncle Davis are very involved in all activities, and he is in the House of Lords."

"Davis who?"

"Davis Patterson, the Earl of Holywell."

"Ah, well, we are in opposing parties. As for seeing them in a social setting, I tend to go to events that support my party. I also tend to not go to very many events, choosing instead to spend time with Helena. Besides, the *ton* is ten thousand members strong," he finished.

"Meaning?"

"Meaning—"

"No, that's enough questions," Helena interjected. "Society is a large, complicated puzzle and it sounds to me like you have even less experience with it than Henry and I do. Shall we just say that fate dealt me a cruel hand, and I have played it the best that I knew how."

"Aunt Aggie will want to see you."

"No, you musn't tell her. It would be too much for her. She has gone on with her life. Look how I live. I'm a mistress to a married man. I would be an embarrassment to her."

"You are not my mistress any longer." Henry grabbed her shoulders and forced her to stand.

"What do you mean? After all these years, are you throwing me over?"

"No. I am going to correct a wrong that never should have happened. I am going to marry you."

"Don't speak such nonsense. Your wife just died. You can't marry now, and you can't marry me ever. I will remain your mistress. Look at all that you can lose if we marry."

"I don't bloody care. Let Thomas take over the title. I have been kept from the true love of my life for too long. We've lost too much. We should have defied our families all those years ago and eloped. I refuse to treat our relationship like it's a curse any longer. We will retire to the country, if necessary, and live the remainder of our days together as we should have done from the beginning, as husband and wife."

"Your son will never speak to you again."

"He rarely speaks to me now."

"And what of your daughter?"

"She has her own family and is deeply ensconced in the *ton*. They will survive. Besides, another scandal will come along to replace this one."

"Oh, Henry, I *do* love you. I think I'll spend some time pretending it will work out as you say."

"It *will*," the older man insisted.

Duncan stood, uncomfortable with the physical display of love the two were showing. "I think I'll just step out for a moment." He left them behind. He walked outside, and in a very undukely fashion, lowered his big frame to the steps.

"Are you all right?" Penelope's voice greeted him. The scent of her cocooned him in something he wasn't quite willing to give a name to.

"I suppose."

"Did you suspect she was alive?"

"No. Did you not mention who you were married to?"

"I honestly can't remember, Duncan. I told her your first name and I might have mentioned your horrible nickname, but all of the rest was merely about the situation."

"I see."

"You don't believe me," Penelope accused.

"You'll forgive me if I find it difficult to believe that you never once, in your several weeks in her company, mentioned me." He felt Penelope brush past him as she moved down the stairs.

"Allow me to tell you something, Duncan Taggart," she said as she stood eye level with him. "I had more things going on in my life than being concerned about you. I was trying to stay alive for one, and for another I was trying to save my mother. Now, I think it would be best if you left since you're just going to be accusatory."

He grabbed her hand as she tried to move up the stairs and pulled her onto his lap.

"Let go of me," she squirmed and struggled against his hold.

"You're making a scene."

"No, *you're* making a scene. Anyone could see us like this."

"Would that be so bad?" Duncan asked.

"I don't know anymore," she said sullenly.

He could feel the rigidness in her body slowly vanquish. "Nothing has changed, Pen. You *will* be my wife."

"How can you say that? After all that's just happened? If your grandfather were still alive, he would never approve."

"My grandfather married a woman less than half his age a few years before his death. Trust me when I say he created his share of scandals for the Taggart family. He just wanted the rest of us to be perfect. I'm done living within society's constraints. I'm going to take my place in the House of Lords while we try to find the killer."

Penelope slipped free of his hold upon hearing this. He looked up to see her staring at him, her mouth agape. "In one breath you tell me you want to marry me, and the next you say you are taking your place in the House of Lords. You can't marry me. You will lose all credibility once they find out about our marriage mishap."

"Who will tell?"

"My grandfather. He would stoop to something like that, you know. He could turn all of the men against you."

"And you think I care about that?" Duncan asked, standing. He gripped her upper arms and lowered his head until his mouth firmly settled over hers. He took the opportunity of catching her off guard to remind himself of how she tasted, how she felt in his arms. After several catcalls and whistles from passing men, he pulled back. "Come with me, please." He rested his forehead against hers and waited on tenterhooks for her answer. Finally, she lifted her head and eased his anxiety.

"Come back tomorrow afternoon. I have to pack and I need to stay tonight and make certain Helena will be all right."

"But—"

"Tomorrow," Penelope interrupted him.

"I prefer you without all of that paint on your face," he said, causing her to pause.

"One must always be ready for her suitors," she replied before disappearing inside the house and firmly closing the door.

Duncan walked to his horse and paid the young boy who watched it. He mounted it and guided it back to the proper section of London, but not to his house. There was somewhere he had to go first. It didn't take long by horseback for him to reach his aunt's house. He almost chuckled at how close the two parts of London were physically, but socially they might as well be different worlds. He stopped in front of Agatha and Davis' townhouse. He had only been here a handful of times since he didn't care for London all that much. He would far rather be in the wilds of Yorkshire.

A man dressed in livery appeared quickly and took his horse from him after he dismounted. Duncan straightened his cravat and shifted his superfine so that he looked presentable. He raked his fingers through his hair, but doubted it did much good. He walked up the steps and his stomach churned nervously. How would Agatha react to the news? Helena didn't want her to know, didn't want to disrupt her life, but she had to know. She had mourned her sister ever since her supposed death.

He moved to grab the knocker, but the door was opened before he could reach it. The butler stood on the other side, looking as stoic as ever.

"Your Grace, it is always a pleasure. Lady Holywell is in the parlor."

"Thank you."

"Of course. If you will follow me."

Duncan did as he was told, afraid to do otherwise. The butler should be a general in the military. Bonaparte would turn and run if he saw him coming.

"His Grace, the Duke of Yorkshire," the man announced.

"Duncan!" A beautiful woman that looked exactly like the one he had just left across town practically flew across the room and into his arms.

"Aunt Aggie, how are you?" he asked, wrapping her in a warm embrace.

"Oh, I'm irritated at my son, as usual, but other than that, I'm marvelous." She pulled him down and bussed his cheek with her lips, then took the handkerchief from his pocket. She rubbed at his lips. "This color of lip rouge just does not look good on you, nephew."

Duncan could feel the flush spread through his body as she tucked it back into his breast pocket and patted his chest.

"Who is she? I thought you had married, but a duchess should not wear that much face paint in my humble opinion. In fact, I'm surprised to see you here. Shouldn't you be begetting the next Duke of Yorkshire?"

"Aunt Aggie!"

"What? Your mother told me to worry over you like you were my own child."

"And what about Reese?"

"Oh, I worry about him for completely different reasons. You're a brooder. Your mother and I commiserated together that you would never find your true love, that you would merely marry to carry on the family name. So, tell me about this new wife. What is she like? I do hope that is her lip rouge that was smeared on you. And why are you in London? You hate it here."

"Her name is Penelope and she is so different from the others," he said as she led him to sit on the settee. "I feel like I'm going to crush this furniture."

"Pish, it's sturdier than it looks. Does she come from a good family?"

"They were at one time. Now…"

"I see. The Scandalous Taggarts will live on. Well, I have learned over the years that society is fickle. Now, why did you come to see me?"

"Is Gray around?" He watched, entranced, as his aunt threw back her head and laughed.

"Oh, dear, Duncan. I could not tell you where my son is at this moment. He could be in Egypt, Italy, India, France, or the house next door for that matter. I'm lucky if I receive the occasional letter telling me where he's been and that he's still alive. I swear that boy will be the death of me. The next time he's within arm's reach, I'm going to do my best to tie him down to someone. Make him respectable."

"Is Bridget or Uncle Davis here?"

"No. Bridget is staying the night with a friend and Davis is at his office," she replied, looking at him strangely. "Duncan, what is it?"

"I truly wish Uncle Davis were here."

"Well, he's not, and I'm a grown woman. Now, tell me whatever news it is you have. Is it Gray? Has he been injured? Or is he—"

"No. No, Aunt Agatha, it's nothing like that."

"It must be serious. You never call me Agatha."

"It is. I thought I saw a ghost today."

"A ghost?"

"Actually, I thought I saw you in the arms of another man."

"What are you talking about Duncan? First you say you saw a ghost, then you say you saw me with some man besides your uncle? You know I love Davis with all my heart. How dare you accuse me of being unfaithful."

"It was a shock to me, too, believe me. The woman I saw is named Helena."

"Helena," she whispered. "No, it can't be. Father said… She… We had a funeral service… She and the babe… You must be wrong, Duncan."

"I saw her myself. She looks exactly like you." Panicked words that Reese spoke the other night when he found Penelope in the park drifted back to him. "I think Reese has seen her, as well."

"She's alive? My twin sister is alive?"

"Yes."

"I can't believe it. I have to go see her," Agatha stood up just as a door slammed shut.

"Agatha! Agatha! Where are you? Agatha Patterson, show yourself this instant."

"Oh, dear. I've never heard him sound like that. Davis, I'm in here."

"Agatha, I want to know… Oh, Duncan, hello."

"Davis, what's the matter?"

Duncan watched his uncle's eyes travel between him and his aunt. "I believe I'll leave the two of you alone. We can talk more about this development later, Aunt Agatha."

"Of course. Tomorrow?"

"I can't. Perhaps the next day."

"It's been thirty years. I suppose another few days won't make much of a difference. Take care, Duncan."

He had walked outside and just mounted his horse when he heard his aunt yelling, "Duncan James Taggart, get back in this house right this minute." Only when he, his brother, and cousins had been in the worst possible mischief did they receive the full name treatment. He walked inside to see his aunt and uncle standing on opposite sides of the room. Both had their arms crossed and were shooting daggers at one another with their eyes.

"What's wrong?" Duncan asked. Never had he seen them so at odds with one another. Both them and his parents had been love matches, which were highly unusual for members of the *ton*, let alone in the same family.

"Tell him. I want you to tell him what you just told me, because he's being an old fool."

"An old fool? When my solicitor tracks me down to tell me he's just seen my wife, in her bed clothes, kissing a man, that is not me, on the stoop of a house, what else am I to think?"

"You're supposed to think that I love you and would never be unfaithful to you, though goodness knows it isn't because I haven't had the opportunities."

"What does that mean?"

"You tell me," Agatha tossed back.

"I want names. I will call every one of them out for a duel."

"You will do no such thing. Now, tell him, Duncan."

"It wasn't Aunt Agatha."

"What? And how would you know?"

"I had been at that house earlier."

"You what? Do you know what type of neighborhood that is? The type of women that live there?"

"Yes, Uncle Davis. My wife is currently living there, with that woman."

"What?!" Both Agatha and Davis asked in unison, staring at him as if he were speaking in a different language.

"The woman the solicitor saw was Helena," Duncan announced.

"What? But that's impossible."

"It seems father lied to all of us," Agatha said.

"Helena's alive?"

"Yes," Duncan answered.

"And the babe?" Davis queried.

"Oh, I didn't even think of that," Agatha said, putting her hands together in a prayer-like fashion against her chin.

"I have no idea," Duncan said. "But does this mean all is well here?"

"Oh, it's far from *well*," Agatha said, giving her sheepish-looking husband a dark look.

Duncan saw that look and thought that he would hate to be Uncle Davis tonight. "Well, I suppose I should go."

"Not so fast, young man."

"I'm almost thirty-five years old."

"I don't care if you are ninety-five. Sit." Agatha pointed to the settee.

"I'd do as she says, son," Uncle Davis added.

"When I need help from you, I'll ask for it," she told her husband. "I want to know exactly what is going on with you."

Uncle Davis was definitely in for a long night. Duncan sighed heavily and lowered himself to a chair instead of the settee hoping his aunt would sit there and his uncle next to her. No such luck. She took the chair across from him, but to Davis' credit, he perched on the arm of the chair refusing to let her get away from him. "I'm not certain where to begin," Duncan said, tunneling his fingers through his hair, his elbows propped on his knees.

"I'd suggest the beginning," Aunt Agatha said.

"You're right." And so he told them everything. By the time he finished, Agatha stood and lit the lamps in the room. He watched as she moved from one to the next without saying anything. Finally, she made her way back to the chair that her husband now occupied. This time she perched on the arm and braced herself against his broad shoulders. You wouldn't have known that they were barely speaking to one another earlier. "Well?" Duncan asked, unable to stand the silence a moment longer.

"I think you definitely have a problem, but Reese is not the culprit."

"How do you know?"

"Reese loved Isabelle. He would have moved heaven and earth to keep her from harm."

"I think I know that."

"It's unfortunate that he didn't come back sooner, before the two of you married. Otherwise, it might have saved a lot of heartache and a life."

"Yes," Duncan could finally allow himself to agree to that.

"So, Penelope somehow fell into Helena's hospitality?"

"It would seem so."

"There is one thing you didn't say about Penelope. Do you love her?"

"I don't know her well enough, Aggie. I know that I care for her."

"I don't suppose I can blame you for being reticent in making a commitment. I'll expect you to pick me up on the way to Helena's tomorrow."

"Aunt Aggie, I told you earlier, not tomorrow."

"And now that I know the reason I am even more determined. I want to meet your Penelope before you marry her. I will stand up as your witness. I also want to see my sister."

"But—"

"Don't argue with her son. It will get you nowhere."

"Yes, sir. I'll be here at noon."

"We'll be ready," Davis spoke up.

"Dear, you don't have to go."

"Darling, do you think I'm going to risk that other man seeing you and possibly sweeping you off your feet? No. I will be going as well. We'll have our carriage ready and follow you there. Besides there must be at least two witnesses."

"You might want to take your seal off of the doors. I mean, considering where we are going."

"Of course. Perhaps it would be best," Davis agreed.

"I should be going," Duncan stood and found his arms full of his fiery aunt.

"I love you so much. I just want you to be as happy as your parents were and your uncle and I are."

"I know," he replied, giving her a gentle squeeze.

"I'll walk you out, son." The two men left the house and walked towards where his horse patiently stood, waiting for him. "She really does love you."

"I know. I think perhaps I have found Helena's baby."

"What?"

"I didn't mention it inside because, well, I'm not sure. I didn't even tell Helena. There are a lot of missing pieces."

"What makes you suspicious?"

"He looks just like Gray. He's an investigator."

"Get me his information. Perhaps I can pay him a visit disguised as a business opportunity."

"Yes."

"Be careful, son. It would kill your aunt if something happened to you."

"I will. Good luck tonight, I think you're going to need it."

"Oh, I have my ways of getting back into her good graces," his uncle said with a smirk. "We'll see you tomorrow."

"Tomorrow." Duncan prodded his horse and they were off, but he couldn't face going home just yet. Instead, he headed to White's to find a dark corner and a full bottle.

Davis walked into the house to find his wife sitting on the settee with silver tear tracks running down her cheeks. He went to her and gathered her in his arms. He rocked her back and forth and attempted to soothe her. She was so tenderhearted when it came to her family, and she had been bombarded with more information than one deserved. So, as any good husband would do, he held her as she cried.

"Where have you been?" she finally asked. "I heard Duncan leave quite a while ago."

"I wanted to give you time to calm down, and I was looking for this."

"What?" she asked, sniffing inelegantly.

He held out a red rose to her. She took it and sniffed deeply. He knew she would smell an exotically sweet and spicy scent. "Careful, there's a thorn near the petals."

"Why on earth would you remove all the thorns but one?"

"To remind myself that despite your beauty, you are still a force to be reckoned with."

"I can't believe you thought I would turn to another man after all these years," she muttered and swiped at her tears.

"I was frightened that perhaps I no longer made you happy."

"Oh, Davis, the only way you couldn't make me happy is if you no longer loved me."

"I do love you, and if you'll let me, I'll show you just how much."

"What's stopping you?"

"Our daughter walking through that door at any moment."

"Bridget is staying overnight with a friend."

"Then let the loving commence," Davis growled as he swung his wife up in his arms.

"We're getting too old for this," Agatha said, laughing.

"Never, darling. Never."

Penelope helped Helena get settled for the evening. "And you didn't suspect anything at all?" Penelope queried. She saw a guilty flush sweep over Helena's face. "You did," she said.

"I wanted to, but I was so afraid. I mean, would fate really lead me back to my family after all these years? Besides, I didn't think they wanted anything to do with me. Remember, they left me in Bedlam and turned their backs on me, or so I thought."

"So now what?"

"What do you mean?"

"Now that you know that they believed you to be dead."

"Nothing's changed. I'm still a peer's mistress, and they are members of the *ton*. Imagine how embarrassing that would be."

"What is your sister like?" Penelope decided to ask and try to get Helena's mind on the good memories.

"We used to look just alike. We loved playing pranks on our nannies and governesses. Jamie, Duncan's father, encouraged our bad behavior. I never really thought father liked us very much. Mother died shortly after our birth. We often were told by him that she sacrificed herself to have us and we both turned out to be girls, not a spare."

"How horrible."

"I suppose he was right," she shrugged, but Penelope could see the bitterness that lingered on her expression. They were alike in many ways.

"As we grew older, Agatha became the mother figure for Jamie and me, despite her being several years younger than him. I didn't know that I would grow wild, but I rebelled against father's tight rein, and I grew to despise my sister trying to always be perfect and encouraging me to do the same. Don't get me wrong, I didn't hate her, I just missed her free-spirit."

"I think I understand," Penelope said softly. Perhaps that was why she and Whitney had drifted apart.

"Agatha tried to dissuade me from seeing Henry. She had found out he was set to be married from her fiancé. But the heart wants what the heart wants. All I knew was that we loved one another, and that was all that mattered. Our relationship was never the same after that, Agatha and mine. Oh, she helped me slip out of the house to meet Henry, reluctantly of course, but she saw that I was going to do it with or without her assistance."

"Did I tell you that I'm a twin as well?"

"No."

"Whitney and I looked and acted nothing alike. She was absolutely gorgeous. She had men knocking down our door for her hand. She was so adventurous. I wished on many occasions I could have been more like her."

"Where is she?"

"Dead."

"Oh, Penelope."

"She tried to murder a woman. She blamed the woman for many things, especially being forced into a marriage with Duncan. When father killed himself after being caught in a treasonous act, no man would come anywhere near us. We were social pariahs. Whitney fell to her death from the top of the Tower of London. That's when mother truly went mad. Whitney was our way out of the poorhouse, and she was mother's favorite. She was everybody's favorite. I miss her so much."

"I've missed Agatha."

Penelope looked up and saw twin tears roll down Helena's cheeks. She felt matching ones rolling down her own face. The two women gathered each other in their arms and let the other cry.

CHAPTER 22

The next day, at the promised time, a knock echoed through the house. Unable to wait a moment longer she beat the housekeeper to the door and pulled it open. "You came back," Penelope said, when she saw Duncan standing on the top stair.

"You doubted me?"

She shrugged instead of answering. She turned her head as he bent down to kiss her, causing his lips to drift across her cheek.

"What's this?" he asked.

"Nothing," she said, rubbing a hand up and down one of her arms. She stood rigid when she saw a woman who looked identical to Helena walking up the stairs behind Duncan. A very distinguished looking man walked beside her. "Is this…"

"Aunt Agatha, Uncle Davis, this is my wife, Penelope."

"I'm not—"

"In every way that counts you are my wife, and they know everything."

"Everything?" she asked, thinking about all that had passed between them.

"Well, almost everything…" He smiled wickedly at her.

"Duncan, stop that," she swatted at his arm.

"It's a pleasure to meet you, my dear." Agatha pushed past Duncan, gathered Penelope in her arms, and hugged her tightly.

"Welcome to the family," Davis gathered her in his arms as well.

"And I'm Bridget, Duncan's cousin."

Penelope looked up to see a gorgeous young woman with sable-colored hair sauntering up the steps.

"What is she doing here?" Duncan demanded.

"Oh, Duncan, you know how stubborn Bridget can be. And we have no secrets in our family. She couldn't wait to meet her aunt and Penelope."

"I thought she was staying at a friend's house."

"That's a story for another time," Bridget said. Followed by the utterance of what Penelope thought was, "stubborn men."

"I'm so excited to have a new female cousin." She grabbed Penelope and hugged her tightly. "Now we can both work on driving the men in our family mad." She winked at Penelope before looping her arm through hers. "Well, I don't know about the rest of you, but I'm ready to meet this long lost aunt of mine. Penelope, won't you lead the way?"

"Umm, of course," she said, feeling bombarded. "Helena, we have guests," Penelope announced as they entered the parlor where the two women had been sitting.

"Who is this?" Helena asked, looking up from her embroidery with a smile.

"Aunt Helena, I'm Bridget, your niece. I've heard so much about you!"

Penelope watched, chewing her thumbnail nervously, as the girl launch herself at Helena. She saw the shock that entered the older woman's eyes. As she awkwardly hugged the young woman in her arms her eyes drifted past Penelope.

"Davis?"

"Helena. It's been a long time."

"Is…"

Penelope could tell that she was warring with herself. She wanted to see her sister desperately, but at the same time she feared the rejection that might be there. She had confided to Penelope that she feared her father had turned her entire family against her. Instead, they had been duped as well. An elaborate scheme that one man had orchestrated. Penelope watched as Davis took one step sideways and revealed a woman that looked identical to Helena.

"Aggie."

"Lena."

Bridget moved aside as Helena stood. The two women rushed across the room threw their arms around one another. They both simultaneously spoke and sobbed. Then they would look at one another and hug all over again.

"Let's give them some privacy," Davis said.

"Of course. This way," Penelope said, leading the trio into the study across the hall. There was another knock. "Pardon me." She opened the door and saw Henry standing on the other side. "Hello, my lord."

"Henry, please."

"Henry. Come in. Umm, Helena is with a visitor. Would you care to join us in the study?"

"Who is the visitor?" he asked before coming to an abrupt halt upon seeing Davis. He turned and looked in the parlor through the doorway and saw the two women hugging and talking. "Davis."

"Henry."

"I thought you were political enemies?" Penelope asked.

"We used to be friends long ago," Davis answered. "I'm sorry to hear about your wife."

"Thank you. Are they all right?" Henry asked, nodding towards the women.

"Yes," Davis answered.

"I'm Bridget," the young woman bounded into the conversation. "This is my father," she wrapped an arm around Davis' waist, "and Aggie is my mother. Who might you be?"

"I'm, well, um…"

"Oh, I'm just teasing. I've heard all the stories, and I think I shall call you Uncle Henry, for in my opinion the two of you should have run off together years ago. I mean, who walks away from their true love?" Bridget chatted, animatedly.

"Would anyone care for tea?" Penelope asked.

"That would be wonderful," Bridget said.

"Duncan, would you mind helping me?"

"What?"

"Now, please," Penelope gritted between her teeth.

"Of course. Gentleman, please don't kill one another. Bridget, behave yourself."

Penelope waited until Duncan joined her in the hall. "Are you out of your mind? I can't believe you brought all these people here. Helena specifically said she didn't want to see her sister yesterday."

"She looks like she didn't want to see her sister," Duncan countered sarcastically, peeking through the open door.

"Men," she muttered and marched to the kitchen. Helena had given the staff the day off, so Penelope made the tea. She walked around the room, gathering items and slamming doors. "Can you at least start the water to boil?" she asked Duncan, hands on hips. She was arranging the cookies and teacakes Cook had left for them on the tray when she felt a hard, warm body behind her. Big hands were on her hips, gently pulling her back against his hardness. Penelope shrugged and tried to step away from him. Instead, she felt herself being spun around.

Warm hands at her waist lifted her in the air and placed her next to the tray she had been working on. The dress she wore was lower cut in the bosom than most women would allow, most women that were in society, that is. She watched Duncan's eyes travel downward. She pushed her chest out just a little further, causing the fabric to dip even lower.

"You are a temptress," Duncan said huskily. He cupped her cheeks in his hands and bent down. He teased her lips with his, gently brushing them back and forth over hers. The kisses grew more heated as time passed. Duncan wrapped one arm around her and moved his other hand to her breast. He cupped it gently, squeezing it. "I've missed you, missed this," he whispered against her temple as the teakettle whistled.

"I thought maybe you could use some…oops, sorry," Bridget's voice filtered to them. "I'll just go back to Papa and Uncle Henry," she said.

"Please tell me she didn't see us."

"She saw us."

"That's not what you were supposed to tell me."

"I'm sorry, but I cannot lie," he said.

"I can't face her." Penelope buried her face against Duncan's chest.

"Of course you can. Believe me, my cousin is no angel." He left her to move the teakettle off the stove to stop the incessant whistling. Duncan looked over to see Penelope trying to wiggle off the counter, causing her dress to inch upward, exposing her legs. "Allow me," he said huskily as he lifted her up then allowed her to slide slowly down his hard body.

A knock sounded. "Who could that be? We have never had this many visitors. Suddenly everyone wants to come here."

Bridget appeared once more in the kitchen. "Duncan," she said hesitantly. "Oh, good," she sounded relieved. "There's a Reverend Jacobs here to see you. Said he was ready to perform the ceremony whenever you were."

"What have you done?" Penelope demanded, turning on Duncan.

"I told you we would be married."

Penelope bristled at his heavy-handedness. "If I wanted to be dictated to I would have stayed under Grandfather's roof."

"Perhaps that would have been best." Penelope took a step back as Duncan snarled at her.

"I think you should leave."

"Not until we've said our vows. Now, come with me."

She fought against the grip he had on her wrist.

"Duncan, I demand to know what is going on," Agatha said, standing in the doorway with her twin. Neither Duncan nor Penelope had seen Bridget sneak out to let her mother and aunt know of the storm brewing in the kitchen.

Penelope took the opportunity afforded to her with his loosened grip and twisted free of his hold. She stepped back, rubbing her wrist more for something to do than because it hurt. She watched the three while her eyes darted about the room searching for an exit.

"Reverend Jacobs is here to perform the marriage ceremony. Penelope has it in her mind that she would rather be my mistress than my wife."

"I've told you why."

"And I've told you it's ridiculous. We're already married in all the ways that matter."

"Except the most important!" Penelope countered angrily.

"It was the machinations of an old fool that kept it from being legal, and I'm attempting to rectify that situation."

"Duncan, let me and Helena talk to her." All three women watched the giant of a man hesitate. "I promise, we will not allow her to run away."

"Promise me you'll listen to them. If after they have talked to you, you still refuse to go through with the wedding, I'll respect your wishes."

"Fine," Penelope said softly, refusing to look away from Duncan.

"I'll be awaiting your decision," he said reluctantly then turned and left the room.

"Shall I pour us all a cup of tea?" Helena asked.

"That would be lovely," Agatha answered.

"No, thank you," Penelope replied. Her stomach churned nervously and she feared she would be unable to keep anything down at this point.

"Come and join me," Agatha patted the empty spot beside her on the bench where the staff took their meals. "So, you are the young woman who has stolen my nephew's heart."

"Hardly that, my lady," Penelope answered with a scoff.

"You are part of the family, so you must call me Agatha or Aggie."

"But I'm not part of the family, or have all of you conveniently forgotten the devious trick Grandfather played? Our marriage was a farce."

"Not all aspects of it were," Helena piped in as she carried the tray over to the table.

"What are you all discussing in here?" Bridget asked from the doorway, sounding much too chipper.

"Is my life to be on public display now?" Penelope asked before placing her elbows on the table and lowering her head until her forehead rested in her palms.

"Now, now," Agatha soothed, patting her back.

"I'm sorry. I just thought the conversation would be more lively than it is in there. Father and Uncle Henry keep eyeing one another suspiciously. The Reverend Jacobs is reading his Bible, and if I didn't know better, I would say that Duncan is pouting."

"I told you he cares for you," Agatha said. "I know my nephew."

"It doesn't matter. Someone tried to kill me."

"Do you fear that Duncan cannot protect you?"

"No, it's not that."

"Then what is it."

"I've had too much murder and death in my life. I just want to live a quiet life where nobody minds that I live to be an old woman. I can't have that life if I marry Duncan."

"Because someone tried to kill you?"

"Yes. Don't any of you see?" Penelope asked, sounding a bit desperate. She watched Bridget sit down across from her and next to Helena, a confused look marring her perfect features.

"No, I don't," Bridget said sincerely. "He cares for you. When Isabelle died, he was angry at the world, but I don't believe it was because he loved her passionately. Everyone knew they were friends growing up and their marriage just made sense. He was mad because of a friend's passing and betrayal. When the other two passed on, he was, well, it is difficult to explain."

"He was saddened for the loss of human life, but he was not invested in the relationship. He was indifferent. I'm not sure what you've done that they either could not or did not do, but you have made him feel again, or rather perhaps for the first time. He's frightened of losing you," Agatha explained.

"Doesn't he see? Don't any of you see?" Penelope asked, looking around the table desperately. "He isn't going to lose me. We'll still be together. Just not as husband and wife. That way no one will have any reason to want to kill me. Why waste their time on a mistress? After all, I can give him children, but not an heir. The titled properties cannot be passed to my children. He's much too wealthy to be able to spend all of his money on me, especially when I have no need for anything." She stared at each woman sitting at the table. If she couldn't sway them to her side, she didn't know what she would do. Penelope took a deep breath before plowing on, "So, tell me why. Why go to all this trouble? Why should I continually put my life in danger?"

"Because I love you, and I think you love me," a deep voice replied from the doorway.

"You're supposed to be in the other room," Penelope accused. She could barely see through the tears clinging precariously to her lashes. How dare he come in here spouting that he loved her when she was trying to distance herself from him? "Don't leave," she said to the other women, but they ignored her and continued on their way. Duncan sat beside her, straddling the bench so he could face her. He wrapped one arm around her lower back and pulled her against him until she rested against his chest. She burrowed her head beneath his chin and let him entwine the fingers of her right and his left hand together.

"You should have told me why you felt the way you did," he said softly.

"I tried to."

"No, you kept telling me how you felt. That you didn't want to marry. I suspected you were a bit worried about your life being in danger, but I didn't realize exactly how deeply your past has hurt you."

"Duncan, please don't make me go through with the wedding."

"All right," he sighed the answer.

"Truly?" she asked, pulling away from him and looking into his eyes. She wanted to see if honesty shone through them.

"Yes."

She let out a sigh of relief. "I want a contract drawn up between us. Just as you would with any mistress."

"And what are your conditions?"

"A small house in a quiet area of London with a small staff. My mother removed from Bethlem Hospital and placed in my care," she said, referring to the asylum by its official name. "I need at least two women with medical experience hired to see to her needs."

"Consider it done."

"Oh, Duncan," she sighed and exuberantly threw her arms about his neck.

"But I want one thing as well, and I want you to agree to it now."

"What is it?"

"I'm not telling you. This is a trust issue. You are going to have to trust that I am not going to bring you into any danger by eliciting this promise from you."

"Without hearing what it is? I don't think so." She retreated from him just as quickly as she had engulfed him.

"Then you'll never see your mother again."

"What do you mean?"

"Your mother is already safely removed from Bedlam. She has four women that are paid very well to see to her needs. In fact she has her own little house and staff."

"Where is she?" Penelope demanded, her back ramrod straight.

"It will be disclosed to you as soon as you sign the contract."

Penelope watched him remove a packet of papers from an inner-pocket in his superfine coat. It fit his form so snugly, she wasn't certain how he could fit anything else in there, even papers. "What is that?"

"This, unfortunately, we will not be needing for the time being."

She quickly snatched the paper from his hand and saw the word *Marriage* scrawled across the top. She dropped it as if it had burned her fingers. "And what is that?" she asked warily.

"This is what you wanted all along, a contract between a man and his mistress."

"But you said you wanted—"

"At this juncture, it does not matter what I want. It matters what has to happen to see us through this particular situation."

"What are you talking about?"

"I'm just fulfilling your request."

"You came prepared didn't you?" Penelope asked. She couldn't keep the hurt from her voice. *You are being ridiculous*, she chastised herself. *You are getting exactly what you wanted.*

"I need something to write with and a witness," Duncan called out.

She warily watched him as he flipped to the back page of the second packet of papers. "What is this?"

"Exactly what you wanted, a contract between a mistress and her protector. Thank you Agg…I mean Helena. It is still difficult to remember there are two of you again. Now, I'll sign."

Penelope watched dumbfounded as he scrawled his name across the page where it indicated he should.

"You sign here."

She looked at where his finger pointed, and followed his arm up to look into his eyes that had hardened the last few minutes. "What am I agreeing to, exactly?"

"That isn't part of the deal. I have given you everything you have asked for. More even. All I ask is that you trust me, just a little, and sign this contract without reading it."

"Penelope, dear, this isn't wise," Helena interceded.

"Listen to my aunt. It isn't wise, but if you don't sign it, you'll never see your mother again, or you could marry me. That would also fix the situation."

"Duncan James Taggart, that is blackmail." Agatha joined them. "I am ashamed of you."

"Stay out of this Agatha," he ordered. "What will it be, Penelope? Do you sign or not? Do we get married? All the decisions are yours to make."

"I thought you said you loved me," she said. She desperately searched his eyes to find the man she had come to know. But he was no longer there. Instead, she was merely involved in a business transaction. It felt so impersonal, so cold, so wrong.

"And I thought you cared for me," he countered, "but it appears we were both wrong."

She jerked the quill from his fingers and signed her name with a flourish.

"Helena, if you will do the honors as witness."

"I shouldn't."

"But you will," Duncan argued.

"What makes you so certain?"

"You have been Henry's mistress for how many years?"

"You may be my nephew, but you truly are a beast. Give me that," Helena demanded. The quill easily came loose from Penelope's limp fingers. She scratched her name on the document and patted the ink dry on all three signatures. "There, you have what you came for, now get out of my house."

"Let's make one thing absolutely clear," he said. "This is not at all what I wanted. This is what *she* wanted." Duncan nodded towards Penelope and she watched him rise from his seat next to her. He picked up both the marriage certificate and the contract. "I'll be back in two hours. Have your things packed and ready. Whatever you don't have packed stays behind." She watched him leave the house through the window with a man she supposed was the Reverend Jacobs in tow.

"What have I done?" she asked the room at large as a sob erupted from her.

"I believe you are dancing with the devil," Helena said softly.

Penelope folded her arms on the tabletop, lowered her head to them, and cried for several long, bleak moments. Somehow she pulled herself together and raised her head to see five concerned faces staring at her. "I suppose I should pack." She stood up from the table and swiped away any trace of tears.

"Penelope, you don't have to do this," Helena argued.

"Yes, I do. I signed a contract, and you witnessed it. If I don't follow through, I'm no better than my grandfather. Besides, Duncan's right. I got exactly what I wanted and I should be happy about it." She sniffed and gave a wobbly smile to the group. "Now, if you all will excuse me, I have a short amount of time to be packed."

"I'll help you," Bridget said, sounding meek for the first time since entering the house.

"I would appreciate it." She proudly lifted her chin and left the room, refusing to shed another tear over the situation.

"This is your house," Duncan indicated as the carriage rolled to a stop several hours later.

"It looks lovely, but I would like to see my mother first."

"You can visit your mother later," Duncan said, trying to remain patient with her. He looked up to see her firmly implanted in the corner of the carriage, her arms crossed, and her chin tilted at a determined angle. "Must we argue about this?"

"I'm not arguing about anything," Penelope denied.

"Damned stubborn woman," he muttered under his breath before opening the hatch to give new directions to the driver. The carriage lurched, causing the occupants to sway. He watched her brace herself against the bench beside her. Duncan fisted his hand to keep from reaching out to steady her. He knew that right now she was angry with him and that touching her might result in him losing a body part that both he and she were very attached to. "We're here," he announced.

"Already?"

"Did you think I would keep your mother very far from you?"

"But you said—"

"I have said a lot of things, but how you interpret them is something else entirely. Shall we?" he asked as the tiger opened the coach's door.

"Yes," she said after clearing her throat.

Duncan stepped down and out of the coach, turned around, and held his hand out for her. He very solicitously helped her out of the coach. Unable to control himself, Duncan wrapped her arm around his. He led her up to a nondescript house in a part of London that was respected but had seen better days. They waited patiently after knocking on the door. When it opened, they were greeted by an older woman who looked quite matronly. Her pepper gray hair was tucked under a mob-cap.

"Your Grace," she said, attempting a curtsy.

"Mrs. Smithers, there's no need for that. How long have we known each other?"

"You had yet to light up your father's eyes with joy," she said jovially.

"Mrs. Smithers, this is Lady Blackstock's daughter."

"Oh, you must be Whitney. She asks for ye all the time, she does."

"I'm Penelope," she answered through gritted teeth. "Whitney is dead."

"Oh, I *am* sorry."

"That's all right," Penelope said.

Duncan could see the tightness in Penelope's shoulders, could feel it in the arm wrapped about his. He patted her gently, trying to convey his support to her. "Penelope, this is Mrs. Smithers. She will be your mother's housekeeper. She worked in our London house for years and wanted to run a smaller household in her twilight years."

"Mrs. Smithers, it is a pleasure."

"Lady Blackstock is a lovely woman. Perhaps you can help me by telling me her likes and dislikes. After you visit with her, of course," she hastened to interject.

"I would be happy to. Do you mind taking me to Mother now?"

"Of course. She's right in here, Miss Presley."

Duncan watched as the two women were reunited. Lady Blackstock sat in a rocking chair, shuffling through something."

"Mother, you look so much better then when last I saw you," Penelope gushed. She was just about to throw her arms about her mother's neck when the older woman's words stopped her mid-step with her arms spread wide.

"Oh, Whitney, I'm so glad you're back. Come look at these fashion plates with me. With the right material, some man is going to find you devastating. In fact, I can see a horde of young bucks fighting over you."

"I'm Penelope, Mother," she corrected the older woman.

"Penelope will be lucky to find a man to take her off your father's hands. She's rather plain, quite loyal, but nothing like you my darling Whitney. Don't you just love this dress? A beautiful pink silk will highlight your fair complexion. And just the littlest bit of lip rouge to entice the young bucks and perhaps the bodice just a bit lower than it should be."

"Mother, Whitney's dead, don't you remember?" Penelope asked hoarsely.

Duncan saw another woman enter the room.

"Your Grace." She curtsied politely.

"How is Lady Blackstock, Mrs. Hawkins?" he asked, addressing one of the women he hired to help care for Penelope's mother.

"Physically, she's a strong and healthy woman now that she's being fed good meals. Mentally, she's broken. I've never seen such a bad case. She rarely has lucid moments. Seems to be living in the past."

"Get away from me!"

"Mother! Stop! Mother! It's me, Penelope."

Duncan and Mrs. Hawkins turned towards the other two people in the room. Penelope was trying to calm her mother, and Lady Blackstock was slapping at her.

"I know who you are. I want Whitney."

"Mother, Whitney's dead, remember?"

"No!"

"Yes, Mother," Penelope sighed.

"I wish it were you!" the woman yelled at her.

Duncan had been watching Penelope start to envelope her mother in a loving hug, but now she stood awkwardly, like a court jester frozen in place. The look on her face was a combination of complete mortification and devastation. Duncan rushed to Penelope's side and wrapped his arms around her. He tried to move Penelope towards the door, but it was as if she were rooted to the spot. "Pen, let's go home," he whispered in her ear.

"Yes, go home, *whore*!"

He felt Penelope jerk at the name as if she had been shot.

"Lady Blackstock, you had best mind your tongue and be lucky that you are not a man, or you would be facing me across the dueling field at dawn."

"Your grandfather paid me a visit and told me all about how you slept with *him*," she spat at Duncan, "outside the bonds of marriage. You have shamed the family name and now we'll never recover. Dear, sweet Whitney would never do such a thing."

"No, you're right, Mother. Instead, Whitney tried to murder someone. That will do nothing to the family name."

Duncan watched as if in slow motion as the older woman drew her hand back and let loose. He couldn't move fast enough and the sound of the slap reverberated on the air around them. Penelope grabbed at her nose and he saw the blood trickling through her fingers along with the red handprint showing up on her cheek. He swooped her into his arms and left the room amid her mother's insane screaming.

"In here, Your Grace." Mrs. Smithers indicated that he should follow her.

Duncan and Penelope found themselves once more in a cozy kitchen. He sat down and perched her on his lap. Mrs. Smithers gently pried Penelope's hands from her nose and instructing her to tilt her head backwards. She then pressed damp cloths against Penelope's nose.

"You've had a recent break, haven't you?"

"Yes." The word was muffled but reached Duncan's ears all the same.

"How?" the woman queried.

"Fell."

"Firm pressure now," Mrs. Smithers advised. "It's not been broken again, but it'll be sore for a day or two."

Lady Blackstock's tantrum was ending, and they could hear her calling for Whitney and crying. Duncan looked down and saw tears clinging precariously to Penelope's eyelashes. He took his thumb and gently wiped them away. "No tears. She isn't worth them, and they will only make matters worse. You are more valuable than one hundred Whitneys."

"How'd you know?"

"I met her once."

"What? When?"

"Soon after your grandfather made the arrangement. Before all of the craziness ensued with the director and his wife. I wanted to know what I was getting myself into."

Mrs. Smithers had disappeared for a moment, leaving the two of them alone. "And?" she prompted.

"I found myself dreading the marriage. Yes, she was beautiful, but she was also selfish, rude, and demanding."

"Where?"

"At a party that you both attended."

"The only one that we attended together was a ball before the Season began almost three years ago."

"That would be it."

"But I didn't see you there."

"No. I avoided being seen, but there was this one young woman that drew my attent—"

"Here now, let's see if we can't get you cleaned up a bit." Mrs. Smithers came bustling back into the room followed by Mrs. Hawkins.

Duncan felt Penelope stiffen in his arms and cursed other people's poor timing. "We're not finished with this discussion," he whispered in her ear.

She pulled away from him. He let her go as the other women helped her stand. He grabbed her waist when she swayed unsteadily.

"I'm so sorry about what happened, Your Grace, Miss Presley. She has not come to the present like that since being under our care. We share reports with each other upon every rotation. It must have been seeing you in a setting that looked like her home that did it."

"You're not to be blamed," Penelope's generous words were muffled.

"If you'll excuse me, I'm going to step outside for a moment."

"Of course, Your Grace," the two older women said almost simultaneously while Penelope remained mutinously silent.

He stepped outside and took a deep breath of air that did not smell like blood. If her mother were a man, she would be dead right now. *How could a parent say that to a child?* he wondered silently. "But then look at what Grandfather did to Aunt Helena," he answered himself. He was going to have to send someone to Yorkshire to retrieve the correspondence between himself and her grandfather, otherwise she would never believe that he had his sights set on her from the very beginning. Duncan paced the length of the block several times. Over and over he wondered why Lady Blackstock had to pick the time her daughter was visiting to ensure her well-being to have her moment of lucidness.

Then there was Penelope's grandfather Lord Bolingbroke. The man had come here to deliberately cause grief. He paused in his stride. If he came here, that meant he knew, of course, that the older woman no longer resided in Bedlam. Somehow, he had found out she had been removed and where she was now being housed. *What else does the old man know?* Duncan wondered. How was he getting his information? Does he know he also bought a house for Penelope? Does he know where it is? Is Penelope in danger? Would he come after Penelope? Would he publicly embarrass her? He would put nothing past the embittered, old man. Suddenly, his hands began to tremble at the thought of Penelope being in peril from so many areas.

The creak of old hinges brought his head up and he saw Penelope being guided from the house and down the front stairs. He jogged over and swept her up.

"I can walk," she mumbled, sounding as if she had a cold.

"Humor me."

She gave him a look but remained silent, as she encircled his neck with her arms.

"We'll take care of your mother, m'dear. Don't ye worry none about it. And don't give a thought to what she said. Any woman would be lucky to have ye for a daughter." The housekeeper patted one of Penelope's legs.

"Thank you," Penelope whispered.

Duncan wanted to kiss Mrs. Smithers upon hearing her kind words. He would find some way to compensate the woman, perhaps an increase in her wages. *Yes, that's what I'll do*, he thought as he carried Penelope to the carriage and helped her inside. He followed behind her after giving the driver instructions. Once they were securely enclosed within the coach and the outside world locked out, he looked intently at her.

"Tell me truly. How do you feel?"

"I've been better," she said, pressing a palm to her cheek.

"Does it sting?"

"Yes, and my head hurts."

"You're going directly to bed upon arriving home."

"You'll not get an argument out of me."

"Penelope, no child should have to hear those words from a parent. I'm sorry you had to."

"I am, too," she replied so softly he strained to hear her. Duncan started to move across the coach to take her in his arms, to comfort her, but she quickly lifted a hand to halt his progress. "Stay where you are."

"But—"

"If you touch me, I'll shatter, and I refuse to let Grandfather win."

He watched her lean back against the squab, look out the window, and withdraw into herself, both physically and emotionally. At that moment he wished things were different between them and cursed her Grandfather and the killer driving a wedge between them. *Am I ever going to be allowed to be happy?* he wondered idly. Duncan watched the light and shadows play over Penelope's beautiful, delicate features.

CHAPTER 23

Two days passed since the incident at her mother's lodgings and Penelope and Duncan had settled into a routine. He stayed with her during the night, holding her in his arms while she slept. She had argued against him staying that first night, but he silenced her by reminding her of the contract. She had held herself stiff against him in an attempt to refuse herself his comfort, but her body had betrayed her. Duncan pursued her physically without overwhelming her. He always made certain she was fully pleasured but refused to fully consummate the relationship once more. Whatever his reasons were for withholding, he did not share them with her. Both mornings she had awoken alone to find his side of the bed cooling and his scent lingering on the pillows.

This morning was no different. Her eyes flitted open against the sun's weak attempt to light her room through the London haze. Penelope found that she missed the bright yellow rays that had streaked through their bedroom in Yorkshire. The way the bed had been positioned, if the drapes were opened, as they often were, the sun would spill across the bed, both warming and waking the occupants. A cacophony of sounds reached her ears. She used to enjoy hearing the hawkers selling their wares, the clip-clop of horse hooves against the stones, and the rumbling of the large dray wagons and carriages rolling down the streets. Now she found she much preferred the sound of the sea birds and other animals that roamed about the countryside, the way the wind sounded, or how the waves crashed against the rocks.

She pushed herself up and slipped from the bed and tugged on a robe to cover her nudity. She strolled to the window and threw it open. She took a deep breath and the offal reached her nose, making her stomach churn sickeningly. Penelope quickly shut the window and took another deep breath, willing her stomach to calm. After a few minutes, her stomach settled.

Nothing about London was the same to her. What she had grown up loving and embracing now annoyed or sickened her, literally evidently. "When did I change?" she asked the empty room as if it could give her the answer she sought. Penelope shook her head and started to turn away from the window when something caught her eye—the barest hint of a shifting shadow. She stepped out of view of the window but continued to study the area. Nothing. "You're being ridiculous, Penelope Anne," she scolded herself.

She performed her morning ablutions and dressed, ready to face the day, when the delicious aromas of food wafted on the air and caused her stomach to growl loudly. She skipped, quite unladylike down the stairs, actually excited about the day ahead, even though she had no concrete plans.

"Good morning, Miss Penelope," Mrs. Jenkins, her lively little housekeeper, greeted her.

"Good morning to you as well, Mrs. Jenkins." Penelope looked at the food on the table. "Everything looks and smells delicious."

"I'm glad you approve. Now, you best tuck into it before it grows cold."

"Yes, ma'am," Penelope said indulgently. It seemed that Mrs. Jenkins enjoyed fussing over Penelope, and Penelope enjoyed the attention. She had never been mothered the way the woman carried out the duty, and she discovered she had missed out on a great deal growing up.

Penelope took several bites and a sip of her tea. She was just lifting another bite to her lips when her stomach did an uncomfortable flip. She put down her fork and pushed the plate away from her with a shaky hand. Beads of perspiration popped up on her forehead and her upper lip. The aromas that had smelled so marvelous only minutes before now struck her as rancid. She looked up to see Mrs. Jenkins enter the room with another dish.

"Miss Penelope, do you not like the food?"

Penelope started to open her mouth, but quickly thought better of it. She pushed back her chair, got to her feet, and rushed out of the room through the door Mrs. Jenkins had just entered through. She took no time to observe her surroundings as she rushed through the kitchen to the back door. Penelope stumbled down the steps and fell to her knees as what little bit she had eaten made a reappearance. A cool, wet cloth was a welcome relief as someone placed it on the back of her neck. She was on all fours as the dry heaves continued to wrack her slender frame. When they subsided, she pushed herself up and made her unsteady way to a bench that sat under a stunted tree in the small garden.

"Here you go, dearie," the housekeeper said, pressing another cool, wet cloth into Penelope's hands.

"I don't know what's wrong."

"Perhaps you've caught something," Mrs. Jenkins suggested.

"Yes. I think perhaps I'll go back upstairs and lie down for awhile. I'm sorry to have ruined your beautiful feast."

"Think nothing of it. Let me help you upstairs." Penelope accepted the woman's assistance gratefully. She allowed the older woman to slip the buttons of her dress free. She removed it and climbed back into the unmade bed in her shift. "You rest," the housekeeper said as she pulled the drapes closed so that Penelope could sleep. "I'll be back to check on you in a bit."

"Thank you," Penelope said gratefully, closing her eyes. Several hours later she woke, feeling rejuvenated. Her churning stomach was non-existent and she found herself ready to face what remained of the day.

On the fourth consecutive day of becoming ill, Penelope looked at Mrs. Jenkins and said, "I just don't understand what's wrong with me. I'm usually so healthy."

"Miss Penelope, I felt the same way when I was expecting my first babe. I was sick all the time. Don't know how I managed."

"What are you talking about, Mrs. Jenkins?"

"You mean you really don't know?

"No," Penelope said, shaking her head negatively. She had a sick premonition that the words about to come out of Mrs. Jenkins would irrevocably change her life.

"Miss Penelope, I believe you're going to have a babe."

"No, it can't be," Penelope whispered.

"Pardon my asking, but have you and His Grace had relations?"

Penelope felt herself blush to the roots of her hair. She turned away from the older woman's gaze, unable to keep eye contact with her. It was like being questioned by her mother. "I've had my menses," she mumbled.

"Was it lighter than usual? A shorter duration?"

Penelope thought about it, worrying her lip. "I suppose it could have been. I didn't really pay much attention."

"Have you and His Grace done anything to prevent a babe?"

"There are things you can do to prevent having a child?" Penelope asked, shocked.

"Oh, dearie, I do think you're going to be a mother."

Penelope looked at her in shock and then her stomach churned once more. After casting up the contents of her stomach for the second time that morning, Penelope sat in shock. At some point she felt Mrs. Jenkins' arms go around her to help her stand and guide her to the parlor.

"Now, why don't you tell me what is really going on between you and His Grace?"

"What do you mean?" Penelope queried, her voice trembling.

"You do not have the demeanor of a mistress. Your manners are too refined."

Penelope ended up telling her everything.

"So we need to determine who is trying to kill you and why."

"Yes."

"And we need to do everything in our power to keep you and the babe safe."

"Yes."

"Are you going to tell His Grace he is to be a father?"

"Not right now." The two women jumped as someone pounded on the door. "I wonder who that could be," Penelope shot Mrs. Jenkins a worried look. There were never any visitors to the small house other than delivery men who came to the kitchen door. Penelope heard someone try to turn the doorknob that was locked. "Perhaps you should see who it is," Penelope said. She followed Mrs. Jenkins into the hallway. As the door opened, she saw Duncan filling the doorway. "Duncan, what are you doing here during this time of day?"

"Warn you."

"Warn me about what?" she asked, confused.

"Danger," he said as he took a faltering step through the front door and collapsed. Penelope dropped to her knees beside him and tried to roll him over. On closer inspection, she saw bruises forming on his cheek bones. His clothes were dirty. He had cuts all over his face. His knuckles had abrasions on them. Even his clothes looked as if someone had tried to cut them to ribbons.

"Miss Penelope, look," Mrs. Jenkins pointed downwards.

Blood trickled down his face from a graze along his right temple, and there was also a tear in his left sleeve. She could see blood soaking the white cloth of his shirt. "Oh, dear God, Duncan, what has happened to you?"

The women somehow managed to drag Duncan's large body inside the house and close the door against prying eyes that might be watching. Mrs. Jenkins slipped out the back and went to Helena's, the only person Penelope knew to seek for help. She had been so upset the day he had taken her to see her mother that even though she knew she lived close, she couldn't give directions to her house to seek aide from one of her nurses. She sat in the cramped hall with Duncan's head resting in her lap while he drifted in and out of consciousness.

As she ran her fingers through his hair, she felt a knot begin to form on the back of his skull. She traced his cheeks with the back of her fingers. He looked so incredibly docile, but she knew an angry beast lurked beneath the surface. When he did regain his strength from this, whoever was responsible would pay if they hadn't already. A groan drew her attention. He tried to quickly sit up, but groaned again as the reality of his injuries hit him. Penelope pushed him back down to the floor. She felt comforted by the feel of his head in her lap once more.

"Safe," he moaned.

"Yes, I'm safe," she said. "Who did this to you?"

He licked his dry lips. "Three…jumped me."

"Where?"

"Down the street."

"Do you think they're still there?"

"Don't…worry," he managed to say.

"How can you tell me not to worry? You collapsed at the door. You look as if you've been beaten and cut for heaven's sake. Do not tell me *not to worry.*" She gaped as she saw the smile that lit his face. *The man had the nerve to smile at a time like this?* she wondered in astonishment.

"You do…care?"

"I never said I didn't," she argued. "Should I send for Reese?"

"No. Grantham. Investigator," he managed to say before he drifted off once more.

Penelope did not have time to give way to the tears she wanted to cry, for at that moment she heard the back door open. "I'm armed!" she called out as a warning, thought it was a lie.

"It's me, dearie," Mrs. Jenkins peeked around the corner. She was followed by another familiar face and two burly men dressed in Helena's livery.

"Thank goodness. We need to send someone after a Mr. Grantham. An investigator. First though, I think you two gentlemen should move His Grace upstairs," she said.

"Right away," the two men said.

"Duncan," Penelope patted his cheek a little roughly to rouse him. "Duncan," she repeated louder this time and slapped him a little harder. He came to looking confused.

"What?" He looked questioningly at her and then squinted at the others in the room. Penelope felt his body tense.

"Easy. They're Helena's footmen. They're going to help you upstairs, but you're going to have to help them as much as you can."

"Anything for you," he said and rolled to his side, with her assistance, and then to all fours.

Penelope watched from the floor as the men heaved him to a standing position. Even though they were big men, Duncan still towered over them.

"Come, my dear," Helena offered her hand to Penelope.

"No. My hands are soiled."

"As if that matters to me. Now, give me your hand and let me help you up."

Penelope did as instructed. Mrs. Jenkins had disappeared. "He says he was attacked."

"Do you doubt him?"

"Not at all," she denied. "I'm worried. If someone was willing to attack him in broad daylight, then what lengths will they go to to harm me?"

"Do they want to harm you?" Helena questioned.

"They were trying to poison me."

"Yes, but I'm beginning to wonder to what end. If they had wanted to kill you to get close to Duncan as we all believed, why would they attack him and nearly beat him to death. That is if this wasn't a random act of thievery."

"You think someone is after Duncan?" Penelope queried. She studied the other woman intently.

"What I think is that we should go upstairs and take care of that nephew of mine. Then we can dissect this situation in more detail once he's on the mend."

"What would I do if you hadn't found me that night?"

"I have a suspicion you would have managed somehow. You're a strong woman, Penelope." The women wrapped an arm around each other's waist and made their way upstairs to see to the patient.

Penelope was just leaving the kitchen after having a bite to eat when a knock sounded at the door. She cautiously cracked it open so she could peek out. A man stood there with a cane in hand that had a wicked looking blade protruding from it. A bloody blade, Penelope noted. She tried to slam the door on him, but he managed to wedge his foot between the door and the frame.

"Get out of here! I won't let you finish him off! Do you hear me?!" She drew the door back and repeatedly slammed it on the man's foot until he was forced to act. But he did the opposite of what she thought he would. He managed to slip in the house. She started to draw back a fist when he spoke, halting her hand mid-flight.

"I'm Grantham."

"What?"

"I was sent for."

"What's going on out here?" Mrs. Jenkins rushed into the hallway wielding a cast iron skillet.

"It's all right, Mrs. Jenkins," Penelope replied. She wearily let her arm drop back to her side.

"Who's that?" the older woman demanded, still not convinced he wasn't the enemy.

"This is the investigator Duncan had me send for."

"Oh, well, if that's the case, I'll go back into the kitchen. You call out if you need me. You'd better not try anything funny with the mistress there, young man."

"No, ma'am," he nodded his head and tugged on his forelock. He waited until the older woman had returned to the kitchen before facing Penelope once more. "She's protective of you."

"Yes," Penelope replied, making no excuses.

"Good. I found this on one of the lower steps." He held out the cane to her.

Penelope took the cane and inspected the top. It was in the shape of a boar's head. She had seen this cane in Duncan's office in Yorkshire. "I never knew there was a blade concealed inside." A small card was placed in her hand. *Dominic Grantham, Investigator*, it read in block letters. "I apologize. It has been a stressful day. Please come in." He stepped further down the hall, and she made certain the door was firmly closed and locked against intruders. She placed the weapon in the corner behind the door. "Follow me. He's resting."

"How is he?"

"He's been better," she said stiffly.

"How did it happen?"

"He managed to tell me he was attacked by several men. I don't know what shape they're in. He simply told me not to worry. He made his way back here to make certain I was safe. When I opened the door, he collapsed in the foyer. Mrs. Jenkins and I pulled him inside." She took a step, swayed, and tightly gripped the bannister. She felt a pair of firm hands on her waist, steadying her. She knew she should pull free from his touch, but he was merely being kind, and she was exhausted—physically, mentally, and emotionally.

"Are you all right?"

"Yes," she said after a moment. She took a deep breath and continued up the steps until they reached the second story. "He's in here." The room was empty except for the man asleep on the bed. Penelope had sent Helena on her way shortly after noon, but only after she accepted the fact that Helena would return to check on them tomorrow. She walked around the bed and leaned over her…what? *My protector? My fiancé? My lover?*

"Are you certain you feel fine?"

"Yes," she answered bringing herself firmly back to the present. "Duncan, wake up. You have a visitor."

"That's quite a menagerie of wounds he has."

"Yes. The physician that came to attend him said that it looked like he had been cut, beaten, and shot."

"And was he?"

"He won't admit it so long as I am in the room," she answered. Penelope took a small vial from the bedside table, removed the stopper, and held it beneath Duncan's nose until he fought his way to consciousness. She replaced the stopper and put the bottle back on the table. She perched on the bed next to him. Penelope gently fitted her right hand within Duncan's right hand as she faced him. "Duncan, Investigator Grantham is here to see you." She felt a gentle squeeze of his hand seconds before his eyelids fluttered open.

"You look a sight," Grantham said, pulling up a chair and taking a seat.

"I feel worse."

"At least you're still with us."

"Yes."

"First things first. The attack."

Penelope stiffened when Duncan swung his gaze at her. "I'm not leaving. If you want me to be your wife, we are in this battle together. Do you understand me? I will not have the relationship my parents had where they lived separate lives. So you decide now. If I walk out that door," she paused nodding to the bedroom door, "we are over. I don't care what the bloody contract says."

"When did you get all fiery?"

"When someone tried to end my life." She felt the squeeze of his hand once more and instead of pulling away from her, he entwined their fingers together and soothingly rubbed his thumb back and forth against her hand.

"I left here and was riding my horse back to the house. I was only a few blocks away when the horse started acting up, favoring one leg. I got down to check his hooves when I was hit from behind. I managed to grab my cane before they dragged me into an alley."

"Lucky thing. How many were there?"

"I saw three."

"Do you think there were more than that?"

"I'm not certain. Two of them held me while the other tried to use me as a punching bag."

"How did you manage to break free?"

"My cane. Somehow I managed to keep a grip of it. I released the blade into the leg of one of the men holding me. It doesn't really matter how the rest of the fight happened. I made it out alive."

"I have a feeling the other men did not." Grantham speculated.

"No, they were not as fortunate as I."

Penelope watched both men turn to look at her as if waiting for her to faint at their words. "Gentlemen, you underestimate me. There are three less men in the world that will harm us. Please, carry on."

"Did you get any information out of them before they…expired?" Grantham asked delicately

"No."

"Dammit. So we have no idea who they were associated with."

"That's not true," Duncan said. "I know exactly where they came from."

"Oh? How's that?" Grantham asked.

"They were all employed by me."

"What?" Penelope asked. This time she had to swallow several times to keep the nausea at bay.

"All three of them worked here at the London house."

"Bloody hell," Grantham said. "That means—"

"Someone is now trying to kill the both of us," Duncan finished.

Penelope was quiet for a moment, trying to assimilate this new information. Finally, she spoke up, interrupting the men's conversation. "Helena thinks otherwise."

"What are you talking about?" Duncan asked.

"Helena wondered why someone would attack you, all of a sudden, if before they had only gone after the women you were married to or about to marry."

"It does seem strange," Grantham seconded. "Have you never had any sort of problem before?"

"No," Duncan answered.

"Curious," Grantham mused.

"And you're certain the men worked for you?"

"I hired them myself last year. We came to town for a few months. I had some business to attend to. There were some repairs that needed to be done to the town house and I hired on some extra help. They had good references."

"References can be forged."

"My gut tells me they were not bad when I hired them, and my gut is never wrong."

"It was this time," Penelope interjected, "and you almost paid the ultimate price."

"I believe that's all for now. We have to piece this together. If you come up with something else, let me know immediately, and I'll do the same."

"Of course." Duncan and Grantham shook hands. Penelope started to rise to show him out.

"You stay where you are," Grantham waved at her. "I'll find your dear, sweet Mrs. Jenkins to let me out," he said mockingly.

"Just stay clear of her pan," Penelope teased, eliciting a chuckle from Grantham.

"You don't tease with me anymore," Duncan accused Penelope after Grantham left.

"He doesn't irritate me," she argued.

"Is that a good thing or bad?"

"I don't know," she pressed on before he could say anything else. "Duncan, you could have been killed. The blood on that walking stick could have been yours. Whoever is responsible for this has to be stopped."

"I know. But for now, I need to do what the physician ordered."

"And what is that?"

"Rest, and I find I do that best when I have a beautiful blonde spitfire beside me."

"You are incorrigible," she said, but found herself lying cuddled next to him, her arm draped lightly across his waist. "Am I hurting you?"

"No."

"You wouldn't tell me if I were," she pointed out, tilting her head back to look in his eyes. He gave her a lopsided grin that caused her heart to gallop. She thought about her secret. How would Duncan feel knowing she carried the possible heir to the dukedom? Would that be the only reason he would want to marry her? He had left her bed every morning, and now that he was hurt, he was encouraging her to stay in bed with him. It seemed like in the boudoir was the only time they had a relationship, and she accommodated his request without hesitation. What did that make her?

"Relax, you're too tense."

"I think I have reason to be."

"Shh. Mrs. Jenkins isn't going to let anyone in, and Grantham is placing guards around the outside. Rest," he coaxed.

Exhaustion claimed her body, and she let herself relax against him. *Regardless, I want to be able to at least have the opportunity to show him I'm more than a body to keep him warm in bed.* Before she drifted off, she managed to cast a silent prayer heavenward, *Please, God,* please*, keep our little family safe. Amen.*

CHAPTER 24

Duncan was with her two weeks. During that time, she fought a fever that ravaged his body, as well as cared for his wounds. They talked when he was awake and lucid and held each other at night. Penelope knew it wouldn't last forever, but she was still shocked when she walked in with a tray of food one afternoon to find him sitting on a tufted bench with curved arms. He had his trousers on and was fighting with a boot. His shirt was draped beside him as was the cravat.

It was late afternoon and her stomach was firmly under control. She was only sick in the mornings and had successfully hidden that fact from Duncan. Another thing she had found was that she wanted Duncan to the point of madness. Perhaps it was lying in his arms every night, smelling his masculine scent. Whatever it was, she was tired of fighting it and keeping her passion banked. *What does it matter?* She thought. *I'm already a fallen woman.*

"Where do you think you're going?" she asked. She shut the door then placed the tray on a chest of drawers.

"I have to report home before they become suspicious."

Her stomach flipped at his words. He was going to walk into danger, not knowing friend from foe. Stubborn, stupid man. He stomped on his second boot, grabbed the cravat, and draped it around his neck. He was just pulling the shirt up one arm when Penelope walked up to him and halted his progress. She tugged the shirt off and tossed it out of his reach.

"I don't think you should go anywhere," she said and pushed him backwards until he was forced to sit back down. "I don't believe you are well enough yet. Besides, you sent word that you were called out of town on business."

"I'm feeling much better," he argued lamely. "And I need to find out who threatened our lives."

"Grantham is on the case, is he not?"

"Yes."

"Do you not want to stay with me? Is a fortnight all you can stand to be with me?"

"No, it's not that at all," he argued, his hands reached out to cradle her hips.

"Then what is it?"

"Being so close to you but not able to make love to you is driving me insane."

"Why aren't you able to make love to me?"

"Because you act as if you don't want me to touch you, let alone make love to you."

Penelope took a moment to think about the last week. Had she acted that way? If she had, it had been to protect him. He had been injured and was recovering. Despite what he thought, he had not been up to strenuous activity of any type. Perhaps he still wasn't, but seeing him as he was, naked from the waist up, had Penelope's fingers tingling to touch him. "I was looking after you."

"If I wanted looking after, I would seek out my aunt. Bloody hell, Penelope, I want a wife and lover, not a mother."

"Perhaps you should lean back," she said taking a step towards him while she slowly pulled up the skirt of her lavender dress.

"Why?" he asked skeptically.

"Because you look a bit flushed."

"Penelope, I told you—"

"Damn you, Duncan Taggart, why can't you just do as your told?" In frustration, Penelope pushed him backwards so that he now reclined against the arm of the bench. It creaked under his shifting form. She worried her lower lip a moment, but decided to throw caution to the wind. She crawled onto the bench on her knees and it creaked once more.

"Perhaps this bench wasn't made for a man of my size," Duncan said.

"I don't care. I have you where I want you and I'm not letting you go," she purred. Penelope grabbed the cravat hanging loose around his neck and pulled him towards her. She shifted closer and allowed her dress to shift lower, showing off the growing fullness of her breasts. Duncan must have noticed as well, for his groan reached her ears. A smile flirted with her lips before she captured his mouth with hers. He made her work for what she wanted, but she finally succeeded in breaking through the barrier of his lips. The moist cavern of his mouth was everything she remembered it had been. She held onto both ends of the cravat with one hand while she threaded her fingers through his dark hair and cupped the back of his head. It felt like they were starving, for soon they were devouring one another.

Penelope was so lost in the kiss that she didn't realize he had been working on the buttons of her dress until she felt the cool air caress her fevered skin. She jerked in pain when he pinched her pert nipples. Her breasts were tender, and what he had meant to be alluring had hurt.

"Softer," she whispered against his ear before nibbling and suckling his earlobe.

"Like this?" he asked, brushing a kiss against one of her alabaster globes.

"Yes," she replied.

"And this?" he asked, laving one tip with his tongue.

"Yes," she sighed, and quickly pulled her arms free of the dress so it slithered down her body to bunch about her waist.

"And what of this?" he asked as he latched onto her and gently suckled.

"Oh, my, yes," she moaned, throwing her head back. She gripped his shoulders, digging the tips of her nails in. Penelope blushed as she felt herself growing wet. He moved to her other breast and gently manipulated the one he just left with his hand. She lifted up while he scooted down a bit. Penelope took the opportunity to lower herself. She felt the ridge of his manhood press against her through his breeches, enticing her, beckoning her.

She shifted backwards so that she could reach the buttons on the placket of his breeches. She broke her connection with him long enough for him to pull the dress up and over her body.

Penelope watched it go flying through the air. "Lift up a bit," she ordered. He did and she pulled his breeches down to his upper thighs, allowing his shaft to jump towards her in greeting. She wrapped a hand around it and squeezed firmly.

"You're killing me," Duncan moaned.

"But in a good way?"

"A very good way. Here, allow me to make you ready."

"Trust me, I'm more than ready." Penelope leaned forward and kissed him, then pulled away. She raised up on her knees and braced herself against one of his shoulders. She felt his hands convulsively squeeze her waist as she lowered herself downward. Penelope kept her brown eyes open and stared into the depths of his deep blue ones. He filled her so deeply this way. Once she was fully impaled, they stayed that way a few moments, merely watching each other. Then Penelope twisted her hips, eliciting a groan from her lover. He attempted to move too, but she halted him. "You let me do the work this time," she said, still gripping his shoulders. "You're still recovering."

"Pen," he said huskily.

She lifted herself and then lowered herself once more, taking all of him within her. She sighed when she felt his hands cup her breasts. His thumbs gently caressed her erect nipples. Penelope continued her slow dance of lovemaking, driving both Duncan and herself mad. "Duncan, help me," she begged as she felt her inner muscles begin to respond.

"How's this?" he asked, manipulating the sensitized bundle hidden at the top of her cleft.

Penelope couldn't speak for the sensations washing over her. Her movements became frenzied as her body was awash with sensations. Shivers raced up and down her spine as she reached her completion, and a soft moan escaped her. She watched Duncan and saw the strain on his face. "Let go," she whispered, using her inner muscles to squeeze his shaft. Penelope felt his body rhythmically jerk upwards, driving him deeper into her causing her to gasp at the sensation.

"Did I hurt you?" he asked.

"No," she shook her head in the negative.

"Good."

He twisted his hips erotically, and she felt his seed explode within her causing her to climax once more. There was a suspicious creak, then they were falling to the floor. Once they had come to a stop, they lay awkwardly, half on the broken bench and half off. Somehow they had remained intimately connected through the short fall. Penelope felt him shaking beneath her.

"Are you all right?" she asked.

"This bench is definitely *not* made for this type of activity," he said, laughing.

"Well, it almost made it," she giggled before leaning forward to kiss him once more.

"What came over you?" he asked after a few moments.

"I decided you were right, I was keeping you at arm's length. Besides, I'm your mistress. Isn't seduction something a mistress should do?"

"Yes," he said, then shifted and slid free of her. He managed to get to his feet and pulled his breeches up, putting himself to rights. "You should get dressed."

He offered her his hand but she refused it. She grabbed her dress, stood, and dropped it over her body.

"You should put something on beneath that dress."

"Why? I'm not allowed to leave this house. I don't know why I even get dressed. You would prefer it if I stay naked and in bed anyway, wouldn't you?"

"I'm not arguing with you about this," Duncan said, pulling on his shirt and doing up the buttons.

"Of course not, you're going to go and put yourself in more danger instead."

"Penelope…"

"No, just go," she said.

"I'll be back in a few hours."

"Of course you will, and damn me, I'll be eagerly waiting for you and begging for your touch."

"Do you mean that?"

"I suppose you'll just have to come back and see for yourself, won't you?" She stepped away from him when he would have pulled her to him for a kiss. "Go."

"We're not through talking about this."

"Yes, we are. You've made your choice."

"Penelope, you know why I have to do this. I have to find the person threatening our future. I will not have your life at risk."

"And what of yours?"

"Mine doesn't matter."

"It does to me," she whispered to his retreating form. Penelope turned and walked across the room to the window so she could watch him leave, but the door never opened. She jumped when she felt a heavy hand land on her shoulder.

"I believe we have some things to discuss that are more important than dealing with my family for the time being," Duncan said.

"I..." The words to tell him he was going to be a father tickled the tip of her tongue.

"Yes?"

"I'm glad you decided to stay," she said instead.

"Me, too."

Duncan and Penelope sat downstairs at the small dining room table as Mrs. Jenkins brought food in for them to eat. Penelope filled her plate and quickly tucked into it, feeling ravenous for a change. Between bites, she managed to ask a question, "Who do you think hired those men that attacked you?"

"First things first, if you ever refer to yourself as my mistress again, I will take you across my knee and spank you until you are unable to sit down. You are my fiancée. Do you understand?"

Penelope arched her brow at him, in an attempt to gauge whether he would really spank her. She decided that yes, he probably would. "Yes."

"Excellent. Now, if I knew who hired those men, I would know who is behind this entire mess."

"I realize that. I just thought that perhaps you have some suspicions."

"I do."

"Well, what are they?" she asked when he acted as if he would say nothing more.

"Reese stands to gain the most from my death."

"Yes, he does, but I truly do not believe he is responsible."

"He's gotten to you, hasn't he? He seems to charm every woman I know, making them for—"

"Stop." She looked at this big, strong man. The man was a duke and oversaw an entire shire. People looked to him for his wisdom. He fought alongside his men against the press gangs to keep them safe. Many feared him, yet he felt like he lived in the shadow of his younger brother when it should be the other way around. Penelope pushed back her chair and walked to him, forcing him to push back his chair as well. She made herself comfortable on his lap. "Reese is nothing compared to you. I cannot fathom what made Isabelle choose Reese over you. Perhaps she was insane. Whatever it is, I'm infinitely glad that things have worked out the way that they have. You're mine, and I'm yours."

"Do you truly mean that?"

"Yes," she said without hesitation.

"Then marry me and there will be no more talk of this mistress business."

"No." She looked at him and watched his expression go from passionate to cold, felt his body go stiff where before he had been relaxed. She knew he wanted her to say yes, but she had too much at stake. Too much that he didn't know about. He gently, but politely, removed her from his lap. Penelope returned to her chair, picked up her fork, and pushed her food around her plate, her appetite once more diminished.

"You should eat."

"Why do you say that?"

"You feel like you've lost weight," he replied before taking a bite.

Penelope didn't know what to say and brought the fork to her mouth, but the food that had been delicious only minutes ago now tasted like sawdust.

"So tell me why you don't believe Reese is the culprit."

"He loves you," she answered honestly.

"I doubt that. We tolerate one another."

"No. I see the way he looks at you and admires you. You're his older brother. He wants to make you proud. I think it was very hard for him to choose between Isabelle and you."

"Not hard enough," Duncan responded bitterly.

"Dammit, Duncan, you cannot continue to live in the past. That's another reason I will not exchange vows with you. Until you let go of your bitterness and realize that, for whatever reason, those women were not meant for you, I refuse to be your wife merely because I am the only one that survived." He started to speak, but she barreled on, "Do you know what it does to me to hear you bemoan the loss of those women in your life over and over? I realize that they were important to you, but bloody hell, I want to be the most important, and until that happens, I *will* remain your *mistress*." In the midst of her tirade, Penelope had stood, pushed her chair backwards, and slammed her hands down on the table causing the dishes and utensils to rattle. Once she had finished, she spun and walked towards the exit.

"Where are you going?"

"To my room. I find I have an explosive headache."

"I changed my plans to stay with you."

"Don't you dare blame me for ruining this evening. All you want is something physical. I want, no I *need*, something more. I thought I could do this, but I can't. So you decide, it's your ghosts or me, but you had better decide quickly."

"And what's that supposed to mean?"

"It means that I have friends that care about me. Friends that will help me disappear."

"And what of your mother?"

"You are seeing that she is cared for. Besides, you heard her when we visited. She despises me because I'm neither Whitney nor Sam. I'm the worth that's embarrassing the family. I have no need to be rejected over and over. I'll take myself and my…" She paused, realizing she almost announced the news about the baby in the middle of her tirade. He would never let her go if he knew there was a babe on the way.

"Your what?" Duncan stood and stalked towards her.

"Just myself. I'll take myself and go where I can start anew. Where scandal will not follow me. Where I can be myself."

"You can't do that," he denied, grabbing her upper arm. "I won't allow you to do that."

"What do you care if I do? You have ghosts to keep you warm."

"What's going on in here?" Mrs. Jenkins asked, entering with a tray of scrumptious looking desserts. "All this yelling is not good for you, Miss Penelope."

"Trust me, the alternative is much worse," Penelope said through gritted teeth, using the distraction to jerk her arm free of Duncan's hold. "The food was delicious, but I am going to lie down."

"But you've hardly eaten."

"I'll eat later, when the company is more pleasant."

"I'm returning home then," Duncan threatened.

"Be certain that the target on your back is painted large enough that it is easy to see," she called over her shoulder as she climbed the stairs. She slammed the door to her room and shortly afterward heard a door slam downstairs as well. Penelope didn't make it to the bed. Her legs gave out, and she slid down the door, landing in a heap on the floor. She leaned her head backwards and looked upwards as silver tears glistened on her cheeks. "Dear Lord, please keep that stubborn man safe."

Duncan left Penelope behind, blinded with anger. How could she throw the fact that she thought of herself as nothing more than a mistress in his face? Then she accused him of not having gotten over the women in his past. Was he ever going to get her to realize that she meant so much more to him than they ever did?

He pushed the thoughts warring within his mind away and instead focused on the fact that someone was trying to kill them. Someone he was close to. Someone who lived in his house. Someone who befriended his wives and fiancée. Reese. First he stole Isabelle away from him, then he lured the others…

Stop and listen to yourself, he accused. *You're blaming your brother because...because why? Are you jealous of him?*

"Yes," he mumbled the reply.

Why? Thoughts swirled around Duncan's mind as he tried to make sense of his anger and jealousy. He walked aimlessly among the London streets before he came to a stop and turned slowly around to determine where he was. A man stumbled out of the door of the house on his left.

"I don't want to see you for a few weeks. Your ribs are bruised pretty good. Did you hear me?" A very fit man called from the doorway.

"Aye, Jackson, I heard ye. Two weeks."

"Perhaps more."

"Aye," the man hoisted himself into a carriage with a groan.

"Are you drunk or lost?" the man in the doorway asked Duncan.

"Lost, I suppose, since I only had a bit of wine with my meal."

"Ah. I'm John Jackson. Which direction can I point you to?"

"Gentleman Jackson?"

"Aye."

"I need to hit something."

"We were just closing…" The famous pugilist halted and studied Duncan a moment. Duncan almost understood what insects must feel like under a magnifying glass, to be inspected so closely and thoroughly. "Come with me."

"Thank you," Duncan sighed, following the man.

"Don't thank me yet. Have you boxed before?"

"No, but I've been in plenty of fisticuffs."

"Good enough. Arnold, get your gloves on." The man led him to a bench along one wall. "Strip to the waist."

Duncan did as he was told.

"Hold out your hands." The man first wrapped his hands in a thin cloth then tugged on some sort of leather gloves. "These'll protect your hands. We use them in practice."

"Fine."

Jackson went over the rules with Duncan while he took care of the gloves. "Do you understand the rules?"

"Yes."

"Good. Albert, this is—" he looked at Duncan expectantly.

"The Du…Duncan."

Jackson looked at him strangely for a moment then carried on. "Duncan, Albert. Have a good, clean fight." The two men knocked gloves then Duncan was stalking his prey. The other man seemed light on his feet, bouncing and ducking, while Duncan just advanced. He swung, and his glove glanced off Albert's chest. Duncan saw a fisted glove coming towards his face. He ducked just seconds before it would have made contact. He came up and delivered a right hook to the man's stomach, causing him to wheeze as the air was forced from his lungs. Duncan took the advantage and stood, landing a left cross on the man's chin. Albert was now both winded and dazed. Duncan sent his opponent to the floor after two more solid punches.

Duncan stood over Albert's prone figure, barely winded from his exertion. "How is he?" he asked, concerned.

"He'll be fine," John Jackson replied. "Where did you learn to fight like that?"

"Back home."

"Where's that?"

"Yorkshire."

"Interesting. Help Albert off the floor," he commanded some men standing around. "Tom, help me put my gloves on." Duncan watched Gentleman Jackson strip to his trousers and boots as well. Soon he was wearing a pair of gloves, too. "Let's see how you fair against me." Duncan must have looked at the man as if he had lost his mind, because the next thing he heard was Jackson saying, "Don't worry, boy, I'll go easy on you."

"I think that should be the other way around, sir," Duncan said before tapping his gloves against the great fighter's.

This time neither man danced backwards, warming up to the battle. Instead, both charged forward, gloved fists lifted protectively. For every blow landed, there was a counter-blow. Both men bobbed and weaved, evading the other, all the while landing significant hits. As time slipped by, neither man noticed the growing crowd of men around them, or the exchange of money as bets were being placed. There was a great amount of cheering and yelling going on, sure to draw even more men in.

Finally, the battle came to an end with a draw, neither man winning. The crowd groaned almost collectively with only a few men cheering. Both contenders were bent over, gloved hands braced just above their knees, trying to catch their breath.

"Water," Jackson managed. The man who had helped him earlier fought his way through the crowd carrying a bucket and a tin cup. Jackson nodded at him, and the man dipped the cup before holding it up to Jackson's lips so he could drink. When he was finished, he nodded in Duncan's direction. Duncan gratefully drank of the refreshing water. The two men made their way through the crowd to a bench where they both sat and leaned back against the wall for support. Jackson held his hands out for Tom to remove his gloves. "Where'd all these men come from?"

"Some were next door, and others were passing by. Then when they realized who was fighting, I heard someone say they were running down to White's to place a bet. I guess they brought the betting here," Tom answered.

"So it would seem," Duncan chuckled. The crowd had started to dissipate when Duncan next held out his hands for the gloves to be removed.

"You say your name is Duncan, but I have a feeling there's more behind that name. I've sparred here before and not drawn a crowd like this. So, come clean, who are you?"

He waited until his hands were free of the bulky gloves then turned to face Jackson. "I'm Duncan Taggart, Duke of Yorkshire. Now, if you had known, you would have gone easier on me, and I didn't want that."

"Perhaps, Your Grace. That is until you started to kick my arse. Then I would have had to fight back to save face. It was a pleasure fighting you. Not many men can say they fought Gentleman Jackson and remained on their feet."

"Well, add me to your small, but elite list," Duncan said, holding his hand out for the other man to take and shake. "Thank you for treating me like someone who just walked off the street."

"That's exactly who you were, Your Grace. Any time you'd like to have another go at it, you know where to find me."

Duncan arrived home late after going to White's with Jackson and having drinks. He was definitely not completely sober as he knocked on the door.

The butler greeted him in surprise. "Your Grace, we didn't expect you home. We thought you were in Yorkshire."

"That's just what I wanted everyone to think," Duncan whispered loudly, tapping a finger against his temple and winking.

"Your Grace, are you drunk?"

"I hope so," he replied before weaving towards the stairs.

"Should I help you upstairs?"

"I'll help him," Reese said, coming from a room off the hall.

"So you can push me down the stairs and inherit the title? No thanks," Duncan gripped the bannister and began pulling himself upwards. He turned awkwardly when he saw Reese move behind him. "I can make it up the stairs by myself."

"I have no doubt," Reese said, holding his hands up in the air.

Duncan turned and started his forward progression once more. Halfway up, he was hit by a wave of dizziness. He wavered and started falling backwards when he felt two large hands firmly plant themselves against his back and give him a shove forward. This process was repeated several more times before he reached the top of the stairs. He made his way down the hall and fought with the doorknob on his bedroom door. Suddenly the door was opening just as he had decided to take a moment to lean against it. He went stumbling across the room, landing face down on the big bed.

He felt his coat being pulled off of him before he was rolled over onto his back. A random thud echoed in his ears followed by another. Then someone was putting a noose around his neck. No, he wasn't ready to die. He had to protect Penelope. Had to marry her. Show her she was the only one that mattered. Duncan started slapping at the hands, tightening the noose.

"Dammit, Duncan, stop. I'm trying to get this bloody cravat from around your neck."

Duncan opened his eyes and saw his brother standing above him. "Trying to kill me."

"Haven't you figured it out yet? If I wanted to kill you, I could have done it a hundred times over by now. Lie still," he ordered.

Duncan did as he was told and heard a rip.

"Damn, I nicked you, but it was the easiest way to get that damned cravat off you," Reese said, pulling the ripped garment free. "I don't know what ham fisted clod tied it, but if it was your valet, you should really seek out someone new."

"Protect Penelope," Duncan managed.

"What in bloody hell are you talking about?"

"She thinks I can trust you."

"When did you see her?" Reese asked, shocked.

"Doesn't matter. Just keep her safe. If something should happen to me."

"Nothing's going to happen to you."

"Almost did," Duncan said as the affects of the drinks he had imbibed in finally overpowered him.

"What are you talking about?" Reese's demand fell on deaf ears. He left Duncan's side only long enough to retrieve his gun from his room. He settled in for the rest of the night to watch over his older brother.

CHAPTER 25

Duncan woke to a pounding head and an aching body. Early morning sun streaked through the windows causing him to squint and look away. What he saw propelled him from the bed. His body crashed into his brother's, breaking the chair and sending them both sprawling. The gun that had moments before lay glinting dangerously in Reese's lap, now skittered across the floor and beneath the washstand in the corner.

"Get off me!" Reese yelled just before a fist made contact with his chin. "Oomph," he grunted.

"You thought to kill me while I slept?" Duncan fisted his hands in Reese's shirt and pulled his shoulders up off the floor. "Why, dammit? Were the others not enough? Are you that desperate for the title?"

"What are you talking about?" Reese managed to get out before Duncan slammed him against the floor.

There was a tentative knock at the door. "Go away!" both men yelled.

Reese fisted his hands together and slammed them into Duncan's sore ribs. Knocked off-guard, and in pain, Duncan released Reese and fell to his side. Reese took the opportunity to scoot out of Duncan's reach. "Now why don't you tell me what the bloody hell is going on?"

"You had a gun," Duncan accused.

"Because I was protecting your sorry arse," Reese answered.

"Why?"

"Bloody hell if I know. I thought I was doing you a favor." He rubbed his jaw and started to stand.

"Wait," Duncan stopped him while pushing himself into a sitting position. He groaned as his body protested any move.

"What is it?"

"Someone hired some thugs to attack me a fortnight ago. They very well could have killed me. Then on the way home last night, I had the brilliant idea to fight Gentleman Jackson."

"Bloody hell, Duncan, why didn't you send for me? You haven't been away on business have you?"

Duncan studied his younger brother and saw genuine concern on his face. "No, I haven't been away on business, I've been recovering."

"Where?"

"I bought a small house here in London for Penelope. I've been there," he answered hesitantly.

"So you did find her that night in the park?"

"Yes."

"You lied to me."

"Dammit, Reese, I didn't think I could believe you, trust you. You stole one woman from me," Duncan accused.

"Yes, Duncan, *one*. One woman that was ripped from my arms, too. I refuse to spend the rest of my life begging you for forgiveness. *I. Loved. Her.* I still do. There isn't a day that goes by that I don't think of her. Can you say that?"

"No," Duncan answered.

"You sound shocked."

"I am."

"Who do you think of every day? Who consumes your mind so that it makes it difficult to function normally throughout the day? Is it Samantha or Frances?"

"No."

"Then who, Duncan? If it isn't any of them, who is it? Who is the one that just the thought of losing her knocks the breath out of you, making you wonder how you would ever survive without her?"

Duncan closed his eyes and leaned his head back against the door as a blonde infiltrated his thoughts. She thought she was plain, but to him she was beautiful. He admired the way she stood up to him when others cowered. The way she looked lying beneath him caught in the throes of passion. The way her brown eyes sparkled with chips of gold—icy, warm, sensuous, and sometimes dangerous. His breath hitched as he felt her hand move towards him to caress his cheek, but when he opened his eyes she wasn't there. He knew a disappointment like he had never known before.

"Who put that look on your face? And I pray to God above that you say the right name, because if you don't I just may have to—"

"Penelope, dammit. It's Penelope. She's everywhere. Things I see, certain smells, specific sounds. Bloody hell, even things I touch remind me of her."

"Good. Now that you've admitted that much, we have something to work with."

"What are you talking about?"

"Your marriage is null. Penelope completes you. There is a difference about you when she's around, a calmness. So the important question is how are you going to woo her?"

"I don't have time to think about that right now. I'm more concerned about keeping us both alive."

"Both?"

"Don't tell me you think it was merely a coincident that Penelope's maid was poisoned? That I lost two wives and a fiancée? That I was attacked, beaten, and if not for a little bit of luck on my part, I might be the one lying dead in the bowels of London."

"Since we have determined it isn't me, who do you think it is?"

"The only other people it could be is Rosalie or Lucy."

"You have to be joking. They're family."

"Family has been known to be murderers before."

"I suppose so," Reese said, still sounding shocked.

"The men who attacked me worked for me here."

"You're kidding," Reese scoffed. When he saw the serious look on Duncan's face he blew out a resigned sigh. "What do we do?"

"I need them out of the house for a while. I need to bring Grantham in to do a search."

"What do you think he'll find?"

"Answers, hopefully."

"Tell me what you want me to do."

"Tomorrow I want you to surprise them with a shopping trip. Take them wherever they wish to go. Buy them whatever they wish to spend money on. Just keep them away for as long as you can. Remember, this is a surprise. I don't want them to be able to leave with anything important."

"Of course."

"And until we find something, we have to be better actors than those on Drury Lane."

"Understood."

Both men got to their feet, Duncan a bit slower than Reese. Reese retrieved his gun and crossed the room to the door.

"Reese," Duncan said, halting his brother before he opened the door. Reese turned and looked at him questioningly. "I never should have doubted you."

"That goes both ways, big brother."

"Duncan, we thought you were away on business," Rosalie said, looking up from her needlework. She and Lucy was in the parlor when Duncan put in his appearance.

"I arrived late last evening."

"I told Mama I heard you and Reese upstairs fighting in your bedchamber."

"A brotherly argument," Duncan scoffed.

"You sounded as if you were going to slaughter one another," Lucy argued.

"You worry too much, little one," Duncan said. He crooked a finger beneath her chin and tilted her head backwards, placing a kiss on her smooth forehead. He then dropped a kiss on Rosalie's cheek before sitting down to visit with the two women. "What plans do you have for today?"

He studied the two women who had lived under his roof for years as they prattled on about their plans. Could one of these two women be responsible for the deaths of four women? And if so, to what purpose? Until he could get Penelope to marry him, Rosalie would continue being the Duchess of Yorkshire. She could not earn a higher title for herself without marrying a prince or a king and either option was highly unlikely. Perhaps she was looking to push Lucy into a title.

"And just how many suitors are coming around?" Reese asked upon entering the room and bringing Duncan back to the present. He, too, dropped a kiss first on Lucy's brow then Rosalie's.

"Enough to keep me entertained," Lucy replied saucily. "Are you jealous?" she asked teasingly, leaning towards Reese.

"I'll always be jealous of any man that gets to spend the rest of his life with you," Reese said, giving the girl a wink.

"Oh, Reese," Lucy said, swatting playfully at his arm. "And what of you, Duncan?"

"What is that?"

"Are you jealous of the men who come to pay court to me?"

"Consider me more the concerned older brother making certain that the men coming around are good enough for our Lucy."

"Duncan, have you had any luck finding Penelope?" Rosalie asked, looking up from her needlework.

"No. She's hiding well, wherever she is."

"Has her grandfather not seen her?"

"Oh, yes, he saw her and promptly dismissed her, but not before she gave him his comeuppance," he said with a grin. "He's a miserable old man and only cares about his title and his money. He's a miser that has run off all his family."

"He sounds just lovely," Lucy said sarcastically.

"You've no idea. Well, if you all will excuse me, there are things I have to attend to."

"Duncan, there is a party later this week that the entire family has been invited to. It would be nice if both you and Reese could attend and escort Lucy and me."

"Rosalie, I would enjoy nothing more," he bowed low before leaving the room. He made his way to his study and had a footman he passed in the hall send for Bolingbroke's former butler, Giles.

"Your Grace, you sent for me?"

"Come in and shut the door, Giles."

"Yes, Your Grace."

"I have a note I need delivered. I only want you or the footman that came with you from Bolingbroke's house to deliver it."

"I'll deliver it myself, Your Grace. If I may ask, have you been able to find Miss Penelope?"

Duncan nodded his head in the affirmative as he said, "Unfortunately, no."

Picking up on the fact that he did not want his find verbalized, the butler said, "Oh, that is too bad, Your Grace. I know you'll find her."

"Thank you," Duncan said. He lowered his voice before continuing, "Tomorrow, my brother is going to take the ladies shopping. As soon as they leave, I want the house cleared of servants."

"Of course, Your Grace."

"It should be a surprise to them that they have the day off. No more than five minutes time to gather the things they'll need for a day out."

"I understand perfectly, Your Grace."

"Excellent. That will be all, Giles."

"Yes, Your Grace." The butler bowed and left the room.

Duncan sat at his desk, fingers steepled, and head pounding. He was ready to put this nightmare behind them and move on with their lives.

"Helena, I'm so glad to see you," Penelope said, throwing her arms around the woman who had befriended her and taken her in.

"And what of me?" Helena's identical twin asked.

"Agatha, I didn't see you there. Of course, I'm glad to see you, too. Come in," she ushered the women in after giving Agatha a welcoming hug, as well.

"We came to check on our nephew," Helena said.

"He left yesterday. We got into an argument when he said he was returning home. I thought it would be too dangerous and well…"

"He's a man and said he could handle the situation," Agatha finished.

"Yes. I might have said some things in anger, but he didn't come back here last night, and I've been worried that something might have happened to him again."

"I'm certain he's fine," Agatha said.

"Yes," Helena chimed in. "Now, for what we really came for. Agatha wants to introduce you to some of her friends since you are to become part of our family."

"Oh, I don't know about that. I don't think that would be very wise. My family is now considered outcasts to the *ton*."

"But you are going to be a duchess," Helena interjected. "You have no idea what a title of such magnitude will do in swaying people's opinions."

"If they didn't want to be my friend before, I don't care to be their friend after I marry Duncan. *If* I marry Duncan."

"Don't speak in such a manner," Agatha chastised her. "Of course you and Duncan will marry and make us great-aunts many times over."

"Who told you?" Penelope whirled on Agatha, demanding an answer. The woman's words had caught her off guard, and she realized too late that she had meant nothing by it.

"What's gotten into you, Penelope?" Agatha asked.

"Oh, dear," Helena said. "Come, sit down," she took Penelope's shaking hand and led her to the settee so that she was sandwiched between the sisters. "Penelope, are you going to have a baby?"

"Mrs. Jenkins believes I am," she said with a sniff.

"But this should be a time of great joy," Agatha said.

"You've never been an unmarried woman expecting a child," Helena explained to her sister.

"It's not even that," Penelope said, "well, not completely."

"What else is it?" Agatha asked.

"What if I have to raise the baby by myself because he gets himself killed?" she asked, verbalizing her fears for the first time.

"Oh, dear, everything will be just fine, you'll see. Duncan has always taken care of the family since inheriting the title," Agatha defended her oldest nephew.

"Yes, he was able to protect three women very well, wasn't he? And what of the other night? Any other man would have been killed."

"But he wasn't," Agatha countered.

"And he might not be so lucky next time. For that matter, I might not be so lucky. And I was being poisoned and didn't know I was pregnant. What if it did something to the baby?"

"Now you're just borrowing trouble," Helena said. "You take one day at a time, do you understand me? That's all you can do."

"Have you told Duncan?" Agatha questioned her.

"No. He has enough to worry about. Mrs. Jenkins is the only other person that knows."

"And she can be trusted with the information?" Helena asked.

"Yes, she used to be Duncan and Reese's nanny."

"Then she will take excellent care of you. Now, no more crying, everything will work out just fine. A baby! It has been so many years since there's been a baby in this family. Oh, I can hardly wait," Agatha exclaimed, clapping her hands excitedly. "Now about that party tomorrow."

"I don't think I should—"

"You definitely should. You will be entering your confinement before you realize it. You need to get out and enjoy yourself before that happens," Agatha said.

"If you insist."

"Of course, I insist. I want Helena to join us, but she has some silly notion about not going out without her dear Henry, and of course, he's still observing the period of mourning for his late wife."

"And what are you doing tomorrow night since you won't be with us?" Penelope asked, wiping at her damp eyes with her embroidered handkerchief.

"Just staying in," Helena replied, a sparkle in her eye.

"I think you're planning something," Penelope said,

"Perhaps, but for now it's my secret. I will share it when it's time. Now, let's go upstairs and decide what dress you are going to wear tomorrow night."

The ladies stood and left the small parlor, arm-in-arm. As they passed the kitchen, the sound of rattling dishes reached their ears. "Excuse me a moment." Penelope stepped inside the kitchen. The smell of yeast tickled her nose and humming reached her ears. "Mrs. Jenkins."

"Oh, Miss Penelope, you frightened me half to death, you did." The older woman had a hand pressed against her chest.

"I'm sorry for that. Miss Helena and Lady Agatha are here. I was hoping you could fix us a tea tray and bring it to my room."

"Of course, Miss Penelope. Right away."

"No rush." Penelope walked out of the kitchen and rejoined the ladies. "Shall we?" she asked and led the way up to her room. The women spent the rest of the afternoon deciding what dress and accessories Penelope would wear to the party. By the time she walked them to the door, she was changing her mind about attending.

Helena looked at her and tightly gripped her hands. "Agatha is right. You need to get out of here for a while. I'll come by tomorrow afternoon to help you get ready, that way you can't back out."

"Thank you, both of you," she hugged them tightly together. "I've never had, well…" she broke off before regaining her composure. "My mother and I aren't very close," she said, remembering the words her mother spewed at her.

"That's just fine, because I find myself lacking in children," Helena said, dropping a kiss on her cheek. Penelope looked up to see the older woman's eyes bright with unshed tears.

"And I have no nieces whatsoever."

"But you have a daughter."

"A daughter who would desperately like the attention I shower on her placed somewhere else, especially when she thinks she is going to be sneaky about something. I swear, she and Grayson are going to be the death of me." She opened the door and called over her shoulder, "I'll see you tomorrow night. Remember the Jersey affair is always the most talked about of the season."

"I'm already sick to my stomach just thinking about it. To parade myself in front of Lady Jersey, one of the preeminent matriarchs of the *ton*. I don't think I can do it."

"You can and you will. Sarah only attacks other people so she can keep them from bringing up her infidelities. Keep your chin up, all will be well. Besides, her parties have become boring the last few years. It's time they got a little exciting."

"All right," Penelope agreed, laughing nervously.

"Davis and I will be by to pick you up."

"If you're certain you want to do this."

"I've never been more certain of anything in my life."

"I'll see you both tomorrow." She waved the women off, unaware they were being watched. "Mrs. Jenkins, I'm going for a walk."

"Oh, you shouldn't go by yourself. Let me get my shawl and I'll go with you."

"All right," Penelope said, stepping outside. The weather was beautiful, and she purposefully left her bonnet inside. It felt wonderful to feel the sunshine filtering through the light clouds. She took a breath and missed the smell of the salt water on the breeze. How had she become so attached to Yorkshire in so little time?

"Ready when you are, Miss Penelope."

The two women began walking after Mrs. Jenkins locked up the house.

"Mrs. Jenkins, do you know where my mother's house is?" The woman remained silent, a look of consternation slipping over her face. "You do, don't you?" Again, silence, and the little woman kept moving onward. The two continued walking in companionable silence. When they had walked quite a while, Penelope said, "Take me to my mother's house."

"Master Duncan would not like that. He told me what your mum did during your visit with her."

"*Master Duncan* is not here, I am. I have some things I need to say to my mother. Please, Mrs. Jenkins."

"All right, but if Master Duncan asks—"

"I promise to take full responsibility," she said.

"This way then," Mrs. Jenkins said reluctantly as they turned a corner.

Penelope had known their houses were close, but she hadn't realized just how close. She followed Mrs. Jenkins up the stairs. The older woman knocked on the door, and it opened a few minutes later.

"Janice, what are you doing… Oh, Miss Presley, it's a pleasure to see you again," the housekeeper from her earlier meeting with her mother greeted them.

"I tried to talk her out of coming," Janice Jenkins said.

"Of course you did, but some things have to be said, isn't that right, Miss Presley?"

"Yes," Penelope said, her voice barely a whisper.

"Your mother is in the parlor and quite lucid today. Nurse Dixon is with her."

"Thank you."

"Come with me, Janice. I'll pour us a cup of tea."

Penelope waited until the women had left the foyer. The palms of her hands were sweating and she rubbed them along the folds of her dress. She straightened her spine before she entered the room. "Hello, Mother. Nurse Dixon, would you mind stepping into the hallway for a moment. I'd like to speak to my mother alone."

The nurse looked concerned, but readily agreed.

"They say you're quite lucid today, so no need to stare out the window and pretend I'm not here," Penelope said. She braced herself for the full anger of her mother's glare when she turned to stare at her.

"What is it you want?"

"I'm here to forgive you."

"For what? I have no need for forgiveness from a slut such as yourself."

"I forgive you for listening to other people above your own child. I forgive you for always loving Whitney and Sam more than me. But most of all, I forgive you for being a terrible mother, for you have shown me what not to be with my own children."

"Get out of here."

"Not before you know that there are people in this world that love and care about me more than you ever did. Women that are willing to be my mother because they *love* me. Women that see past my faults and love me anyway. I am sorry you have chosen to hate your own child, for you are not just removing me from your life, but also any future grandchildren."

"I'm too young to be a grandmother," she scoffed.

"You're *not*," Penelope said meaningfully, staring at the woman who had given her life.

"You…you…" she sputtered.

"I merely stated a fact," Penelope said. "I will see that Duncan keeps you in this house and continues to see to your needs, because you did the same for me for twenty years. I do want to thank you for giving me life, but you will never see me again. It's better this way."

"I despise the fact that it was my sweet Whitney that perished that day and not you, and that the blood of this family will be carried on through the bastard you carry in your belly."

"Don't you think I know that?" Penelope asked, refusing to give into the tears pricking the backs of her eyes. Her hand twitched with the urge to slap her mother. "I just wonder why? I loved Whitney, too, but she was selfish and took and took and took. All I ever did was help the family. I gave up my entire Season, except that one ball for her to make a match."

"She was older," her mother said.

"By *five* minutes. No, you are not going to do this to me. I'm not going to argue with you. I hope the rest of your life is uneventful and without pain. Goodbye, Mother." Penelope walked out as something crashed to the floor and shattered, followed by a string of expletives. "Mrs. Dixon, I believe you are needed."

"What happened?" Mrs. Jenkins asked as she waited in the hallway.

"Something long overdue. I'm ready to return home."

"Yes, Miss Penelope."

The two women left the house. They rounded the corner and the full impact of what she had done struck Penelope fully. She had completely cut ties with her family. Well, Sam was still out there somewhere, but who knew where he was. For all intents and purposes, she was alone. Utterly and completely alone. And if something happened to Duncan… She began to shake uncontrollably at the thought.

"Miss Penelope, are you all right?" Mrs. Jenkins' voice seemed to come to her from a long tunnel. Her vision got fuzzy at the outer edges. She took a step and stumbled. "Miss Penelope!" The last thing she saw was an angry looking beast of a man stalking towards her, then everything went blissfully dark.

CHAPTER 26

What the bloody hell happened?" Duncan asked as he scooped an unconscious Penelope up in his arms just before she crashed to the ground. "Why are the two of you outside?"

"She fainted, Master Duncan. She wanted to go for a walk and considering her con…"

"Her what?"

"Nothing, Your Grace," she said using his official title and not her moniker for him in her agitation.

"What are you hiding from me, Nanny Jenkins?" Duncan demanded.

"Not here. Bring her into the house," she said. He followed her inside. "Take her upstairs," she ordered. "I'll bring some tea and biscuits right up."

Duncan carried his precious cargo up the stairs. He studied her face and could see the lines of stress that had etched themselves into her features. He had done this to her. By choosing her as a bride, he had done this to her. He nudged open the door to her room and carried her to the bed. He dragged a chair over and sat beside her, taking her hand in his.

"Duncan?" Penelope's eyes fluttered open.

"How do you feel?" he asked, squeezing her hand.

"So tired," she whispered, closing her eyes once more.

Several long minutes later, Mrs. Jenkins entered the room with a tray.

"Has she not woken yet?" she asked worriedly, sitting the tray down.

"Briefly. She said she was tired and closed her eyes once more. Should I try to wake her?"

"No. Let the poor mite sleep. She's been worried half sick about you, and she had a tiff with her mother."

"Is that where the two of you were?"

"Yes. She said she had something she had to do. We were already out for a walk and she caught me off guard."

"Why did you leave this house? You know the danger she's under."

"And I know a person can go mad being kept prisoner, even if it is for their own safety. Come with me a moment."

"But, Penelope—"

"Will be fine. She fainted and now she's asleep. It's her body's way of saying she's had too much to deal with. Come, we must talk."

He watched his former nanny walk out, clearly expecting him to follow her. Duncan placed a kiss on the palm of Penelope's hand. He stood, removed her slippers off her feet, then pulled a light blanket over her. He bent over and brushed a kiss on her soft, pliant lips.

"Love you," she murmured on a dreamy sounding sigh.

He paused and studied her. Her lips had tilted up on one side in an adorable half-smile. His body was responding to her close proximity. Was she speaking of him? Why couldn't she say it when she was fully conscious?

"Wonderful father," she sighed before burrowing beneath the blanket.

He sucked in a breath. What was that supposed to mean? He had done nothing to prevent a child. They had thought they were legally married. Could there be a child on the way already? *No, she had her courses*, he reminded himself thinking back to the pile of soiled cloth he had found. There was a fine tremor to his hand as he reached out to shake her awake, to demand an answer.

"Master Duncan," Nanny Jenkins called from the doorway, waving him to follow her.

He followed on shaky legs, allowing Penelope's bedroom door to remain open enough so they could hear if she needed one of them. They reached downstairs and went into the kitchen.

Mrs. Jenkins poured something into a mug and brought it over to the heavy, wooden table.

"You're going to need this, I think." She added a dash of something from a bottle.

"Is she going to have a babe?" His words sounded shaky and hollow to himself.

"Yes, but how did you know?"

"She just said something in her sleep."

"Oh, dear. You look quite putrid. Take a drink," she ordered.

He did and felt the burn of whisky with just a little bit of tea trail down his throat. "I'm going to be a father." He lifted a shaky hand to his face and scrubbed it.

"You should be happy," Mrs. Jenkins said.

"I am, I think. I'm just frightened. Someone has tried to kill both of us."

"Tried and failed. That is what you need to focus on."

"My child will not be born a bastard," he said, conviction in his voice.

"She won't marry you until you find out who is threatening your lives. And she can't know that you know about the babe. She's not prepared for you to know yet. You must respect her wishes."

"But—"

"I know, you want to be a father more than anything."

"No, Mrs. Jenkins, I want to be married to Penelope and spend the rest of my life showing her how much I love her more than anything. The baby is going to be a wonderful bonus."

He watched his former nanny sit down across from him. "I was so worried."

"About what?"

"That you just wanted an heir, and Miss Penelope was a means to that. She's been through so much lately, she deserves to be loved for who she is."

"I agree."

"Your mother and father would be so proud of the man you've become. They were worried you were just marrying Isabelle to secure an heir."

"I was in a way. She was a good friend, and I didn't mind being married to her. I didn't have to leave Yorkshire. It was convenient...and wrong."

"And the others?"

"It was just to beget an heir, until I saw Penelope."

"What do you mean? I thought you were to marry her sister."

"I was, but I wanted to see what I was getting myself into. Word had traveled as far north as Yorkshire about Miss Whitney Presley. I was beginning to regret the agreement I had entered into, sight unseen. So, I traveled to London and attended a ball. Whitney was surrounded by men and shamelessly flirting with each and every one of them. She disappeared on several occasions, each time she returned she looked a little more worse for the wear, if you'll pardon my plain speaking."

"And that's what turned you away from Miss Whitney?"

"That and the quiet blonde that tried to fade into the background. She would notice Whitney missing, go find her, and bring her back. Each time the blond was given a tongue lashing by Whitney, but she ignored her and continued watching over her."

"I'm guessing the blonde was Penelope."

"Yes. I was instantly attracted to her," he said, feeling a flush creep across his face telling his old nanny all of this. "She was pretty, and from the conversations I overheard her involved in, she was intelligent. Whitney was vapid, or at least she acted that way. We all attended an opera the next evening. While Whitney entertained gentleman caller after gentleman caller, Penelope had nothing but eyes for the opera. Between acts she would surreptitiously wipe at her tears. Then her father killed himself, forcing me to write to her grandfather. I did everything but beg the man to be able to marry Penelope instead of her sister and was denied at every turn."

"Is that why you delayed the wedding initially?"

"Yes. I had hoped to use the period of mourning to wear the old man down. Then Whitney was killed, and well, matters took care of themselves."

"Have you told Miss Penelope this?"

"No. She wouldn't want to hear all this."

"I think she would. I'm not proud of it, but I eavesdropped on her conversation with her mother today. She's completely cut ties with the woman. She told her she would continue to ask that you see she's taken care of, but she has washed her hands of her. If you ask me, the woman didn't know what a wonderful daughter she had in Miss Penelope."

"I agree. I'm going to go upstairs. I'll make sure she eats when she wakes up if you will send a full tray up."

"Of course. Remember, you aren't supposed to know about the babe."

"Yes, ma'am." He winked and brushed a kiss on the older woman's brow. "Mrs. Jenkins, will you be our baby's nanny once it is born?"

"I would love nothing more, Master Duncan," the older woman said huskily.

He bounded up the stairs and let himself into her bedroom then firmly shut the door. He stood there for a long while, studying Penelope, the woman of his dreams, the love of his life, and the mother of his child. The emotions he felt threatened to overwhelm him.

He had a renewed sense of purpose to determine who was threatening his family. He would see that they paid for their sins and that his fledgling family remained safe from harm.

Penelope blinked her eyes open to almost total darkness. The faintest sliver of light from the moon spilled through the curtains. Heat emanated from behind her and she felt a heavy hand resting on her hip. She inhaled deeply and smelled Duncan's cologne on the air. She felt her body relax against his, and that's when she realized they were both nude beneath the covers.

Her eyes flew open at that thought, and her mind frantically ticked backwards as she tried to remember what had led her to this position. Helena and Agatha had come by. She and Mrs. Jenkins had gone for a walk. She went and saw her mother, and bid the woman who had given birth to her adieu for the last time. On the way home, the shock of what she had done had struck her, and then she had seen Duncan bearing down on them looking like an angry, hulking beast, and that was the last thing she really remembered.

Who had undressed her? Had she said anything she shouldn't have? Was everything all right with the babe? Her breathing suddenly became erratic, panicked.

"Shh, everything's all right," Duncan whispered against her ear as if he could read her mind.

She felt his calloused palm high on her abdomen, pulling her closer to him. His hair roughened chest caressed her smooth back and his growing erection nestled against her derrière.

"Do you know you scared years off my life when I saw you collapse?"

"I didn't really collapse," she argued, looking over her shoulder at him.

"You've been asleep for hours."

"I suppose I was exhausted. I haven't been sleeping well lately, what with worrying about everything."

"I'm sorry you are having to worry about any of this. This is not what I imagined our life would be like when we married."

Penelope opened her mouth to point out that they weren't married, but closed it once more. She refused to dwell on the negative of the situation any longer.

"You're so bloody beautiful," he whispered against her, taking her earlobe gently between his teeth and suckling.

Penelope angled her head to give him greater access to her ear and neck. Her breath hitched when she felt the arm beneath her body shift so that his hand could capture her breast. She bit her lower lip at the sensations that were washing over her. She felt him grow larger against her and her body grew excited. The hand that had been resting on her abdomen worked its way downward, dipping into her navel, teasingly. She felt his hand spread out, almost protectively over the area between her hips. No, that was just wishful thinking on her part. There was no way he could know he would be a father, that there, where his hand paused for just a moment, their child grew.

Then his hand was moving onward and all she could do was feel and relish the sensations. She sucked in a breath as his finger made contact with the spot that he already knew how to manipulate so well. Her hips wiggled as he slowly stroked that spot.

"Are you ready for me, my beauty?" he whispered enticingly in her ear.

She nodded her head, unable to make words form.

"What was that?"

"Yes," she moaned. Her skin felt like it was crawling in anticipation of what was to come.

"Are you certain?"

"Yes," she whispered hoarsely.

"You're going to have to help me. My hands are full at the moment," he said.

She turned her head and looked at him, shock registering on her face. "I ca—"

"Don't say you can't. I remember just a few days ago when you were very forceful in what you wanted."

"But not like this."

"Do you want more of this," he asked as he took her lips and teasingly dipped his finger into her wet, heated channel.

She moaned into his mouth and let her bottom push more fully against him. "Please," she begged against his lips.

"Move your right leg over mine."

She did and whimpered as this move allowed him to manipulate her more easily. "Now what?" she asked breathily.

"Take me in your hand and guide me home," he whispered as he kissed the nape of her neck.

She felt so close to exploding with every continued touch of his hands and his kisses. Penelope reached beneath the blanket, then she felt between them and wrapped her hand around his full arousal. She rubbed her hand up and down, slowly.

"You're killing me," he whispered against her ear.

"We wouldn't want that, would we?" she asked, and then she guided him where she needed him most. She lost her breath as he eased slowly into her. She tilted her hips slightly to take as much of him as she could and dug her short nails into his buttocks, pulling him tightly against her. He was everywhere, touching her, manipulating her body, and making it sing just for him. Then she was exploding, and the contractions of her channel were caressing him, but she could feel the tenseness in his body as she slowly relaxed. "You didn't…"

"No, my beautiful Penelope, that was for you and you alone. Now, we start all over because next time I will be with you, flying among the stars."

"You make me feel so special, and not just here," she waved her hand to encompass the bed. "No one has done that before," she whispered.

He pulled away from her, rolled her over onto her back and kissed her thoroughly, leaving her breathless. "But you are special, my beauty. In a thousand different ways, you are so incredibly special, and I plan on spending the rest of my life showing you." He ever so slowly slipped inside her once more and began to move within her, awakening her body to the delight of his touch again.

A long while later, after they were both sated, he pulled her close and wrapped his arms about her. They fell asleep, their fingers and bodies entwined.

The old man shuffled about the empty house. For the first time in his life, he didn't have servants to see to his every need. He had finally run everyone off. The only people that came around were those that he paid for their services. No one else wanted to be around him and the feeling was mutual.

A thick envelope lying on the floor of the foyer caught his eye. There was a wax seal, but nothing was embedded to give him an idea of where it came from. He flicked a yellowed nail beneath it, broke the seal, and removed a piece of folded paper. He opened it and quickly scanned the contents.

My lord,

It has come to my attention that your granddaughter will be attending Lord and Lady Jersey's ball tomorrow evening. I have included an invitation that will guarantee your admittance. I need your assistance removing her from my life. Please do not disappoint.

A friend.

The old man pulled free an invitation and several bundles of paper money.

"Rubbing shoulders with her betters, is she? That little slut will rue the day she came into my house and embarrassed me, then stole my servants and my silver. Thank you, friend.

Tomorrow night will be quite an entertaining evening indeed." He cackled like a maniac.

CHAPTER 27

"I can't believe we found nothing," Duncan railed. He and Grantham had spent the last few hours searching the house for any clue whatsoever that would tell them who was behind the killings.

"That's not true," Grantham countered.

"You have a handful of ashes you collected from a fireplace."

"I have a bucketful of ashes I collected from several fireplaces. There were also some pieces of paper in them. I'm hoping I can piece them together."

"And what's that going to do besides give you a puzzle to work on at night to keep you from being lonely?" Duncan snarled.

"I hope, *Your Grace*," Grantham said sarcastically, "to be able to come away with a clue that will aid us in determining who the killer is. Now, if you'll excuse me, I have other cases to see to."

Duncan watched the other man leave his study and then shortly heard the front door shut behind him. He walked over to his desk, ready to swipe all the items from it, then he paused as he considered the mess that would leave for the staff members. Suddenly he felt deflated and drained. He collapsed into the leather chair behind his desk. It creaked as it took on his large frame.

"Dammit," he said to the empty room. "Penelope, I promise you we will find the responsible party, then we will be able to live out our lives together free of worry."

Duncan didn't see the figure lurking in the shadows of the hallway or the sly smile that crossed the hidden face.

The next afternoon, Penelope attempted not to fidget while Helena worked on her hair.

"Calm down. You're going to be the diamond of the ball," Helena tried to soothe her.

"I doubt that. These people are going to be staring and pointing and whispering."

"About how beautiful you are."

"About my past. I can't do this," she said shivering. Her palms grew damp and beads of sweat appeared on her brow.

"Calm down this instant," Helena ordered.

"That's easy for you to say," Penelope said. "You get to stay home in the comfort of your house and spend the evening in Henry's arms. I have to face *them*, the *ton*."

"And you will do beautifully. Now close your eyes."

Penelope did as she was ordered and felt something wet drag across her upper lid near her lashes.

"Do not blink," Helena ordered once more.

Penelope did her best to obey. Something was rubbed roughly against her cheeks, then along her lips.

"There. No, do not look yet. Not until you are completely dressed," the older woman warned. Penelope remained where she was as she watched Helena retrieve a claret colored gown from the wardrobe. She helped Penelope into it and did up the buttons in the back. "These are going to look beautiful on you," she said as she opened a box.

Penelope saw a flash of diamonds lower before they were fastened around her neck. "It's too much."

"Stop arguing. They are mine to do with as I wish and I wish for you to wear them and enjoy them. You look gorgeous," Helena said as she attached ear bobs for her as well. "Now you may look in the mirror."

Penelope turned and took a few steps before she saw her reflection. Helena had performed pure magic with her hair. When she moved, her hair sparkled from the additional diamonds that had been strung through her updo. The twinkling was echoed at her ears and her throat. Her eyes had been rimmed with something that made them appear sensual, almost sleepy looking. And the dress made her look like a seductress.

"I can't wear this," she said, attempting to tug the low neckline up.

"You can and you will."

"I'm positively indecent."

"You are positively *beautiful.*" Helena walked closer and slapped at her hands. "Now, stop that." She righted the dress and readjusted the neckline.

"My breasts are going to spring free before the night is over."

"Only if my nephew lures you into a dark corner."

"Helena!"

"Is he going to be there?"

"We didn't talk about it," Penelope answered, blushing.

"If you aren't already with child, you will be soon. The pregnancy has made your breasts more abundant. It is one of the side effects of having children. The men will adore you, and the women will hate you."

Penelope studied herself in the mirror once more. "I can't do this," she said, her chest heaving with every nervous breath she took.

"You can."

"Why didn't I realize when I was younger that I disliked going out in society so much? Being stared at and judged is horrible."

"Perhaps you did."

"Why do you say that?"

"Didn't you say that after only a few parties, you let your sister be the one that the family indulged for such events?"

"Because she was the one most likely to make a successful match."

"I think you're not being completely honest with yourself. I also believe you underestimate yourself. Here are your gloves."

Penelope tugged on her gloves as she tried to push Helena's words from her mind. She watched as Helena clasped a diamond bracelet over the fabric of her glove and about her wrist.

"You're a beautiful young woman, and once you put my nephew out of his misery, you are going to make him a wonderful wife. I only wish I had had a daughter like you."

"Helena," Penelope whispered, tears misting her eyes.

"Now, none of that. We don't want you ruining what we've spent ages working on." A knock sounded below. "That'll be Agatha and Davis. Are you ready?"

"I suppose so," she said and followed the older woman out of her room and down the stairs. They entered the parlor to find Henry, Davis, and Agatha all politely chatting like they had been life-long friends. She halted, feeling like a deer caught in the hunter's line of sight. She worried her lower lip and wrung her hands in front of her.

"My darling Penelope, you look absolutely enchanting," Agatha gushed.

"I predict your dance card will be full within five minutes of walking in," Henry said.

"I do hope I won't have to call anyone out on your behalf," Davis said with a fatherly smile.

Their words made her relax.

"Are you all coming?" Bridget asked as she entered the house. She paused when she saw Penelope. "I don't know how I'm ever going to find a husband," she said, sounding forlorn. "All the men are going to be agog over you and not see any of us mortals. Aunt Helena, how did you manage to make her look like a goddess? Mother, I'm letting Auntie get me ready for my next ball."

"Over my—"

"We'll see," Agatha said over her husband's protest. "Now, shall we go?"

"Here's your cloak, dear," Helena said. Penelope allowed her to wrap a fine black wool cloak about her shoulders and secure it at her throat. "Enjoy your evening, love," Helena hugged her tightly and brushed a kiss on her cheek.

"I'll try." She gave the other woman a tremulous smile before she followed the others out of the house and into the waiting carriage.

Helena was wrapped in Henry's arms as they rattled down the street. She hoped that Penelope was able to relax enough to enjoy her evening. She had also meant what she had told her, she wished she had a daughter like her. If her nephew had anything to say about it, soon she would be her niece via marriage, and she could still dote on her. She would also see that, once the time came for the babe to be born, that she had the best care possible. Helena made a promise to herself that Penelope would not lose her child as she had and would be able to be the mother of many if she so chose.

"What's the matter?"

She could feel the vibration of Henry's chest when he spoke. "Just thinking."

"My solicitor gave me this the other day." He handed her an envelope.

"It's addressed to me."

"Yes."

"It's been opened."

"I read it. I'm not proud of my actions, but I had to know what it said. I didn't want it to upset you, but there's no way past it."

She looked at him warily as she pulled the letter free of the envelope. She tilted it so that she could read it by the swaying carriage lantern.

Dear Helena,

For years I hated you. Not because of your closeness with my husband, but because you had been lucky enough to find true love, and so had he. I married our dear Henry knowing he loved another and for years I let that turn me into a bitter woman. You see, I, too, was in love at one time, but my father would never have approved my marrying Thomas. He was the gamekeeper's son on my father's estate, and we had grown up together.

I found myself devastated by the fact that Henry, being a man, could easily be with the one that he loved while I was denied my darling Thomas. I ask two things of you, Helena. First, love Henry with your whole heart as I never could. He deserves to be happy as do you. You especially have suffered at the hands of society and all because you were unable to truly be with the man that you loved.

"I will," Helena said, as silent tears slipped down her cheeks. She blinked rapidly so that she could finish reading the words of the woman she had considered her rival for so many years.

Thomas and I have exchanged letters these many years. He never married for he said he couldn't when his heart had already been taken. Please deliver this final letter to him, and tell him that I died with his name on my lips and engraved on my heart. I ask that you take it to him, because he is the one that coaxed me into seeing you as a victim as much as we were after my horrible actions. I hate what society does to people.

"What horrible actions?" Helena asked.

"Keep reading."

I have left letters for my children, trying to explain to them my relationship with their father and urging them to follow their heart in their relationships. I have also told them that their father is a wonderful man. It is I they should despise for I have kept them from their family. I wish you and Henry all the love and happiness for all the rest of your days.

I also ask your forgiveness for what I am about to tell you. Your family truly thought you and the child died in childbirth. I alone was responsible for your placement in the asylum and all the lies, not your father. Also, your son is alive. Thomas can tell you where to find him. I am so sorry for keeping the three of you apart all these years. I have asked God's forgiveness. Now, I beg for yours.

Ruth

"No," Helena denied, shaking her head. "This can't be true."

"She wrote me a letter saying much the same thing," Henry said. "I have no reason to doubt a dead woman."

"No!" Helena screamed, letting everything she was feeling come out in that one word. She felt Henry's strong arms wrap around her. Their tears mingled together. She clutched her fingers in his coat lapels as if she would fall into an abyss if she let go.

Later, she wasn't certain if it was hours or minutes, she came back to herself. There was something different about the sounds she heard. She pulled away and looked out the window and saw darkness where she should have seen the lights of London.

"Where are we going?"

"To Gretna Green. I'm going to do what I should have done thirty-one years ago. I'm going to marry you, then we are going to find our son."

"But what about your children?"

"My children are old enough to tend themselves. They can be miserable if they want. I sincerely hope they take their mother's words to heart, but I am tired of living by society's dictates. You are the love of my life, and I wish to spend our remaining years together."

"I love you, Henry," she said.

"And I love you, my darling, beautiful Helena," he said, before he kissed her deeply and passionately.

Penelope wrung her hands the entire way to the ball.

"You have to calm down," Agatha said. "Everything is going to be wonderful. You are absolutely stunning, and people are going to be envious of you."

"I don't know…"

"If anyone does anything untoward, you just find me. I'll take care of them," Davis said.

"Thank you," Penelope said, her full lips tugged up into a lopsided smile.

"And I'll be right beside you," Bridget chimed in. "Maybe some of the men that are going to swarm you will see me and sign a few of my dance slots."

"Perhaps I should have brought my gun, after all," Davis growled.

"Oh, Papa, you know you want to be done with me and all the headaches I cause you," Bridget said impishly.

"You're my little girl, and you may stay with us as long as you choose."

"Davis, bite your tongue. I want grandchildren to spoil, and goodness knows Grayson isn't in any hurry to give them to us. We're here. Now, stop fidgeting, Penelope, and put on a smile. You have to make them at least believe that you care nothing about what they think. And remember, you are better than they are. Why even Lady Jersey is known to be unfaithful to her husband."

"But she is one of the elite members of the *ton*."

"Which means nothing. Now, come along," Agatha called over her shoulder as she descended from the carriage with the assistance of a footman.

Penelope exited followed by Bridget then Davis. They joined the queue of people waiting to enter the house. The line moved rather quickly, and once she crossed the threshold a footman waited to take her cloak. She stiffened her spine, undid the button, and removed it with a flourish. There were several gasps around her at the décolletage she revealed, but she merely tilted her chin up in response and dropped the cloak into the servant's hands.

She could see the host and hostess greeting their guests. Her heart beat so loudly, she felt certain those standing around her could hear it. She started to press her hand to her throat, to hide her fluttering pulse, but forced her hands to hang loosely at her sides.

"Sarah, this is Miss Penelope Presley. She is practically like a daughter to me. Penelope, allow me to introduce you to Sarah, Lady Jersey," Agatha announced.

"Lady Jersey," Penelope said, curtsying respectfully. She was standing once more when she heard a gentleman speak.

"And who is this vision of beaut—oof," the man standing beside Lady Jersey asked before he was elbowed in the ribs.

Agatha repeated the introduction to Lord Jersey, who took a step away from the reach of his wife's elbow.

"You are a thing of loveliness, my dear. Remember, it is polite to save a dance for your host."

"Of course, my lord," Penelope bestowed one of her bewitching smiles on the man and allowed him to take her hand and drop a kiss on the back of it.

"You've won over one gentleman already," Bridget said.

"The gentlemen aren't the hard ones," Penelope countered.

"Well, I wouldn't say that," Bridget said, impishly, wagging her eyebrows.

"Oh, you should behave. Do you want your mother, or rather *your father*, to overhear you discussing men's endowments?" she whispered.

"I suppose not, but you are almost as red as your dress," Bridget teased.

"Girls, quit dawdling. I see some ladies I would like to introduce you to. Come along."

"We best follow along," Bridget sighed. "I'm sure they are some boring matrons. Mother has spent years trying to make the Taggarts acceptable in the eyes of society."

They followed Agatha to a group of women that seemed only a few years older than they were.

"Pardon my interrupting," Agatha said.

"Oh, Lady Holywell, it's always a pleasure to see you," a dark-haired beauty warmly welcomed the older woman. She introduced her to the group of women, some of whom knew her already.

"Your Grace, may I introduce my daughter, Bridget? And this is Miss Penelope Presley, my soon-to-be niece."

Penelope had only been half paying attention earlier, but she noticed a beautiful blonde, that stiffened slightly at her name. She studied the woman and tried to place her. A sense of déjà vu swamped her, and she weaved slightly. She felt a hand grip her arm.

"Pen, are you all right?" Bridget whispered worriedly.

"Yes," she said, straightening. "I'm sorry, you look very familiar. Have we met?"

"Yes, under circumstances I wish I could go back and change," the woman said, her throaty voice washing over Penelope.

"Miss Graham," Penelope said as it all came rushing back to her.

"Mrs. McKenzie now."

"Yes, I had forgotten. You look well. Very…," she paused as she searched for the perfect word, and finally said, "serene."

"Marriage and motherhood will do that to a person. Miss Presley, I am truly sorry for all that happened. It was never my intention to—"

"You needn't apologize for something that was not your fault. My father made his choices as did my sister, and they have paid the ultimate price for their sins."

"You have paid a price, too, if the rumors I hear are correct."

"I have found out that I am a survivor," she said proudly, tilting her chin defiantly.

"I believe you are. Allow me to introduce my sister-in-law, the Duchess of Hawkescliffe and her sister-in-law, the Countess of Blackburn. And this is our dear friend, the Viscountess Southerby."

"It is a pleasure to meet you all," Penelope curtsied.

"Don't look now, but I believe you have been spotted," the Duchess of Hawkescliffe said in a raspy voice that Penelope imagined most men found quite alluring.

"By whom?"

"I believe every unattached man here, and some that *are* attached."

"Not our husbands, mind ye, they know better," the beautiful red-headed countess said in a Scottish burr.

"Indeed," the blonde viscountess agreed.

"Ladies," a dandy of a man bowed low upon approaching the group. "Please put me out of my misery and introduce me to this vision of beauty that has graced our presence."

"Miss Presley, this is Mr. Beau Brummell, dandy extraordinaire," Lady Hawkescliffe introduced the man sarcastically.

"Why, Lady Hawkescliffe, you make it sound like a disease. Miss Presley, it is a great pleasure to make your acquaintance." He bowed low, took her hand, and dropped a kiss on the back of it. He stood straight and tall once more, the curls of his hair looked haphazard, but Penelope knew he had probably spent more time getting ready for tonight's event than she had. "Might I see your dance card, Miss Presley?"

"Mr. Brummell, you do know who I am, don't you? Who my father was? My sister?"

"Of course."

"And you still wish to dance with me?"

"Those of us who carry a bit of scandal with us are often the most interesting and honest people about. Now, your dance card, if you please."

She handed it over, bemused by this man that had the Prince Regent's ear. Penelope watched him scratch his name down, not just once, but twice.

"We want to give them something to talk about, but not fly in the face of convention. Sarah would kick me out on my arse, and while it is fun teasing her, I wouldn't want to send her into apoplexy. I'll be around in a bit to claim my first dance. Until then." He flicked the card back to her, kissed the back of her hand once more, and then left.

"He didn't even ask for my card," Bridget whined.

"Because he knows your father would challenge him to a duel at dawn. I'm afraid he might be challenged by that nephew of mine," Agatha clucked nervously. "Now come with me and let's find you a nice young man to dance with."

"I don't want a nice young man," Bridget could be heard saying as her mother tugged her away from the group. "They aren't any fun."

"I'm afraid Agatha is going to have her hands full with Bridget," Penelope said worriedly.

"I'm sure she can handle her," Lady Hawkescliffe answered, chuckling.

Before anything else could be said, another gentleman approached Penelope for a dance, then another. Within minutes her dance card was full, and she was being escorted from the group for her first dance. She couldn't even remember the name of the man standing across from her for the quadrille. The music started, and she went through the motions of the dance.

Her mind wandered, trying to figure out who the killer was, and why they wanted Duncan dead. She was certain it wasn't Reese, regardless of what Duncan believed. Reese only wanted to please his older brother and make up for the betrayal he had served him when he fell in love with Isabelle. No, it had to be Rosalie or Lucy, but which one?

She was on her fourth dance of the night and no closer to determining who the killer was. She found herself waltzing in the arms of Mr. Brummell. The man chatted nonstop about the most inane things. Did he not realize she was trying to solve a murder, several in fact? And he had taken two spaces on her dance card? Why had she let him?

They turned a corner and suddenly came to an abrupt stop. Penelope looked over her shoulder and up to see Duncan's furious features. She found herself sandwiched between a brute of a man and the dandy who had her in his arms. *No, this isn't happening*, she thought to herself.

"I didn't know you were going to be here," she said breathlessly.

"Would it have stopped you from coming if you had? Stopped you from dancing with the likes of him?" he snarled.

"That's not fair, and Mr. Brummell has been a perfect gentleman."

"I'm sure he has," he said sarcastically.

"He has, as have all my dance partners thus far," she said. She watched as his face grew more furious.

"Say ol' chap, won't you let us finish this dance? After all my name is on her dance card," the dandy said.

Penelope looked at him, askance. Did he not realize how angry Duncan was? Did he not realize he was poking the *Beast*? Did he not understand that the *Beast* could strike quickly and lethally?

"Do you mean this dance card?" Duncan ripped the card from around her wrist and tore it into pieces.

"Yes, that was the one," Brummell replied cockily, unfazed. "But it's all right. I believe I had signed up for number four and number twelve, both waltzes. Wasn't that correct, my dear? You see, I have an excellent memory."

"Unhand my wife," Duncan snarled.

"I'm not—" the room grew deathly quiet. Even the musicians had stopped playing to observe what was happening on the dance floor. Every eye in the room was on the trio.

"You are in every way that matters," he growled. He pulled her free of Brummell's grip and wrapped her up in his own arms. "Start the music," he ordered. The musicians quickly began playing and he twirled her about the dance floor.

"Everyone is staring at us," she whispered.

"I can't believe my aunts dressed you up like this," he said.

"What's wrong with the way I look?" she asked indignantly.

"Your charms are practically revealed for all to see."

"So?"

"So? I am the *only* one that gets to see you like this." He pulled her close as they made a turn and grazed the back of his fingers across the top of her bosom.

"Duncan," she whispered, scandalized. She looked around frantically to see if anyone saw what he had done. "Haven't we caused enough scandals?"

"Oh, I don't know," he said and continued moving her around the dance floor.

"Duncan, the music has stopped."

"Has it?"

"Yes." She stopped, forcing him to stumble to a halt as well. Penelope walked off the dance floor with Duncan trailing behind her. She walked to a corner, and he followed her. She turned on him, her finger raised like a scolding governess, but before a word could escape, Agatha was beside them.

"Duncan James Taggart, what was all that about?" Agatha demanded, hands on hips.

"What are you referring to?"

"What am I referring to?" she mimicked. "That spectacle you made of yourself on the dance floor. *That* is what I'm referring to, young man. Do you realize who Penelope was dancing with?"

"I know who that dandified bastard is."

"You watch your mouth," she scolded as she frantically looked around. "That's *Beau Brummell*, and he has the ear of the Prince Regent."

"And since when did you care about something like that, Aunt Aggie?"

"Since I'm trying to make a match for your cousin!" she whisper shouted.

"My behavior is not going to affect Bridget's chances of making a match. Uncle Davis' money will see that she makes a good match."

A gasp sounded behind them, snapping their heads around. The trio saw Bridget standing there, a hurt look on her face.

"Is that what you think Duncan? That no one wants me for me? Only the money my father has will see that I'm married?"

"No, Bridget, that's not what I'm saying. I was merely—"

"Go to hell, Duncan," Bridget whirled around and ran through the open doorway that led to the terrace.

"Come with me, Duncan. You're going to apologize to your cousin and tell her what an idiot you are. Do you understand me?"

"I didn't mean—"

"I don't care what you meant. She is fully aware of the stigma attached to our family. Her greatest fear is she will never find someone who loves her for herself, someone that is willing to look past all the scandals. There will always be someone that knows our family's background. Some mother who will use that knowledge to see that her daughter makes a proper match over Bridget, and your words just reminded her of that. Now I don't care what you have to say to her, or what you have to do to convince her that she *will* marry for love, but you are going to do it. Now."

"But—"

"Go and check on her," Penelope said. "Your aunt is right. It is so much harder for women. Go. I'll be fine." She pushed Duncan towards the terrace doors.

"You had best be here when I return."

"I will be," she promised. Penelope walked to the room where the food was laid out. She poured herself a cup of punch and sipped it. Men walked by her and leered at her while the women sneered. The women also flicked their skirts away from her as if they would become soiled if they touched her.

"I would like for you to leave," a cultured feminine voice said.

"Lady Jersey," Penelope said, curtsying politely.

"Stand up. You and that terrible man have caused enough of a scene. I want you to leave."

"But I promised—"

"I don't care what you promised. Please escort her from the premises," she turned to the liveried footmen standing behind her.

The two men had just gripped her upper arms when there was a commotion in the ballroom.

"There she is. Arrest her!"

Penelope's insides quivered as she saw two men approach her. "You'll be coming with us, miss," one man said, as he grabbed her upper arm where the footman had relinquished it.

"What for? What have I done?" Penelope demanded, as she tried to twist herself free of the hulking brutes on either side of her.

"You've stolen from this man. His servants and his silver. For that you must be arrested."

"But I…"

"Yes?" one of the men asked.

Penelope thought about Grandfather's poor, ill-abused servants. Someone had helped them escape the tyrant that stood before her. If she had to take the blame, she gladly would. They were safe now, and she would keep them that way.

"I'll go with you," she said softly. The sound of gasps reached her ears. She looked behind her and saw several women faint into the arms of nearby gentlemen. Others were pointing and gawking at her. She stiffened her shoulders and turned to leave the house with her head held high. The men led her out to a cab that stunk of refuse and unwashed bodies and forced her inside. One man climbed inside with her while the other climbed onto the seat next to the driver. The dingy vehicle lunged forward as it pulled away from the Jersey's townhouse and the party going on inside. Penelope held herself stiffly as she watched the house fade into the darkness. She wondered vaguely if Duncan would believe that she hadn't run off on her own.

CHAPTER 28

Bridget, where are you?" Duncan stomped through the garden looking for his errant cousin. "Bloody hell, Bridge, I'm sorry for what I said. The words were spoken in haste and not meant to offend you. I was merely trying to make a point to Aunt Agatha."

"Oh, do go away Duncan," he heard a sniff from the shrubs next to him.

"Bridget? Come out from there right now." He watched her emerge from her hideout. "What were you doing there?"

"Avoiding you and mother."

"I am sorry for what I said."

"You were right."

"No, I—"

"Please, Duncan, don't lie to me. You spoke the truth. It's much easier for men to marry for love than it is us women. Four Seasons have already passed me by and still I find myself unmarried. *Four*," she stressed the word, holding up her hand with her four fingers spread wide and her thumb folded across her palm. "What am I to do Duncan?"

"Take fate into your own hands," he suggested before he pulled her into his arms and hugged her tightly.

"I think you're right, Duncan." She pushed away from him just as her mother walked up.

"There you are!" Agatha exclaimed.

"Yes, Mama, I'm here."

"And did—"

"Duncan apologized. Now, we should all go back inside. Perhaps we won't cause anymore scandals this evening." They all three laughed.

"You two go on, I need a moment to myself," Duncan said. He watched his aunt and cousin walk to the house, took a deep breath and released it. Penelope was right. He had embarrassed her in front of everyone, and all she had been doing was dancing. However, he couldn't help himself when it came to Penelope. Seeing her in Brummell's arms had made him crazy. She belonged to him as no one ever had before. He owed her an apology for his behavior.

He took a deep breath and then let it out slowly. Duncan approached the terrace to find a blonde pacing back and forth. She was pretty, Duncan noted, but not as beautiful as Penelope. His footstep sounded like a gunshot on the terrace step, causing the woman's head to jerk up.

"Your Grace," the woman quickly curtsied.

"I'm sorry, but I don't believe we've met."

"No, but I know Miss Presley. In fact, I feel some responsibility for the predicament she finds herself in. You see, I'm the woman her sister was fighting with when she fell to her death. I'm Mrs. McKenzie."

"I see," he said stiffly, all kindness gone from his voice, his posture stiff.

"Your Grace, you may be angry all you want later, in fact, I very probably deserve it for Miss Presley has been the victim far more often than not, including tonight."

"You are speaking in riddles, madam."

"Miss Presley was just taken by Runners."

"You jest," he scoffed.

"No. An old man came in accompanied by two Runners. He pointed at Miss Presley and said she should be arrested. When she questioned them, they cited that she had stolen his servants and his silver. She did not deny the accusation and was forced to leave with them."

"No!" Duncan roared ferociously.

The woman took a hesitant step away from him.

"What's going on out here?" a man with a thick Scottish brogue spoke. He was equal in height to Duncan and his hair was just as dark. "Cassie, are you all right, love?"

"Yes, Mack. He just found out the Runners have taken Miss Presley away."

Duncan watched the woman called Cassie step into the haven of the other man's arms and found his arms ached with emptiness.

"What has she done?"

"Not what they believe," Duncan said bitterly. "Pardon me, I have to go."

"Mack, can you help her? She has suffered so much because of me. Perhaps we could help her this little bit?"

"You're right. I believe I could be of service, Your Grace."

Duncan eyed him suspiciously. "And what can a commoner such as yourself do that I, a Duke, cannot?"

"Perhaps I should introduce myself." He held out his right hand to Duncan, refusing to bow. "Stuart McKenzie at your service, Director of the War Office. Most people, however, call me Mack or Director."

Duncan reluctantly took the other man's hand in a firm handshake. "I apologize for my earlier comment, Director."

"You're worried about your woman. I have first hand experience with that feeling. Now, let's see what we can do about getting her back, Your Grace."

Duncan was forced to follow the couple into the ballroom. Bridget rushed up to him, her eyes looked wild.

"Duncan, Penelope's been arrested," Bridget said. "Everyone's talking about it. It happened while we were in the garden."

"I know. I'm going to get her back."

"And then what?"

"And then I'm going to pay her grandfather a visit."

"Don't do anything either of you will regret. You and Penelope belong together. She needs you *alive*," Bridget stressed.

"Thank you for that reminder." He winked at her before turning to catch up with the McKenzies.

"Duncan, Penelope's been arrested," Lucy ran up to him, a frantic look on her face.

"I'm taking care of everything. You stay and enjoy yourself," he dropped a kiss on her forehead and turned once more to leave the Jersey's ballroom.

Duncan joined the McKenzies in their carriage since he left his behind for Reese, Rosalie, and Lucy. He fidgeted nervously as they traveled through the London streets.

"I've been arrested before. She will be fine," Mrs. McKenzie said, trying to comfort him.

"Cassie, I don't think that's what the man wants to hear, love," the Director said, chuckling. The carriage came to a stop a short time later. "Wait here," Director McKenzie ordered as he stepped from the carriage.

"I'm coming with you," Duncan said.

"Well, I'm definitely not staying out here by myself," Cassie announced.

"Fine, then," Mack said as he helped his wife from the carriage. Duncan followed them. Duncan watched as McKenzie beat on a door. They waited but no one answered. McKenzie pounded once more.

"Bloody hell, I hear you! What do you want?" A man yelled from a window above them clad in a nightshirt and sleeping cap.

"Barton, let us in, we need to speak to you," McKenzie called back.

"That you, Mack?"

"Aye."

"I'll be right down." They waited on the steps for the man to come down. Barton opened the door and ushered them in. He had tugged on a velvet robe over his nightshirt. "Well, what is it?" Barton asked once they were all in his small study.

"Barton, this is the Duke of Yorkshire. His fiancée was arrested by your Runners earlier this evening on false accusations."

"Says who?"

"Me," Duncan spoke up.

"I'm sorry, Your Grace, but evidently the charges were substantial enough that my men believed she should be taken into custody."

"And I'm telling you those charges are false," Duncan argued.

"Explain yourself," Barton said before yawning widely.

Duncan quickly explained how the servants had sought refuge at his house for fear of their life, with his assistance, after they had helped Penelope. Then he told them how they had forced Penelope to take the silver because she had no money with her and how it had all been stolen when she fell.

"And that's all?" Barton asked.

"Not exactly," Duncan cleared his throat and looked uncomfortable at having to admit his stupidity to the people in the room. Best get it said as quickly as possible. He took a deep breath and blurted everything out. "Presley sent his granddaughter to marry me with a false marriage certificate, of which Miss Presley, as well as I, believed to be real. I had already transferred five thousand pounds into his account with the agreement I would transfer five thousand more after the marriage ceremony."

Barton had perked up at this information. "Of which I am supposing you did, Your Grace?"

"Of course. I am a man of my word," Duncan said proudly.

"And did Presley ever purchase a new marriage certificate to rectify the situation?"

"No, he did not. In fact, he refused. I am the one who purchased the marriage certificate."

"I see. And why is the young woman not your duchess yet?"

"Well, Mr. Barton, it appears that someone murdered the previous women in my life, and then tried to murder both Miss Presley and me. She refuses to marry me until the culprit is caught, and for good reason."

"How many wives?" Barton asked curiously.

"Two and a fiancée," Duncan replied stoically.

"Bloody hell, young man. That's quite a number for a man your age."

"Well it isn't as if I'm Henry the VIII and ordered them beheaded in the castle square."

"Most people would still consider you to be bad luck."

"Yes, sir, they do."

"This interests me. I would like to help you solve this conundrum you find yourself in."

"I have an investigator looking into the situation."

"Name?"

"Grantham."

"Good man. Been trying to get him to join my men for several years. Still, I find your situation quite intriguing. I would like to help you find who is responsible for the murders and attempt on your life. Now, give me a moment while I go and change clothes. I believe we have a visit to bestow on Lord Bolingbroke."

"And my fiancée?"

"Yes, your fiancée," Barton agreed as he left the room and disappeared up the stairs.

Duncan paced the confines of the small room.

"Barton is a good man," Mack said. "He'll set things right."

"I hope to hell you're right."

The cell door clicked loudly, making Penelope jump. Her grandfather stood on the other side with the Runners flanking him. She had held herself tall and proud as they guided her through the corridors, his laughter following after her. Now he stood across from her grinning a most unholy grin.

"This is exactly where you belong, you interfering little chit," Bolingbroke said. I should have done this to you instead of sending you to Yorkshire. It would have saved us all a bit of trouble."

"But how would you have gotten all that money to save your precious title?"

"I could have bent your brother to my will."

"Yes, you were so successful with that, weren't you?" Penelope asked sarcastically. "That's why he disappeared for lands unknown. Sam is just as sick and tired of your machinations as I am. He was not eager to live in your shadow and become the next Lord Bolingbroke."

"I've heard enough. I do hope you rot in here, for not even your precious duke can get you out of the charge of theft."

"You mistreated them for years and refused to pay them. They deserved to be out from under your cruelty," Penelope countered heatedly.

"I'll not stand here and argue with a criminal. Gentlemen, I do believe we are done here."

"I despise you!" Penelope yelled at his retreating figure, gripping the bars of the cell tightly. "Duncan won't let you get away with this. He won't!"

"Screaming won't help ye none, dearie," a weathered feminine voice drifted to her from the next cell. "No one cares about us."

"How long have you been here?" Penelope asked tiredly.

"Long enough."

"Let me out of here," Penelope growled, shaking the metal door to her cell.

"Ye ain't goin' nowhere," another woman said, laughing hysterically.

A cacophony of voices cackled and mocked Penelope for her naïvete. She walked to the cot shoved against the wall and sat down. It creaked loudly and she hoped it wouldn't collapse beneath her slight weight. She huddled on the filthy piece of furniture, drew her legs up close to her, and wrapped her arms around them. The inmates' laughter echoed off the stone walls. She rested her forehead against her knees and covered her ears with her hands. She thought she must look like what her mother had looked like that day in Bedlam, but couldn't stop herself from rocking back and forth.

"I will not turn into my mother," she said softly. "I will not turn into my mother," she chanted the words over and over. An overpowering aroma of human filth reached her and made her stomach churn sickeningly. Penelope slipped her hands from her ears to cover her nose and her stomach. She felt some relief when the smells diminished. "Your Papa is going to rescue us from this…this—" she whispered the words and rubbed her churning stomach with her other hand.

"Hell hole I believe is the phrase you're looking for."

A familiar voice had her head snapping up. "Duncan!" she exclaimed as she jumped up and just as quickly sat back down when a wave of dizziness overtook her.

"Open this damn door," she heard Duncan order. Before she knew what had happened, Duncan's bulky frame knelt in front of her. One big hand cupped her cheek while the other cradled her hands in his left. "Your hands are freezing."

"Are they?" she asked, staring into his powerful sapphire-colored eyes. They had stripped her of everything but her dress and shoes when she was brought in. She had no gloves, and the beautiful jewelry Helena had given her to wear was gone.

"Yes. We are getting you out of here."

"How? I was arrested. The entire *ton* witnessed it."

"Well, not the entire *ton*," he teased.

"How can you joke about this?"

"I would like to have seen Lady Jersey's face. I imagine that was a sight to behold," a gentleman standing near the opening of the cell commented snidely.

"Who's that?" Penelope asked.

"Our guardian angel," Duncan said.

He dropped a tender kiss on her forehead then lifted her into his arms. "Duncan, put me down," she ordered. "I can walk."

"Humor me, love," he said, winking at her.

"What's the meaning of this?" a familiar voice reached her ears.

"I will face Grandfather on my own two feet, Duncan. Put me down, now," Penelope ordered pushing away from him until he was forced to let her body slide down his. She turned and saw the now familiar Runners dragging her fighting grandfather down the corridor towards them.

"What's this? Why is she out of her cell? What am I doing here?"

"Good evening, Lord Bolingbroke."

"Who're you?" he demanded belligerently.

"Barton. I'm in charge of the Runners. It has come to my attention that you were not entirely honest with the information you gave my men when they brought this young woman into Newgate."

"I don't know what you're talking about," the old man blustered.

"First of all, you said this young woman took your servants when in fact the Duke of Yorkshire here helped them to escape your brutality."

"A man has the right to treat his servants as he sees fit," Penelope's grandfather said indignantly. "And what about the silver?"

"Stolen by ruffians on the street," Barton answered. "Now I have a question for you Lord Bolingbroke. If a man entered into a contract with you and didn't follow through what would you do?" Barton questioned.

"Why I'd have him thrown into—"

"Yes?" Barton asked.

"Nothing." Lord Bolingbroke pursed his lips.

"I believe it is more than *nothing*," Barton emphasized. "It's about ten thousand pounds and a false marriage. Not only did you not follow through with the contract you settled into, you basically stole money from His Grace, and worse, you mocked God and the sanctity of matrimony."

"Now, see here," Bolingbroke puffed up his chest and turned a purplish red.

"No, you see here," Barton said. "I will be seeing the magistrate about this; however, until that time, you will spend some time in here to consider what you've done."

"This is all your fault, you little bitch!"

Penelope found herself being spun around as Grandfather lunged towards her. She heard a crunching sound and looked in time to see the old man crumple to the floor after coming into contact with Duncan's fist.

"We'll take care of everything from here, Your Grace. Perhaps you can come and see me tomorrow, and we can talk more about your predicament."

"Yes, sir," Duncan nodded then swept Penelope into his arms once more, despite her earlier protest, and walked out of Newgate.

Duncan placed Penelope into a carriage opposite of Director and Mrs. McKenzie then climbed in after her.

"What are they doing here?" she asked, scooting over so he had more room.

"Director McKenzie was instrumental in getting you released from Newgate."

"Thank you, Director McKenzie," she said and nodded her head in acceptance of his good deed.

The ride was quiet and Duncan knew Penelope was uncomfortable. She kept shifting and fidgeting. He took her hands in his and rubbed them, trying to both warm them and soothe her.

"Where are your gloves and jewelry?"

"I have no idea. They took them upon admitting me to Newgate."

"I'll see that they are retrieved for you first thing in the morning," Director McKenzie interjected.

"Thank you." She sat quietly, allowing Duncan to warm her. She studied the couple sitting across from her. "I am sorry. I'm afraid I smell rather rank. I do hope I'm not dirtying your coach," she said.

"Of course you're not, Miss Presley," Mrs. McKenzie waved away her concern.

Silence ruled the carriage once more until they finally rolled up to her little house after what felt like a interminable journey. Duncan stepped down from the coach, causing it to list to the side before righting itself. He turned and placed his hands about Penelope's waist and lifted her down.

They were almost to the door when he felt Penelope turn and look behind them. She tugged him to a stop. "What are they doing?"

"They're coming inside."

"Why?" Penelope demanded.

"They have agreed to serve as witnesses for our wedding."

"Our what?!"

CHAPTER 29

Oh, Miss Presley, I was worried about ye, I was, when ye didn't show up."

"It's been quite an adventurous night, Mrs. Jenkins. I'll tell you all about it later. Would you mind showing Mr. and Mrs. McKenzie to the parlor? I must have a word with His Grace."

"Of course," Mrs. Jenkins said and led the couple into the parlor.

"There should be another gentleman arriving shortly with a cleric," Duncan informed her.

"A cleric? Here?" Mrs. Jenkins asked.

"Indeed," he said before turning to follow Penelope's retreating figure.

"Shut the door," she ordered when he entered the room.

"Why?"

"Because I wouldn't want our guests overhearing me call you ten kinds of a fool. I can't believe you are attempting to force me into this marriage again. I told you I refused to wed you until the danger was past."

"I'm tired of not having my ring on your finger. Do you think you would have been treated the way you were tonight if you were truly a duchess? I want the world to know that you belong to me."

"I think you did a fairly good job of seeing that everyone knew that at the ball, don't you?" She crossed her arms beneath her burgeoning bosom.

"You're beautiful," he said.

"Stop it," she ordered, shifting, fisting her hands, and holding her arms straight down at her sides. "I will not be swayed by your words. I will not let you charm me into falling into line with your plan. I'm fighting for my life. I'm fighting for our ch…"

"Our what?" he asked, his voice pitched low.

"Nothing," she muttered, turning away from him. She felt him behind her and closed her eyes as his hands settled tenderly on her shoulders. Her head fell backward against his chest as he began to tenderly massage the tension from her.

"Our child?" he whispered.

She stepped and twirled away from him, but her feet got caught up in her dress. Penelope teetered precariously before strong arms wrapped around her, securing her to him.

"Careful, you don't want to hurt yourself…or the babe," he finished.

She pushed away from him. "How do you know? You're not supposed to know. How long have you known?"

"Does it matter?"

"I suppose not," she slumped onto the leather settee. She felt him sit next to her. He wrapped her up in his arms and held her close. "Duncan, I do—"

"If the next words coming out of your mouth have to do with marriage in the negative, then you should just not say anything at all, because I won't hear of it. I'll not have my child born a bastard."

"Of course that would be your greatest concern. You must have your heir, musn't you?"

"Penelope, that isn't fair. This is our future we are talking about. *Our child.* Doesn't that mean anything to you?"

"It means *everything* to me," she bit out. "I'm the one that's doing everything in my power to keep *your* heir alive."

"I don't bloody care if it is a boy or a girl. I just want it to be healthy and you to be alive in the end. Is that too much to ask?"

"You tell me."

"What is that supposed to mean?"

"Oh, I don't know," she said, rubbing her brow.

"Penelope," he said, taking her hands in his. "I desperately want to be with you. I want us to be a family. I love you."

Penelope's heart pattered frantically at his words before reason struck her. He was just waxing poetic, telling her words that he believed she wanted to hear so that she would acquiesce and marry him, and she was tired of fighting. "All right, Duncan."

"All right, what?"

"I'll marry you, but please, there is no reason to tell me that you love me. We both know this union was beneficial to both parties from the very beginning. As an added bonus, I now have Mother and Grandfather out of my life, which I must thank you and Mr. Barton for. And you have a possible heir on the way. Everyone is a champion. Well, perhaps you did lose some money to Grandfather for purchasing me. I am sorry about that."

"I'm not." He cupped her cheek. "You are worth a king's ransom."

"Duncan, anyone that heard us arguing at the ball will know that we are not married."

"And?"

"And. People will know the babe is something of a seven month miracle."

"Don't worry, the *ton* will expect it. After all, you *are* marrying into the *Scandalous Taggarts*." He wrapped one arm around her shoulders and leaned her backwards so that he could kiss her. His other hand rested lightly, low on her stomach, where their child grew.

Penelope found herself surrendering. They were in this together, come what may. She cupped his cheek and kissed him back. A soft knock sounded, breaking them apart.

"The minister has arrived," Mrs. Jenkins called through the door.

"We'll be there in a moment," Duncan called. "Are you ready to become the Duchess of Yorkshire?"

"I suppose."

"You suppose? You'll be known all over England as the beauty that tamed the *Beast of Yorkshire*," he teased.

"You're not a beast," she argued softly.

"I'm glad you said that. Come, love, let us go and say our vows."

Penelope let him tug her up from the settee. "Duncan," she said.

"Yes?"

"Promise me we'll make it through this alive."

"I will lay down my life for you and our child if it should come to that, Pen," he said.

She looked up and could see the passion, honesty, and emotion in his eyes. "Then I'm ready to become your wife." She watched Duncan bring her hands up to his lips and kiss them passionately. "Let's go," she said softly, a winsome smile on her lips as she led him across the room and out the door.

A few days later, Penelope sat alone in the wood lined study. Her feet were curled under her on the settee, and an open book lay spread out on her lap. She sat there, reflecting on how her life had changed. When Grandfather had first told her she would have to marry the *Beast of Yorkshire*, she had thought she was receiving a prison sentence. Every clip clop of the horse's hooves as she left London had felt like someone driving a nail into her coffin. Then she had met him.

It was true he could be brutish at times, but he was so much more. He cared about his people and fought alongside them. Most importantly, he loved his family. If he didn't, his brother's betrayal would not have hurt him so much. And he cared about her. Every night, and sometimes during the day, since their wedding ceremony he took her body to extreme heights with his tender explorations. He made her feel as if she were being worshipped like a goddess from bygone days.

He had also continued to tell her he loved her even though she told him repeatedly that he didn't have to. That she, in fact, preferred that he didn't. He had ignored her, and she didn't know whether to be angry or rejoice. Those three words had felt like a balm to her soul, especially since she had never heard them directed at her before. She had overheard her mother and father speak them many times to her siblings, but never were they spoken to her. Now, she basked in the knowledge that someone loved her, or at least pretended they did.

"If he makes me feel this special, he'll make you feel like a prince or princess," she said softly, patting her tummy lightly.

Penelope languished about, enjoying the sunny afternoon. Her mind drifted to the three other women that had come before her. "Thank you all for having been a part of Duncan's life, for making him into the man he is now. I will love him enough for all of us. And if you did not love him, then you should have." *Now I have begun talking to myself,* she thought. *If anyone heard me they would question my sanity and cart* me *off to Bedlam*. She could not suppress the shudder that slithered up and down her spine.

She had just started to drift off when some random memory popped into her mind. *I never left Samantha's side. We had become quite close and she had confided in me that Duncan frightened her. She felt much more at ease with Reese. When she fell ill, I nursed her myself.* Lucy's words echoed in her mind like a gong.

Penelope thought through more of her conversations with Lucy. Lucy who had seemed so warm and welcoming. Could she be the one responsible for the deaths of those three women? Women who more than likely considered her their friend. Who never thought to suspect her. But why? Did she love Duncan? At first, she thought perhaps she did, but now she wasn't so certain. There were many times she had witnessed her flirting with Reese. She occasionally had said something flirtatious to Duncan, but it had seemed almost forced and unnatural. She knew that Duncan did not care for Lucy in that manner. How, then, had Reese acted to Lucy's flirting. Had he flirted back, or had he merely been kind and attentive to a young woman who had grown up under their roof?

"Oh, no," Penelope said. She stood up and paced the room, nervously nibbling at her thumbnail. Duncan had left her earlier, after kissing her until her toes had curled. When she questioned him, he had told her that he had a meeting with Grantham and Barton. Both men had become active participants in finding the murderer.

What if they were at the house now? What if, at this very moment, Lucy was serving them all poison-laced tea? What if Lucy decided to use a gun this time?

"Mrs. Jenkins!" Penelope called, practically flying across the room. She could hear the tremor of fear in her own voice.

"What is it, child? You look as if you've seen a ghost."

"I have to go to the townhouse immediately."

"Oh, no. His Grace wouldn't like that one bit."

"Mrs. Jenkins, please, I think I know who the killer is. I'm afraid Duncan could be in danger. He doesn't know. He would trust this person explicitly. She would truly be the last person he would suspect. I love him. I can't lose him, don't you see? Not now." The older woman still looked unsure. "Please, help me."

"All right, Your Grace, I'll find a hack for you while you gather what you need."

"Thank you." Penelope hugged her tightly.

"Just make sure His Grace doesn't have me hung for not keeping you here. I want to live to be your babe's nanny."

"I won't allow him to harm a precious hair on your head," Penelope said before slipping upstairs.

The trip to the townhouse was long and slow. Penelope tried to play out every possible scenario in her mind as to how this confrontation could happen. She had to protect herself, but she also had to find the truth. The hack rolled to a stop in front of the over-sized house, and she sat there, staring.

"Miss, is this the right house?" the driver called down to her.

"Yes," she called back. "I'm just gathering my courage," she muttered to herself. She exited the hack and paid the driver.

"Would ye like me to wait?"

"No, thank you."

He nodded and drove off, leaving her on the walk to stare at the door that seemed to loom tauntingly at her. A thick fog had begun to roll into the city from the Thames, which just made Penelope jumpier than she already was. What had proved to be a beautiful day just hours before was quickly turning into the opposite before her very eyes. She took a deep breath, slightly lifted her skirts, and walked to the door. Though she was now the Duchess of Yorkshire and had every right to walk into the house unannounced, she still found herself lifting her hand to rap on the door. It was opened by her grandfather's old butler.

"Oh, miss, it is so good to see you!" he exclaimed. "We've been worried about you, we have."

"I've been perfectly fine, Giles. Did you all settle in all right?"

"Yes, Miss Penelope. Some of the other servants heard that you had been taken to Newgate. But I told them, 'not our Miss Penelope. She's too fine a soul for that to happen to.'"

"Well, that is sweet of you to say, but I was taken to Newgate. Grandfather, however, has ever so humbly, and justly, taken my place."

"Say it isn't so," the old man said, covering his mouth with a white gloved hand.

"It is," she said and saw a look of relief wash over his face. "Where is everyone?" she asked, looking around the rooms leading off the foyer.

"Oh, yes," he cleared his throat. "This is the servants' day off and the ladies are out shopping."

"Are all the servants gone?

"Yes. Well, except for the four of us. We don't fit in too well and have no one to visit, so we run the house while the others are out."

"Excellent. And Reese?"

"Upstairs in his room. Came home last night reeking of whisky and women, pardon my language, Miss Penelope."

Penelope reached out and squeezed his hand. "I must search Lucy's room. I don't know what exactly I'm looking for, I just know that it has to be here, whatever it is."

"Can we help you?"

"It would be best if you didn't. On the off chance that I'm wrong, I don't want you to be a part of this."

"But Miss—"

"I'll brook no argument. I will need someone stationed at a window that can give a shout out to me when Lucy and Rosalie arrive. I don't want to be caught snooping if I can't find anything."

"Of course. We'll all watch. I'll station someone at a window that looks out in every direction."

"Perfect. Now, if you'll excuse me, I have a murderer to catch."

"A murderer?" Giles asked startled.

Penelope ignored the old man and practically skipped up the stairs. She entered Lucy's empty room and turned in a slow circle studying every nook and cranny.

"Where would I want to hide something important?" she mused quietly. Under the bed was too obvious. She tossed back the rug and stepped on the ends of boards to test for loose ones. Again, nothing. Penelope opened drawers and shifted clothes, always careful to put things back the way she found them. She went through the wardrobe and still came up empty handed. She dug through the nightstands, but could find nothing of importance there either. She searched the entire room a second time, this time checking beneath the mattress and the bed. She also checked the window trim to see if any boards were loose.

Frustrated with not finding anything, she sat down heavily at the dressing table. She idly picked up item after item, using the time to think and consider the situation. Perhaps she was wrong. Perhaps Lucy was exactly what she seemed—an innocent young woman. It could be that she looked to Duncan and Reese as brothers, much like her own relationship with Sam. She opened a large silver container. Inside were several glass bottles. When she removed the stopper of the first one, she got a whiff of Lucy's aromatic perfume that she was inclined to wear. Penelope replaced the stopper and the bottle before picking up the next one. Belladonna. So Lucy performed the same beauty rituals she had watched Whitney perform, using the plant to dilate her eyes. She shook her head sadly and placed it back in the silver container. She picked up the third bottle, and stopped a moment, holding it in mid-air. Penelope slowly put the third bottle back, not seeing what it was. She stared at the second one once more.

Belladonna. She remembered when she had procured the bottle from the apothecary for Whitney. The old man had warned her about using it overly much. What exactly had he said?

"Do not ingest it, even though you can. It can make you extremely ill. Physically ill. Do you understand me, young lady?" She had answered that she had, then took the bottle and left. When she had repeated the warning to Whitney, her sister had merely looked at her as if she had grown another head.

"You twit. Of course, I'm not going to drink it. I want to attend the ball, not be forced to stay here with you casting up my accounts or worse."

"Worse?"

"Did you not hear about that silly, stupid girl two Seasons ago? She found herself unmarried and increasing. She heard what belladonna could do when drunk as a tea. One evening, she feigned illness and stayed home. She added it to her tea and was dead within the hour. It was not a pretty death either, from what I understand."

"How sad."

"She knew what she was doing. There's a reason they call it deadly nightshade,*" Whitney said coldly. "Besides, if you're going to act as a trollop, you should do things that will prevent a child."*

"Whitney!"

"Oh, come now, Penelope, don't be so naïve."

Whitney had been no angel. Penelope continued to finger the bottle as the conversation between Whitney and herself played through her mind over and over again. Then Duncan's words about how both Samantha and Francis had passed away. Samantha had fallen ill and her health never improved. Lucy had even mentioned that only days before her death, Samantha had gone blind. Francis had drunk poison rather than marry Duncan. What type of poison had she ingested? Then there had been her maid, Mary. It had appeared she had drunk poisoned tea.

"What am I going to do? I can't take you with me because she will know immediately that you're missing. I'll check Rosalie's room and see if she has any." Penelope stood and made certain the room was exactly as she had found it before crossing over to Rosalie's. After a quick search of the dowager duchess' cosmetics she found no belladonna. It had to be Lucy.

"Miss Presley, she's just arrived," her grandfather's former maid announced in a stage whisper.

"I'll be right down." Penelope entered the hall and smoothed shaky hands over the skirt of her dress. She nervously patted her hair and then straightened her spine. "Get a hold of yourself," she ordered. She was at the top of the stairs when the door opened to reveal Lucy entering. “Good afternoon, Lucy,” she said, a smile on her lips that didn’t reach her eyes.

Duncan was in Barton’s office discussing his situation. Grantham had not been at his office when he stopped earlier this afternoon, so he had come on his own. He was tired of this hanging over them like an axe ready to fall. He had gone over every situation with Barton, but they were at a stalemate. Who was the culprit? Rosalie or Lucy? How did one decide?

What if they were wrong and it was, in fact, Reese? Perhaps he and Isabelle had had a lover’s quarrel. Did she struggle out of his hold, slip, and fall to her death? Could it be that Samantha had truly fallen ill and never recovered, and that Francis had chosen to take her own life rather than face a lifetime with him? But then there was the death of Penelope’s maid and the attack on him. He tunneled his fingers through his hair, frustrated.

“We have to decide upon a culprit,” Barton said. “These women did not die at the hand of an apparition. I know it’s difficult to accuse a woman, but some of the most dangerous murderers throughout history have been women.”

“So you say,” Duncan said.

“Yes. Now, let’s look at the facts. Poison is a woman’s weapon. We know for absolute certainty that two of the women, your fiancée and the maid, lost their lives due to poisoning.”

“Yes,” Duncan agreed. He could not eradicate from his mind the scene he had walked in on that day. He kept seeing Penelope lying there, lifeless, instead of the maid.

“Your second wife had fallen ill and never recovered. That could have been nature or it could have been poisoning as well. There are many poisons that can make it seem one has the lingering death,” Barton continued.

“I understand.” Duncan paused and tried to collect his thoughts before continuing, “What of Isabelle? What of her death?”

“I have several thoughts on it. It could have truly been an accident, a slip of the foot that plunged the poor woman to her death.”

"She was surefooted, especially along the cliffs. She had been raised around them here entire life, and they were her favorite place to be. No, I refuse to believe it was merely an accident."

"Then someone must have been with her, or come up on her. Pushing someone to their death is a coward's weapon, but extremely successful in most cases," Barton said. "And then there was your mishap. You do know we have gangs in this town, don't you?"

"I've heard."

"However, most of them are young boys who work together to disable their target and then relieve him of his pocketbook. You were brutally beaten by grown men. Most would not have survived, let alone killed his attackers. You were either very determined or very lucky."

"I'd like to think a bit of both," Duncan said, rising to stand. He paced Barton's small office. "The men were my own footmen. Someone turned them against me."

"I do not think your brother is the murderer. I think it a bit of bad luck that he has always been present when the ladies have died, but like I said earlier, poison is a woman's weapon. If your brother had been responsible, we would be looking at murders caused by strangulation or shooting."

"Does speaking of death in such a way ever get old?"

"It's my job, Your Grace," Barton said, tilting his chin proudly. "Yes, I wish we saw less of it, but I am proud of the work that my men and I do. We do our utmost to keep the people of London safe."

"I apologize, I did not mean to offend. It's just that I'm so tired of thinking about the dead and murders. I just want to get on with my life," Duncan said, feeling years older than his almost thirty-five years.

"I under—"

"Gentlemen, I apologize for being late. I had something to do. Your Grace, I do believe I know who the murderer is, but we must hurry back to your house."

"Why?"

"Because your wife is there with them trying to get a confession."

"Bloody hell, let's go!"

CHAPTER 30

Penelope, is that you?" Lucy asked, squinting up the stairs.

"Now, surely it hasn't been that long," Penelope said. She felt like her shoulders were up by her ears with tension and forced herself to ease them lower. *Relax or she will suspect something is afoot before you can get any information out of her.*

"I'm just surprised to see you here," the younger woman said. "What are you doing up there? Does Duncan know you're here?"

"No," Penelope answered honestly, ignoring Lucy's first question altogether. "But I decided that I could hide no longer. After all, I am the Duchess of Yorkshire, and that carries with it a certain amount of power, doesn't it?"

"What do you mean you are the Duchess of Yorkshire?" Lucy asked, halting almost mid-step. "Haven't you been in Newgate all this time?"

"No, thankfully I did not have to spend long in that horrid place. Duncan rescued me and that night he wore me down and convinced me to marry him. We had a quiet ceremony several days ago."

"That's wonderful!" Lucy exclaimed, but it sounded rather false to Penelope.

She pulled Penelope into what seemed to be a friendly embrace, making her second guess herself. There was only one way to force her hand. "Yes. He has promised to lay down his life for me and the babe," she let purposefully slip. And there it was, the almost imperceptible tightening of Lucy's body. A breath held slightly longer than necessary. The ever so slight gasp she couldn't contain. This time Penelope's smile was real when she pulled back and looked at the other woman. Real, because she finally knew who was behind all the tragedies. Now she only had to get her to admit to them.

"A new babe! Oh, Mother is going to be so excited. Is Duncan excited?"

"Ecstatic."

"Do you think it will be the heir?"

"I honestly don't know, and Duncan has told me he doesn't care. Can you believe that, a duke not caring whether his child is a boy or girl? I believe he would be perfectly content letting Reese inherit the title if it were to come to that someday, far far in the future, of course," Penelope added very pointedly. She looked around curiously, "Where is Rosalie?"

"Oh, she ran into a friend while we were shopping, and they went for tea. I need to run upstairs and refresh myself. Why don't you send for tea and we can have a nice visit while everyone is away."

"That sounds wonderful. I've missed you a great deal. It's nice to have another woman close to my own age to visit with. It reminds me of all the times my sister and I spent sharing secrets," Penelope lied glibly.

"I feel the same," Lucy said with a smile and hugged her tightly once more. "I'll be but a few moments."

Penelope watched her sedately move up the stairs. Perhaps she was wrong, for Lucy didn't act like a killer. But then again, she was putting on the greatest act of her life, as well. She shook herself out of her reverie and found the servants gathered in the kitchen.

"What did you find, Miss Penelope?" the butler asked anxiously.

"I believe Lucy is the one who has murdered the other women," she said furtively. A chorus of gasps greeted her. "I know it seems farfetched, but a woman in love is often times quite desperate."

"What do you want us to do?" Mrs. Giles asked.

"I need a tea tray brought into the parlor as soon as it can be made."

"Of course, I'll start it right away." Mrs. Giles moved away from the group, filled the kettle with water, and put it over the fire. Then she began gathering up the other necessary items while the others continued talking.

"I need you," Penelope looked directly at Giles as she placed a card and money in his hand, "to go to Investigator Grantham's office. Tell him my suspicions, and that he needs to come right away. Slip out the back so that Lucy doesn't see you and take the fastest horse possible." She was so thankful she had kept Grantham's calling card from the night Duncan had been attacked.

"Consider it done, Miss Presley." He gave a smart salute as if he were a soldier and then slipped from the house.

"And what of us Miss Presley?" the footman asked, indicating the maid and himself.

"I need you to be within hearing distance. If I give a distress signal, I need your assistance immediately. Do not hesitate to harm or seek to end Lucy's life. Do you understand?"

"Yes," the footman said solemnly.

"There is a good possibility that she has some of the other servants on her side."

"She does, Miss Penelope," the maid spoke up. "I walked in on her with one of the footmen the other day. She doesn't know that I saw anything," she hastened to say.

"This is good to know. Reese is still asleep. He needs to be told what is going on. He can be of help, but he must stay out of sight if we are to get her to confess to anything."

"I'll take care of his lordship," Mrs. Giles said.

"Thank you, Hortense. I guess I should go." She took a step and hesitated.

"What is it, Miss Penelope?"

"I'm frightened," she admitted to herself and the others.

"You are a strong young woman. We will be there should you need us," Hortense said encouragingly.

"Thank you." Penelope took a deep breath, held it, and let it out. She left the kitchen and made her way through the house to the large parlor. She beat Lucy by only a few minutes. "What did you purchase today?" Penelope asked from the chair she was sitting on.

"The normal baubles," Lucy waved her question away. "More importantly, I want to know everything about the wedding.

Mother is going to be incensed that it was not a lavish church wedding. Neither one was, in fact."

"Under the circumstances, we thought it better this way."

"You mean the babe?"

Penelope nodded her head. "And my family's history."

"Oh, that," Lucy said airily. "Do you forget you married into the *Scandalous Taggarts*?"

"How could I?" Conversation paused while the maid carried in the tray of tea and other goodies. Penelope reached forward and chose a plain biscuit to nibble on.

"To be increasing, you look very thin, almost gaunt," Lucy observed.

"Yes, well, I haven't felt all that wonderful," she said. "Just in the last few days I have not woken up casting up my accounts."

"I've heard some women say the morning illness can be quite horrible."

"Morning?" Penelope asked incredulously. "At the beginning, mine lasted almost all day. But enough of me. How is the Season going for you? Have you caught the eye of any eligible young men?"

"Yes," Lucy bobbed her head in affirmation. "In fact, I have many admirers."

"I would think you would be more excited than you sound," Penelope prodded.

"It seems the one man that I want doesn't know I even exist. At least not in that manner, and I don't know what to do."

This is it, Penelope thought. *I have to ask the question in such a way that she thinks I have no suspicions about the truth.* "Is it anyone I know?" she asked innocently.

Lucy hesitated in answering. She used the time to pour the tea. "Yes, you know him," she finally answered.

Penelope picked up her teacup and took a sip to wet her dry mouth, then put it back down. "Is it Duncan?" she asked warily. She mentally girded herself for the answer. She knew Lucy's love had to be one of the two men. It stood to reason it was Reese since Duncan's life had been threatened as well, but there was always the chance they had been wrong in their summation. The attack on Duncan could very well have been an accident. It also boded well for her to appear to be the jealous wife.

"No," Lucy denied. "I could never tie myself to the *Beast of Yorkshire*," she said.

"He is not a beast or the *Beast,* and I truly wish everyone would stop referring to him as such. He is a kind man that does everything in his power to take care of this family and those under his care," Penelope countered heatedly.

"Of course he does. I did not mean to offend. I've just heard him called that for so long that sometimes it just slips out."

Penelope pursed her lips and nodded her head once in acceptance. "So that means that your feelings are for…"

"Reese," Lucy admitted. "I have loved Reese since Mother and I came to the household when I was merely a girl," she announced proudly. "He has always been so kind and attentive to me."

"I see." Penelope stood and walked to the window, looking towards the square. She pulled the sheers back and studied her grandfather's empty house across the way. Soon it would be put up for auction in an attempt to pay his debts, but he had borrowed far too much from Duncan for that to happen. She thought of Duncan's family and how close knit they were, even his long lost aunt, and a deep sadness overtook her. She had never been loved like that. Which family was normal? Hers? His? She didn't care anymore. She was just glad she was now a part of the *Scandalous Taggarts* if it meant she was loved and taken in with open arms. Penelope also felt great sadness for Lucy, who didn't realize it, but was throwing away so much by her actions.

She turned around and studied the younger woman. Had she given her enough time to lace her tea with the belladonna? Surely she had.

"Did you hear anything I said?" Lucy asked.

"I'm sorry, my mind drifted. What were you saying?"

"I was asking if you thought that Reese could ever love me?"

"He does love you, Lucy."

"Like a sister. I want him to love me like the woman I have become."

"Well, I—"

"I don't believe he knows all I've done for him."

"What do you mean?" Penelope asked curiously.

"Nothing," Lucy said. "Please tell me, how can I entice Reese to stop turning to whores and see *me*? Oh, but look who I'm asking. Didn't you live with a woman who has been a man's mistress for almost thirty years?" Lucy asked snidely.

"How did you know that?"

"You know everyone underestimates me. I will go to any length to get who, or what, I want."

"And what do you want Lucy?"

"Reese and to be his duchess."

Penelope turned her back to Lucy once more. She slowly walked the perimeter of the room towards the doors.

"Where *are* you going, *dear friend*?" Lucy snarled near her ear.

"I was just—"

"Seeking help? I think not."

"Ow!" Penelope's hands flew up to the back of her head where Lucy's fingers had entwined themselves in her hair. She was forced to walk backwards and found herself shoved into a chair. She rubbed her tender scalp and looked up into Lucy's crazed eyes. "It's difficult to be a duchess when you're in love with the second son," Penelope said.

"That can easily be rectified. Accidents happen all the time."

"Why aren't we moving?" Duncan demanded.

A Runner returned to them with a report, "A dray cart has overturned with casks of ale littering the roadway."

"Then have the driver back up," Duncan ordered.

"Not possible, Your Grace. There are several conveyances behind us and more being added each minute."

"Damn you for having your office on one of London's busiest thoroughfares," he threw the accusation at Barton.

"It wasn't my choice," the man said to Duncan's retreating figure. "Where are you going?"

"If I have to travel by foot, I will, but I will not just sit here while my wife's life hangs in the balance."

"Perhaps we should follow him and keep him from doing something he'll regret," Grantham said.

"Yes. Men, follow us!"

Duncan led the procession through the streets of London. He felt a hand on his arm trying to halt his progress. "Let go of me," he growled, trying to shake the hand off.

"Dammit, man, stop and look around. We are past the traffic and still have much distance to travel. Let's get another hack. The travel will be faster this time," Grantham said.

"He's right, Your Grace," Barton seconded.

"Fine, but we keep moving until we can flag one down."

There was mumbled agreement among the other men that included two Runners.

"It was you, wasn't it?" Penelope asked, sounding surprisingly calm. "You killed them. Not because you were in love with Duncan, but because you are in love with Reese."

"Yes, I am in love with Reese," Lucy verified a second time.

"You're a smart girl not admitting to the murders. You know that when they bring you to trial they will find you guilty and hang you."

"I love him so very much. We would make a most elegant Duke and Duchess of Yorkshire. Not like that brute that you married. He would do better as a servant than a duke. How fickle fate can be, don't you agree?" Lucy asked.

"Duncan is a wonderful duke and I don't believe that Reese wants the title."

"Of course he does, he just doesn't realize it yet. Once he realizes the power that comes with the title, he'll change his mind. I just need to show him."

"Do you realize the amount of responsibility that also comes with such a title?" Penelope inquired.

"Such as?"

"The protection of those that live along the bay from the press gangs."

"And put his life in danger? They can do very well on their own. Besides, we will live in London, and I will be the belle of every ball and envied by every woman."

"But what of all the tenants in Yorkshire? They are going to need Reese's guiding hand."

"We have the steward to oversee that," she brushed off the concern. "I'm done with all of this talking. You are going to be so overwhelmed with the duties of being a duchess and the worries of motherhood that in a moment of insanity you are going to drink this poisoned tea."

Penelope took the teacup that Lucy forced into her hands.

"No one is going to believe that."

"You think not? Need I remind you that your father committed suicide, your sister stalked another until she herself was killed, and that your mother spent time in Bedlam?"

"No," Penelope replied stoically.

"Good, then drink up."

"Before I do, at least humor me and tell me about the others. And then there was the attack on Duncan. Am I correct that you were behind that as well?"

"Drink!"

"You're a coward then?" Penelope taunted. "Are you truly ashamed of what you've done? Do you regret killing the others?" A sharp sound from outside, like that of a gunshot, drew their attention.

"What was that?" Lucy asked, sounding nervous for the first time, her back to Penelope.

"I don't know," she answered honestly. She made no attempt to move, fearing Lucy's instability and what she might do.

Lucy spun around and approached Penelope with venom in her eyes. "Drink it now, bitch!"

"Don't drink it!" Duncan yelled as he charged across the room. The door bounced off the wall as he forcefully shoved it open. He dove towards Penelope as he watched her tip her head back to take a sip of the tea. He bumped her arm just enough to cause her to lose her grip on the cup. It tumbled from her fingertips and flipped through the air until it landed on the plush rug with a soft thud. It laid harmlessly on it's side, unable to hurt anyone any longer as it's contents emptied out.

"Duncan! What are you doing?" Penelope asked, exasperated.

"Trying to save your life. I believe Lucy is the killer and is trying to poison you," he said, pushing himself up.

"Of course she is, but I was fine. I switched the cups when she wasn't looking."

"You're brilliant!" he crowed as he stood to his full height and pulled her into his arms. Neither was very concerned with the woman creeping across the room towards the exit. She had put the teacup full of the poisonous liquid down on a shelf as she passed and was just about to leave the room when her progress was halted.

"What's all this racket about?" Reese asked upon entering the room, looking rumpled and unkempt. He grabbed Lucy as she stumbled into him in an attempt to stabilize her.

"Don't let her go," Duncan ordered.

"Why? And who are they?" Reese asked, nodding to Barton, Grantham, and the two Runners.

"She's the one who has been trying to kill Penelope. These men are here to arrest her."

"What? You jest, big brother. Little Lucy here wouldn't do something like that."

"Let go of me," Lucy demanded, twisting in Reese's grip, desperate to be free.

"That teacup has poison in it." Penelope nodded in the direction of the poison-laced cup.

"I don't believe it."

"If you would like to try it to confirm our suspicions, go ahead, but I wouldn't suggest it," Duncan said.

"Lucy, is it true?" the dowager duchess' voice sounded hollow as she entered the parlor, fresh from her shopping trip.

"It's all lies, Mama! I would never harm anyone, let alone dear, sweet Penelope," Lucy said imploringly.

Reese pulled Lucy further into the room and away from any means of escape. "Perhaps we should hear Duncan out," Reese suggested.

"Can't you see? He's just trying to put the blame on someone else to take the suspicion off of himself," Lucy argued.

"Duncan, please tell me why you believe my daughter was trying to poison Penelope."

"This," Grantham said, holding up a piece of paper with a jagged left side. It looked as if it had been ripped out of a book.

"What's that?" Reese demanded.

"It looks to be a piece of paper," Duncan said.

"I found it in the fireplace when we searched the house last week. I was able to piece some of it back together. A little *puzzle* I've been keeping myself entertained with at night, you know, to keep me from being too *lonely*," Grantham said, looking pointedly at Duncan. "Evidently Lucy burned her diary, or had one of the servants burn it."

"You've been going through our things?" Rosalie asked, sounding offended.

"Yes," Duncan replied with no remorse. "The lives of my wife and child are at stake, and I would do anything to protect them, even die for them."

"Wife and child?" Rosalie asked.

"Yes," Penelope answered this time, standing closer to Duncan, if that were possible.

"I see," Rosalie said tightly.

"Well, what does it say?" Penelope asked on tenterhooks, hoping that they might actually be able to put this part of their lives behind them soon.

Grantham cleared his voice as he began to read the elegant, feminine script, "*Today we received word that another would be coming. I am both horribly angry and relieved. Duncan is such a powerful man, but, well... They say the young woman coming is actually the sister of who was actually supposed to arrive here to take her place as Duncan's wife. I cannot believe he is willing to add one more scandal to the Taggart name. My step-father would have been disgraced by his behavior, and all because of a woman.*

"*I am unsure how to carry forth with number four. Should she meet a similar fate as one of the previous women, or should something unique happen to her? If only the gamekeeper had kept his promise and...*"

"And what?" Reese wanted to know.

"Her journaling ends there. There were some additional pieces in the fireplace, but all were too small to make anything out of."

"What did you mean by it, Lucy?"

Penelope saw the crazed look in the younger woman's eyes as she pulled against Reese's firm grip. "I thought she was in love with Duncan and wanted him and the title for herself," Penelope answered.

"You thought?" Duncan asked. "What happened to change your mind?"

"She has admitted to loving Reese and, of course, wanting the title. For a very long time, apparently."

"What?" Reese asked, shaken.

"You have been so blind to me and my feelings for you," Lucy accused. "I would be such a wonderful Duchess of Yorkshire. Mama agrees wholeheartedly, don't you, Mama?"

"I don't know what you're talking about," Rosalie said, an ashen pallor to her complexion.

Duncan gave the Runners an almost imperceptible jerk of his head and soon they were also holding Rosalie. Penelope might be convinced that Lucy was the only culprit, but he was not so certain.

"I don't understand," Reese said.

"Sometimes you can be such a dimwit," Duncan said, irritated at his brother's gullibility. "Anyone with eyes can see that Lucy has been moon-eyed over you ever since she and Rosalie joined our household."

"But I thought she was interested in you," Reese accused.

"Evidently that was an act to throw everyone off," Duncan countered.

Several things happened at once. The men engaged in an argument resulting in name calling and a resurrection of the past, and Penelope moved closer to Reese and Lucy in an effort to calm the tension in the room. Lucy grasped a letter opener from a nearby table, whispered a shaky, "I'm sorry," then drew back and plunged the weapon into the fleshy part of Reese's leg. Reese yelled, relinquished her, and dropped to the floor. Lucy took a step towards Penelope and entwined her fingers in the thick, blonde mass of hair. She held the bloody weapon against Penelope's alabaster throat.

"Lucy, let her go," Duncan commanded, moving towards the women.

"Stay where you are," she said, pushing the dagger-like weapon further against Penelope's neck.

"Please, do what she says," Penelope pleaded as she tried to lift her chin higher and away from the weapon.

"Reese, are you all right?" Lucy asked, giving him a quick glance before returning her attention to the others in the room.

"I've been better. Now, tell me Duncan isn't right. You're not in love with me. I'm not the Duke of Yorkshire, Duncan is."

"But you could be," she countered.

"Only if Duncan were…"

"Dead," Lucy finished. "It wasn't anything personal towards you, Duncan. I loved you like a brother, but I wasn't *in* love with you."

"That doesn't explain why you killed my two wives and fiancée. Why you tried to murder Penelope."

"I attempted to get the gamekeeper to kill you and make it appear to be a hunting accident on several occasions. He took what he wanted from me, but he wouldn't follow through with his promise. That was part of the problem, Duncan. Your servants are loyal and those that might be persuaded fear your power and authority. So I decided I must bring outsiders in to take you away."

"The gamekeeper. You killed him, too, didn't you? He had asked to meet with me that last day. We thought he had run across poachers, but it was you."

"I had to stop him before he told you what I was doing."

"Dammit, Lucy, why?" Reese demanded.

"Because I would do anything for you, Reese. For us and our future."

"We have no future. I don't love you like that," he argued from his prone position on the floor.

"You killed Francis to make it look suspicious. Everyone always assumed she committed suicide, but I remember people saying she didn't leave a note behind, which always left room for doubt. Then someone would have to investigate and possibly find Duncan guilty of murder," Penelope surmised.

"You're brilliant and I truly believe we could have been great friends," Lucy said, a tinge of sadness in her voice.

"I don't—" Duncan started to say, still having difficulty believing that this slip of a young woman standing before them could have killed so many people.

"Duncan, she wanted you to hang for murder so your brother could inherit the title free and clear," Penelope clarified, irritated that the men were still not wanting to believe the truth before them. "Never, *ever*, underestimate what a woman will do to reach her desired goal."

"You should listen to her, Duncan. Penelope is so much better than all of the others combined," Lucy added.

"Isabelle was special as well," Reese argued.

"*I* am special!" Lucy raged, spittle flying from her lips. "Do you truly think you were the only one she had an affair with?" Lucy challenged her beloved. When he gaped at her like a fish out of water, she continued, "Well, you weren't. She had a string of lovers. I caught her on several occasions dallying with footmen, stable hands, and one of the villagers."

"I don't believe you!" Reese exclaimed.

"No, you wouldn't," Lucy said sadly, looking down at him.

"Who?" he demanded to know. "Name them now."

"They've all moved on," she said. "No need for you to waste your time and life fulfilling old grudges."

"Explain about Samantha. You befriended her. When she fell ill you nursed her. Was it all just an act worthy of Drury Lane?"

"She had mentioned what a weak constitution she had, how she got the ague so easily. It wasn't difficult to lure her outside when I knew a storm was approaching. She grew ill, just as she predicted she would. And yes, I nursed her, but the soup and tea was laced with belladonna."

"Belladonna?" Reese asked.

"People wouldn't question a woman having such a poison on hand. You see, many women use it to dilate their eyes for fashion. Too much ingested can kill a person," Barton said.

"Mama, I'm sorry to have shamed you, but you always did tell me to set my mind to what I wanted and let nothing step in my way until I received it. Perhaps I took it to heart just a little too much. Remember me fondly, and that I will always love you."

"I love you, too, my darling girl. We'll get you the best barrister money can buy."

"No one can keep the hangman from stretching my neck, Mama, not even you." She looked around the room at each one of them, acknowledging both the love she felt for them, and how she had wronged them. "Take care of them," she whispered in Penelope's ear.

Penelope felt the grip on her hair easing and was suddenly propelled across the room until she crashed into Duncan. He wrapped her securely in his arms, holding her close. Penelope twisted and saw Lucy's intent and screamed, "No!"

Too late, she watched the younger woman lift the bottle of belladonna from her pocket. She undid the stopper and quickly drank down the liquid before anyone could reach her.

"Good-bye, everyone. Reese, I love you so—"

"Let me go, you brutes," Rosalie struggled free of the Runners and rushed to Lucy's side as she collapsed, trying to ease her through her last moments on earth. They all watched, unable to turn away as the young woman was overtaken by vomiting and convulsions. Rosalie willed and begged her to fight against it, to stay with them, but it was futile.

When it was all over, Penelope felt the warm, strong arms of Duncan around her, giving her strength. She looked briefly at Rosalie and felt pity for the older woman who had been clueless about her daughter's machinations and was now mourning her only child. Then she found herself studying Reese. He still sat on the floor, propped against the wall. He had staunched the blood flow on his thigh, but now his hand was covered in the warm, sticky liquid. He looked like a man haunted by both the past and the present as he stared at Lucy's lifeless form. She wanted nothing more than to be away from this house and the horrors associated with it.

"Duncan?"

"Yes, love?"

"Take me home."

"Of course. Barton, can you take care of this?"

"Yes, Your Grace."

"We'll be there in a trice, love," he told her.

"No, take me to Taggart Hall."

CHAPTER 31

They had been back at Taggart Hall for almost a week. Her grandfather's servants were now here with them and enjoyed the wilds of the moors. They received a letter from Rosalie saying that she was so very sorry for all that had happened and was taking a ship to America. She said that she hoped new scenery would make it not so difficult to live out the rest of her days without her dear Lucy. Penelope found herself truly wishing the poor woman happiness in her new life, knowing she had been just as much a victim as anyone else. She had merely done what she believed was best for her daughter. Lucy had been a wonderful actress, keeping her true nature hidden from so many.

Duncan had felt it his responsibility to keep her abed and see to her every need. On many occasions, they had made love, celebrating life and the fact that they had come out the victors. Duncan continued to whisper words of love to her, and Penelope desperately wanted to bask in them, but she believed now he felt obligated to her because of the babe. So she gave herself to him physically and enjoyed their being together, but held on tightly to her emotions when, in truth, she wanted to shout them for all to hear.

One morning, they were lying among the rumpled bedclothes, catching their breaths after a particularly exuberant bout of lovemaking when a hesitant knock sounded at the door.

"Yes?" Duncan managed to get out.

"There's a messenger here. Said he's to give his package to the Duke of Yorkshire and none other."

"I'll be right down." He rolled over and kissed Penelope passionately before getting out of the bed.

Penelope watched him as he strode across the room, gloriously naked. She rolled to her side and propped her head up in her hand, lusting over her husband. "That's a pity," she said, as she watched him pull on a pair of breeches and a billowing white shirt.

"What is?" he asked as he buttoned first the breeches and then the shirt.

"Covering up that handsome body of yours," she said.

"You are insatiable," he said.

"I understand it is one of the side effects of being with child for some women."

"I'm glad you're one of those women," he growled and stalked towards her. "Now, be good." He kissed her once more then left the room.

She was drifting off to sleep when he returned a short time later. His expression worried her. She raised up on her elbows, holding the sheet to her breasts. "Duncan, what's wrong?"

"Pen, I love you with all that I am."

She fell against the bed. "Do we have to do this now?"

"Yes."

"Fine. I know you believe you do."

"No, I know I do."

"Duncan—"

"You should read these." He tossed a stack of bound letters on the bed beside her. "Start from the top one and work your way down. I believe you will find them very interesting."

"Where are you going?"

"I have things to see to," he said over his shoulder.

Penelope studied the door that he had slipped through, then picked up the brick of letters. That was her father's handwriting on the first envelope. She quickly untied the bundle and curiously flicked through the letters. After the first one, the odd letters turned into her grandfather's spidery writing. The others were in Duncan's broad script. There were more of Duncan's than there were of Lord Bolingbroke's. It seemed as if some of Duncan's letters had gone unanswered. She opened the first letter and began reading.

Duncan was at the stables saddling his horse when he heard a rider approaching. Not wanting company, he kept working the rigging on the saddle.

"Good morning, brother."

"I guess today is not the day for me to have peace and solitude."

"What?" Reese asked.

"Nothing. What are you doing here?"

"I'm going away for a while, but I wanted to clear the air between us before I did."

"There's nothing to say."

"There is everything to say. For a long time, you thought I was the killer."

Duncan mounted Cyclops and put his heels to him. They bounded across the land, running from Reese's accusations. In his peripheral vision he saw Reese and his horse moving up. They were running full tilt for the cliffs when Duncan turned towards Reese, forcing him to turn as well to keep him and his horse from being trampled on. They slowed their horses to a walk.

"What the bloody hell was that about?"

"What?" Duncan asked.

"You nearly ran me over."

"And you would have gone right off the bloody cliff."

"I don't have a death wish, Duncan. Besides, I was just keeping up with you."

"Fine. Yes, I thought you were the killer, and I regret that. Now, do you have something else you would like to discuss, or was that it?" Duncan studied Reese who had suddenly become very quiet and pensive. "You have my attention. You had something to tell me."

"Do you really think Isabelle had other men?" he asked, sounding insecure for the first time in his life.

"I don't know, Reese. She was not pure when she came to me," Duncan said.

"Oh." They walked their horses in pregnant silence. "I'm leaving."

"So you said. Where are you going?"

"I don't know."

"What are you going to do?"

"Again, I don't know."

"Well, as long as you have a plan," Duncan said, chuckling.

"You love her, don't you?" Reese asked curiously.

"With all of my being," Duncan answered immediately and emphatically.

"Take care of her and don't let her slip away."

Duncan nodded his head, his throat constricting with emotion.

"Be sure and name my niece or nephew after me," Reese teased before turning his horse. "Goodbye, Duncan. Take care."

"You, too."

Penelope stared at the papers strewn across the bed. She heard a plop and noticed a tear had fallen on the one she held, smearing the ink. She lifted a shaky hand and swiped at the tears she hadn't realized she shed. She scurried from the bed and went to the wardrobe and pulled out one of her plain dresses. Penelope pulled it on and did up the buttons and lacing. She quickly scraped her fingers through her hair and pulled it back with a ribbon tied at her nape. She slipped on a pair of shoes then crossed to the bed and scattered the letters until she found the two that she wanted.

"Miss Penelope, where do you think you're going?" Hortense asked.

"I have to find my husband. We have unfinished business," she said.

"I don't know that it's wise for you to be out alone. This is wild country, miss."

"Isn't it glorious?" Penelope asked, dancing the older woman in a circle. She hugged her tightly before sprinting out of the house. She was running to the stables when she heard a familiar voice.

"Ho, there, it looks like a sea nymph has come to land."

"Reese, what are you doing here?"

"Just making peace with my brother and saying goodbye."

"Why? You don't have to leave."

"I do. You and Duncan deserve the chance to start a life together without any interference. Besides, it's time I made a name for myself. Perhaps I'll create a new identity for myself so that no one will know who I am."

"And what good could come of that?"

"Probably none, but it proves to be an adventure," he said with a boyish grin. "And where are you going in such a rush?"

"To find my husband," she said.

"I left him not too long ago near the cliffs."

Before, that would have bothered her. She would have thought he was trying to get close to Isabelle's memory, but not after reading the letters. "Will you take me to the ruins?"

"Why?"

"Because I need to see Duncan."

"But I told you where I left him."

"I know. Please, Reese," she begged.

"Come here." He kicked his foot free of the stirrup so she could put her foot in. Then he held his hand down so she could take it, and with very little energy on her part, she flew through the air and landed sitting across his lap. "To the ruins you say?"

"Yes."

"To the ruins," Reese said, turning the horse and spurring him into action.

They flew across the moors, and Penelope relished it. The sun was warm on her skin and she loved the smell of the fresh, salt air. It was so very different from London and she knew that this is where she and Duncan would spend the majority of their lives, raising their family and growing old together. Reese started to slow the horse, and she opened her eyes and saw why. The ruins loomed before them and stalking towards them was her husband, who didn't look particularly happy.

"I think you should let me down here. I'll walk the rest of the way."

"I'm not scared of him. Besides, nothing happened."

"All the same, I'd rather not lose any more family." She hugged Reese tightly and gave him a kiss on the cheek. "Take care of yourself, Reese."

"Take care of him," Reese said.

"I will." Suddenly Duncan's deep voice reached their ears.

"Bloody hell, unhand my wife! I'll challenge your sorry arse to a duel. Pistols or swords, you name your preference."

"Here we go," Reese said, rolling his eyes.

Penelope giggled. "I'll calm the *Beast* while you disappear. Don't worry, all will be well." Penelope was once more standing on the ground when Reese turned his horse and rode off. Duncan ran past her, still raging at his brother's retreating figure. Penelope sighed and started walking the short distance to the ruins.

"Your lover left you behind."

"He's not my lover."

"I saw you kiss him."

"You saw me give him a brotherly peck on the cheek and wish him well." She whirled on Duncan, her golden brown eyes flashed with emotion. "If you would stop acting so beastly and jumping to conclusions then you would have seen past that red haze of anger you always carry with you." She turned back around and marched to the old abbey, leaving Duncan to either stand and stare at her or follow her. He followed her.

"It's not anger, it's jealousy, if you must know. I worry you will grow tired of me," he admitted. He quickly changed the subject before she could comment. "Why are you not in bed? You should be resting," Duncan advised.

"Duncan, I'm going to have a baby, that doesn't mean I'm an invalid," she argued.

"Fine, then what are you doing here?"

"Sometimes I wonder," she muttered.

"What?"

"These, I came because of these." She held the two letters aloft.

"You read them."

"Yes. Did you mean them?"

"Every word."

"Read this part to me."

"Why?"

"Please. I just want to hear the words."

He took from her hand a letter that he had written to himself, as silly as that sounded. It was the night he had first seen Penelope at the ball during her Season. Her one and only ball, and he had felt moved to put pen to paper, to remember everything about that night. He cleared his throat and began to read, "*She was the most bewitching creature I have ever seen. She stood in the shadows, as if they could hide her beauty. I watched her for what seemed forever. I could see things about her that the others could not. There was a bit of desperation around her eyes that reminded me of myself. She looked like a lost soul, as if she wanted to belong to something or someone. I was yelling curses inside that I was affianced to another. I moved around the room to hear her voice. It swept over me like water on the parched ground. I asked a passerby who she was. It took several times before I finally had my answer. Imagine my delight when I found out that this fey creature was my fiancée's sister. Perhaps there is hope. I will plead my case with the old man, for her father is useless. Tonight I went to the ball with my shoulders drooping with the weight of the world and I return feeling as if I were walking on air. Did I mention that I found out her name? Penelope. I will dream of her until she is in my arms.*"

"And now this," she ordered huskily.

"*Lord Bolingbroke, I understand that we had an agreement. That I would marry your oldest granddaughter, but as I have explained, things have changed. It is Penelope that I have fallen in love with. I cannot, nay, I* refuse *to marry one when I am in love with the other. You have denied my request to marry her more times than I care to count, even though I offer you double the amount for what I was willing to pay you to marry Whitney. Penelope is worth a king's ransom to me; therefore, I am offering four times the amount to marry her. That is £10,000. If this is not accepted, I would suggest you hire armed guards, for I will be taking her as my own with or without your blessing or approval.*" He looked at her doggedly as he folded the letters once more.

"Is it true?"

"I would not have written them if it weren't."

"And the others?"

"All true."

"You felt this strongly about me from one chance encounter?"

"I couldn't take my eyes off you that night. You seemed so sad yet so strong. You were smart and kind. You were everything I ever wanted in a wife, in a lover, in a friend."

"Truly?"

"Penelope, I cannot apologize for my previous relationships. Living through what happened brought you to me. But I have said goodbye and put them where they belong, in the past. You are my present and my future. I love you so much that my heart is bursting and I want to shout it for all to hear." He turned away from her and looked towards the channel. "I love Penelope Anne Taggart with all of my soul!"

"Duncan!" she scolded then saw the smile that lit his handsome face.

"What?"

"I love you so much!" she finally managed to say. "I've wanted to tell you for so long, but feared that I was competing with ghosts, and you could never love me as you did them."

"I turned Isabelle into a false saint, and the others I merely mourned their untimely passing. You, Penelope, you are the love of my life, the mother of my future children, and the one I want to grow old with."

"I love you," she choked out and found herself in his arms, being spun around. When they stopped spinning, he kissed her deeply and passionately and for the first time in her life she felt like she was home.

EPILOGUE

"I have to get out of here," Penelope told Agatha and Helena.

"But, my dear, you could have that baby at any moment," Agatha argued.

"Agatha, she knows what she's doing. Besides she'll take Duncan with her."

"Of course, I will," Penelope said crossing her fingers behind her back. Her dear, sweet, loving husband was one of the reasons she had to escape, if only for a few hours. Everywhere she turned around, he was there. It was because of him that their house was full of family. He had invited everyone out to keep her company before the baby arrived. He was underfoot, she was tired of being pregnant, and she hurt, everywhere, but most especially her back. She had not been without a backache for almost a week. What little sleep she got was when Duncan rubbed her back at night in their bed.

"Your buggy is ready, Your Grace," a footman announced.

"Thank you. Are the blankets still on the back?"

"Yes, Your Grace."

"Where's Duncan?" Agatha asked worriedly.

"He's meeting me at the buggy," she lied. The footman followed her out of the house and helped her into the conveyance.

"Was I supposed to get His Grace? I thought you said—"

"You did the right thing. I'm just going for a short drive to clear my head. I'll be back soon."

"Yes, Your Grace."

Penelope slapped the reins against the horse and they clip-clopped down the drive. The spring day was warm and sunny. A barely there breeze caressed her face, and the sun kissed her cheeks. Her back spasmed uncomfortably, and she reached around with her free hand and rubbed at the spot. She drove to her and Duncan's favorite spot in the world, the ruins of the old abbey. Just as it came into view, the ache in her back intensified once more, taking her breath away. Her fingers fisted in the reins, causing the horse to whinny in agitation. She willed her body to relax, and the back ache seemed to go away, leaving only a memory of the pain. She pulled the horse to a stop, and managed to lower her ungainly form to the ground.

She tethered the horse to a thin column before strolling around the grounds. Penelope had just reached their favorite lookout point when she felt an odd shift within her. This time the cramp in her back had her crying out in pain, and she gripped the stone window tightly to keep from falling to her knees. When it passed, she rested her head against the frame and worked on recovering her breath.

"No, baby, you can't come now. Not here," she rubbed her stomach and felt the oddest thing. Her stomach grew hard and it was synchronized with the back pain she felt, followed by a burst of water. When the pain had passed, tears pricked her eyes. "Your Papa's going to kill me."

"Yes, he is," Duncan said. "What were you thinking of, going riding on your own like that?"

"You've been underfoot and everyone watching me all the time was driving me a little mad. You were hovering, and I had to get away for a bit, but Duncan, listen to me—"

"I only hover because I love you and worry about you," he said then broke off when Penelope bent at the waist and moaned, resting her head against the bottom of the crumbling window. "Penelope, what have you done?" Noticing for the first time that the lower half of her dress was soaked.

"The baby's coming," she said, panting after the pain passed.

"We must get you home," he said, panicked.

"I'm afraid he isn't going to wait."

"I'm going to ring your neck."

She knew he was teasing, of course, hopefully. "Can you please do it now? I hurt so bad," she said, tears shimmering on her lashes. "Oh, here's another one."

"You are strong and can do this," he encouraged her. He rubbed her back as the pain ebbed, peaked, then left her drained.

"You have amazing hands," Penelope sighed.

"I know. That's why you're in this predicament."

"Oh, Duncan," she giggled and it quickly turned into a groan.

"Another one?"

She nodded her head and he rubbed her back. "The blanket and oilskin are on the carriage. Get them."

"But I don't want to leave you."

"Trust me when I say I'm not going anywhere. Go," she waved him away. He had been gone less than a minute when the most powerful contraction yet ripped through her body. She could not contain the scream that was ripped from her. This one had been different, more intense, and she found she wanted to push, to expel her child from the confines of her body.

"What is it?" Duncan ran back to her, arms full.

"I think the baby is ready to make its appearance."

"But it hasn't even been a half an hour. Aren't these things supposed to take hours, days even?"

"The backache I've been having," she explained.

"For days?" he asked, both livid and shocked.

"Blankets," she gritted out as her body was caught up in another pain. She could feel her child moving downward and wondered how it could simultaneously be the most amazing and torturous thing to happen to her.

"I'm here. What do you want me to do? Do you want to lie down?"

"No. I couldn't move if I wanted to. Kiss me," she ordered. And he did, first on her lips, then on her forehead, making her feel loved and cherished. "You're going to have to deliver our babe."

"But I've never done this," he said. "Well, at least not with humans."

"See, of the two of us, you have the most experience."

"Dear Lord, help us all."

But Penelope didn't hear him because she was caught up in the struggle of delivering their child. She no longer had a respite between the pains as they washed over her, one on top of the other. She did what her body was ordering her, and together she and Duncan welcomed their baby into the world.

"She's beautiful, isn't she?" Penelope asked Duncan.

"She's not quite as beautiful as her mother, but it's a close thing," he said.

They were now back home in their bedroom. Everyone was examined and announced to be in fit health, including Duncan. Right after being found, he had very nearly passed out. He would deny it until his dying day, but it was one of the things that endeared him so much to Penelope.

"When you have healed from your ordeal, I am taking you over my knee." Duncan sat facing her, his hand braced next to her opposite hip.

"That would be something new," she said saucily and winked at him.

"What kind of an example are you setting for our daughter?"

"I'm showing her how much her parents love each other," she said.

"And I do. I love you so much, Pen. I was so frightened that I was going to lose you. It was all happening so fast, I was certain something was wrong." He kissed her passionately and rested his forehead against hers.

"Nothing wrong, I just didn't realize I had been in labor for days. I'm sorry I worried you, but I am glad that you arrived when you did," she said over their sleeping daughter. She cupped his cheek with her free hand.

"Me, too," he said. "I have something for you." He held out a box for her.

"You hold her while I open my present," she said, passing her daughter into her husband's very capable hands.

She opened the box to reveal a stunning necklace. "It's to replace your mother's pearl necklace. I know that I promised I would have it fixed, but I just don't want something from her gracing your beauty and kindness. This is mother of pearl and it comes from the same place as the pearl, but I think it is much more interesting to look at, like you."

"It's beautiful, thank you," she said huskily.

"I should be thanking you. Look at all you have been through since coming to marry me."

"You saved me," Penelope said. "I love you so very much."

"And I love you."

She swiped at a lone tear that was threatening to fall.

"Here, let me take care of that." Duncan shifted slightly so he still cradled his daughter and could retrieve a handkerchief.

"What is this?" Penelope asked, looking at the stained, tattered piece of fabric.

"You mean it doesn't look familiar?"

She took it from him, spread it out, and studied it. "This my handkerchief from the night Helena found me."

"I found it. I missed you by minutes that night. I nearly went mad when I saw it lying in all that blood. My imagination went wild. I took it home that night and cleaned it the best I could and have carried it every day since just so I would have a part of you close to me."

"Why are you giving it back now?"

"I thought, despite what I said, you might want something to remind you of your family."

"You keep it. I have this precious little girl to remind me of you anytime I wish. The two of you, and whatever future children we have, are my family—in all ways that matter."

"You are my everything," Duncan said huskily, kissing her once more.

"And you are mine." She returned the kiss, and their lips clung together. Finally Penelope pulled back. "What are we going to name this sleeping beauty?" she asked, peeling back the blanket slightly as they studied the face of their newborn with the rapt attention and love that only new parents can.

"Well, since she was born at the abbey and perhaps conceived there…"

"I think Abbey is a beautiful name. And I think she should also have the name Victoria for your mother. From all you have told me, she would have loved having a granddaughter," Penelope said.

"Yes, she would have. We are a family now, you, me, and our Abbey Victoria."

"You have made all my dreams come true."

"I love you my *beauty*."

"And I love you my *beast*."

BOOK LIST

The Reluctant Lords Trilogy:
A Traitorous Heart
A Thin Line
To Love and Protect

The Rogue Agents Trilogy:
Taming the Wicked Wulfe
Seducing the Ruthless Rogue
Enticing the Weary Warrior

Those Scandalous Taggarts:
The Beast of Yorkshire
Wild Lord Taggart - coming 2016

All books can be read as stand-alones; however, you will see repeating characters throughout the two trilogies. To purchase or read more about any of these titles, please read the excerpts at the end of this book, or click here.

AUTHOR BIO

I grew up in the Panhandle of Texas, but have always been fascinated with the land of my forefathers – England, Scotland, and Ireland. I also classify myself as a true romantic, and find I frequently dream of greater than life heroes that leave me thinking – that is what love should be like. So, I work on creating love stories with strong women and stronger men, and let the battle of wills ensue. I am currently busy writing my fourth book in my little cottage in the woods of North Texas with my cat, Ajax, to keep me company.

I would love to hear from those who read my books. I can be contacted at: tammyjo@tammyjoburns.com

To keep up with my new releases and sneak peeks of upcoming books, sign up for my newsletter here.

My website is Tammy Jo Burns

I can also be followed on the following social media networks:

Amazon Author site – Tammy Jo Burns
Facebook – tammyjoburnsfanpage
Twitter - @tammyjoburns
Pinterest – tammyjoburns
GoodReads - tammyjoburns
Instagram - @tammyjoburns

I truly hope you enjoyed this book!

Warm wishes & happy reading,

Tammy Jo

Made in the USA
Charleston, SC
12 October 2016